ACCLAIM

"Full of mystery and intrigue, *Sanctified* is a satisfying third installment to V. Romas Burton's Legacy Chapters. An ensemble cast of familiar, beloved characters becomes even more endearing as they fight together against the growing threat to the lands and people they love. Inner strength, faith, and friendship take center stage in this epic tale of magic and adventure you won't want to miss."
—CRYSTAL D. GRANT, award-winning author of Christy Finalist *Shadowcast*

"In *Sanctified*, the third installment of the Legacy Chapters series, plot lines seamlessly converge through moments of mystery, adventure, and sweet romance. Burton brilliantly weaves together a beautiful story of family, identity, and hope with characters who exemplify wisdom, inner strength, and meekness that is anything but weakness."
—TABITHA CAPLINGER, author of Carol Award Finalist *The Wayward*.

"Perfect for any fantasy lover who enjoys reading retellings...*Fortified* is definitely a must read in my book."
—KATHLEEN BIRD, Clean Fiction Magazine

"*Fortified* is a riveting, beautifully-written adventure filled with intrigue, betrayal, strife and one woman with enough faith and bravery in her heart to face it all."
—CASEY L. BOND, author of *Where Oceans Burn*

Sanctified

THE LEGACY CHAPTERS
SANCTIFIED
Quill & Flame
PUBLISHING HOUSE
V. ROMAS BURTON

To anyone who has been told you're not good enough, you are.

Chapter One

Ida, Vlacklear Academy, Before the Battle of Edo

Don't cry, don't cry, don't cry, Ida told herself as she shuffled down the white stone corridor. The black academy uniform wrapping tightly around her small frame felt more like a prison than the Fortress ever did.

This is where you were always supposed to be, she chided herself, doing her best to suck back the tears brimming in her eyes as the headmistress of Vlacklear Academy led Ida to her chambers.

But as she took in the stark-white hallway lined with a blood-red carpet, Ida wanted to do nothing more than race back to the Fortress where she, oddly enough, felt safe. Until Warden Hazor requested her presence in his office. Ida recalled the memory like it was yesterday. In fact, it was only yesterday that her entire life unraveled. Again.

The warden had just returned from a meeting with the King's Council where Devora and Nadia were sent to the battlefront. Almost as soon as the news reached Ida's ears, a knight escorted her to Warden Hazor's office.

"Enter," the warden commanded.

"Ida Shabawn, as you requested, sir," the knight said with a bow before leaving Ida defenseless against the ruthless Warden Hazor.

Ida clasped her hands in front of her, doing her best to seem strong and confident like Devora always did. Though, even when she tried her hardest, Ida still couldn't stop her lips from quivering and her fingers from fidgeting. Fear rippled through her veins. Had she done something to evoke the warden's wrath? Since entering the Fortress, she had done everything within her power to comply with his rules.

Ida rubbed her thumb over her wrist, the wire bracelet from Nadia still snug from when Sir Jacques tied it there. Warmth spread through her cheeks as she recalled the memory of the knight's touch, but she shook it from her mind. That desire could never be.

Warden Hazor set down the crinkled parchment he was reading and studied her with his coal-black eyes.

"Why are you here, Shabawn?" His deep voice held authority like no other.

Ida clasped her hands tighter. "You requested my presence, sir," she replied barely above a whisper.

The warden stroked his mustache. "Why are you here"—he repeated—"at the Fortress?"

Ida's lips opened to reply, but no words came out. As her mind processed the warden's question, she suddenly realized what he was asking. Not why she was at the Fortress, but what made *her* special enough to have categorized for Vlacklear.

Almost two months ago, King Atol switched the color patterns for those participating in the annual Categorization Call. Those who should have categorized for the prestigious Vlacklear Academy were sent to the Fortress, the prison-turned-military academy. Warden Hazor wanted to know what in Ida's blood made her stones stack in Vlacklear's color pattern.

Ida closed her parted lips. She had wondered the same thing when she categorized for Vlacklear. She wasn't noble, she wasn't even a layman. She was worse than that. And she could never disclose what she really was if she wanted to live.

"I'm not sure, sir," Ida finally replied.

Warden Hazor's dark gaze narrowed as he leaned back in his chair, crossing his arms over his wide chest.

The silence between them lengthened. Ida swore she could hear her own sweat rolling down the back of her neck. She absentmindedly ran her thumb over the wire bracelet again, a gesture she had picked up since Sir Jacques urged her to take the concealed weapon not more than two weeks ago.

Had it only been two weeks?

The kind knight with the beautiful eyes seemed to be everywhere she was lately. Not that Ida minded. When she was at her lowest in Grenly, taken from the home she held dear, Sir Jacques treated her with kindness. He didn't have to be gentle or comforting to her, but he was. Unfortunately, she couldn't return his kindness.

"Read this," Warden Hazor commanded, snapping Ida out of her daydream. The warden pushed the parchment he was previously reading toward her.

A series of inked swirls and lines of a foreign tongue glistened up at Ida. The symbols easily translated in her mind, just as any foreign language had always done.

Ida whispered a prayer to Tunri, knowing He was the one who had granted her this ability before she read about a battalion of Kadeshian troops heading toward Tenton's borders. Ida held back her gasp. Not only was Kadesh threatening to take Maldove Palace, but they demanded the Tentonian Seer be handed over to them or they would strike with full force.

How did they know about Devora so soon? It was not long ago that Ida and the rest of the Fortress learned of Devora's true identity, after her eyes turned violet when she won the game of Kings against Captain Blake. How had word spread across the border so quickly?

Ida's toes tapped in her boots as she bit her lip. *Did Warden Hazor really not know what the parchment said? Why would someone send him such information in a tongue he couldn't understand?*

Then again, Ida deciphered plenty of parchments she wasn't sure she understood. Somehow, the words just came to her. It was something she had always been able to do, a gift Tunri had blessed her with since before she could remember.

But Ida learned at an early age to keep her mouth shut about such abnormalities. She refused to allow anyone to get hurt again because of her.

"I'm sorry, sir," she replied as calmly as she could. "I'm not sure what tongue that is."

Warden Hazor didn't blink as he analyzed her.

Ida couldn't help but squirm under his scrutinizing gaze. She'd thought Captain Blake's judgmental stares were bad, but they were nothing compared to the warden's.

After what seemed like an eternity, Warden Hazor shook his head. "Pity. I suppose I have no need for it then."

Reaching for the flickering candle nub at the edge of his wooden desk, Warden Hazor grabbed the parchment.

Ida's pulse raced. She couldn't allow him to ignore such important information, especially concerning Devora.

The flames licked the edge of the paper.

"Stop!" Ida cried out, snatching the paper from the warden's hands before the flames could devour it. "A battalion of Kadeshians is coming and they want Devora." Adrenaline pumped through Ida's veins, allowing the next words to tumble from her lips before she could stop them. "I won't allow you to send her to them, sir. Just because she's a Seer doesn't mean she's evil. She deserves to be protected, too."

The moment the last word left Ida's lips, the blood drained from her cheeks.

How could I have spoken to the warden of the Fortress like that?

Taking a step back, Ida placed the parchment on the table and bowed her head. "My deepest apologies, sir. I was out of line with my actions and words. I will accept any punishment you deem necessary."

But what happened next was not a lashing or a strike, but a deep chuckle. After another moment passed and Ida had yet to be reprimanded, she hesitantly glanced up.

"I wasn't sure if there were any Translators left, but with Atol's focus completely on the Seer, he's placed you right in my hands." Warden Hazor chuckled again. "What a fool."

"Sir?" Ida questioned. She'd never heard anyone speak so brazenly about the king before.

Warden Hazor smoothed out the parchment. "You passed my test, Shabawn. But now you're going to have to pass an even harder exam."

The next twenty-four hours flew by as Ida filled out a large stack of papers, was scrubbed cleaned and dressed in a restrictive black uniform, then swept from the Fortress and thrust into a carriage.

Ida blinked back her tears once more, touching her slicked back curls tamed into a tight bun at the top of her head. She could see the Fortress from across the murky lake. It was in the distance, but still visible.

Is Sir Jacques still there? Will he even notice I'm gone?

But all those questions fled her mind as the carriage pulled up to her new home: Vlacklear Academy.

Chapter Two

"Breakfast is at seven. Your first class is at eight," the headmistress chirped cheerily.

Ida hesitantly nodded at the tall thin woman, her thoughts trying to move past everything that had happened in the past twenty-four hours. Based on her jutting shoulders and hook-like nose, Ida expected the woman to be harsh and cruel. Instead, she gave her a kind smile.

"I pray Vlacklear is everything you desire it to be." She then noticed Ida's lackluster reply before adding, "Chin up, my dear! Vlacklear has amazing opportunities, even for a scholarship student like you." She patted Ida on the shoulder before continuing to lead her down the empty hall.

Black wooden doors lined the walls on both sides of the austere hallway. As Ida took in the chilling atmosphere, the headmistress chatted on about how male and female students had separate living quarters and must not enter each other's rooms.

Yet, as soon as the woman turned her back, a door at the far end of the hall squeaked open. A male with shining black hair peeked out and looked both ways before slipping out of the room and down the hall.

Ida shook her head in disbelief that the prisoners in the Fortress obeyed the rules better than the students at the prestigious Vlacklear Academy.

Probably because Warden Hazor or Captain Blake would have them hanged if they disobeyed. Ida chuckled to herself at the thought.

While the headmistress continued prattling on about more rules and regulations, Ida considered what the woman said earlier.

Even for a scholarship student like you, the phrase rang in Ida's ears. She knew the headmistress was trying to be kind, but the words still stung.

How many times had she heard that phrase?

Someone like you *wouldn't understand.* You're *too poor.*

People like you *have no idea. You have no class.*

Ida blocked out the past insults. Only those who truly knew *what* she was took the opportunity to try to break her. Then she'd cry and cry, not knowing what else to do.

"Don't listen to them," Ama would say, stroking the tight ebony ringlets away from Ida's tear-stained face. "You are worth more than fifty of those *chinctas.*"

Ida smirked, thinking about Ama's, her mother's, nickname for foolish people. The word *chincta*, derived from the old Tentonian words *chinck* and *tah* or blind and bat. Ama always said fools were no better than blind bats.

Ida took in the headmistress' rigid form and tight black bun as the woman continued explaining about order and decorum at Vlacklear.

Is she a chincta? So far, the woman had been kind to Ida, but after Josef, Ida knew not to trust pretty words so readily.

The headmistress finally stopped her monologue when they reached the end of the hall. A black wooden door, like all the others, stood before them. But, for whatever reason, Ida felt that this door was lonelier than the rest. Standing by itself at the end of the hall, Ida never thought she would relate to a slab of wood so much.

Blinking, Ida pushed the thought aside. She was never alone. Tunri was with her. He had been there in her darkest days before the Categorization Call and the Fortress were even a thought. Tunri was there when Josef was taken from her before he was ever really hers. Ida still remembered Josef's warm smile and sparkling eyes. Eyes that she dreamed about at night. Eyes that were closed forever.

"And that is that!" the headmistress said happily. She clasped her long thin fingers in front of her and gave Ida a wide smile that seemed a bit forced. "Do you have any questions, my dear?"

Ida shifted her focus to the bird-like woman. She couldn't tell if the headmistress was actually kind or forcing herself to be. Either way, Ida was exhausted and just wanted to be left alone.

Taking a breath, Ida recited, "I think I remember everything. Breakfast is at seven, my first class at eight, wear my uniform, comb my hair, listen, take notes, complete my assignments, return to my room by nine, lights out by ten."

The headmistress beamed. "It's no wonder you're here! What a smart young lady you are. Please don't hesitate to reach out to me if you need anything."

As soon as the woman was halfway down the hall, Ida breathed a sigh of relief.

She wasn't sure why, but she preferred Warden Hazor's and Captain Blake's cool frankness instead of this woman's saccharine personality.

Facing her door, Ida gripped the golden knob and twisted. The dark wood creaked open revealing a blindingly white room. An arched window with scarlet drapes welcomed her into the small space. On the far left stood a singular cot with a dark red blanket and white pillow. To the right, sat a sturdy wooden desk. Ida glanced down at her new academy boots sinking into the plush red rug adorning the stone floor.

Though there were luxuries in this room she had never seen before, an uneasiness crept up her spine.

Why is everything the color of blood?

Shivering, Ida thought of her cell in the Fortress. It was dark and plain, but it had become comfortable. She had just started to use different ribbons from Hestia to decorate her space when Warden Hazor ordered her to Vlacklear.

"You'll be a student from Lower Grenly," she remembered the warden saying. "Your story is that you're on scholarship."

Sighing, Ida flopped onto her new bed. How Warden Hazor had gotten her into Vlacklear on scholarship, Ida had no idea. But she was here now, and she had to complete the mission he had given her.

Students like you.

Ida scrunched her nose at the thought. Usually, she could blow off comments like that but, for some reason, the way the headmistress was overly kind dug beneath Ida's skin.

Maybe it was because Ida couldn't figure out if the woman was insulting her status as a "scholarship student" or her home, Lower Grenly.

Ida remembered how Devora treated her the first time they met. Devora sneered at Ida just like all others outside of Lower Grenly. Ida had been so upset and shaken by the experience, especially after First Lady Medee had given her the basket of food in the first place.

At the time, Ida couldn't understand how the First Lady's daughter could be so different from her mother. But Tunri told Ida to trust, so she did. And to her surprise, Devora had been sent to the Fortress, just like Ida. Tunri wanted Ida to show Devora mercy and grace, just like He had shown her many times.

Ida sent a prayer up to Tunri for her Seer friend, hoping that she was safe on the battlefront.

Present

A few weeks passed since that first emotional day and Ida was finally getting used to her life at Vlacklear. She'd chosen to sit in the back of her classes and still got lost when trying to find the dining hall. But Ida loved her work study job in the greenhouse. The beautiful plants and humid temperature reminded her of home.

Stretching from her bed, Ida dressed in the black academy uniform, hating how restricting it was. For the past few weeks, she'd dreamed about wearing her training uniform from the Fortress again, although it was itchier than the fine academy uniform.

Ida ran a hand through her wild curls and frowned. She despised having to confine her hair *every* class day. But the warden said she needed to blend in, so Ida would try to keep doing just that.

With a wince, Ida dipped her fingers in the cold, thick goop and ran it through her ebony ringlets. She cringed as the slimy substance tamed her voluminous curls. Ida hated having to suppress her wild hair.

"Do your best to blend in," Warden Hazor's voice rang in her mind. "If anyone discovers your real purpose at Vlacklear, it'll be both of our heads."

Taking a breath, Ida tried to calm her frantic nerves. She would only have to be here a few more weeks. She was almost halfway through searching Vlacklear's library for anything regarding a lost prophecy. The problem was that the workload for Vlacklear was so heavy, Ida barely had time to execute her plans for the mission.

With a frown, Ida twisted her slick curls into a high bun atop her head, abhoring its resemblance to the headmistress.

After mulling over her introduction to the headmistress a few weeks back, Ida decided she didn't like forced kindness. Staying away from the too sweet and accommodating woman was the best course of action if she wanted to complete her mission from Warden Hazor quickly and quietly.

Placing the lid back on the clay jar, Ida straightened her uniform and headed out the door. As soon she left her room, she noticed a gaggle of girls clogging the hallway.

"Are they here?" Jane from Ida's Ballroom Etiquette class said, standing on her tiptoes to see above the crowd.

"I'm not sure, but that's what I heard," Victoria, a Second Year, responded, craning her neck.

Ida frowned. How was she supposed to get to breakfast on time if there were so many people in her way?

Ida had done her best to not get too close with anyone at Vlacklear, but she still tried to learn the names of the girls living on her hall and be kind to them. She was already so worried for Devora and Nadia on the battlefield, making sure to pray for them every night. But when Warden Hazor took her away from Reese and Hestia, Ida's heart nearly shattered. She didn't want to inflict any more pain on herself by making more friends.

However, Ida did want to make it to breakfast on time.

Gathering her courage, Ida asked Victoria, "Excuse me. Who are you looking for?"

The girl spun around and stared at Ida. She had beautiful strawberry-blonde hair, just the right amount of light brown freckles scattered over her small nose, and, just like Ida, her poor hair was slicked back into the same atrociously high bun. Ida passed the girl in the hall before and knew she was a Second Year. Victoria had always been kind and introduced herself a few days after Ida entered Vlacklear.

Yet Ida still felt the girl's scrutinizing stare, much like she had when Devora first laid eyes on her. Ida's former insecurities about her upbringing crept into her thoughts again.

Poor.

Scum.

Worthless.

Ida blinked the words away and gave Victoria a soft smile. As if a spell had broken, the girl smiled in return.

"You haven't heard of the Sandje sisters?" Victoria asked, still trying to peer over the crowd of people. The group was slowly thinning out. "They're one of the richest families to attend Vlacklear. We heard they just transferred here."

Ida frowned, not recalling the name. She shook her head.

"Oh," Victoria replied, pushing back a stray lock of her strawberry-blonde hair behind her ear. Ida thought a harsh remark would follow. Instead, the girl grinned. "I remember you! You transferred here too, yes? A few weeks ago?" Before Ida could nod, Victoria continued, "We heard new students were coming to Vlacklear after the king changed the categorization colors. Apparently, there are too many vacancies here and the school board needed to fill them."

"Yes," Ida agreed hastily, thankful she didn't need to come up with a lie. She wasn't the best at thinking on her feet.

"I'm thankful your group has been better than the ones who came before," Victoria added, seeming to enjoy talking.

"What do you mean?" Ida asked, curious. If King Atol hadn't switched the color categorizations, Ida, Devora, Nadia, Hestia, and Reese would've all attended Vlacklear together.

The strawberry-blonde leaned in and whispered, "The students that enrolled over the summer were originally meant to attend the military academy."

"Is it bad they came here?" Ida questioned.

"They're brutes!" Victoria squeaked. "They only care about conquest and the next siege. There's no place for them here at Vlacklear where scholars are bred." She crinkled her nose in disgust as she took in the crowd of flocking females. Sighing, the girl focused back on Ida. "I may have introduced myself before, but if not, I'm Victoria Heading, daughter of Governor Charles Heading and First Lady Starr Heading of Ballear. In case you didn't remember." Victoria stuck out her hand in greeting.

Ida stared at the hand. Victoria held so much confidence, just like Devora. No wonder Devora could speak to Captain Blake and Warden Hazor so forwardly. Just like Victoria, as a governor's daughter, she had been taught to do so.

Ida took the hand and shook it once. "I'm Ida."

Up close, Ida studied the freckles dusting Victoria's petite nose as the girl frowned. "Just Ida? That's it?"

Ida lifted her shoulders and gave a warm smile, hoping it was convincing enough. "That's it."

Victoria eyed Ida suspiciously until a large girl, almost the size of One Shot, barreled through the crowd.

"Move out of the way!" the large girl bellowed; her voice deeper than any female Ida knew.

"Watch out!" Victoria cried, grabbing Ida's arm, and yanking her against the wall.

The hefty girl pushed and shoved the others to the sides of the hall, making a path.

Ida's heart raced at the sight of the large girl. Her thoughts immediately went to Babshee, the giant who had attacked Ida's and Devora's carriage convoy when they were first sent to the Fortress. Babshee had been captured and imprisoned in the Fortress after that. The last time Ida had seen the giant was when

Captain Blake sent him back to Level Five after he broke free of his chains while fighting Devora.

Is this girl related to Babshee somehow?

But Ida didn't hear the thick accent in the girl's booming voice that she had in Babshee's.

"Thank you for that," Ida breathed once the possibly giant girl passed them. "Who was that?"

Victoria nodded. "That's Louise. She's usually harmless. But don't get in her way of breakfast. She was supposed to go to the Fortress. But, well—" Victoria looked at Ida and shrugged.

Ida nodded in understanding before studying Louise's toned arms and muscular physique as she torpedoed down the hall.

That's probably what Captain Blake was expecting, but instead he got all of us. Ida thought of Devora and her opinions, Nadia's inventions, Hestia and her flirtatious nature, and Reese's calculations. No wonder the captain was angry all the time. They were nothing like the usual military academy students.

"No, you don't need to worry about Louise," Victoria continued. "But there are some people you should worry about. Mainly Sergio."

"Sergio?" Ida questioned, trying to remember if she'd heard the name when the class prefects took attendance in each class.

"Ugh, I can't stand him," Victoria said, sticking out her tongue. "He's a Third Year so you probably haven't seen him much in your classes but watch out for him."

"I see," Ida replied, realizing the politics at Vlacklear may be far more complicated than those at the Fortress.

"But don't worry," Victoria said, linking her arm through Ida's. "Stick with me and you'll be fine."

Ida was taken aback by the girl's open care. Unlike with the headmistress a few weeks ago, Ida believed Victoria to be sincere in her kind intentions.

Victoria smiled again then glanced at the pathway Louise created. "Oh look, we can finally get a look at the Sandje sisters on our way to breakfast."

Ida turned toward the crowd that gathered to see the Sandje sisters. It was strange how everyone wanted to gawk at someone because they were rich. Rich people still had two eyes, two ears, and a nose. Unless their wealth had made the sisters magically sprout another head or foot, Ida wasn't sure what the big deal was.

But as Victoria flanked her right side, Ida was able to see what the fuss was about. Standing in the middle of the crowd, one giggling and the other brooding, were none other than Hestia and Reese.

Chapter Three

Ida, Vlacklear Academy, Juro

Ida fumbled her steps as she caught sight of Hestia and Reese in the center of all the other girls' attention. Though she was glad to see her friends, Ida had no idea why they were suddenly at Vlacklear Academy, too.

Am I not working fast enough on my mission? Did Warden Hazor send them to help me?

"No one knows about your mission," the warden had told her. "And don't tell anyone unless you're certain they can be trusted and can assist in achieving your goal."

If Hestia and Reese are here to help me, why didn't the warden tell me about them coming to Vlacklear?

Ida glanced back at Hestia and Reese, unsure what to do. Gone was their Fortress attire, replaced with the same form-fitting black academy uniform as Ida and the rest of the girls in the dormitory. But something was different. Ida wasn't sure what it was, but with their hair tied in identical intricate knots at the top of their heads, Hestia and Reese were stunning.

No wonder everyone is flocking to them, Ida thought.

She wasn't sure whether Warden Hazor wanted her to talk with Hestia and Reese or not. And, surprisingly, Ida was okay with that. At the Fortress, no one cared about how much money you had or what you were wearing. People only cared if you could fight well and if you would protect them on the battlefield.

But at Vlacklear, Ida was brought back to her upbringing where she was the poor girl who no one wanted to be friends with. No one but Josef.

Ida took another look at Hestia and Reese and kept walking. It was better they didn't know she was here. She needed to focus on her mission and get back to the Fortress with the information Warden Hazor needed as quickly as possible.

As Victoria prattled on about different historical facts about Vlacklear, Ida took in her surroundings, still not used to them. Unlike the dark stone of the Fortress, Vlacklear Academy's halls were comprised of pure white marble. The more Ida looked around at the walls, the more her eyes hurt. The white wasn't comforting but blinding.

A plush red carpet ran down the middle of the hall. Ida remembered when she first walked upon it, expecting the color to change when they left the girls' dormitories. But it never did. Almost every carpet at Vlacklear Academy was blood red.

A shiver ran down Ida's spine as she took in the scarlet carpet and crimson drapes against the golden light fixtures. It may be that she had gotten used to the Fortress' dingy décor, but everything in Vlacklear was almost *too* tidy. There were no smudges on the window, no creases in the rug. Everything was perfect.

Ida nodded as Victoria asked her a question, not knowing what it was, but hoping it would invite the girl to continue to talk. Luckily, Victoria enjoyed hearing her own voice.

Warden Hazor warned her that Vlacklear wasn't everything it appeared to be. But when Ida prompted for further information, the warden said no more. So, Ida had done her best searching through the library when she had a few spare moments. But so far, she had come up with nothing to tell the warden.

The sugary scent of cinnamon swirling through the air interrupted Ida's thoughts. Her stomach let out a growl. While Vlacklear kept her nerves on end, the food was miles better than the prison mush at the Fortress.

"And this is where we sit in the dining hall," Victoria said, concluding her seminar on Vlacklear that Ida barely listened to.

Ida looked at the rows of wooden tables lining the white hall. If she could block out the bright walls, which she had tried to do every day for the past few weeks, it almost felt like the Fortress.

"Okay, Vic, I think you talked her ear off enough," a male voice said, and Ida jerked around to find a boy with curly brown hair standing right next to her.

"Who are you?" Ida asked with surprise.

Victoria rolled her eyes. "Ugh, this is Patrick. Ignore him."

Ida glanced between Victoria and Patrick.

Patrick grinned at her and said, "I'm Patrick. Don't ignore me, I'm the fun one." He extended his hand.

Ida couldn't help but crack a smile and think the statement was one Nadia would say.

Reaching out, Ida shook his hand. "I'm Ida."

Patrick nodded with understanding. "One of the new transfers, huh? Glad you found ole Vic here to show you the ropes."

Ida didn't bother explaining that she had already been there for a little while. It was easier to let people believe what they wanted about her. Instead, she only smiled, like she usually did.

Patrick wrapped a gangly arm around Victoria's slim shoulders. And though she shoved him off, Ida swore she caught a blush on Victoria's cheeks.

"Well, Ida, Vic—" Patrick glanced at both girls before rubbing his hands together. "Let's get some grub."

Victoria rolled her eyes with a scoff and sat down at the table without getting any food. Ida didn't understand why Victoria didn't want to eat, but *she* wasn't going to pass up the chance for another delicious meal.

Ida allowed Patrick to whisk her to the line for breakfast. He handed her a red tray then grabbed his own before layering plates of food on it. Ida stared at the tray. Red again. Though she had been here for a bit, she still couldn't get used to all the red.

"Aren't you going to get anything?" Patrick asked, trying to balance a plate of eggs on top of a plate of cinnamon rolls. He had already stuffed one of the rolls in his mouth.

Ida giggled and decided on a cinnamon roll and a bowl of fruit.

The gooey cinnamon sugar scent filled Ida's nose. She couldn't wait to dig her teeth into its soft crust. Giddiness tickled Ida's nerves as she thought about her soon-to-be delight.

As she sat back with Victoria, who opted only for an apple, Ida licked her lips. Reaching out, she grabbed the cinnamon roll. Cinnamon sugar oozed onto her hands. Completely entranced by the roll, Ida hardly noticed the figures coming toward her. Just as she opened her mouth to take a bite, she heard her name yelled across the dining hall.

"Ida!"

Ida froze, the delicious delight of her cinnamon roll forgotten as it fell from her hands. Slowly, Ida turned to see Hestia hurrying toward her with Reese not far behind.

It wasn't that Ida didn't want her friends to find her. She planned on finding them later, in a more private manner. No, it was all the faces of judgment staring at her throughout the dining hall. Ida remembered the first time she entered the Fortress' dining hall. She was so frightened she dropped her bowl of mush. But the prisoners didn't laugh or jeer at her. They simply kept on eating their food until Sir Jacques helped her clean up the mess.

So far, she had kept a low profile at Vlacklear. No one looked twice at her, and Ida was happy with that. But with Hestia's and Reese's fame, that would all come to an end.

As Ida took in the smirks on the faces of the nobles around her, Ida preferred the indifference of the prisoners.

Before she had a chance to reply, Hestia wrapped her long arms around Ida and gave her a tight hug.

"Why didn't you tell us where you went?" Hestia whispered in her ear. "We've been worried sick!"

"It was a secret," Ida managed to reply.

Understanding dawned on Hestia, and she quickly released Ida and took a step back. "Ah yes, my good friend, Ida, from summer lessons." Hestia added a forced laugh causing Reese to roll her eyes.

"Good to see you again, Ida," Reese said smoothly, giving Ida a deep bow like she was someone of authority. Reese clanked the beads of her abacus against each other. "I hope your family is doing well."

Ida's brows rose at Reese's proper manners. *What happened to the rude girl with the abacus?*

Reese gave Ida a pointed look and Ida realized she hadn't responded. The dining hall returned to its soft murmurs, but a few people still eavesdropped on the conversation, mainly Victoria and Patrick.

"Ah, yes," Ida replied, her hands clasped in front of her as she rubbed the wire adorning her wrist. "My family is well since...summer lessons. Thank you for asking."

Reese nodded politely as Hestia bounced on her toes in excitement. A cough sounded from behind Ida, and she spun around, realizing Victoria and Patrick were still staring at her.

"T-these are my classmates," Ida fumbled. "Victoria and Patrick."

Victoria sprang up like a daisy, immediately thrusting her hand toward Reese. "I'm Victoria Heading, daughter of the Governor of Ballear. I've read all about your father's investments and how he procured his wealth. It's an honor to finally meet you."

For the first time since she met Reese, Ida watched the girl stutter for a response.

"It's great to meet you, too!" Hestia barged in, shaking Victoria's hand vivaciously.

Victoria returned Hestia's enthusiastic smile. "Would you like to join us for breakfast?"

"I thought you'd never ask," Hestia chirped as she slid next to Patrick. "What's your name?"

"Patrick," he replied between bites. Though judging by his tone, Patrick had no intention of getting to know Hestia or Reese better.

Reese quietly sat next to Ida as Victoria chittered on about Duke Sandje's latest investments.

Ida turned to Reese. When they first entered the Fortress, Reese said nothing but rude comments and insults. But, as time went by, Ida witnessed Reese's demeanor soften until she started to care about those around her.

But as Ida took in Reese's slumped posture and hardened gaze, Ida knew something had changed.

"Is everything all right?" she whispered to Reese.

Reese didn't speak but shook her head while sliding the beads on her abacus one at a time.

"Oh, we must get going!" Victoria said, bouncing up from the table. Ida noticed her apple hadn't been touched. "Ida, what's your first class?"

Ida fished out the parchment from her pocket. Though she knew her class schedule, she always forgot the room number, so she kept a copy of it with her.

The headmistress told Ida she was already behind with her studies and needed to load up her classes if she wanted to keep up with the rest of the students in her year. Ida had no idea how she could've been so far behind when all the other students hadn't begun classes much earlier than she had. But, as always, she kept her thoughts to herself.

Unfolding the parchment, Ida read: "The Fundamentals of Learning Advanced Battle, Room three zero five."

"Wow, that's a mouthful," Hestia replied as she wolfed down her plate of eggs. Reese nudged her in the ribs and Hestia quickly straightened and politely wiped her mouth with her napkin.

Victoria beamed. "Patrick and I have a class in the same hall so we'll walk with you." She turned to Hestia and Reese. "It was a delight meeting you both. I'd love to have lunch together, as well."

"That would be great!" Hestia replied. It was her turn to elbow Reese in the side. Reese mechanically nodded but stayed silent.

Worry danced around Ida's heart for Reese, but she couldn't spare her friend a second glance before Victoria whisked her away with Patrick shuffling behind.

Once they left the dining hall, Victoria looped her arm through Ida's and asked, "Why didn't you tell us you knew the Sandje sisters?"

"She just met us, Vic," Patrick groaned as he shoved his hands in his pockets. "She doesn't have to tell us anything."

"It was just a question, Patrick," Victoria hissed.

"I apologize, Victoria," Ida replied, doing her best to impersonate Devora. "When I met Hestia and Reese, they didn't reveal their birthright to me. We were all equal at summer lessons. The topic never came up, and I never asked."

Ida knew she stretched the truth, but she was happy it wasn't an outright lie. They *were* all equal at the Fortress and the topic *hadn't* come up. Ida also hadn't intended for the comment to be a jab at Victoria's noble upbringing but felt guilty when Victoria winced at the statement all the same.

"Sounds like wherever you took your lessons had some sense," Patrick said. Lacing his hands behind his head, he strolled on Ida's left. "Everyone here will judge you for who your parents are and what they do. They don't care about who *you* are and what *you'll* do. Isn't that right, Vic?"

Victoria said nothing as the trio rounded the corner of another white hall. Their steps were silenced by the plush red carpet, but Ida could still hear the tension thickening between her and Victoria. She knew Warden Hazor didn't want her to stand out, but Victoria had reached out to Ida so kindly and openly.

"Our class is here," Victoria said softly, not meeting Ida's eyes.

Ida usually didn't speak her mind so freely. She always relied on others to stand up, and she would rally behind them. But there was no one else there.

Taking a breath of bravery, Ida explained, "I didn't mean to offend you with my comment, Victoria. I was just explaining that, as someone who doesn't have such a distinguished background, being on the same level as Hestia and Reese was nice." Ida reached out and squeezed Victoria's hand. "There's nothing wrong with being proud of who you are and where you come from."

Shock covered Victoria's face before it melted into a smile. "Thank you, Ida. We'll come by after your class and walk with you again if that's all right."

Ida smiled with a nod; thankful she was able to diffuse a tense situation by herself.

"Come along, Patrick, we're going to be late."

"Yes, ma'am," Patrick replied with a salute, winking at Ida as Victoria prattled on about how she knew the three of them were going to be good friends.

As Victoria and Patrick turned down a different hall, Ida headed toward the third door on the right. And although she had been attending classes for a few weeks, Ida always felt nervous entering the classroom.

Courage, Ida, she told herself. *You've done this many times before. Courage and don't cry.*

Taking a breath, Ida forced her legs to carry her into the room. Each of the chairs was already filled, and Ida quickly realized she was the last one to arrive. She typically arrived early, even with getting lost in the halls, and claimed a seat in the back.

But eating breakfast with Victoria and Patrick and the shock of seeing Hestia and Reese had made her late.

Heat tinged Ida's ears as she slunk into the last available chair at the front of the room. Thankfully, all the judgmental stares were behind her now and she had gotten there before Prefect Eric took attendance. Ida witnessed many times when he marked people tardy, although they were in the classroom. If you weren't in your seat at the correct time, you were tardy.

But as Ida took out her parchment, quill, and ink, she noticed Prefect Eric was nowhere to be found. Professor Trudoe was sometimes late or had Prefect Eric teach the class in his stead. But never had the prefect been absent.

Not five minutes after she sat down, the door to the room burst open, causing several students—including Ida—to jump.

"My apologies, first years. I got lost trying to find my way here. This castle is a labyrinth if I ever saw one."

If Ida were made of ice, she would've melted into a puddle on the floor. Her heart rate increased rapidly as she tried to divert her eyes from the sandy blond hair and hazel eyes she'd come to adore.

"Welcome back to the Fundamentals of Learning Advanced Basics, or FLAB, as I like to say," Sir Jacques said to the class with a wide grin.

Chapter Four

Matthias howled in pain as his wolf form shrank back into his human body. He wasn't sure what day it was anymore. He had been searching for Devora for what felt like weeks and found nothing. The scent of the purple rose he'd left for her kept him on her trail for a while, but it suddenly stopped. Matthias tore through Tenton, searching everywhere for her, but came up empty-handed.

Growling, he slammed his fists on the muddy ground, his muscles still raw from his transformation. It had gotten easier—his curse to change into a wolf—over time. But that didn't mean the pain was any less.

Droplets of rain slammed onto his naked form, feeling like spears of ice instead of the harmless water they were. It always took a few days for his body to recover and that was if he transformed *willingly*. When he was first cursed, the wolf would spring out any time it pleased, leaving Matthias defenseless against its will. So many innocent lives were lost because he couldn't control the raging beast inside of him.

With a groan, Matthias stood, trying to get his bearings. In his wolf form, his senses heightened, and he could always determine his location based on scent. But once he was human again, he had to use basic deductive reasoning. A sheet of rain poured over him and Matthias swiped his chestnut hair out of his eyes. First things first, he needed to find clothes.

Matthias trudged through the mud-caked ground, trying to ignore his bare feet sinking into the squishy soil. Frigid rain rolled down his skin, soaking him to the core. At least he knew he wasn't in Grenly or Yekel. Typically, their rainstorms were humid and warm. That fact alone led him to believe he was somewhere in northern Tenton.

A warm orange light glowed in the distance. Relief encouraged Matthias' cold form to move toward the light. Once he was dry and clothed, he could refocus on finding Devora. His stomach released a guttural growl, squeezing in pain. His transformation burned a lot of energy. Being in his wolf form for an extended period took a toll on his human stomach too.

The thought of warm bread and butter, roasted chicken and potatoes, and a slice of cocoa cake had saliva almost dripping from Matthias's mouth. Even his hungry daydream was far better than the raw rabbits he'd been eating for the past few weeks. Once he was dry, clothed, *and* fed, he could refocus on finding Devora.

Matthias approached the thatched cottage. Now that he was closer, a waft of freshly baked goods spiraled from the cracks in the door and he refrained from breaking it down. Sucking in a breath, he did his best to cover himself with his hands before knocking.

Rain splattered down on him from the roof just as a young woman open the door.

"Good day," he started after realizing he wasn't sure what time of day it was. "My name is Captain Matthias Blake and I'm in need of some clothes and refreshments if you could spare any. I will be sure to compensate you royally upon my return to the capital."

The young woman with tight black ringlets stared wide-eyed at Matthias before she slammed the door in his face.

Blinking, it took Matthias a moment to realize what had happened. He glanced down at his muddied bare body and sighed. At least the girl didn't kill him on sight. That would've been his first reaction to a naked man knocking on his door during a storm.

Matthias began to move to a different home when he overheard a conversation inside.

"That has to be him. I know it, Pa," a female voice said.

"Are you certain?" a deep male voice responded.

"I don't like it, Mara," another younger sounding male voice commented. "Why would he appear in such a state?"

The flurry of papers rustling sounded and then the female, Mara, said, "It must be. Ben wrote about a captain in his letters."

Matthias strained to hear over the howling wind of the storm. He wished whoever was inside would decide whether they were going to let him in. At this rate he was going to die of hypothermia.

Another moment passed and the door creaked open to reveal a tall middle-aged man. His long thin arms held out a thick woolen blanket.

"Please come in, Captain Blake."

Matthias swiped his dripping hair out of his eyes and hastily took the blanket. As he stepped into the cottage, the warmth of the humble home instantly made him feel at ease. He was thankful there were still gracious people in Tenton. After all his time in the Fortress and Maldove Palace, he had forgotten they existed.

"Thank you, sir," Matthias bowed, making sure to keep his shivering form completely covered. "I owe you a great debt."

Once he straightened, Matthias noticed the man's features. Long thin arms, pale skin, straight black hair. He tilted his head to the side. *Is this One Shot's father?* If that were true, then Matthias was just outside of Ballear.

"I hear you know my son, Benjamin?" the man who looked almost exactly like One Shot, asked.

A crinkle of papers alerted Matthias to the couple standing as far away from him as the small room would allow. The young woman who first answered the door gripped a stack of papers in her hands so tightly, Matthias thought they may rip in half.

That must be Mara. One Shot had told Matthias what happened to his sister and why One Shot was in the Fortress. Matthias never blamed One Shot for his actions as he would have probably done the same if it were his sister. Or worse.

Mara's face was whiter than a sheet, eyes larger than the moon as she stared at Matthias. Matthias studied her to find her belly just barely swollen and his sharp gaze softened.

The man next to Mara was tense, his arm wrapped protectively around her shoulder. Probably her husband, One Shot's former friend. Matthias was immediately reminded of the warden's wolves back at the Fortress. It had taken him a bit of time to convince them he was a friend, and he would do the same here.

Clearing his throat, Matthias did his best to seem respectable even in his weathered state. "Yes. Benjamin has been a crucial aid in the recent events regarding the war against Kadesh."

Mara elbowed her husband in the stomach. "See? I told you," she whispered as the man winced from the jab.

"Where is he now?" One Shot's father asked. "We haven't heard from him in months."

Matthias shifted the blanket around his shoulders, wishing he could continue this conversation fully clothed. But he'd endured worse than this and would soldier on.

"Unfortunately, I cannot share his current whereabouts as it would comprise his and others' safety, sir." Mara gasped and Matthias added, "Please rest assured that he is safe."

One Shot's father relaxed at the comment and gave a nod. "Let's get you some dry clothes and maybe you can tell me why you've shown up at my bakery bare as a newborn babe."

Heat rose up Matthias' neck at the comment while Mara snorted, trying to hold back a laugh.

"Mara, please get Captain Blake some food. I'm sure he's hungry."

"Any nourishment would be most appreciated, sir," Matthias responded, doing his best to control his ravaging hunger.

As One Shot's father and Mara shuffled about, Mara's husband eyed Matthias like he was a criminal. He crossed his hands over his chest making sure Matthias knew he wasn't completely welcome here.

Matthias was impressed. If he wasn't trying to find Devora, fight a war, and save his kingdom from tyrannical rule, he would recruit the man on the spot.

Straightening his stance, Matthias dipped his head. "I assure you, I am no threat to your family, despite what my sudden and alarming appearance may indicate."

The man's gaze narrowed, and his stance stayed alert, but he dipped his head in acknowledgment.

One Shot's father stomped into the room "I'm not sure these will fit, but it's the best I can do."

"I appreciate your kindness, sir," Matthias responded as he took the clothes.

"Name's Byron. No need to call me sir." But the older man smirked at the title. He thrust his thumb over his shoulder. "Spare room's back there, if you want some privacy. Mara will be out with your food in a moment."

Matthias bowed deeply, thanking Tunri he had been guided to a family of a friend, not a foe.

After he was dried and clothed, Matthias remembered he'd left Devora's imperial opal ring with One Shot. His neck felt bare without the chain there, keeping the ring safe so it wouldn't harm her or anyone else. Once Matthias ate a hot meal, he would be on his way back to his father's vineyard, Totem, and would take the ring back. If One Shot listened to him, then he, Nadia and her friend Rae, and Tristan should all be there with the others who fled from Yekel.

Matthias combed damp hair out of his face with his fingers. He needed all of them to help find Devora. His wolf senses usually didn't fail him when tracking people, but he wasn't dealing with an ordinary woman. She was extraordinary in every definition of the word. He just prayed he'd have another chance to tell her so.

Straightening his shoulders, Matthias strode back into the room where he met One Shot's family. The cottage was cozy and warm. A wooden table rested against the far wall with three chairs around it. Framed cross-stitch patterns hung from the walls and Matthias wondered if One Shot's mother had made them. One Shot never mentioned his mother, so Matthias didn't ask, assuming it was an off-limits topic.

A crackling fire flickered to the left, and it was then Matthias noticed the adjacent room was the kitchen. He took a step to see beyond that and found a small gathering area where different baked goods were displayed. Reaching back in his memory, Matthias recalled Byron mentioning he was in a bakery.

When Matthias was first thrown into the Fortress and befriended One Shot, the giant-like man explained his love for baking. Matthias had scoffed and rebutted that his new friend could bake all he liked but if he wanted to survive the Fortress, a cake wouldn't save his life. He then taught One Shot the fighting techniques he'd learned when he previously studied at Vlacklear. The giant man was an astute student and a fast learner. Matthias never understood why he didn't use that to get out of Level Five.

"Your meal is ready, sir," Mara said with a small nod toward the table.

Her initial fear had fled her face and was now replaced with open curiosity. Matthias could see the questions building, waiting to escape her mouth. He smirked, remembering Devora having the same look.

"There's no need for the formalities," he responded. "I am grateful for your kindness and hospitality."

Matthias strode toward the table where a plate of warm chicken, fried potatoes, baked carrots, and a roll waited for him. Mara had also set down a warm cup of coffee and Matthias swore she was a saint. He felt like ripping into the food with his hands. But the three sets of eyes staring at him kept his animal instincts caged.

As he sat down, Byron and Mara joined him, leaving Mara's husband standing. Matthias would've offered him his chair, but he knew the man wanted to be in the most powerful position in the room. Matthias couldn't blame him for that.

"So," Byron began once Matthias enjoyed a few bites of the food. "What brings you to Snoken in the middle of a rainstorm?"

Matthias swallowed a bite of the freshly made roll. "I was tracking an important member of my troop when the storm hit, and I lost the trail."

Matthias knew half-truths, and sometimes full-out lies, were a necessary evil when fighting a war. He couldn't reveal everything to anyone.

Byron nodded. "And your clothes?"

Matthias sighed, deciding he had to tell a partial truth. "I cannot give you a believable explanation, sir. But I can assure you, I do not make it a point to stalk around naked. Especially in rainstorms."

Mara snorted again, trying to cover up her laughter.

Matthias quirked a brow but found himself smirking. How different Mara was from her brother. Matthias was thankful to see she'd healed from her past and prayed One Shot would be able to do the same.

Byron's lips ticked up at the end as he nodded. "All right, son. No need to be so serious. I was merely curious. From what Benjamin has told us, you helped him a lot. For that, Mara and I are grateful."

Worry cinched Matthias' throat. *What has One Shot told them?* Yet judging by their open, accepting faces, One Shot had spoken highly of Matthias. Something he was unaccustomed to.

"One—er Ben has been an asset and a good friend to me as well," Matthias added softly.

Once Matthias finished his plate of food, the trio chatted more about the bakery, One Shot, and the storm, until Mara brought out a cocoa cake. White sugar coated the top and Matthias' heart immediately yearned for Devora.

"This is Ma's recipe," Mara explained as she served her husband and Byron a slice. "Ben loved making it. He even memorized all the ingredients and measurements."

"Yes," Matthias nodded, thanking Mara for the slice she handed him with a nod. "I've had his before."

The three of them stopped and stared at Matthias.

"Ben bakes in the Fortress?" Mara's husband asked with a look of shock.

"Ben is baking again?" Mara whispered at the same time.

Matthias placed his fork down. "He did, as a favor to me, for a friend of mine." Matthias' heart squeezed at the word *friend*, knowing what he felt for Devora was so much more than friendship.

Mara clasped her hands together, a soft smile coming to her face. "After everything that happened, Ben refused to bake again. I was so angry at him for so long." She placed her hand on her husband's shoulder. "But Tunri has used Jonathon to help me through my pain and anger. I wish I could see Ben again and apologize for cutting him out. He was always the better baker of the two of us." Her eyes misted when she added, "He loved it."

Matthias thought about Devora enjoying the cocoa cake after Round Two of the Regulus Protecti tournament. How he wished he could taste the cocoa on her lips after she enjoyed the dessert. He was a fool to have wasted his precious time with her. Swallowing deeply, Matthias cleared his throat and tried to refocus his thoughts.

"I want to apologize to him, too," Jonathon said, finally relaxing enough to sit next to Matthias. "I didn't support him when I should have. If I would've vouched for him in court, he wouldn't have gone to the Fortress."

Matthias studied the man before him. A fierce loyalty radiated from Jonathon, reminding Matthias so much of himself.

"Perhaps," Matthias replied, thinking of One Shot's remarkable marksmanship. "But, from what I've witnessed, the Fortress has assisted Ben in more ways than one."

"Really?" Jonathon asked as he took out a piece of wood from his pocket.

Matthias nodded and Jonathon relaxed more as he pulled a small blade from a sheath on his belt.

"Another piece of cake, Captain?" Mara asked. She then noticed Matthias' focus on Jonathon's whittling. "Oh, don't mind him. He has a goal to carve the baby every animal he can think of." Mara rubbed her stomach lovingly. "We already have fifteen of them."

"And we'll have plenty more if I have anything to say about it," Jonathon replied with a grin. Mara leaned down and kissed him tenderly before serving Matthias another piece of cake.

But it wasn't the adoration between the couple that had Matthias fixated on Jonathon—though he was envious of the man's happiness. It was his blade. Sturdily gripped in Jonathon's hand was a blade with a handle made of imperial opal.

Chapter Five

The air fled Ida's lungs.

First Hestia and Reese. Now Sir Jacques is here too? How many more undercover students is Warden Hazor going to send?

"Ah yes, FLAB, my favorite subject," Sir Jacques repeated, evoking a ripple of laughter from the students. "And though I wish I was the one teaching you the wonders of FLAB, I am only a newly appointed, lowly prefect." He bowed his head in mock shame, while the class moaned in disappointment. "Unfortunately, Prefect Eric had to return home for familial matters. Your professor will be here shortly. Until then"—Sir Jacques shrugged the leather bag off his shoulders before rifling through it. Once he pulled out a piece of parchment and stick of charcoal, he glanced up— "time for attendance."

Ida's breathing slowly returned to normal as Sir Jacques rattled off a series of names. But when he called out hers, her heart stopped.

"Miss Ida Shabawn?"

The way he said her name made her pulse race. She wanted to crawl into a hole and hide from his attention while wanting to throw her arms around him and kiss him at the same time.

Slowly, Ida lifted her gaze to his as she replied in a soft voice, "Present."

His hazel eyes landed on her in the front row and held her stare for what seemed like an eternity. But as much as Ida wanted the moment to last, it was gone in a blink.

The knight gave her a quick wink and Ida thought her heart would burst as he continued down the list of students' names.

Sir Jacques had to be here because Warden Hazor sent him as well. But was she supposed to talk to him about her mission? Or hide it like she did with Hestia and Reese? Why wasn't the warden clearer about these things?

Confusion and anxiety brewed like a storm in Ida's mind, and she couldn't focus on anything Sir Jacques said until Professor Trudoe came into the room. He was a stout man with a receding hairline and nasally voice. Once Professor Trudoe's dull lesson explaining the origin of the stone used to build Vlacklear started, Ida was reminded why the class enjoyed Sir Jacques' presence so much more.

Ida couldn't help but track Sir Jacques as he placed the attendance parchment on the professor's desk and sat in a chair against the far wall. His presence was extremely distracting, and Ida couldn't focus at all on what the long-winded professor was saying. She comprehended a few remarks Professor Trudoe made that sounded important. But when she hastily went to scribble them down, she couldn't help but glance at Sir Jacques and find him watching her. He gave her a warm smile; the same one she'd come to adore when he collected the taxes in Grenly. Ida would soon be a puddle if she looked at him anymore.

Once her pulse calmed and her skin cooled, Ida was able to think rationally. She needed to push her emotions aside and talk to Sir Jacques or Hestia or Reese. She needed someone to help her with this mission. She couldn't do it alone. But together, they may be able to make it through the rest of the books in the library.

"All right, students," Professor Trudoe announced near the end of the class. "Before we end our class today, the headmistress has some questions she'd like all students to answer about their time here at Vlacklear. Prefect Jacques will administer the questions. Remember to complete your reading before the next class."

The professor packed up his bag and exited the class before anyone could respond. As soon as he was gone, Sir Jacques stood from his chair and strode before the class.

"All right, students, please take out a blank piece of parchment."

"Do we really have to answer the questions?" a tan boy with black hair asked. "The professor doesn't seem to care at all."

Ida didn't know much about him other than all the girls giggled and tried to get his attention. Similar to how the girls acted with Sir Jacques at the Fortress.

Sir Jacques smiled but it was tight. "It is my responsibility to follow Professor Trudoe's instructions, not question them, Sergio."

Ida's ears perked up at the name, remembering Victoria saying something about a student named Sergio, but couldn't recall the details. Prefect Eric only called out each student's last name, so Ida had never known any of her classmates' first names until today.

Groans erupted from the students, but they each took out a piece of blank parchment all the same.

"And I was going to say you were the best prefect at Vlacklear," Sergio whined.

"While I'm flattered," Sir Jacques replied, facing the blackboard, his voice laced with a dark tone Ida rarely heard from the knight. "As I said before, I am not the professor."

Ida blinked dazedly as Sir Jacques wrote the questions on the blackboard with a piece of chalk. His angular shoulders dipped into his thin waist as he wrote each letter in beautiful cursive.

Has he had private lessons? Ida thought.

Because she lived in Lower Grenly, Ida had to attend public lessons with the rest of the Lower Grenly children. The teachers of the public lessons usually didn't care what the kids learned as long as they stayed out of trouble. Because of that, Ida's penmanship was horrific. Thankfully, her gift with different dialects and languages helped her learn how to read on her own. Maybe that's why she categorized for Vlacklear. Yet, she still couldn't figure out how her categorization worked, especially since she wasn't born in Tenton.

Sir Jacques set an hourglass on Professor Trudoe's wooden desk. "You have thirty minutes to answer these three questions starting now."

The scribbling of quills on parchment filled the room while Ida stared at the board. How could she answer these questions?

Question One: What do you hope to accomplish at Vlacklear Academy?

Ida gripped the quill in her hand, black ink staining her fingertips. *Should I answer truthfully?* She still didn't know who she was supposed to trust. Tears welled in her eyes at the stress Warden Hazor placed on her, but she sucked them down. If the Fortress had taught her anything it was to be strong and hide your weakness. She decided to move on to the next question.

Question Two: Why do you want to be at Vlacklear Academy?

Ida frowned. *Isn't that the same question?* She shook her head. Maybe she wasn't smart enough to be at Vlacklear. She didn't have private lessons like Devora and apparently Sir Jacques. She could barely hold a quill and couldn't memorize things nearly as fast as others. Tears threatened to spill over again, but Ida held them back. Barely.

She finally made it to the final question but was even more confused than before.

Question Three: If you could do anything with your life, what would it be?

What is the point of these questions? Ida didn't know what she wanted to do with her life, but she did know she wanted to do nothing but crawl back to her room and hide. She felt as if everyone else knew who they wanted to be and had their future planned, and Ida was just trying to survive. Quills scribbled back and forth, spiraling Ida deeper and deeper into herself.

What would she do with her life if she had the choice? A question that seemed so simple but held so much weight.

She dreamed once. She'd dreamed so many dreams. But all that was taken away. As soon as Josef was gone, Ida's life shifted into survival mode. Hiding from a war, taken from her home. Not that Ida didn't appreciate what Ama had done for her, but she wasn't her real mother and Ida knew it.

Ida always feared what the people of Lower Grenly would say if they knew her true origin. Would they kill her on sight? Throw stones at her until she bled out? Either Ama's plan worked and no one in Lower Grenly found out about Ida's birthplace, or the people of Lower Grenly chose to look the other way and say nothing.

Yet as Ida glanced at the studious faces around her—writing paragraphs of all the wonderful things they wanted to accomplish at Vlacklear and do to change the world—Ida knew these people would do nothing but condemn her for her true nationality.

Daring to peek at Sir Jacques, she found him thumbing through a thick leatherbound text. Ida blushed at how handsome he looked with his slicked-back blond hair and crisp white tunic. A black jerkin, matching slacks, and boots completed his elegant Vlacklear attire. Ida noticed that upon the jerkin, a golden V was embroidered on the left side, displaying Sir Jacques' position as a prefect.

Ida had never seen Sir Jacques in anything other than his training uniform and his armor. She always loved it when he came to collect taxes in Grenly. Not that she enjoyed their hard-earned coin going to a king who didn't care about them, but Sir Jacques would always greet Ama so kindly. He wasn't rude and brash like some of the other tax collectors in the past. Ama encouraged Ida to greet him at the door, but she would only cower in the corner where she couldn't be seen.

She'd always admired Sir Jacques from afar because that's where it was safe. Her heart couldn't handle suffering the loss of another knight. And besides, why would a knight of the Fortress want to be with her, a poor girl from Lower Grenly?

A quick look at the hourglass and Ida knew she only had a few minutes left. She quickly scribbled a few sentences down until Sir Jacques called time.

"All right, students, place your parchments next to the hour-glass on the way out. Don't forget about the reading assignment. You'll be happy you learned about all the wonders of FLAB."

The students snickered again as they filed before the desk. A few gave her inquisitive looks as they passed by but said nothing.

Gathering her courage, Ida did her best to hold her chin high like she'd seen Devora do many times. Once all the other students exited the room, she strode to the desk.

As Ida placed the parchment down, Sir Jacques quickly laid his hand over hers.

"Ida, I'm so glad you're okay," he said softly.

Ida's skin burned with delight at his soft touch.

"I am many things right now, Sir Jacques," she whispered, not trusting herself to look at him for fear she may burst into a sobbing mess. "But I'm not sure if okay is one of them."

After he didn't speak, she steadied herself and glanced up. Concern laced his angular features, and the tears Ida was trying to hold back almost fell. *Why does he care about me?*

"I need to talk to you, privately," Sir Jacques said, his voice low. "About why you're here. About why we're *both* here. And other news that hasn't reached public knowledge yet."

Ida's brows rose, hope digging her heart out of the sorrow it was falling into. Had Warden Hazor provided her with someone she could trust and confide in? The heavy weight she held lightened as she nodded.

Sir Jacques squeezed her hand once, rubbing his thumb over the wire bracelet. "Meet me in the library tonight after dinner. We'll call it tutoring in case anyone asks." He winked at her again, and Ida's cheeks filled with heat.

"Okay," she said, feeling bashful. "I'll see you then."

As she regretfully pulled her hand away, Sir Jacques called out to her again.

"Keep that bracelet close. If anyone finds out why you're really here, you may need it."

Victoria and Patrick waited outside her class, just like they said they would. Ida's heart warmed at their quick loyalty.

"Already getting into trouble?" Patrick asked with a smirk.

"I'm sure that's not true," Victoria piped in, though her face was covered with concern. "She's not like you."

Patrick smiled proudly and Ida laughed, thankful to release some of the tension she'd been holding.

"Apparently, I need extra tutoring," Ida lied. "Since I came later in the term, I'm behind."

Patrick and Victoria nodded with sympathy.

"We've both been there," Victoria sighed, fixing a stray strawberry blonde strand trying to escape from her tight bun. "Vlacklear is heavy with its academic standards. It's difficult to keep up. As long as you don't have the lowest average in your class before the Assembly, you should be okay," Victoria said with a shrug.

Ida's brows furrowed. "What happens at the Assembly?"

Victoria and Patrick shared a look.

"If you have the lowest—" Patrick started before Victoria clamped her hand over his mouth.

A group of prefects, all wearing the same golden V emblem on their shirts, strode by them, casting suspicious glances.

Victoria gave them a winning smile until they all passed.

"Do you want to be sent to the Tower, Patrick?" Victoria hissed.

"I've already been before, Vic," Patrick bit back. "And I'm fine."

Victoria's face fell as she twisted her hands. "We're not all as strong as you."

Patrick's face softened. "Vic, I didn't mean—"

Victoria cleared her throat and faced Ida, blocking her view of Patrick. "Anyway, shall we go to our next classes?"

Ida studied the pair, completely confused by the exchange that just occurred. Why couldn't she have the lowest average before the Assembly? What was the Assembly? What was the Tower?

But Ida wasn't used to cornering people and making them answer her questions, so she only nodded, and the trio headed down the hall. As they took a right at the adjacent corridor, a group of girls passed by them. They took one look at Victoria and Patrick, then Ida and burst out laughing.

"Ignore them, Vic," Patrick said, his hands in his pockets as he strolled next to Victoria. "You know they're trying to get under your skin."

Victoria nodded solemnly as she tightened her arms around her books, but Ida swore she saw tears building in her eyes. It was a look Ida constantly held after categorizing for the Fortress.

Ida's next class was Ballroom Etiquette. Surprisingly, she found this class fascinating. More fascinating than Patrick, who kept falling asleep beside her, apparently did. Ida had never been to a ball but always dreamed of wearing an enormously poofy gown and being swept off her feet by a dashing stranger.

Ida sighed to herself. *Like that would ever happen.*

After Ballroom Etiquette ended, Ida and Patrick made their way to the dining hall where they met Victoria for lunch. As Ida entered the hall, Hestia immediately found her and linked arms with her.

"Ida, we need to exchange schedules to see if we have any classes together."

Ida nodded and took out her schedule, hoping they did share a class until she saw the looks of the others around them. Looks she had seen many times before. Judgment, disgust. The whispers soon reached her ears.

"Who is *that*? And why is she with one of the Sandje sisters?" a girl with a tight brown bun asked.

"I heard she was a scholarship student," another one with auburn hair sneered. "From *Lower* Grenly." The girls erupted in a fit of giggles.

Shame closed over Ida like a cage. This is exactly what happened with Josef. Josef was taken away because of her. Because *she* wasn't good enough. Ida wouldn't let that happen again.

Ida stepped away from Hestia. "Maybe we shouldn't spend so much time together."

Hestia looked at her in shock. "What? Why not?"

Ida shook her head. "Warden Hazor told me to keep a low profile." She winced at another lie but knew Hestia would understand.

Hestia's eyes grew wide with understanding. "Really? He told us the exact opposite."

Ida's head whipped around. "What?"

"Hello," Reese said, coming up beside Hestia and Ida. She took one look at Ida's downcast face and sighed. "Is Ida trying to get rid of us? There was an eighty-seven point five percent chance she would."

Hestia nodded. "I think so, but it's not going to work."

Reese shook her head then looked at Ida. "We're raising suspicion so I think we should reconvene sometime later."

"Yes, I was trying to get her schedule," Hestia replied in an annoyed tone.

Ida stared at the twins in bewilderment as she handed them her schedule. *How did they know I was trying to run away and hide?*

"We may not all be Seers, but we have keen eyes and ears as well." Reese sighed as she read Ida's schedule. "We grew up in this world, Ida." She motioned to the people around them, who, thankfully, had lost interest. "We know what these people are like. The Fortress was the first time anyone really saw us as individuals and not a package. Not a door to get to our father."

"Ah ha!" Hestia said with a grin as she peered down at the two pieces of parchment. "We all have the last class of the day together."

Ida peered down at her schedule to see Hestia's manicured finger pointing to the word Horticulture.

Reese scrunched her nose. "Horticulture? In Juro? It's practically winter all the time here."

"There's a greenhouse," Ida said with a smile.

"Hopefully we can talk a bit more freely there," Hestia added.

Hestia handed Ida her class schedule, then squeezed her hand.

"Don't hide from us, Ida. We're your friends, regardless of where any of us comes from."

Reese nodded. "We'll see you in Horticulture."

Ida watched the twins saunter over to a table filled with laughing students. As soon as they saw Hestia and Reese, they immediately kicked two people out to make room for them.

Ida shook her head, not understanding why, out of all the influential and affluent people at Vlacklear, the rich Sandje twins still wanted to be her friends.

Chapter Six

Ida, Vlacklear Academy, Juro

After lunch with Victoria and Patrick, who questioned her about her relationship with the Sandje twins again, Ida finally arrived at the class where she felt comfortable: Languages and Foreign Tongues. Ida sighed with relief; thankful she could finally be in her own element again.

The teacher, Professor Mal, was an elderly woman with white and gray hair braided into a long plait down her back. Unlike the headmistress, this woman's eyes were warm and kind, inviting all her students to be courageous and ask questions. Ida loved the class since day one and couldn't wait to learn more.

Seated in the front of the class as she had been in Sir Jacques' class, Ida felt her worries and woes slip away as Professor Mal's soft voice explained the intricacies of the Tentonian dialect and how it differed from Kadeshian. Though Ida's penmanship was worse than how the chickens scratched on Ama's farm, she took lengthy notes. Her mind had been ready to learn for so long. Because of her social status, she was never given the chance. It was as if she was a wilted lily, finally receiving the water and nourishment she needed.

As Professor Mal concluded with their assignment for that evening, the petals of Ida's mind felt alive and well, ready to absorb more information tomorrow.

Blowing on her parchment, Ida was careful not to smudge the letters when a bronzed hand snatched the paper from her fingertips.

Ida's head whipped around to find the boy with ebony waves and sun-kissed skin from FLAB, assessing her notes. She tried to recall his name as his green eyes roved over the words, narrowing as he continued reading her notes.

"Excuse me," Ida said, embarrassed that someone had seen her horrible penmanship. "May I have my notes back?"

"Of course," the boy said with a charming smile that Hestia would've loved. "I've been watching you since you transferred here. You always seem really into what the old crone is saying." The boy handed Ida the parchment.

She grabbed it hastily and stuck it in her bag. Whoever this boy was, she already didn't like him. "I enjoy studying languages."

The boy sat on the table, peering down at Ida with piercing eyes and a wicked grin as he crossed his hands over his chest. "Is that so? Maybe we could study together sometime."

The hair on Ida's arms rose, and it wasn't because of the chilled northern climate. Thankfully, Hestia and Reese appeared in the doorway.

"Ida, we came to walk with you to Horticulture," Hestia announced before she saw the boy peering down at Ida from his spot on the table. Hestia's brows raised; her lips parted in surprise.

Reese's demeanor changed as well, but instead of surprise, a dark look passed over her face. Stalking into the room, she grabbed Ida's books off the table. "Come on, Ida. We don't want to be late."

Not knowing what was happening, Ida darted up and hurried behind Reese, who grabbed Hestia's arm as she stormed by.

As Ida dashed out the door, she peered over her shoulder. The boy stayed seated on the desk with his wicked smile. With a quick wave, he gave her a wink, sending Ida's nerves in a frenzy.

Once the girls were far from the classroom, Reese slowed her fast pace. Hestia ripped her arm out of Reese's stone grip.

"What was that about, Reese?" she hissed, rubbing her wrist. "You almost broke my arm."

Reese ignored Hestia's whines as she turned to Ida. "Ida, do you know who that is?"

Ida shook her head, only remembering him as the boy from FLAB and not his name.

Why is Reese so upset?

"I didn't think so. There was only a seventeen point three percent chance that you did." Reese rubbed her eyes with her fingers, clinking her abacus with her other hand. "That's Sergio Amata. His father is a duke in the eastern region. Their family is closely connected with ours."

"Oh," was all Ida could say, ashamed that she had already forgotten Sergio's name from earlier. Something bad must have happened between the two families for Reese to react so harshly. "Are your families feuding?"

"Reese was betrothed to Sergio before father sent us to the Fortress," Hestia explained as she fussed with her bun on top of her head.

"What?" Ida exclaimed. But if Sergio was Reese's betrothed, why did Reese act so hostile toward the suspicious yet attractive boy?

"Shh!" Reese cried at the same time.

"Baba wanted to marry her off to save our family from our crippling debt," Hestia blabbed, frowning as a long strand of her black hair fell between her eyes. Frowning, she twisted the strand around her high bun then continued. "Since she's ten minutes older than me, he wanted to marry her off first. But honestly, I think he's always wanted to get rid of us the moment he could."

"Hestia!" Reese cried, slapping her hand over Hestia's mouth.

Ida's eyes grew wide in understanding. Hestia and Reese weren't the rich twins everyone thought they were. They may be just as poor as Ida.

"Is it bad that people find out about your family's debt?" Ida whispered.

Hestia bit Reese's fingers, causing Reese to yank her hand away from her twin's mouth.

Hestia stuck out her tongue. "Blah, what soap do you use? It tastes horrible." She then turned to Ida. "Reese doesn't want anyone to know because this school is full of gossips. As soon as Baba knows we're here, he'll try to marry us off again. The king bailed Baba out before, when Baba agreed to willingly send his daughters to the Fortress for a handsome sum. But I doubt the king would do it again." Hestia shrugged. "Though, because we were sent to the Fortress, the betrothal may be void, but that wouldn't stop Baba from trying to arrange another marriage once he knew where we were."

Ida's mind swirled with all this new information. Hestia's and Reese's father was *paid* to send them to the Fortress? Did the twins categorize for Vlacklear and then were victims of King Atol's categorization change? Or did they even have a choice to Categorize at all?

The questions piled in Ida's mind, but she found her tongue tied. As if *she* could question anyone about their family history. So, as the girls entered Horticulture, Ida stayed silent.

As Ida sat with Hestia and Reese—the twins deeming it fine for them to sit together since the class was small—Ida was pleasantly surprised to find Professor Mal, not her professor from the past few weeks, Professor Fortua, teaching Horticulture, as well.

"Budget cuts," Professor Mal smiled as recognition dawned on Ida's face.

Ida returned the smile and nodded in understanding. As Professor Mal began to take attendance for class, the clacking of footsteps came from the hall. The chatting of the seven students in the class stopped as soon as Sergio stepped through the door.

"Apologies, professor. It seems I lost my way," he said smoothly. "I only just transferred into this class today."

Professor Mal gave him a sharp look over the rim of her glasses. "You've been here for three years already Mister Amata; I hardly believe that. Nevertheless—" she gestured to the open space beside Ida— "you'll receive my grace only once and this is it."

Sergio placed his hands before him, as if he were praying, and bowed in thanks. As he strode by Ida and sat down, a soft floral scent of lilacs and sage wafted from his clothes. Ida frowned at the smell, knowing it wasn't a typical masculine scent.

"Hey, new girl," he whispered, and Ida wished she'd sat between Hestia and Reese.

"Hello," she replied politely, not wanting to make more conversation than necessary.

The situation between Reese's and Sergio's families seemed complicated enough and Ida didn't need any more complications in her life.

Professor Mal started teaching, and thankfully Sergio didn't speak to her again. Ida paid close attention to the professor's explanation on which plants flourished in a cold climate and which didn't. It baffled her that *any* plant could survive the cold conditions of the northern region. Produce was easy to come by in Grenly because of its warm and humid climate. Unfortunately, many of the people in Lower Grenly grew the produce and most was lost to the king's tax.

In order for Ida's family and many others to pay the tax, they had to sell their produce to the citizens of Upper Grenly or to vendors passing through on their way to other citadels, such as Yekel or Ballear. The succulent passion fruit Ama grew was ripe and delicious, but Ida knew they could hardly ever enjoy it because the best fruit always went to the highest paying customers.

Ida sighed, focusing on the black ink staining her cocoa-colored skin. That's how it always was. Those with the most money always got the best, with nothing left for the rest of them.

Ida thought of First Lady Medee and her garden. How she took it upon herself to grow her own food to give back to those of Lower Grenly. Ida always admired the First Lady, hoping to one day rise out of Lower Grenly and give to others as the First Lady had given to her. Before Ida's Categorization Call, First Lady Medee invited Ida to her garden and began teaching her the basics of gardening and caring for different flowering plants and fruits. Ida couldn't believe that a noble such as the First Lady would take notice of a mere peasant such as herself, but the kindly lady had all the same.

Drumming her fingers silently on the table, Ida's mind wandered back to her Categorization Call. When she categorized for Vlacklear, she, Ama, and Jil were ecstatic. If Ida could succeed at Vlacklear, she could finally pay back Apa's and Ama's kindness of all those years ago. Sadness layered over Ida's heart as she thought of Apa. He'd died in a battle a few years after he brought Ida home with him. Ida remembered being so scared and frightened of what Ama would do to her once Apa was out of the picture. But Ama always treated Ida with kindness and love, just like Apa wanted.

A warm, strong hand laid over Ida's tapping fingers and she froze. Eyes wide she glanced over to Sergio who'd placed his hand over hers, much like Sir Jacques had earlier. However, Ida's heart didn't soar like it had with Sir Jacques. Instead, she snatched her hand back and hid it under the desk.

"Apologies, but your tapping was distracting," Sergio whispered too close to Ida's ear.

Ida leaned away, unnerved by how comfortable Sergio was being in her personal space. She had been here for weeks. Why was he just now deciding to befriend her? "I'll stop."

He nodded, but stayed painfully close to Ida, making it impossible for Ida to focus on Professor Mal's lecture.

When the class was about to conclude, Professor Mal said, "Dress warmly for tomorrow, we'll be visiting Vlacklear's greenhouse where you all can check on the plants you decided to grow and nurture as your final assignment. For those of you just joining us today, I suggest you choose a plant that sprouts quickly."

Once she dismissed the class, Hestia and Reese darted out the door, no doubt trying to get away from Sergio. Ida bolted up too, ready to flee, when he called out to her.

"Hey, new girl."

Irritated that this annoying boy wouldn't leave her alone she spun around. "I've been here for weeks, so I'm hardly new anymore and I have a name. It's Ida."

A spark of excitement lit Sergio's eyes and Ida realized her annoyance enticed him more.

"Ida," he purred. "A beautiful name."

"What do you want?" she asked, doing her best to impersonate Devora's authoritative look and stance. "I have somewhere to be."

Though she had to have dinner first, she wasn't lying. She had her meeting with Sir Jacques later that evening. If Ida was lying, it would clearly show on her face. That's why she never engaged in a game like Kings as Devora had. Whether she had a good hand of cards or bad, her opponent would know right away.

Ida thought of Sir Jacques' kind smile and mesmerizing eyes. He was the exact opposite of Sergio, right down to their contrasting coloring. And Ida adored Sir Jacques even more for it.

She'd seen how all the female recruits at the Fortress—save Devora, Reese, and Nadia—fawned over Sir Jacques. He could easily have taken any one of them for himself. But he didn't. Not only was he handsome on the outside, but his heart was even more beautiful. Ida just wished that it could be hers.

"Tell your *friend*," Sergio started, emphasizing the word "friend" as if it was impossible Reese would associate with Ida. "That I won't tell her father she's here."

Ida froze at the statement. She didn't know Sergio that well, but she'd heard of others like him. There was something telling her that he wasn't going to keep the twins' location a secret for free. Unfortunately, Ida knew all too well that nothing in life was free.

"I'll pass that along," she said coolly, hoping to end the conversation swiftly and escape. Yet, as she hurried toward the door, Sergio continued.

"But for my silence, you have to help me."

Ida's heart sank, knowing this was coming. Spinning around, she asked, "Why would you need my help?"

Tunri, why won't he just leave me alone?

Sergio sauntered toward her, and Ida's stance went rigid. Though she wasn't the best fighter in the Fortress, she'd learned her training well enough to be able to defend herself if need be. The wire bracelet with spiked ends rubbed against her wrist, reminding her of her other defense, as well.

"I read your notes in Foreign Languages and Tongues. Your penmanship is terrible, but you're smart. Help me with my work for that class and I'll keep the Sandje twins' secret safe." He placed a finger on his lips before giving a sly grin.

Ida bit her lip, not wanting to involve herself in this tangled mess. And though Sergio *said* he wouldn't say anything, Ida was smart enough to know he would only keep his mouth shut for so long.

Why would he need my help anyway? I thought everyone at Vlacklear was smart.

But the thought of Reese having to marry the sleazy boy in front of her sent a shot of fury down her spine. All because Reese's and Hestia's father needed money. Why did everything seem to always return to that one thing?

Before Ida could think the better of it, she nodded, "Fine. But only for that class."

Sergio's wicked grin returned. "I'm forever in your debt, Ida." Before she could react, he snatched her hand and gave it a kiss.

Ida's skin crawled under the sloppy kiss. She hastily pulled it away and rubbed it on the side of her dress.

Sergio only laughed as he swaggered out of the room.

Ida ran a hand over her slicked hair, her heart plummeting to her feet. What had she just agreed to?

Chapter Seven

Ida, Vlacklear Academy, Juro

Trying her best to push Sergio from her mind, Ida raced to the greenhouse. As a scholarship student, she was required to choose a work study program. No one wanted to tend to the greenhouse because of the harsh weather they'd have to endure outside. So, to have some peace, Ida took the position readily.

Ida clutched her black cloak tight as she hurried through the chilled wind. The peaked glass roof of the greenhouse was just ahead. She quickened her steps, ready to be among the peaceful plants. After everything that had happened today, she needed a break from people.

Ida breathed a sigh of relief as soon as she entered the greenhouse. Though she missed many aspects of the Fortress, Vlacklear's greenhouse was one place she did enjoy at the academy. The warm, humid air brought joy to her heart, reminding her of Ama's and First Lady Medee's gardens. Though the greenhouse was nowhere near Grenly's lush gardens, Ida still enjoyed tending to the various plants.

Placing her cloak on a nearby chair, Ida pushed up her sleeves and got to work. There was something therapeutic about working in the dirt. She loved being close with the material Tunri created. She had learned many people chose to admire Tunri for his grand creation of the Edo desert and the Maren Ocean. But Ida preferred to see Tunri's greatness in the small things of creation. The intricate designs on the petals of a flower. The way a tomato plant could hold dozens of tomatoes, yet each one was still different. And the alluring scent of various herbs. While she enjoyed cooking with rosemary and thyme, lavender was her favorite to smell.

Smiling, Ida strode to the lavender plant and inhaled. She knew the scent was calming, and she was thankful for that. Her mind was a whirlwind and needed peace.

As if Hestia and Reese weren't enough of a surprise, then Sir Jacques showed up too. Ida shook her head as she checked on her lily.

Professor Fortua told her that growing a lily in the north would be nearly impossible and that she should pick another, heartier plant. But Ida knew what type of lily she wanted to grow. It was a special bulb, one First Lady Medee had blooming all over her exquisite garden. The desert lily the First Lady procured would only thrive in the hottest temperatures.

Ida glanced out the glass of the greenhouse, cringing at the frost collecting in the corners. Professor Fortua was probably right. And maybe Ida was crazy. Yet as she went to check on her planted bulb, a blossom of hope filled her chest. There, within the sand of her clay pot, a tiny sprout had sprung.

Ida hadn't realized how late it was getting and knew she needed to eat dinner before meeting with Sir Jacques that evening in the library. She hastily wiped the sand and grime from her hands as she fled into the dining hall where Victoria and Patrick were waiting.

"I wish we had some classes together," Victoria pouted as she placed a small green salad on her plate.

Ida frowned at the tiny portion of leaves. Vlacklear had every food imaginable for its students to eat. Why was Victoria eating so little? In Lower Grenly, when food was available, you ate it and didn't think twice.

"She's probably already sick of us eating with her at every meal," Patrick snorted, piling his tray with various meats.

"That's not true," Ida said quickly. "I enjoy both of your company. Thank you for befriending me so quickly."

Victoria smiled wide.

Ida picked up her tray filled with potatoes, chicken, and green beans. Her eyes traveled down the line to desserts, and she remembered the cinnamon roll from earlier. She had been so caught up with seeing Hestia and Reese—or rather Hestia and Reese finding her—she never got to enjoy the delicious treat. Thankfully, there were fresh ones for dinner. Before she could think twice, Ida snatched up two cinnamon rolls and followed Victoria and Patrick to a long table by the far wall.

Once seated, Ida took in the dining hall. Students chatted with one another, some laughing, some debating. A card game was underway at another table and Ida almost felt like she was back at the Fortress.

"What are you thinking about?" Victoria asked, stabbing her fork in her salad but not eating any of it.

"Just home," she replied quickly before diving into her potatoes.

"Let her eat in peace, Vic," Patrick said, his mouth full of roast duck.

Victoria stuck her tongue out at Patrick, then kept her mouth closed.

Ida giggled before taking another spoonful of potatoes. They were hot, buttery, and delicious. Ida didn't care if she ate anything else because the potatoes were a dream.

The students around them became silent and Ida resurfaced from her potato heaven to find Hestia and Reese gliding into the dining hall. From the outside, the two were the image of elegance. They held their heads high and walked with all the grace Ida wished she had.

Sighing, Ida focused back on what Victoria was saying about a jousting tournament coming up. The twins and Ida decided to stay separate at mealtimes to avoid arousing suspicion. They would later meet up after Ida had her tutoring with Sir Jacques, but it was still difficult not being able to speak with her friends.

The twins were like magnets, immediately attracting everyone's attention as they fluttered into the dining hall. Even Reese seemed to be playing more into her role than before as she smiled and giggled at something a squat boy with broad shoulders said. Though, Ida could still see Reese clacking her abacus beads beneath the table. All eyes were on the twins except Sergio's, who kept his eyes locked onto Ida.

The potatoes turned to ash in Ida's mouth, but she forced them down. He grinned at Ida and gave her a small wave.

Victoria leaned over to Ida. "Why is Sergio Amata waving to you? Do you fancy him?"

"Vic," Patrick warned, pointing a fork with a meatball on it at her. "Don't pry."

"What? No, of course not!" Ida replied quickly, hating how the exquisite potatoes were now upsetting her stomach. "I barely even know him. He's just in some of my classes."

"Watch out for him, Ida," Victoria chided in a motherly tone.

"For once, I'm going to agree with Vic on this one," Patrick added. "He's no good, Ida."

"So, I've heard," Ida muttered under her breath.

Her decision to help Sergio sat like a rock in her stomach and she suddenly wasn't hungry anymore. But, because she knew the abundance of food in her life wouldn't last forever, Ida finished her dinner quickly and stood.

"I have tutoring tonight," Ida explained before Victoria could question her on where she was going and why. She enjoyed the girl's company, but for Ida to accomplish her mission from Warden Hazor, she had to learn how to dodge them better. "One of the prefects in my classes offered to help me with my assignments."

"That's a smart decision, Ida," Victoria said with an approving nod.

Ida remembered her conversation with Victoria and Patrick earlier, about having the lowest average and something about a place called the Tower. The question was on the tip of her tongue before Victoria continued talking, and Ida lost her confidence.

"Let me know if you'd like any additional help with any assignment."

"Thank you, Victoria," Ida said with genuine thanks. She wasn't sure why Victoria and Patrick were being so kind, but Ida would try to think the best of it.

Ida's agreement to assist Sergio in Foreign Languages & Tongues, crept back into her mind. She held back her shudder. Hopefully her rash decision wouldn't come back to bite her later.

As she placed her tray on a table by the exit, a hand caught her by the elbow.

"Hey, new girl." Sergio's velvety smooth voice rolled over Ida like a bad omen.

Ida pulled her elbow away, giving Sergio a wide berth as she headed toward the open door, trying to leave him behind. "I thought I told you my name."

"Oh, I remember it," he said, trailing behind her. "Ida. A beautiful name meaning prosperous."

Ida's steps faltered. "I thought you needed help in languages. If you know the meaning of my name, you're obviously smart enough to figure out the class assignments on your own." Ida didn't know where this sudden confidence and sass came from, but she liked it.

Sergio grabbed her hand and pulled her back. He was mere inches from her face, the same lilac and sage scent twirling off his uniform around Ida's nose. Now that he was so close, Ida studied his dark emerald eyes full of mischief. His skin, not as dark as hers but still darker than the citizens of Juro, held no flaws.

Ida swallowed as Sergio leaned closer, her brief confidence dissipating into fear. The only boy she'd been this close with was Josef and that had been years ago. It was almost as if her time with Josef was more a dream than a memory. His soft smile, the kindness in his eyes. Had she really been in love? She couldn't have been. She was so young, *too* young, just a child. But to a child who had nothing, Josef was everything. And it was all gone the instant his mother found out about her.

Ida pushed the memory from her mind and the tears that came with it. She pulled away from Sergio.

"I will help you with your assignments and nothing more," she whispered and hurried down the hall, leaving Sergio speechless and alone.

Once Ida turned the corner, she allowed her tears to flow freely. All the confusion and anger and pain she'd been holding on to since Warden Hazor gave her this awful mission finally exploded. Luckily, Ida knew where the library was and burst through its doors, doing her best to quiet her sobs.

The library was quiet, as all good libraries should be. Ida stifled her cries until she found a plush chair by a window in the back. She wasn't supposed to meet Sir Jacques for a little while, so she curled into the chair and silently wept to herself.

She wept for Ama losing Apa and taking on another mouth to feed. She wept for Josef, who lost his life because he was in the wrong place at the wrong time. She wept for Devora, not knowing whether she would return from battle alive. And she wept for herself, wishing she was stronger and more confident. Maybe then her circumstances would be brighter.

Soft footsteps approached her, and Ida hurriedly wiped her eyes with her hands. Of course, someone from Vlacklear would find her crying and jeer at her for it. She had done her best to stay strong at the Fortress and would only cry once she was alone in her cell. But her emotions were too heavy to bear lately, and they were spilling out.

"Ida?" Sir Jacques whispered; his voice heavy with care.

"Sir Jacques," she croaked, her throat scratchy from sobbing. "I thought we were meeting later." Her eyes stung with tears as she tried to blink them away.

Sir Jacques took a step forward and placed a plate with two cinnamon rolls on the table before Ida. Once he set the textbooks next to the plate, he crouched before her.

"I know this mission is not ideal," he started, his voice so low Ida had to strain to hear it. "But I know the warden sent us here to protect us." Standing, he ran a hand through his sandy blond hair. It was no longer slicked back as it had been this morning, but unkempt and messy. Just the way Ida liked it.

"The warden is ruthless, but he does care for his soldiers." Sighing, Sir Jacques crossed his hands over his chest. "Or I may have misjudged your tears, and you're actually horribly undone by my terrible jokes in FLAB."

Ida's laugh broke through before she could stop it.

Sir Jacques grinned. "There's that smile."

Ida looked away, knowing her face was probably redder than the roses in the greenhouse, but didn't hide her grin.

"Now," Sir Jacques continued. "We have a lot of things we need to discuss if you want to catch up to the other students." Giving her a wink, he extended his hand down to her.

Butterflies erupted in Ida's stomach as she delicately placed her hand in his and stood. After picking up his stack of books and plate of cinnamon rolls, Sir Jacques led them to a large oak table in the back of the library. Ida's search for the lost prophecy hadn't led her to the back shelves yet. There were so many books about Vlacklear's history she had no idea where to begin. So, when she arrived at Vlacklear, she decided to start at the front.

As Ida followed Sir Jacques, she thought the shelves of books would end, but instead there was a separate section of books beyond the wall of the library. Only an iron door with three slats at the top allowed her to see so much.

"What is that?" Ida asked, her heart sagging as Sir Jacques released her hand.

Sitting at the table, Sir Jacques placed his books down. "Vlacklear Academy has the largest library in all Tenton. There are texts here that are hundreds of years old." Sir Jacques pointed to the books beyond the wall. "That is the Restricted Section of the library, rumored to hold all Tenton's history. Even those things which have been struck from other texts."

Ida's eyes widened as she recalled Warden Hazor's mission.

"The prophecy to undo the king and queen lies in Vlacklear's library. Find it and translate it as quickly as possible."

Shivers raced down Ida's arms and legs. The warden never explained she would have to break in somewhere to get the prophecy.

Of course, it would be something like that, Ida. That's why you're undercover.

"First things first," Sir Jacques said, "You must not call me Sir Jacques anymore. Here, I am only a lowly prefect." He stuck out his lower lip to pout and Ida giggled. "Second—" he slid the plate between them. Cinnamon swirls of delight danced from the two pastries. "These are my favorite, so I thought you'd like one too." He smiled. "It may also help me with the whole 'do not fail your mission, Jacques, or I'll skin you alive' threat."

Ida's eyes widened. "Is that what the warden said to you?"

Jacques shrugged before he took a bite of the cinnamon roll. "More or less. He won't do it though. I hope."

Ida grabbed the cinnamon roll; thankful she was finally able to enjoy the sugary delight. "He's frightening."

Jacques nodded in agreement. "He has to be. Or the Fortress would run wild."

Ida considered the statement, realizing Jacques was right. Why would criminals and soldiers listen to a weak, cowering leader? They needed a strong, fearsome commander like Warden Hazor. Not someone like her, always crying in the corner.

Ida sighed and ate the cinnamon roll, wishing she could be someone else.

Jacques wiped his sticky fingers on his handkerchief, then offered it to Ida. Ida blushed and stopped herself from licking her fingers before using the handkerchief.

Smiling, Jacques pushed the stack of texts between them.

"So, I hear you've been hiding something."

Ida's gaze shot up, thinking Jacques had found out about her agreement with Sergio. Fear struck her heart, and it took her a moment later to wonder why she would be fearful of Jacques' thoughts on Sergio.

"I have?" she asked, trying to sound as innocent as possible.

Jacques opened the first textbook and slid it to her. "Can you read this?"

Ida hesitantly lowered her gaze to the pages. Swirls and lines of archaic Tentonian texts stared back at her. She whispered her prayer of thanks to Tunri for her gift before she blinked and the symbols rearranged, translating to the modern tongue she knew.

Ida sighed and nodded. *Who knew Warden Hazor was a gossip?*

Reaching out, she ran her finger along the first line. "In the days of King Solt, first chosen king of Tenton, all gifted persons alike cooperated and created the nation of Tenton."

"Amazing," Jacques whispered, studying Ida with admiration. "Have you always been able to translate different texts?"

"Since I can remember."

"Just written text? Or can you translate language auditorily?"

Ida thought back to when Babshee attacked her and Devora in their carriage on the way to the Fortress. She translated his words instantly for Devora to understand. Ida was trying to keep her gift a secret, but it slipped out. Luckily, her time in the Fortress didn't force her to translate anything. So how Warden Hazor found out about her, she didn't know.

"I can translate any language written down or spoken," she finally answered.

"Amazing," Jacques breathed again.

"You already said that," Ida replied with a smirk, enjoying his full attention and admiration.

"Well, you are. I mean—" A tint of red covered Jacques' face, leaving it a shade of cranberry.

Ida remembered Captain Blake referencing something about Jacques' face turning red and she giggled.

Jacques cleared his throat. "Your gift. It's amazing. First, Lady Devora and now you. How many other gifted people were in the Fortress?"

Ida shrugged with a smile, deciding not to tell Jacques about Nadia and her tinkering gift, hoping he would figure it out on his own like she had.

Jacques pulled his gaze back to the ancient language. "These are books I was able to procure from a reliable source. They were formally in the Restricted Section. The only people allowed to check out books from the Restricted Section are those with the king's clearance."

Ida frowned. "So why didn't Warden Hazor just check out what book he needed himself?"

Jacques pinched the bridge of his nose with a sigh. "It would've been nice if it were that simple, right? His clearance got revoked after Devora and One Shot escaped from Level Five."

"What?" Ida gasped. "Why was Devora locked in Level Five?"

Jacques rubbed his eyes with his palms. "Right. That was what I needed to tell you first."

Ida lips stayed parted in shock, waiting for Sir Jacques' explanation. *Devora is a criminal? But why? Hadn't she been sent to the battlefront to save Princess Haden and Tenton?* That was at least what Ida had heard at the Fortress after Devora had won the Regulus Protecti tournament. What had happened since then?

"You know I don't go on many covert missions, but I wish the warden would tell everyone the same thing," Jacques grumbled.

"Hestia said Warden Hazor told them to make themselves known while he told me to keep to myself," Ida offered.

Jacques groaned again, massaging his temples. "Yes, having to keep track of those two has been a nightmare, especially considering our families' past relationship."

"What?" Ida asked again, feeling like she was the dumbest person in Tenton for asking the question so many times.

Jacques sat up straighter as if something slipped out that shouldn't have. He pulled on the collar of his tunic. "Ah yes, that's a story for another time. But let me tell you about Devora first before we begin planning."

Ida's mind swirled as Jacques started to explain what happened during the Battle of Edo and at the ball honoring Devora afterward when the clacking of heels came toward them.

Jacques froze mid-sentence, his posture turning rigid as he masked his panic and faced the headmistress.

Chapter Eight

Byron was more than willing to lend Matthias one of his horses. Matthias said he would return the steed as soon as he was able, knowing he wouldn't be traveling too far from Snoken.

Deep pools of rainwater dotted the empty streets of the small village. The sun was just beyond the horizon, dawn barely peeking over the rolling hills. The people of Snoken were still asleep and Matthias was glad for it. Tunri had blessed him by leading him to One Shot's family. Who knew what another villager might have done when a naked man arrived on their doorstep?

Matthias tightened his grip on the straw-colored horse's reigns, clenching his jaw. It was bad enough that he was cursed to turn into a wolf, but once he transformed back, it was almost worse. The excuses he had come up with when he was back in his human form were embarrassing and degrading. Matthias could almost hear the witch laughing every time he was left defenseless and alone with each change.

Pushing the thought from his mind, Matthias kicked the horse with his heels, sending it into a gallop. He needed to get to Totem and fast.

After an hour or two, the soft, rolling green hills of his home greeted him. Matthias held back the urge to weep. So many memories of love and loss decorated these hills. But he clamped down on his sorrow. Now wasn't the time to dwell on the past. His mother was still missing and now Devora was too. He wouldn't rest until he found them both and knew they were safe.

A man with graying chestnut hair strode down one of the hills and Matthias instantly recognized his father. Matthias swallowed back his tears again. It had been months since he was able to break away from the Fortress to visit his father and Totem. And now with King Atol's tighter leash around him, Matthias didn't know when he would be able to visit again after today. He had already been gone from the palace too long.

After dismounting the horse, Matthias approached his father. He suddenly felt like a young boy again: scared, confused, and lost. He didn't know what to say or how to react, but his usual stoic demeanor immediately melted away when his father pulled him into a tight embrace.

"Welcome home, son," Liam Blake, Matthias' father, gently said.

Matthias wrapped his arms around his father, realizing the last hug he'd received was from Devora. The ache in his heart grew more and he clung a little closer.

Ever since he stepped foot in the Fortress, Matthias had to be strong and unwavering. Not that he minded. It was usually easy for him to stay guarded and emotionless. But some days—especially at night—it was more difficult to maintain the tough appearance.

But here, in Totem with his father, Matthias didn't have to be the captain. He didn't have to be second to Warden Hazor. He could just be Matthias, a farm boy from the countryside.

Liam pulled back, assessing Matthias with the same gray eyes they shared. "I see a lot has happened over the past few months."

Matthias nodded, not trusting himself to speak without his voice wavering.

Liam smiled gently and patted Matthias on the shoulder. "Come, we're just about to eat. Life's gotten a lot more interesting around here since your other friends and brother arrived."

Matthias pulled Byron's horse along, remembering he'd sent Nadia and Tristan to Totem before he led the battalion to recapture Yekel. It was a relief to know that, for once, Tristan listened to him. Maybe Nadia was keeping his brother in line.

As they crested the hilltop, the rolling vineyards of Hacana Farm stretched before him. His mother had named it when his parents first got married and only had a handful of vines to tend. *Hacana* meant peace. And that was exactly what Matthias was fighting for.

"I'm sorry for not informing you of Tristan returning or of my own return," Matthias finally said, finding his voice.

Liam waved him off. "I figured once your brother showed up, you wouldn't be far behind. It's been that way since you were both children. Tristan running off into trouble and you following behind him, trying to clean it up."

Matthias couldn't help but smirk. Even when he told Tristan to his face that they weren't family, they both knew it wasn't true. Tristan was his little brother and Matthias would always see him as such.

"He isn't any less of a handful now than he was then," Matthias murmured.

"I agree," Liam chuckled. "I'd say he's worse now."

Matthias laughed, feeling himself relax. He'd missed his father. In the early days when his mother was first taken to the palace, his father was the brothers' lifeline. The three of them stayed close together, hoping and praying to be a united family once again.

Once they were over the next hill, far from the main road, the canvas tents of Totem came into view. Pride swelled in Matthias' chest as the different citizens of Tenton buzzed around the makeshift village. Most of whom were sentenced to death by the king's unfair laws.

"You've done something wonderful, son," Liam said, patting Matthias' shoulder again.

"I've done nothing," Matthias replied, watching Tinkers from Yekel argue about which tool was better for shaping metal. "You've tended and grown this place. It was only my idea."

"And a wonderful idea that's saved many lives and families," his father replied. "Come. I know you wish to speak with your friends."

Matthias descended the hill with his father, handing off Byron's horse to a former soldier of the Fortress who was falsely accused of treason.

"Welcome back, sir," the soldier said, saluting Matthias before he guided the horse away.

Matthias nodded, then followed his father to his childhood home. To an outsider, the pale wooden boards of the humble home looked simple. But to him they were everything in the world. One day—he prayed—he would be able to live on this land again. He thought of Devora, also praying he wouldn't live here alone.

Running a hand through his hair, Matthias did his best to smooth the wrinkled white tunic and pants he borrowed from Byron. Straightening his shoulders, he pushed open the wooden door.

"Are you saying I would lose?" Tristan gasped; his voice laced with offense.

"Of course, you would lose," Nadia replied immediately. "We all know you can't really fight."

Tristan snorted. "I only fight when I have to."

"Like when the Street Rats attacked you outside of Yekel?" One Shot's deep voice countered.

Nadia laughed outright. "Exactly!"

"I'll have you know; I studied several forms of fighting at Vlacklear," Tristan began, and Matthias had heard enough.

Clearing his throat, he entered the small kitchen, a wave of memories swirling into his mind. His mother making jam by the windowsill. He and Tristan smashing grapes in the corner, laughing as the fruit squished between their toes.

"Did you really, Tristan?" Matthias asked, causing Nadia to scream as he stepped behind her. "Was that before or after you dropped out?"

Tristan stood before the circular wooden table, a spoon in his hand, as if he were conducting an orchestra.

Tristan lowered the spoon. "Welcome back, brother," he said, donning his usual sly grin. "I was wondering when you would make it here."

"Cap!" Nadia said, springing up from her chair. "Did you find her?"

Matthias' heart wrenched in his chest. He'd followed Devora's rose scent until it was gone. After that, he looked everywhere he thought she could be but never found her. His logical self already condemned her to death, but Matthias refused to believe it. How could Tunri have kept her safe and hidden for sixteen years and then allow her to be killed now? No, she was still alive, Matthias knew it, and he would do everything in his power to find her again.

"I did not," he strained, unable to hide the regret on his face.

Nadia's face fell. "Oh." She fiddled with some new contraption in her hand. "Well, if there's one thing I know about Dev, it's that she's strong. Wherever she is, we'll find her."

Matthias nodded, thankful for Nadia's grace in his moment of weakness.

Clearing his throat, Matthias took a breath then turned to One Shot. Warden Hazor and Jacques knew of his curse already and now One Shot did too. Matthias knew he could trust his longtime friend, but it was still difficult to pretend like One Shot hadn't seen him transform into a gray wolf before his eyes.

Matthias extended his hand to One Shot. "Thank you for making sure those who wanted a new life from Yekel made it here safely and for helping Tocha round up the Kadeshians."

One Shot's dark eyes stared into Matthias' own as he grabbed the other man's forearm and nodded. "Of course."

Matthias released One Shot before noticing the woman next to him. Her hair was short like Nadia's had been, but it was so blonde, it was almost white. Matthias vaguely remembered seeing her with One Shot before he approached the crumbled Temple of Pahga in Yekel. His mind then pieced it all together. This was Rae. The woman who defeated and killed General Yada, the Kadeshian general responsible for sieging Yekel five years ago. And, judging by One Shot's proximity to her, this woman also held the heart of his tall friend.

"Am I correct that you were the one who defeated General Yada?" he asked, assessing Rae.

There was a fire in the woman's eyes, one he'd seen in Devora's, as well. It was a look that told Matthias everything he needed to know about Rae. She was a fighter, a survivor, and wouldn't allow anyone to take advantage of her.

"It was actually the statue of Pahga," Rae replied matter-of-factly.

Matthias nodded, then bowed deeply. "It is to you I owe my thanks."

When he righted himself, the entire room was silent. Rae's eyes were wide with disbelief.

"Because of your bravery," Matthias continued. "Tenton has reclaimed Yekel. We are a united nation again. When I return to the capital, I will make sure you are duly rewarded and honored for your courage."

Rae blinked in shock before One Shot placed his large hand over hers. Matthias noted the gesture but said nothing.

"That's not necessary," Rae finally said, her voice a whisper.

Matthias was about to speak when Nadia interceded. "I think what she means, Cap, is that Rae would rather stay safe and away from the public. At least for the time being."

She looked to Rae who nodded, keeping her fingers locked into One Shot's.

Matthias' brow furrowed, but he nodded.

"Please feel free to reward me," Tristan butted in, his mouth full of buttered bread. "I played a crucial part in the plan."

Nadia rolled her eyes.

"You also almost blew our cover several times," One Shot muttered.

Tristan ignored the comment.

Pulling out the chair beside One Shot, Matthias shook his head. "You've already been compensated for your efforts, Tristan. Stop being greedy."

Tristan scrunched his nose like he was five summers old again and ate the rest of his food.

The rest of the meal went by fairly peacefully. From the corner of his eye, Matthias noticed Rae studying him. Nadia and Tristan bickered more, and One Shot stayed silent. It wasn't until Liam returned that Matthias realized so much time had passed.

"I know you need to return to the capital soon, but you need to see something before you go," he said to Matthias.

"Oh, are you going to show him?" Nadia said, clapping with delight.

"Show me what?" Matthias said standing.

"It really is amazing," Tristan added in with a grin.

"I'll go with you," One Shot stood, hunching so he could fit in the home.

"Follow me," Liam replied, disappearing out the door.

One Shot looked to Rae. "Do you want to join us?"

Rae eyed Matthias then shook her head. "No, I have to help Mami with some things." She squeezed his hand, nodded to Matthias then darted out the door.

Matthias didn't know why, but he got the feeling Rae didn't like him. He was familiar with the look she gave him. But usually, he received that look after people had already gotten to know him or he punished them for disobedience. This woman just met him. Even *he* hadn't had enough time to make her dislike him yet.

Matthias followed One Shot out of the house and into the field. People from all regions of Tenton busied about. Some tended to the vineyard, others worked on their own projects. But everyone had a place and a purpose.

Matthias strode next to One Shot, Liam a few paces ahead.

"She seems nice," he offered to the tall man.

"She is," One Shot replied.

Silence laid like a barricade between them.

"I'm sorry about Devora," One Shot offered after a while.

Matthias sighed. "Me too. But Nadia is right. Devora is strong. I'll find her one way or another."

Liam continued walking and greeting workers along the way. Matthias enjoyed seeing his father happy. There had been so many years of sorrow and hardship. The creation of Totem not only helped those wrongfully accused, but his father as well.

"Where's Vinn?" Matthias had sent the large white elk Devora freed from the Fortress with Tristan and Nadia. Though his family's land in Ballear was vast, he was confident he would have seen the giant elk by now.

"I can only assume he's looking for Devora, as well," One Shot replied. "He was already gone by the time I made it here from Yekel."

Matthias frowned, remembering the elk from his childhood. Vinn always loved the farm when he spent time with his mother. It seemed the giant white elk-like creature enjoyed the company of Seers. He prayed Vinn would be more successful at finding Devora than he had been.

"How long have you been able to change into a wolf?" One Shot asked suddenly.

Matthias blinked in surprise but was glad the question had surfaced. "Not while we were cellmates. But soon after I won *Victor Omnia*."

One Shot nodded. "Why?"

Matthias rubbed the back of his neck. It was something he'd wondered as well. After he'd won *Victor Omnia*—another one of Warden Hazor's tournaments to weed out the strong from the weak—he was sent to King Atol and Queen Leza to be knighted. Before his ceremony, he was approached by an elderly woman, claiming to be one of the queen's handmaidens. She did something to him; the details have always been hazy. But he was later told by the king and queen that his new "abilities" would help in serving his kingdom.

Matthias pushed back the horrid memories of the lives he'd taken while in wolf form. For the first year he couldn't control it at all. But he then realized, whenever he was about to shift, King Atol needed him to complete a task. Almost as if he *knew* when Matthias would turn. After that realization, Matthias worked hard on controlling his transformation cycles. But what helped the most was the imperial opal ring from Devora. Though it did drain some of his energy, the imperial opal kept the beast silent and tame.

Matthias realized he hadn't answered One Shot's question. "I'm still trying to figure that out."

One Shot nodded and was silent for a moment, then said, "It was cool."

Matthias smirked as his father finally stopped in front of a tent on the edge of Totem. A man with bright blond hair like Rae's stepped out from the tent. A wide smile filled his face.

"Captain Blake, welcome back." The man bowed deeply. Once he stood, he added, "My wife just left with my daughter, but when they return, you must meet them!"

"He just met Rae, Lucas," Liam said. "But I want you to show Matthias what you've been working on."

Lucas' eyes lit with excitement. "Yes, yes!"

He ushered Matthias and One Shot, giving One Shot a pat on the shoulder as he passed by.

Behind the tent sat a type of mechanism Matthias had never seen before. Fused within a pyramid of metal rods was a series of rings intertwined with one another to create a sphere. The design was simple yet complex at the same time. Matthias was confused about its purpose until the stone of the rings glinted in the mid-afternoon sun.

"What is this device?" Matthias asked, his eyes analyzing the imperial opal rings in the center of the pyramid.

"I don't have a name for it yet," Lucas replied. "But it can nullify imperial opal."

Chapter Nine

"Good evening, headmistress," Jacques responded to the crow-like woman giving them her usual forced smile.

Ida couldn't believe how quickly Jacques' persona changed from kind and caring to cold and controlled. She remembered how he'd dealt with Niche and his gang when they took Devora's sash before they were sent to the Fortress. That was the first time Ida had ever seen Jacques threaten anyone. But she supposed after working in the Fortress for so long, he had to learn to deal with unsavory characters and hide his emotions or risk being punished.

As Ida schooled her features into a calm mask, she noticed how Jacques pulled the restricted texts away from her and attempted to conceal them behind his elbow. But as Ida glanced up at the headmistress, she knew the woman's keen eyes hadn't missed anything.

"Prefect Jacques," the headmistress said cheerily. "I'm surprised to find you in the library with a student at this hour." Her gaze raked over Ida. And though her smile shone, her beady eyes bore nothing but judgment. "We wouldn't want anyone to get the wrong idea."

Ida lowered her gaze, fumbling with the hem of her sleeve. Of course, a male and female student together, alone, in the back of a library at night would look suspicious. But what was even worse, the headmistress' words cut Ida to the core. What would people think if she were *really* with Jacques? Especially if they knew about her gift and upbringing.

In the corner of her eye, Ida noticed Jacques straighten in his chair.

"I thank you for your concern, headmistress." The knight plastered on a dangerous smile. "But I was the one to offer to assist Miss Shabawn. The Assembly is sure to come around soon, and I wanted to make sure she was caught up in her general studies before then." He tipped his head at her. "I already asked Professor Trudoe for his approval, and he agreed. Did I need yours, as well?"

The headmistress narrowed her eyes at Jacques but didn't spit the venom Ida was so sure would come out of her mouth. Instead, her smile widened further, like a cat biding its time before it caught its prey.

"Your edification of Miss Shabawn is acceptable, Prefect." She laid her gaze on Ida, and it felt as if a whole mountain would fall on top of her. "I am anticipating your attendance at the Assembly, Miss Shabawn."

The headmistress didn't spare them a second glance before she stalked back out of the library, her black heels echoing among the countless shelves of books.

As soon as she was gone, Jacques let out a breath. He turned toward Ida, running a hand through his shaggy hair. "That woman terrifies me, and I've dealt with some pretty terrifying people."

Ida kept her gaze down as she said, "I thought Captain Blake was bad."

Jacques chuckled. "Captain Blake is a kitten compared to the headmistress. And that smile." He shuddered.

Ida couldn't help but giggle, imagining Captain Blake as a little kitty playing with yarn.

"Are you all right?" Jacques asked.

"Yeah," Ida said finally lifting her gaze.

Her heart almost leapt out of her chest at the tenderness and care welling in Jacques' eyes. *Is it really for me?*

"Don't listen to what that crone said. No one is going to think anything is going on between us."

"Right," Ida said after a moment, pushing away her hopes that Jacques would want to be with someone like her. "Of course. That would be inappropriate."

It may have been the flickering of the lanterns in the windows, but Ida could've sworn Jacques' cheeks were turning red, again. He suddenly cleared his throat and pushed the restricted texts back between them.

"As I was saying, Warden Hazor's access to the restricted library was revoked because Devora escaped from Level Five of the Fortress."

"But why was she even there in the first place?" Ida cried. The last she'd heard, Devora was a hero.

Jacques furrowed his brow creating a crease between them. "It's complicated. But as far as I know she's safe."

Ida quirked a brow at Jacques, knowing he was hiding information, but she decided not to probe.

She glanced down at the stack of restricted texts, their titles smudged and hardly legible. "Okay, so someone *else*—not Warden Hazor—had these restricted books and couldn't decipher them?"

The knight nodded, opening the worn leather binding of the book at the top of the stack. "Since your gift was discovered, he was hoping you would be able to read them."

Ida raised her brows. "And do I get to know *who* this someone else is or is our friendship based solely on secrets?"

Jacques looked taken aback by her frankness but then smiled brightly. "I would like there to be no secrets between us at all, Ida."

Ida felt her cheeks heat and took the text from Jacques' hands. His rough fingers brushed against hers, and she had to fight to keep the butterflies in her stomach controlled.

Grabbing the flickering candle on the table, Ida dragged it closer. "So, *who* am I translating this for?"

Jacques focused on a spot on the table. "Captain Blake, Warden Hazor, Lady Devora and possibly all of Tenton."

Ida's head shot up. "What?"

Jacques shrugged. "No more secrets." Ida waited and he continued, "The reason the king wanted to rid Tenton of all Seers was because his wife received a terrifying prophecy from a Seer. No one knows what the prophecy was because it's said to have been stricken from all Tentonian texts. However—" Jacques tapped the open pages in front of Ida— "apparently that isn't true and there is a record of it somewhere."

Ida nodded, remembering the warden telling her a quick version of the same story. "And you think the prophecy is here, in this book?"

"I don't know what to think, Ida," Jacques explained. "I am a soldier and knight of the Fortress. I follow orders." His voice tightened as it had in class earlier that day. "I'm good at following orders."

Ida bit her lip, unsure of how she felt about being a part of defying the monarchy of a kingdom she really didn't belong to. *Should I tell Jacques? Should I tell him that I wasn't born in Tenton?* How would Warden Hazor feel that the person he chose to unveil the prophecy was born a Kadeshian?

As Ida parted her lips, Jacques gently laid his hand over hers. "I know this is scary and confusing. But rest assured I have told you everything I know. When I find out further information, I will make sure you aren't left in the dark again." He gestured to the darkening library around them with a smirk and Ida giggled.

"So, am I actually going to get help with my studies or am I just going to translate restricted texts while you sit and eat cinnamon rolls?"

Ida blushed at her playful banter. In the Fortress, she tried to stay hidden and not draw any attention from any soldier or prisoner. But maybe it was because Jacques needed her, or the fact that she was alone with him, Ida felt she could be bold.

Jacques chuckled. "I believe I brought the cinnamon rolls to share. But yes, I will help you with your studies, if you need it. However, from what I've heard from the other professors, you and Reese will catch up just fine. Hestia though..." Sir Jacques trailed off.

"What about her?"

Jacques rubbed the back of his neck. "Let's say that the Assembly isn't kind to those who don't perform well in their classes."

Ida wanted to ask more about the Assembly and what Victoria had said to Patrick about the Tower, but a group of students burst through the library doors. Ida jumped and quickly shut the aged book. Her fingers tapped nervously on the worn cover. The group sauntered in and out of the bookshelves joking and laughing.

Why are they here if they're just going to be loud?

A few of them broke off to different tables before Ida looked up and caught Sergio's eye. She inwardly groaned as the sleazy boy sauntered toward them. Ida swore she saw Jacques stiffen beside her.

"My prosperous Ida. You've only been here a few weeks and you already have your nose in the books?" He playfully wagged a finger. "Come join me and my friends for some fun."

Ida held back her frustration. Never had a person irritated her as much as Sergio. If Devora were here, she would've already put him in his place. And that's what Ida intended to do.

"No, thank you. I need to focus on my studies if I want to do well."

She wished she could think of something colder and biting to say like Captain Blake, but polite frankness was the best she could do. Unfortunately, Sergio didn't get the hint.

"You have plenty of time before Assembly. Come on." He went to reach for her arm when Jacques shot up.

For a moment, Ida feared the knight's Fortress training would take over and Sergio would be splayed all over the bookshelves. She'd seen Jacques snap back and forth between a kind man and a vicious soldier. And if she were honest with herself, it scared her.

"Ah, Prefect, I didn't see you there." A mischievous glint twinkling in Sergio's eyes.

"Sergio, if you spent as much time in your books as you did trying to engage every pretty girl in conversation, you would be at the top of your class."

Ida's eyes widened, not hearing any other word besides "pretty." *Jacques thinks I'm pretty?*

But Sergio only laughed. "Right you are, Prefect. But I only have one life to live, so I'm going to live it how I want."

Something in the statement struck Jacques. Ida noticed how his posture went rigid, almost as if Sergio had hit a personal nerve.

"That, I can understand," Jacques replied less forcefully than before. He then turned to Ida, his face a swirl of emotions, none of which Ida could decipher. "Miss Shabawn, may I escort you back to the woman's dormitories?"

"No need, Prefect," Sergio butted in before Ida could reply. "I can escort Ida."

Jacques nodded tightly before grabbing a book from a nearby shelf. He placed it on top of the restricted texts and gave her a wink. "These are all the books that should help you catch up to the other students."

"Thank you, Si—er—Prefect Jacques," Ida replied, her hopes falling to her feet as the knight bid them goodnight and walked away.

Why couldn't I speak up? Why did I let Sergio trample all over me? And why did I let Jacques leave?

Because that's what she did. Ida Shabawn didn't create a fuss or fight anyone. She drifted through life, trying not to be noticed.

"My friends and I are having a bonfire later, if you'd like to come," Sergio said quietly. He played with an invisible string on his sleeve almost as if he were nervous.

Ida frowned at the invitation, still irritated that Sergio had cut short her meeting with Jacques. Hopefully she would be able to decipher some of the text in the books so she could see the knight again.

The future of Tenton is resting on your shoulders and all you want is to see Jacques again? she thought to herself. But it was the truth.

Ida shook her head, hurrying to grab the three restricted texts and other book into her arms.

"Maybe another time." And before Sergio could protest, Ida slipped through the bookshelves and out of the library.

Chapter Ten

Ida, Renta, Kadesh- Nine Years Ago

"You know you're my best friend, right, Ida?" Josef asked.

Ida giggled. At only seven summers, being anyone's best friend was exciting, especially if that someone was an older boy of ten summers.

"Of course," she said between giggles. "But I hope it's not just because I'm the only person you talk to here."

Josef laughed. "Well, that's part of it."

"Hey!" Ida replied, smacking him on the shoulder.

Josef jerked away with another laugh, causing Ida to chase him around, breathing through bouts of laughter. It had always been like this. Just the two of them, best friends and maybe something more when they were older.

Shoulders heaving, Ida slowed her pace. Josef was so much faster than she was.

"Okay," she breathed. "You win."

Josef grinned in triumph before striding up to her and sitting on the ground. He reached up and pulled Ida down beside him, and the two of them lay down and looked up at the clouds. Ida loved it when Josef came to visit. His laughter and jokes made Ida almost forget about the orphanage behind them. Almost.

"Are you going to leave?" Ida asked Josef. He was the only friend she had in the world. She didn't know what she'd do without him.

He violently shook his head, collecting sand and dust in his dark curls. "Never. Are you going to leave?"

Ida shook her head. "I don't plan to."

"Good," Josef said, taking her hand in his. "Then we'll be together forever."

"Josef?" a shrill female voice shrieked. "What in Pahga's name are you doing in the dirt? And with an orphan no less?"

Josef jolted up, sand falling from his hair. "Mother, this is my friend, Ida."

Ida sat up slowly, trying to deflect the sting of the word. Orphan. No one could ever look past that word to see who Ida really was.

Fine turquoise silk and jewels wrapped around the woman's curvaceous body. Ida glanced away, not realizing Josef came from a family of such wealth. He always dressed so simply. Ida just assumed he was the son of a humble merchant.

"Come along, Josef." The woman hurried, keeping her gaze averted from Ida.

"But mother—" he started before his mother shot him a look so deadly, Ida thought Josef would be instantly incinerated.

Furrowing his brow, Josef stood. "I'll come back soon," he whispered to her. "Promise."

Ida nodded quickly, trying to be strong, trying to hold back her tears. But it was no use. The tears came anyway. She cried as Josef walked away. She cried as she heard his mother forbidding him to associate with someone "like her." And she cried even more when Josef never returned to the orphanage.

Months later a battle against Tenton flooded into the capital city of Renta. Homes, businesses, and the orphanage were burned to the ground. It wasn't until days later that a Tenton soldier found Ida curled in a ball under the wreckage.

"There's a child!" a voice with an unfamiliar accent called out.

Ida soon felt the weight of the wooden planks over her lift, but she was too scared to move.

"Is she alive?" another voice asked.

"Who cares? She's Kadeshian. Let's put her out of her misery."

Ida squeezed her eyes shut. She didn't know much about religion, but a local priest would come by to read stories to the orphans about a God named Tunri. Most of the older orphans followed the Goddess Pahga, but there was something about the stories of Tunri that brought peace to Ida's weary heart.

Don't let me die, Ida prayed, hoping someone would listen.

"Hold your weapons," a commanding voice boomed.

Ida winced as heavy footsteps came toward her. Soon a gentle touch landed on her shoulder.

"Everything is okay now; you don't have to hide."

After a moment, Ida uncurled herself and stared into the eyes of the enemy. Five Tentonian soldiers stood around her. Some looked angry, others looked bored. But the man crouching before her studied her with kind eyes.

"Where are your parents?" he asked, his brown hair tinged with white splayed across his forehead, slick with sweat.

"I don't have any," she whispered as more tears fell from her eyes.

"Captain, I think—"

The man stood, his eyes narrowing at the soldier. "I've heard enough of your thoughts, Telel. The child goes with us. I will find accommodations for her."

The soldier stepped back and saluted. "Yes, Captain Hazor, of course."

The next few days flew by as Ida was taken from the only home she ever knew to her new home in Grenly. The captain who saved her found her a place with a kind couple in Lower Grenly. After he dropped her off though, she never saw him again.

It was weeks before Ida spoke to her new family, though they were nothing but kind to her. But one day, Ida heard a young girl around her age screaming about a viper escaping from the jungle. Ida rushed back inside to find the viper in the back of her new home, a few feet from her new baby sister, Jil. Grabbing the closest branch she could find, Ida fended off the viper until Clara, her new ama, found them. With the force of a bear, Clara beheaded the viper with a machete Cyrus, her new apa, used when foraging in the jungles. After that incident, Ida fell into Clara's arms, weeping about everything. When the tears finally stopped, she told Clara all about the orphanage, how she didn't know her parents or why they didn't want her. And she sobbed about Josef. How he didn't come back and didn't care that she was in an entirely new place.

Clara listened with the patience of a loving mother, stroking Ida's tight curls. "I don't know much about Kadesh or their customs, but I know that you are a very special girl, and we are so thankful Tunri brought you to us."

Ida enjoyed her new life in Lower Grenly. Often, times were hard, and money was tight, but she was loved and that was what mattered most. Then one day, they received news that Cyrus, her new apa, had been killed in action in the latest battle with Kadesh.

Clara, Ida, and Jil wept for days, not knowing what to do. But the strangest part of the news was a piece of parchment the messenger gave to Ida.

"Captain Shabawn was too injured for the medics to move him," the messenger explained. "His dying wish was for his girls to know he loved them all and to give this to Ida." The messenger handed a crumpled piece of parchment to Ida, looking worn from years of creasing.

Ida hesitantly took the letter, unable to open it until years later.

It wasn't until Ida was about to participate in the Categorization Call that she opened the old parchment, recognizing her apa's handwriting.

Ida,

It has been many years since we've spoken but know that I've thought about you every day. It was fate that I met your adoptive father on the battlefield. He is now the one writing this note for me.

I'm so sorry for the way my mother treated you that day and that I never came back. I was young and confused. I went back after the battle of Renta was over and was devastated to find the orphanage destroyed and you gone. When I was old enough to join the military, I did, hoping it would one day bring me back to you. And it has.

I've always loved you, Ida.

The note tapered off; two dates written at the bottom. It took a moment for Ida to realize they were Josef's birth and death dates. She cried even more. Tears continuously flowed from her eyes for the next week. Though she was meant to start at Vlacklear Academy, she was sent to the Fortress. A giant attacked their caravan and Ida felt more alone than she had in a long time.

But there was one person who was kind throughout all the struggles. His hazel eyes and blond hair were a contrast to how Josef looked, but Ida found the same gentleness in Jacques' gaze as she had Josef's. And that was when her fear took over. She couldn't get close to another person like Josef, the heartache was too hard. Though Jacques was desirable, Ida had to stay away.

Chapter Eleven

Ida woke up the next morning from a fitful night of sleep. It had been a while since she dreamt about her early childhood in Kadesh. Each year caused the memories to fade even more, but she still held on to the note from Josef.

Rising from her bed, Ida ran her fingers over her scalp. The roots of her hair stung from being forced into the required tight bun every day. Thankfully, she could wear her hair however she wanted in her room.

Ida left the note from Josef at home, knowing it would only haunt her with the past as she began her new life in the Fortress. She didn't know where the new path would lead but after she finally reached the Fortress, she accepted it. Tunri sent her to Tenton, then the Fortress, and now Vlacklear for a reason. She just had to continue to trust He would protect her, and she would be unharmed in the end.

Stretching her arms above her head, Ida's eyes locked on to the texts from Jacques laying atop Sergio's Linguistics homework she'd already completed. Somehow "helping" Sergio turned into completing all his assignments for him for the class. Ida knew it was a risk, but if it kept the sleazy boy's mouth shut about Reese and Hestia, Ida would continue to finish his assignments.

Sighing, Ida moved Sergio's homework aside and studied the worn covers of the books from Sir Jacques. She needed to translate them soon. But even with the urgency and knowledge that all she had to do was open them and translate, Ida hesitated. What would she find in them? Would she be discovered and tried for treason? Would she be killed?

Ida was brought into Tenton unnoticed. She didn't know how she'd gone undetected all these years, but no one suspected her of being any different than any other citizen of Lower Grenly. The soldier who left her with Ama and Apa also procured her a bag of categorization stones, as well. So, when the other Tentonian children practiced their categories, Ida did as well.

Ida sighed as she ran her hands over the cover of the extra text Sir Jacques placed on top. It was newer than the restricted texts so she could read its title easily: *Prose of Old: A Collection of Stories and Poems from Ages Past.* Ida studied the green binding of the book, curious as to whether Jacques picked this book by chance or on purpose.

Classes were finished for the week and the students had two days off before they had to return to them. Usually, the libraries were filled with everyone studying and trying to earn the best marks. And if the suspicions Ida had about the Assembly and the Tower were true, she intended to do the same. Except, instead of studying in the library, she decided to stay in her room. Even eating breakfast in the dining hall would risk running into Sergio again and that was something Ida definitely did not want to do. Thankfully, she had a plan to wait until breakfast was just about finished, and the dining hall was nearly empty—to rush in, grab whatever was left to eat, and hurry back to her room, hoping not to be seen.

Content, Ida sat back on her bunk and opened the book. Elegant print ran along the parchment pages. The words were Tentonian although some of the earlier age dialect and slang were scattered throughout.

The first entry was a poem:
By night I see the stars,
By day I see the sun.
Although you are not near,
On your every word I'm hung.

Ida frowned and checked the title again. It didn't specify that the poems were about love. After Sergio ruined her time with Jacques and her dreams about Josef, Ida didn't want to read anything about love.

She flipped through the pages until she got about halfway through the book. The title of a short story immediately caught her attention: *The White Elk.*

Ida's eyes grew wide, remembering the giant creature One Shot, Sir Conan, and Devora faced in the final round of Regulus Protecti. While Sir Conan tried to kill the elk-like creature—and failed—One Shot had bowed before it, vowing not to harm the elk: thus, getting disqualified. Devora was the one who freed the elk. The last Ida had seen of the creature was when it busted through the Theater doors and escaped the Fortress.

But seeing this story intrigued her to know more about the great animal. Settling against her pillow, she read:

Legend has told of a mystical elk roaming the lands of Tenton. Whiter than the snow in the north and swifter than the winds of the south, the elandi *is a creature few have seen.*

Ida was immediately enraptured by the story. Her mind easily translated the word *elandi* into the word *spirit.* But Ida had seen the elk with her own eyes. It wasn't a spirit, but a real creature. Even more curious, she focused back on the text.

The elandi *roamed free for centuries, under the protection of the Seers. But when the Seers disappeared, the* elandi *lost its ethereal form and was vulnerable to attacks and capture.*

Ida gasped. The elk had to have been captured by Warden Hazor and locked in the Fortress. But why would he do such a thing?

Ida read on, but the story diverged into a tirade about the monarchy, and she wondered why this book was still allowed on the shelves with such outspoken opinions. Scanning the page again, Ida searched for an author, but the text didn't provide one.

Flopping the book on her lap, Ida peered out her frosty window. She didn't know why, but something about this information struck her as important. Yet before she could dwell on it further, a loud knock pounded on her door.

Squealing, Ida hurriedly hid the restricted texts under her bed, praying it wasn't the headmistress at the door.

Smoothing back her wild curls as best as she could, Ida creaked open the door. "Hello?"

"Why weren't you at breakfast?" Hestia cried, barging into Ida's small room. Reese was two steps behind.

"Lower your voice, Hestia," Reese chided, shaking her abacus in the air. "There is at least a thirty-three point six percent chance that people are still sleeping."

Hestia rolled her eyes then smiled as she took in Ida's room. "You've got a nice room, Ida. The end of the hall is so much better than the middle. People are always passing by, knocking on our door, wanting to socialize." Hestia sighed as she dramatically slumped on Ida's bed.

Ida giggled. She missed her friends. "I'm sure your raging popularity is a terrible burden."

Hestia placed the back of her hand on her forehead, feigning exhaustion. "It is, but someone must rise to the occasion."

Ida laughed again and this time Reese rolled her eyes.

"I never thought I'd say this," Reese added, "But I miss the Fortress. At least there I knew whether people liked me or hated me. They told me right to my face. Here, everyone is a liar."

Ida sympathized with Reese, having felt the same way many times since coming to Vlacklear Academy.

"Oh, let's not talk about anything dull," Hestia said, throwing Ida's pillow at Reese's head. Reese swiftly caught it, and Ida was impressed.

Hestia snorted then continued, "We came here to invite you to watch the jousting tournament with us."

"Jousting?" Ida asked. "I didn't know jousting tournaments were still held in Tenton."

Ama had told Ida about jousting when she'd seen a group of men traveling with their lances and horses from Lower Grenly to a tournament in Ballear. It was an age-old tradition from when Tenton was first founded. Over the years, the tradition faded away. Occasionally, a citadel would host a tournament for entertainment, but Ida couldn't remember the last time a jousting tournament had been held in Grenly.

"It's just for fun!" Hestia squealed with delight.

"And by that she means she wants to watch the male students participate," Reese deadpanned.

Hestia rested her hands on her hips. "Well, why else would I want to go?" She reached out and grabbed Ida's hands. "Please, please come with us. There will be loads of other girls so no one will be suspicious about us being there together."

Ida glanced at the restricted texts under her bed. She *did* need to read them, but after a night of little sleep, she really only wanted to rest her mind.

"Okay, I'll come," she replied. Before she had even finished her sentence, Hestia grabbed her wrist and was tugging her out the door.

"Wait!" Ida cried. "I need to fix my hair."

"We don't have to wear that awful bun when there aren't classes, thank Tunri!" Hestia said with a grin. "And your hair always looks lovely. Now come on!"

Hestia galloped toward the indoor racing course housed in the basement of the academy. Because of the harsh northern

weather, the school kept all their extracurricular activities in-
doors.

Ida's legs strained as she tried to keep up with Hestia's long
strides with Reese bringing up the rear.

When they entered the racing course, a slew of girls was
already in the stands, cheering for a rider in a blue tunic atop
a black horse.

"Come on," Hestia urged, pulling Ida and Reese down the
stairs and into the stands. "We need to get good seats."

Ida followed Hestia without a fuss, curious as to who the
popular rider was. Reese trailed in behind them.

Hestia slid next to Victoria, who was on the edge of her seat,
biting her nails as she watched the competitor who was jousting
against the blue tunic rider.

"What did we miss?" Hestia asked.

"Oh!" Victoria said, surprised and excited that one of the
Sandje twins was talking to her. Her voice then flattened as she
said, "Sergio's won four rounds already."

Reese winced at the mention of Sergio but kept her comments to herself as she sat on the other side of Ida, fiddling with
her abacus.

Victoria then glanced over Hestia. "Hi, Ida."

Ida waved and sat down, noticing how Victoria's gaze was
glued to the rider in the red tunic. If Victoria bit down on her
nails any harder, she was going to draw blood.

"Is everything okay?" Ida asked Victoria.

Victoria put on a fake smile. "Of course, I'm just worried that
Patrick will get hurt and I'll have to do his assignments for him."
She rolled her eyes but stayed focused on the red tunic.

Ida followed her gaze, recognizing Patrick's lanky physique
beneath the red tunic. *So that's why she's so worried.* Ida suspected there was more going on between them.

"No one has beat Sergio?" Hestia snorted then leaned over to
Victoria. "Did you see anyone else? Anyone about this high with

shaggy blondish hair?" Hestia held her hand an inch or so up above her head.

Confusion drawled over Victoria's face as she shook her head. Hestia's shoulders slumped.

"Who are you looking for?" Ida asked, curious.

"No one," Hestia sighed. "I just thought I saw someone I knew earlier this week."

Soon, Sergio charged toward Patrick and landed a blow straight in his chest. Victoria let out a cry but quickly covered it up. Patrick landed on the ground with a thump. For a moment, he didn't move, and Ida was worried. But when he bounced back up, took off his helmet, and gave Victoria a thumbs up, she released a thankful breath.

Victoria scoffed, but smiled anyway, shaking her head at him.

"Is that your boyfriend?" Hestia asked Victoria, waggling her brows.

"Patrick? Ew, no," she said, but her cheeks were rosy. "Just a friend."

Hestia lifted a brow. "Too bad. He's cute."

"Hestia," Reese hissed. But as usual, Hestia ignored her sister.

Ida smiled, feeling at home with Reese and Hestia by her side. Though, her heart missed Devora and Nadia dearly and she prayed that Tunri would bring them all back together soon.

Excited to watch the next match, Ida focused back on the track. Dread knotted in her stomach when she noticed that Sergio had seen her and was coming her way. This time she outwardly groaned. *Why won't he leave me alone?* He hadn't noticed her for weeks and now, within the past week, he was everywhere.

Cupping her hair behind her ear, Hestia turned to her and asked, "What's the matter?"

But before Ida could reply, Sergio was already there.

"My prosperous Ida," he cooed, causing all the girls around them to eye Ida as a threat. "What brings you to the tournament?"

Ida rubbed her palms over her knees, hating the nickname Sergio called her. Everyone knew she was a scholarship student and anything but prosperous. Was he mocking her because she was poor? "Just taking a break from studying."

"Always studying," Sergio tsked. "You need to make time for fun. Have dinner with me tonight."

The girls around Ida, Hestia included, gasped, anticipating her response.

Heat crept up Ida's neck. She hated being the center of attention. All her life she tried to blend in and not make a fuss. Because of Sergio and his unwanted attention, she was the center of *everyone's* focus. And, in this case, that wasn't a good thing.

"I don't think I can—" she started before Sergio interrupted.

"What about a wager then," he grinned. "If I win the next round, you'll have dinner with me. But if I lose, I won't ask you to dinner again."

Ida held back her frustration at his insistence. Didn't he realize she didn't want to know him more? But she knew if she didn't bend now, Sergio would continue to berate her. Ida glanced past Sergio's shoulder to see the next rider suited up for the joust. There was something familiar about the rider's gait but with his helmet on, Ida couldn't see who it was.

After another moment, she sighed. "Very well."

Sergio grinned in triumph before rushing back down the stairs. And then the whispers started.

"What does he see in *her*? She hasn't even been at Vlacklear that long."

"I heard she was a *scholarship* student. Can you imagine? The head of the Amata fortune in the hands of someone like *her*?"

As the girls chittered around her, Ida wanted to crawl into herself and hide. She didn't ask for Sergio's affections. She didn't want them. She didn't even want to be at Vlacklear or the Fortress. She just wanted to go home.

"And she hangs out with Heading," another girl added. "Did you know Victoria used to be the size of a cow? I would die of embarrassment if I had ever been *that* huge!"

Ida glanced over at Victoria. *That's why she never eats in the dining hall.* How many times had these girls made fun of her?

Ida was impressed that Victoria's face was a mask of stone as she stood. "I think I'm going to check on Patrick."

"You will not," Hestia said, more forcefully than Ida had ever heard before.

Victoria stared at Hestia in shock and sat back down.

"Hestia," Reese suddenly said quite loudly. The girls quieted down, wanting to hear what one of the Sandje twins had to say. "Did you know that in ancient times, those who spoke harshly of others without reason had a seventy-two point eight percent chance of being drawn and quartered?"

Hestia's eyes widened as a mischievous grin split her face. "Why no, dear sister. Do tell me more. In full detail."

As Reese explained the horrors of ancient punishment and questioned whether they should be reinstated, the gossiping girls around them paled and quickly steered their conversation away from Ida and Victoria.

After Reese finished her monologue, Ida leaned toward Reese and said, "Thank you."

Reese nodded, her face calm but her eyes ablaze with fury. "They only talk about you like that because you allow it, Ida. You are so much more than any of them."

Ida's emotions swelled in her chest. Reese never showed her true feelings to anyone. To be complimented in such a way tugged at Ida's heart.

Reese glanced at her and scoffed. "No tears, Ida. I only speak the truth."

Still, Ida reached out and squeezed Reese's hand. To her surprise, Reese returned the gesture.

The starting horn blew, drawing all eyes to Sergio and his unknown opponent. While Sergio wore a striking light blue—Ida learned through the chattering girls it was his family's color—his opponent wore a beautiful light green. There was some discussion as to whose family color was light green, but a conclusion was never made. But the beautiful shade reminded Ida of her small desert lily growing steadily in the greenhouse.

The green rider aimed his lance toward Sergio's chest, but at the last minute, Sergio dodged. The girls cheered and Ida balled her hands into fists. If the green rider didn't win, she would have to endure a whole evening with Sergio. Alone. She didn't want to think of what plans the sleazy boy had for that evening. Ida ran her fingers around her wire bracelet. If she had to use it on Sergio in self-defense, she would.

The next round, Sergio tried to strike the green rider in the head. But the rider was swift and able to deflect the blow. Ida's hope returned. Maybe she wasn't doomed to have dinner with Sergio after all.

The girls around them were all on the edge of their seats. Some were entranced by the green rider, but most of them were worried that Sergio would lose. Yet, at the same time, they didn't want him to spend a whole evening alone with Ida.

The final round was upon them, and all the girls waited with anticipation. Not a single one spoke as the two riders galloped toward one another; lances ready to strike. Ida couldn't help it, but she reached out and grabbed each of Hestia's and Reese's hands.

"Don't worry," Hestia whispered, keeping her eyes glued to the match. "We won't leave you alone with him. We'll figure something out."

The words comforted Ida's fearful mind until the snapping of wood breaking filled the air. A yell ricocheted against the stone walls of the track. Some girls cried out; others gasped. The only one who was pleased was Ida, for the green rider had knocked Sergio off his horse.

Fuming, Sergio launched up from the ground and threw off his helmet before stomping toward the green rider, who still sat upon his horse.

"I say, sir, if you are to defeat me, at least give me the dignity of knowing who you are." Sergio oozed formality, but his stance was rigid with fury.

"Gladly," the green rider replied.

The entire track seemed to silence as the rider took off his helmet, revealing the sly smile of Jacques.

Chapter Twelve

Matthias, Totem, Ballear

Matthias whipped around, removing his focus from the intricate machine. "What did you say?"

Rae's father, Lucas, strode to the machine, twisting a screw a few more times. "It neutralizes imperial opal."

"And how do you know this?" Matthias questioned, casting a scrutinizing glance at the machine.

"I gave him the imperial opal ring you gave me," One Shot cut in. "I know it was Devora's but the only way we could be certain the machine would work was to test it on the real stone."

Matthias' resolve faltered at losing the ring from Devora, but his mind moved too quickly to dwell on it. *A device that could nullify imperial opal. Could it be true?*

"How do you know it worked?" Matthias asked, wanting to be absolutely sure this device worked before he divulged the rest of his plan.

"Some of my fellow Tinkers agreed to be test subjects, as well as my daughter," Lucas replied. "They each wore the ring for an hour to understand its full effects before I used the nullifier on it. After the ring went through the nullifier, each volunteer wore the ring again and none of them felt the effects as before. It was just a ring."

Matthias cupped his chin. "Your daughter, Rae, has a gift, as well?"

The man shook his head. "No. Unfortunately, she has experienced the power of a larger source of imperial opal, so I knew she would know what its drain felt like."

Matthias tilted his head to the side, casting a glance at One Shot. The tall man nodded his head in confirmation.

"What do you think, son?" Liam asked, his eyes bright with hope.

Matthias looked at his father, remembering all the long days and even longer nights of his care and love. He was glad to see that his father's hope was still alive and well.

"This is excellent work," Matthias said, turning to Lucas. "It will be pivotal in the near future."

"Thank you, sir," Lucas replied, wiping his hands on a cloth hanging from his belt. "I only wish I had more imperial opal to test it on. In my short time at the palace working for the king, I learned that imperial opal is something the monarchy craves, but I don't know why."

Matthias frowned, wondering if Rae would be able to shed some light on the subject. For whatever reason, the woman didn't like him, but that never stopped Matthias from asking the questions he needed answered.

"Very good," Matthias said. "I will check back with you before I leave for Juro."

Liam stayed with Lucas to chat about the change in seasons as Matthias and One Shot strode back to the house on the hill.

"I'd like to speak with Rae," Matthias told One Shot.

One Shot was quiet for a while then replied, "She's been through a lot, Matthias. Try to be...less intense."

Matthias' frown deepened. "I'm not going to order her to run laps around the vineyard, One Shot. I just want to know about the imperial opal."

One Shot sighed, rubbing the back of his neck. "Yeah, I figured that. There was a floor-to-ceiling statue of the Goddess Pahga, in the Temple back in Yekel. It was made of imperial opal."

Matthias' brows rose in surprise. "The whole statue?"

One Shot nodded. "From what I understand, Rae's former...captor forced her in front of it. After that, something changed in Rae." The tall man kept his hard gaze forward. "But that's all she's told me, and she *likes* me."

A smile ticked at Matthias' lips. "Yes, I can see that the feelings are mutual for you."

Red crept up the pale skin of One Shot's neck, but he didn't say anything further.

When the two reached the wooden home, Rae and another woman sat on the porch, dying different pieces of cloth. Matthias had never seen such radiant colors. Blues, brighter than the sky. Greens, fresher than the grass. A vivid purple lay across Rae's lap and Matthias immediately wanted to have it for Devora.

If he ever saw her again.

He pushed the thought from his mind. He *would* see her again. He would find her and his mother, even if it killed him.

"Hello there," the other woman said as Matthias and One Shot approached.

As soon as Matthias saw her, he knew the woman had to be Rae's mother. The two were practically copies of one another.

A kind smile rested on the woman's lips as she waited for an introduction.

Matthias bowed low. "Good afternoon, ma'am. I am Captain Matthias Blake, Liam's elder son."

At his voice, Rae's gaze shot up. Her eyes narrowed at seeing him but then softened as she glanced at One Shot behind him.

"It's nice to officially meet you, Captain. I'm Sara. Liam speaks of you often. Only good things," she added with a wink before coughing a few times.

Matthias smiled. "He is too good for this world, ma'am. The best father a son could ask for."

Before Matthias could ask any further questions, Sara erupted into another fit of coughs. Rae quickly offered her mother a drink of water, concern covering her face. Sara coughed a handful more times before she smiled back at Matthias.

"Are you all right, ma'am?" he asked.

Sara nodded. "Of course, I'm just getting used to the new environment of Ballear." With another kind smile she asked, "Is there something we can help you with?"

Matthias glanced at Rae, who hadn't broken her lethal stare since he approached them. "I was wondering if I could speak to your daughter. I have a few questions about Yekel, and I feel she's the only one who can answer them."

Sara turned to Rae. "Well, *mija*? Are you just going to leave the man standing there?"

Rae huffed, setting the fabric down. Her hands were stained a shade of lilac, reminding Matthias of Devora yet again.

"Only if Ben stays," she finally said.

"Of course," Matthias replied swiftly.

Rae gave him an odd look before her mother stood to find her father.

Once she was gone, Rae asked, "You know his real name?"

One Shot carefully sat on the porch beside Rae. Even sitting a few steps lower than where Rae sat, he was still almost as tall as her.

"Matthias was my cellmate in the Fortress," One Shot told her.

Rae's eyes widened in shock. "What? But you're an officer."

Matthias rubbed his eyes with his fingers before seating himself in Sara's chair. "That is a very long and complicated story. But, yes, One Shot—Ben—and I were cellmates. I still call him One Shot per his request."

Rae studied Matthias, the harshness of her gaze softening slightly. At least he'd said something right.

"What do you want to know about Yekel?"

Matthias took a breath, trying to find the tact that Jacques always accused him of not having. How would Devora phrase it? He tried to think of the kind yet forward words she would use.

"I understand you spent time in the Temple of Pahga," he began. At Rae's immediate rigidity, Matthias feared she would refuse to speak. But One Shot grabbed her hand and held it, relaxing her tense state.

"While I can't imagine the horrors you experienced there, I would appreciate it if you could tell me more about the imperial opal statue."

Rae took a deep breath, clenching One Shot's hand in her own purple-stained one. "The statue of Pahga came when Kadesh sieged Yekel. They placed it in there and encouraged sacrifices to the goddess."

Matthias leaned forward. The cabbage-lemon scent of the purple dye pierced his nose, but he kept his attention focused on Rae. "What kind of sacrifices?"

"Female sacrifices," she whispered. "All ages. Kadeshians didn't care if they were fifteen years old or a few days old. It was horrible." Rae looked down at the fabric in her lap. "While I was there, General Yada forced me to take *menta*, an herb known for causing hallucinations, and placed me before the statue of Pahga."

She paused, keeping her eyes down.

One Shot whispered something to her, but she shook her head. Matthias waited patiently, hoping Rae would continue.

Stifling a breath, Rae looked up at him, tears glistening in her caramel eyes. "I don't know how it happened, but it felt as if pieces of my soul were being ripped out of me. The statue somehow drew them out and took them."

Matthias sat back in his chair, hating that his suspicions were correct. "Thank you, Rae. I appreciate you sharing this information with me. If you don't mind, may I ask you one more question?"

"Matthias—" One Shot started to protest, but Rae cut in.

"It's okay, Ben. Go ahead, Captain."

"Did you happen to meet an elderly woman there?" Rae's whole stature changed, and Matthias knew she'd met the hag. His lips thinned. "Thank you, Rae." He stood from his chair and bowed to Rae before descending the porch steps.

Matthias suspected where all the threads of this tale began but he prayed it wasn't true. The hag, the imperial opal, the power of the stone. He'd seen the same power before, had endured it when he was just a young knight being cursed to shift into a wolf every full moon. Sometimes even more. And all the evil led back to one place. One person.

The stomping of footsteps followed behind him as Matthias made his way down the hill.

"Matthias, wait," One Shot said, catching up to him in four strides.

Matthias stopped.

"What does an old lady have to do with anything?" One Shot asked. "And what about the imperial opal?"

Matthias sighed, wanting to think and plan a bit more before divulging his idea to One Shot. He knew his friend's history and wasn't sure he'd be keen on helping.

"The hag is a story for another time. But regarding the imperial opal, I have a solution as to where we can find more to test Lucas' machine."

One Shot's brows rose. "You do?"

Matthias nodded, keeping his gaze plastered on the horizon. "I do, but I'll need your help in retrieving it and returning a horse."

One Shot gave a confused look at the mention of the horse, but replied, "Of course. I'll help in any way I can."

Matthias pushed out a breath, knowing One Shot would be compliant.

"I learned of a hidden cave filled with imperial opal not far from here."

One Shot's eyes darkened. "Where?"

Matthias faced his friend, never having been one to sugarcoat things. "It's about a mile from your home village. I need you to retrieve some for me."

Chapter Thirteen

Ben, Totem, Ballear

"I'm coming with you," Rae declared, already packing her sack with a handful of scarves.

Ben had just returned from his conversation with Matthias and explained everything to Rae. His mind shouted at him to say no and flee from the task. But his heart took hold of his tongue and he agreed. After four years of being away from home, he would finally see his family again.

"You don't know Snoken like I do," he said. "I don't want anything to happen to you."

Rae flicked her hand at him as she stuffed a pair of pants and a tunic into her bag. "Oh please. It can't be any worse than the Temple."

Ben wanted to argue with her, but he knew she was right. Rae had defended herself for years as her former alias, the Crimson Cord, a street fighter in the Dark Market of Yekel. But that wasn't what worried Ben. It was all the people he grew up with. Would they chase him out of town or just insult him from afar like they always had?

Ben ran a hand through his shaggy black hair. He didn't want Rae to see that part of his past. He didn't want her to know the soiled parts of him.

Rae stopped packing and analyzed his face. "Do you really not want me to come?"

Ben couldn't bear to see the worry in her eyes. They'd only begun their fragile relationship a few weeks ago and though things were going well, it would be a long time until she fully trusted him.

Sighing, Ben decided—as he always decided when with Rae—to tell the truth.

Sitting down on the cot inside Rae's family's tent, he explained. "I'm worried that your opinion of me will change if you meet the people I grew up with."

Rae placed her sack on the floor and joined him. Her arm and leg rested against his own and Ben welcomed the closeness. He understood and respected her hesitancy toward physical touch. But every time she smiled at him or made him laugh, the yearning in his heart intensified.

"I don't care what other people think about you or about me." She placed her head on his shoulder and Ben turned into a statue. He didn't want to move and risk her leaving his side. "I only care about what you think of yourself."

Ben cautiously leaned his cheek against the top of her head. While she was the Crimson Cord, Rae had previously shorn her hair short. But since she left Yekel and the Crimson Cord behind, she decided to grow it back out again. It was already growing fast, and Ben loved the vibrant yellow-white shade of it.

When Rae didn't pull away from him, Ben relaxed a bit more.

"I'm still working on how I feel about myself," he confessed.

Rae chuckled. "Me too, but about me. I know how I feel about you."

Ben swallowed, his throat suddenly becoming dry. "Care to share?" he managed to say.

Rae hummed and then, to Ben's dismay, stood up. "Not quite yet."

Ben smiled at her new flirtatious demeanor. When he first arrived in Totem, Rae was still stiff and skittish, as if every person in this new place was ready to harm her. Though Ben understood her reactions, it burdened his heart to see her still filled with so much fear.

Yet, eventually, after more time spent with her mother and father, Ben was able to get glimpses of Rae as she might have been before Kadesh seized Yekel. And he was enjoying it greatly.

"So," Rae said. Facing him, she placed her hands on her hips. "Am I coming or not?"

Two horses were saddled for Rae and Ben the next morning. One Ben recognized as Clove, his father's horse. Matthias had yet to explain how he met Pa and Mara, but Ben assumed he would find out the details eventually.

Rae wrapped a dark brown scarf over her vibrant hair before mounting the other white and brown speckled horse beside Clove.

"No bright scarves today?" Ben asked, nodding to the cocoa-colored scarf. "Are you worried about the trip?"

He always loved the vibrant colored scarves Rae wore. Whether over her head or around her neck, the color she picked for the day usually defined her mood. When she wore blue or yellow, she was happy. Purple, she was content, green she was upset. But ever since they came to Totem, Ben had yet to see her wear crimson again.

Rae kept the crimson cord from her former disguise beneath her scarves at the bottom of a trunk. Ben wondered if she'd ever bring out the disguise again.

Rae sighed as she tucked the ends of the scarf around her neck and shoulders. "I figured we didn't want to be noticed. And yes, I am worried."

Ben made sure Rae was secure on her horse before he grabbed Clove's reins. "We'll be okay," he replied, trying to convince himself, as well.

Though it had been over a month since his and Devora's escape, King Atol's soldiers were still patrolling the different regions for them. Although, they cared a lot more about finding Devora than him.

"Are you going to walk all the way there?" Rae asked, frowning down at him.

Ben nodded. "I'm too large for Clove to carry me the whole way. I'll walk for now and maybe ride in a bit."

Rae's frown deepened and before Ben could protest, she dismounted her steed.

"What are you doing?"

She brushed a stray hair from her eyes. "It's a nice morning, I feel like stretching my legs." Rae grabbed her horse's reins and took a few steps forward. Glancing over her shoulder, she said, "You coming, slowpoke?"

Ben grinned and took two steps toward her. "Right behind you."

The walk to Snoken took longer than anticipated, but Ben didn't mind. He and Rae talked about all sorts of things: new pastry ideas, Ben's friendship with Matthias, and his childhood in Snoken.

"Not everyone was cruel," Ben commented as they crested another hill.

He stopped to let Clove nibble on some grass. Rae came beside him and let her horse do the same. Just beyond the next hill sat a sleepy village, quaint albeit small.

"My friend, Jonathon, was always there when I needed him," he added, keeping his gaze fixated on the thatched rooftops ahead.

"He's the one who married your sister?" Rae asked, stroking her horse's neck.

Ben nodded, hoping Mara wouldn't turn him away after what he'd done.

"Hey," Rae said, grabbing his hand and squeezing it. "It's going to be okay."

Ben turned to her, trying to find the hope and strength Rae always seemed to have. But the weight of the past slumped his shoulders even more.

"I hope so," he mumbled.

Rae squeezed his hand again. "It will. Plus, you have me now." She grinned.

Ben couldn't help but chuckle. "I can see where Nadia got all her confidence."

Rae nodded in agreement then laced her fingers through his. "Come on. Sometimes the only way to confront a situation is head on."

They continued and before he knew it, Ben was right outside his childhood home. On their way into town, several people glanced their way—many of whom did a double take. He was a few inches taller than when he was last here. His hair was longer too. Ben pulled the hood of his cloak over his head, hoping to hide his face and the crossbow attached to his back.

Rae glanced up at him, her warm eyes full of care. Ben knew she would defend him against any of the townspeople and that's what worried him. Rae was a fierce fighter, and he didn't want her to get into harm's way because of him. She'd already been through enough. He couldn't ruin another person's life because of his mistakes.

"Ready?" Rae asked.

Pinching his lips together, Ben nodded. He held his breath and knocked on the door.

Quick footsteps rushed toward the door. Before Ben could lower his hand, it swiftly opened.

Shocked, Ben froze in place, unable to speak or lower his hand from where he knocked. Mara stood before him. No longer a young girl, but a woman. He glanced at her swollen belly, even more shocked. A woman about to be a mother.

"Ben?" Mara's eyes went wide before tears clouded them. "Is it really you?"

A few people who'd been walking through the village stopped and openly eavesdropped on their conversation.

Rae's hands reached out and lowered Ben's still outstretched fist. "Hi, I'm Rae. May we come in?"

Mara's eyes immediately went to Rae, surprise written all over her face.

"Mara?" a male voice called from inside. "Is that Linus with my butter order? He was meant to be here an hour ago."

Ben braced himself as Pa came to the door. It had only been a few years, but Pa had aged, and Ben's heart sagged. Ben knew he'd put a lot of stress on his father when he shot and killed the four men who violated Mara. Pa's life was another one Ben had ruined.

"Benjamin?" Pa asked with the same shock as Mara. "You're—you're here? But how?"

Ben, still at a loss for words, was thankful Rae insisted on coming.

"Hello, I'm Rae," she said again with a warm smile. "I'm a good friend of Ben's. May we come inside?"

Ben noticed Rae take a hesitant glance around. It was then he realized that more people were casually lingering around the bakery.

Pa glanced at Rae and blinked as if unable to comprehend her presence. Thankfully, Mara broke the trance.

"Yes, yes, of course," Mara butted in, wiping the tears from her cheeks. "Please forgive us. It's been quite a while since we've seen Ben."

"Thank you," Rae replied with a kind smile.

As Pa and Mara disappeared inside, Ben found his words.

"I can't do this," he breathed, feeling the world closing in around him. The memories were too much. So much joy, so much pain. It was better when they were buried. Then they couldn't hurt him anymore.

Ben had spiraled into depression before when he first entered the Fortress. It's why he didn't mind being on Level Five. No one bothered him there and he could dig deeper and deeper into his regret. But that all changed as soon as Matthias came into his life.

While Ben was forlorn and defeated, Matthias was a raging fire, unwilling to be beaten down. Ben always admired that about him and wished he could hone some of that fire for himself.

"Ben, look at me," Rae commanded. Her small, chilled hands cupped his cheeks. "You can do this. You *need* to do this." He started to shake his head when she pressed her palms firmer, squishing his face. "I've seen how people react when they're disgusted with you or feel pity. Your sister and father held none of that in their faces. Give them a chance to explain what they've been through these past years too." She released his face but kept her gaze boring into his own.

Ben wanted to get lost in her eyes and think of nothing but them, but he knew she was right. Like Matthias, Rae was a tornado of flame. No one would bring her down. Ben was just thankful that she allowed him to stay in her life.

"Okay," he whispered.

Reaching out, Rae offered her hand, knowing he needed her support to walk through his former home again. He took it and nodded thanks.

As the two strode through the threshold, the warm, welcoming scent of freshly baked bread overwhelmed Ben. He'd smelled it so many times growing up, he never thought it would bring him so much joy. Before he could stop himself, he started to weep.

"Ben?" Rae asked, worry crossing her features.

"Ben?" Mara repeated, walking forward with a tray of pastries in her hand. "Are you all right? I brought out your favorite scones."

Ben fell to his knees, unable to bear the weight of his guilt, the weight of Mara's kindness after everything he'd done.

"I'm so sorry, Mara," he sobbed into his hands. "I beg for your forgiveness, though I don't deserve it."

Mara dropped the scones to the floor and rushed over to Ben, wrapping her small arms around him. Tears soon fell from her eyes as the siblings wept together.

After they cried, Mara rubbed her nose and stood. "Come, all these tears aren't good for a pregnant woman. Apparently if I want to have a happy baby, I must be happy myself."

"All the time?" Ben asked, his eyes burning from all the tears. "That sounds difficult."

Mara gave a small smile. "It's not. Not anymore." She wrapped her hands around Ben's waist in a hug. "Although it was difficult for me at first, I've already forgiven you, Ben. You're my brother and you always will be."

Ben squeezed his little sister tight, wishing he could take away all the pain he caused her. He knew he couldn't but was thankful to see the strength she gained while he was in the Fortress.

"We love you, Benjamin," Pa said from the corner of the room.

Pa had always been polite, not one to intervene in other's affairs. When they were children and quarreled, Pa always told Ben and Mara to work things out among themselves and make it right. Ben always thought his father loved him, but sometimes questioned it when Pa was distant.

But as Pa strode forward and embraced Ben in a hug as well, Ben knew Pa truly meant it.

"I'm so sorry for the trouble I've caused," he muttered. "Is there anything I can do to make it right?"

"Yes, there is," Mara said, releasing him from her grasp, her face serious.

Worry gripped Ben's heart, but he would do anything for his family.

"You can start by telling us who your lovely friend is and why you're here," Mara continued with a bright smile.

Chapter Fourteen

Ida, Vlacklear Academy, Juro

Ida stared in bewilderment as Jacques removed his helmet and held it against his side. He defeated Sergio in the jousting tournament. But why was he even participating?

"Prefect Jacques?" Sergio questioned, his charming persona faltering for a moment before he slipped it back on. "Who knew you were so skilled with a lance? I never thought a Fourth Year would still joust. It's an honor to compete against you."

"Likewise," Jacques clipped, his usual kind smile vacant from his face.

Ida's palms began to sweat as Jacques' gaze turned to her. Before she could greet him, Sergio jumped into the stands and sidled up beside her. The rest of the girls leaned in, trying to get close to Sergio. But Ida wanted nothing other than to get away from him.

"Now, Jacques, let's make our next round a bit more fun, what do you say?"

Jacques shifted his hazel eyes to Sergio, a hardness overtaking them as Sergio wrapped his arm around Ida's shoulders.

"Whoever wins the next round gets to enjoy a lovely dinner with Ida."

Ida was stiff as stone, not knowing how to react to Sergio's forwardness. Devora would shove him away then tell him off. Nadia would probably have some contraption to get rid of him.

She looked to Hestia and Reese for help, but it seemed the other girls were bombarding them with questions. Ida was all alone.

"Now, wait a moment," Victoria piped in, and Ida's hope returned. "You said that if you lost the last round, you would leave Ida alone."

Victoria gave Sergio a patronizing glare as she crossed her hands over her chest.

"Careful, Sergio," Jacques said tightly. "You don't want to make a promise you can't keep. If you already said you'd leave Miss Shabawn alone, I suggest you keep your word."

Worry clouded Ida's thoughts as she analyzed Jacques' tone. Though he looked incredibly handsome in his jousting attire with his hair messy, his face was as serious as a statue. And when he looked like that, Jacques turned deadly.

Sergio smiled wider, almost too wide. His arm tightened around Ida's shoulders. "I intend to be a perfect host to Ida when we dine together tonight."

Ida wanted to cry out and say something about the injustice of all of this. Did anyone even care what *she* wanted? Sergio lost to Jacques already, he should accept his defeat and move on. But try as she might, Ida could not form the words. Thankfully, she did find a small bit of courage and slowly inched away from Sergio.

Victoria tried to speak up again but was drowned out by the group of girls cheering for another match that had started on the other side of the track.

Jacques gritted his teeth then turned to Ida. "I will only accept these terms if Miss Shabawn approves of this match."

To Ida, the room quieted so much so that the only noise she heard was her heart racing inside her chest. Even though Ida scooched away, Sergio's warm arm still hung over her shoulders, like a weight ready to smash her if she disobeyed.

Why was Sergio trying so hard to win her affections? She was just a poor girl from Lower Grenly. No, not Lower Grenly. From Kadesh, which was even lower than Grenly.

You are enough, something inside of her said.

Ida blinked. She'd never heard the statement before, had never dreamed of it being associated with someone like her. Ida was never enough. She would always be an orphan. She would always be poor. And if someone like Josef was too good for her, Jacques would be too good for her, as well.

Yet, as the negativity clouded her mind, the phrase wouldn't leave.

You are enough.

You are enough.

Am I enough? Ida thought.

Before the dismal thoughts could invade again, Ida found her courage. Straightening her shoulders, she shoved Sergio's arm off.

She lifted her chin like she'd seen Devora do many times and said, "I will dine with whomever *I* choose. A silly competition isn't going to make my decisions for me." While she was still feeling brave, she added, "But if you want to compete to have dinner with each other, be my guest."

Jacques' eyes widened, his lips parted in shock at Ida's outburst, but a glimmer of admiration twinkled in his eyes.

But Ida couldn't dwell on the beautiful sight, before her embarrassment took over. Heat crept into every crevice of her body as she spun around and fled from the indoor track.

"Ida!" Jacques' voice called from behind, but Ida didn't stop.

All those laps Captain Blake made her run finally kicked in and she raced as fast as she could away from Jacques, unsure if she could ever face him again. She ran and ran and ran until she was outside of the Academy.

A brisk wind slapped her across the cheeks, ceasing her steps. Her breath came out in hard pants, small white puffs escaping her lips.

They were never allowed to leave the Fortress, and now that Ida was in the freezing cold, she could see why. The winds howled around her, but there was something welcoming about the biting air. Ever since she came to Vlacklear, her thoughts were muddled and clouded. Finally they were clear.

Wrapping her arms around herself, Ida trekked further away from Vlacklear toward the greenhouse. She always loved it when Professor Mal had class in the greenhouse. It was as if all her problems and worries disappeared when she was tending to the plants.

Ida's fingers tightened around the chilled metal handle. She yanked the door open and stalked inside, slamming it behind her. She wished she hadn't made the agreement to help Sergio with his Linguistics work. Though she had completed his assignments so far, she despised him to no end and the agreement felt like a ball and chain forever tying her to him. But she couldn't allow Reese's and Hestia's location to be exposed. Who knew what would happen if Sergio yapped to the twins' father about their whereabouts? Would Reese be forced to marry Sergio? Or would her father find another unworthy suitor? And what would he do with Hestia? Another arranged marriage?

Grabbing a metal watering can from the corner, Ida started sprinkling the plants. A variety of blooming greenery stretched out before her. Some were vegetables: mixes of tomatoes, various lettuces, and carrots. Others were plants: ferns, boxwoods, and hollies. Ida continued down the rows, noticing how some plants fared better than others. Scraggles of dying vines sprawled from the tomato plants and the lettuce was wilted. The boxwoods seemed okay, but they were sturdy plants.

Finally, Ida made it to where her plant resided. Professor Mal praised her efforts, which was more than her former professor did. The small desert lily sprout seemed a bit taller than last time, but nowhere near where Ida would like it to be.

"A seed must be broken to create a beautiful flower," Professor Mal told her yesterday during Horticulture.

Sighing, Ida glanced at the other blooming plants of her classmates then stared at the small sprout. It seemed as if all the other plants grew fine and didn't need to be broken anymore. Why was her lily subjected to such cruelty when it had done nothing other than want to live?

Tears stung Ida's eyes and she wiped them away. Crying over a plant was silly, but Ida knew Professor Mal was speaking beyond the desert lily.

Shaking her head, Ida patted her little sprout, wishing it a bright future. Professor Fortua, her former instructor, said it would be extremely difficult to germinate a lily in the northern region, even in the greenhouse. But after First Lady Medee had given Ida a tour of her gardens, Ida dreamed of the day when she could have her own garden filled with delicious vegetables and gorgeous flowers.

"I truly believe you will have your own garden one day, Ida," First Lady Medee said with a kind smile.

Ida smiled at the memory then let it falter. That was right before she ran into Devora. Ida had lost track of time and needed to get home to help Ama with dinner. Ida was in such a rush that she didn't even see Devora. She remembered being so frightened and surprised that the same girl whose vision had saved Jil's life could be so cruel. But later, when she shared a carriage with Devora, Ida knew, somewhere inside, Devora was just as kind and caring as her parents.

Ida's thought deepened more as she sprinkled some manure on her lily. Where was Devora now? Was she all right? Ida couldn't imagine being hunted by the kingdom.

Closing her eyes, Ida said a prayer for Devora, praying Tunri would guide her way even when the darkness seemed to win.

As Ida was tidying up the greenhouse, the metal and glass door squeaked open. As fear lodged in her throat, Ida kept her grip firm on the broom. Quickly, she ducked into a corner by some potatoes. She may not be the Defender of Tenton, but she learned enough at the Fortress to fend off whoever followed her into the greenhouse. And if it was Sergio, maybe she would enjoy it.

Steady footsteps came toward her. Ida took a reassuring breath, remembering the training she had with Jacques. It felt like years instead of weeks ago. The gait of the intruder paused, and Ida used it to her advantage.

Lunging out of the corner, she twirled the broom and smacked the intruder in the chest with its handle. The intruder grunted and Ida recognized him too late, for the broom swung again whacking Jacques in the head.

"Ow!" he cried, rubbing his head while grappling for the broom. When he locked his grip around the handle, he wrenched it with all his might, pulling Ida along with it.

She didn't release it in time before she, too, smacked into his chest. With her nose smashed against the toned muscles, Ida fantasized about this scenario working out differently than what was presently occurring.

"I thought I'd find you in here," Jacques said, only slightly pulling back from her.

He was only a breath away and Ida didn't mind. Although she thought her heart would burst from excitement.

"I'm sorry," Ida said, trying not to become a weeping mess in front of him. Again. He probably thought she was nothing but a walking waterfall. Almost every time Jacques saw her, she was crying.

"Sorry for what?" he asked, a crease forming between his brows. "Sorry for standing up for yourself against a pompous playboy?"

Ida giggled at the comment, suddenly feeling proud of herself. "I'm sorry for attacking you with the broom."

Jacques held the broom like a staff. "Ah yes, but you executed your technique so well. Captain Blake would be proud of you, lieutenant."

Ida's grin dipped at her title. While playing student at Vlacklear, she'd almost forgotten her true purpose. She needed to find the correct book that held the prophecy Queen Leza received sixteen years ago.

"What's the matter?" Jacques asked, concern crossing his features.

"Nothing," Ida said shaking it off. Some leaves and dirt had fallen into her charcoal ringlets when she hid from Jacques. Now that she had noticed them, she was even more mortified.

Hastily, Ida reached up and started pulling the leaves from her hair. She'd gotten all but one out when Jacques' fingers caressed her own.

"Allow me," he breathed, plucking the last leaf from a curl right by her temple.

The curl sprung back, landing across her cheek. Ida couldn't breathe as Jacques brushed his fingers across her cheek and tucked her hair behind her ear.

"I've missed seeing your hair like this," he said, his voice suddenly husky. "Untamed and free."

Ida knew she needed to breathe or else she might pass out, but she didn't want to miss one moment of Jacques' adoration by needing oxygen.

"The headmistress doesn't agree with you," Ida whispered. "She likes everything well kept, not a hair out of place."

"I couldn't care less what that horrid woman thinks," Jacques said, leaning forward.

Ida's heart jumped from her throat to her stomach all in one fell swoop. Was this really happening? Was Jacques going to kiss her?

His luscious lips just barely brushed hers when the greenhouse door opened again.

Ida let out a small yelp in surprise, and Jacques immediately snapped into his rigid military posture.

"I won't tell anyone," Professor Mal said, waving her wrinkled hand at them, a gentle smile on her lips. "I just wanted to pick some beets for my dinner."

If Ida wasn't so horribly embarrassed, she would have laughed for Jacques' face was the same shade as the beets Professor Mal was picking.

"Forgive us, Professor," he said with a deep bow. "We'll be on our way."

Professor Mal gave another wave but slipped Ida a wink before Jacques grabbed Ida's hand and hurried out of the greenhouse. He didn't say another word until they were back inside the warm walls of Vlacklear Academy.

Though his face wasn't as red as before, there were still hints of pink blotting his cheeks.

"Miss Shabawn," he started then bowed so low, Ida thought his forehead would touch the floor. "Please forgive my forwardness. I shall not succumb to my desires so easily again."

Ida stared at the knight in bewilderment. He was apologizing and bowing to *her*? Like she was a noble or some kind of royalty. But she was nothing. She was just Ida.

"You don't need to apologize," she said shyly, tugging at the hem of her sleeves. "I didn't move away," she added softly.

Jacques stood tall, taking in her statement. He licked his lips, as if trying to find the right words to say. "While that is true, I did not behave like a proper gentleman or a knight. Forgive me?" He gave her his winning smile that Ida adored and could never say no to.

"Of course," she said. Ida realized then she didn't want her time with Jacques to end. "However," she added, hoping he would agree. "Even though you didn't joust against Sergio for dinner with me, you can join me for dinner all the same." She finished all in one breath.

Jacques' brows rose up his forehead before Ida hurriedly added, "Plus I can tell you what I've learned in the texts, and we can read them more."

Jacques smiled and offered her his arm. "Well, Ida, that's an offer I can't refuse. Shall we?"

Grinning from ear to ear, Ida took his arm, believing that maybe for Jacques, she was enough.

Chapter Fifteen

Ida, Vlacklear, Juro

Agreeing to meet up in the library, Ida and Sir Jacques retrieved their dinners separately. In the dining hall, Ida ran into Reese and Hestia, who peppered her with questions of her whereabouts after the joust. Ida said she had to finish her job in the greenhouse and was off to study in the library. Though Hestia wished her a good night, Ida knew Reese could see through her.

It wasn't a total lie. Ida did have homework to finish for tomorrow, although it was trivial since it was for Linguistics. Unfortunately, that was the class she had with Sergio. Who knew what he would demand tomorrow after she'd embarrassed him in front of everyone at the jousting tournament?

Sighing, Ida shook the thought from her mind, focusing on seeing Jacques again. After passing by her room to retrieve the restricted texts, Ida hurried to the library. Parts of her sandwich were all over her tray by the time she made it to the table in the back.

Jacques was already there, his elegant brow furrowed as he read a thin book. He nonchalantly bit into an apple, and Ida found it the most attractive thing in the world.

Shaking her head, Ida strode forward, trying to keep her tray balanced atop the stack of books.

Upon hearing her footsteps, Jacques glanced up. A warm smile adorned his face all the way to his eyes. Ida couldn't imagine that someone like her would make him feel that way, but her heart soared all the same.

"Welcome back," he said, standing to take her tray from the books. "It looks like your dinner's trying to run away."

Ida giggled at the remark. "I had a little trouble carrying my tray and the books." The three restricted texts and extra fourth book were so thick, they reached Ida's chin. And that was when she held them at her waist.

Jacques placed her tray down on the wooden table and grabbed the texts. After setting them on the table, he pulled out the chair next to his and motioned to it. "Care to join me?"

"Of course," Ida replied, blushing.

After she sat, Ida's nerves took over. Should she dive right into telling Jacques what she'd learned about the elk from the Fortress? Or should she try small talk first? Ida bit her lip, fumbling with her fingers in her lap. She was never good at small talk. She remembered feeling so nervous when she rode with Devora in the carriage all alone. What could she say to a girl who hated her for no reason?

Thankfully, Jacques was excellent at talking. "So," he said after he swallowed another bite of apple. "Have you learned anything from the texts? I know it hasn't been long since I gave them to you, but I'm curious."

Ida stretched out her fingers and decided to place them on the table. Picking at the pumpernickel bread of her sandwich, she confessed, "I haven't opened the restricted texts yet, but I did open the extra one you put on top. Did you pick that one on purpose?"

Jacques shook his head. "No, I was just trying to cover them so Sergio wouldn't see. What did you find out?"

Ida grabbed the text from the top and thumbed through it until she found the passage about the giant elk. Pushing the pages towards Jacques, she watched his eyes scan the page.

"Do you think this is the same elk from the Fortress?" he asked.

Ida nodded. "It must be. I've never seen any other elk, giant or otherwise. My question is why Warden Hazor would cage such a beautiful creature that is so important to Tenton."

Jacques shrugged. "It's in his nature."

Before Ida could stop herself, she blurted, "No, it's not. He's not as awful as everyone thinks he is."

Jacques stared at her, taken aback. "Ida, Warden Hazor is ruthless and cruel. The only way to stay in his good graces is to comply without hesitation. Why do you think criminals don't even try to escape from the Fortress?"

Ida pinched her lips shut. She shouldn't say anything more or else her secret would be revealed. What would Jacques say? All the kindness he'd shown her would vanish and he would leave her. Just like Josef had.

Ida could never let Jacques know she was really Kadeshian, and it was Warden Hazor who'd saved her. Up until her time at the Fortress, she had no idea who Warden Hazor was. But as soon as she saw him standing outside the Fortress gates, Ida remembered him immediately. But why he had stayed so closed off to Ida all these years, she had no idea.

"You're right," she said quietly. "I was just thinking of someone else."

Jacques narrowed his gaze at her. He knew she was lying. But he didn't question her, and Ida was grateful for that.

"Let me take a look at one of these," she said quickly, keeping her gaze focused on the restricted texts.

She pulled the thick, leather-bound book in front of her. The front cover thunked on the table. Swirls and slants of the ancient Tentonian tongue stared back at Ida. She blinked, fascinated.

She'd never seen a language so beautifully transcribed. As soon as she whispered a prayer of thanks to Tunri, the script started to dance across the page, rotating around until Ida could understand them. Of course, to Jacques, the words were still foreign. Only a Translator had the pleasure of watching different dialects shift and shape to show their meaning.

Ida could feel Jacques' gaze burning into her as she translated the text. But she needed to fully concentrate to use her gift completely.

In the seventh year of King William's reign, the crops were fair and the weather bright.

Ida's eyes continued to scan through the pages, searching for something, anything about a prophecy. But as she got halfway through the book, there were only crop reports and weather patterns recorded throughout the entirety of King William's reign.

Sighing, she closed the book and rubbed her eyes. Even with only three restricted texts, this was going to take a while. Still, she reached for the next text. It wasn't until she was halfway through King Rupert's tax reports that she realized Jacques hadn't said anything in a while.

Hesitantly, she glanced over at him. A look of awe and fascination covered his face as he studied her.

Ida suddenly felt shy. "What?"

Jacques closed his parted lips. "Did you know your eyes turn the most beautiful shade of gold when you're translating? Like autumn leaves just about to fall."

Ida was at a loss for words. Where was this forwardness coming from? Though she didn't mind Jacques' advances in the greenhouse, she never thought he would be so open with his feelings.

"Thank you," she said, lowering her eyes. "And yes, I did know. Jil always wanted me to translate things so she could see my eyes turn gold." Ida smiled, thinking about her little sister.

"Jil is your sister?" Jacques asked.

Ida nodded. "Yes, she's wonderful. So carefree and strong and brave. She's seven years younger than me and I wish I could be more like her." Ida laughed, then her mood sobered. "I miss them. My family, I mean."

Jacques nodded. "Hopefully, when this is all over, you can see them again."

Tears started to pool in Ida's eyes, but she held them back. Now was not the time to cry.

Pushing King Rupert's text away, Ida grabbed the last text, hoping it was something more than monarchy reports.

Taking a breath, she prayed for Tunri's guidance and opened the book. The script in this book was different. Though it was still ancient Tentonian the handwriting wasn't the same as the other two. Usually, a king had a personal scribe that notated everything the king wanted to be recorded. Ida recognized the same penmanship throughout King William's and King Rupert's texts.

But as she thumbed through this text, all the entries were comprised of different strokes. Some were long and elegant, others sharp and rushed. It was almost as if a collection of people wrote in this book. But why? Was it some kind of journal?

Anticipation clawed up Ida's spine as she waited for the language to translate.

I've finally seen it. The great elk has blessed me with its presence. I praise Tunri for this sign of blessings in our futures. Only He can direct the spirit of this nation and with the sight of the great elk, good tidings are near.

"Jacques," Ida whispered. "Jacques, I found something."

Jacques blinked his bleary eyes. Ida hadn't realized how late it had gotten or how low the nub of their candle was. She still hadn't finished her homework, but that was the least of her worries now.

"What is it?" he said, leaning toward her. The sweet scent of honey and apples enveloped Ida in a warm hug, and she scooted closer.

"Right here," she pointed to the page. "It talks about the giant elk again and that it's a sign of blessing from Tunri. Something else about the spirit of Tenton, but I'm not sure what that means."

Jacques furrowed his brow. "Does it say anything about the prophecy?"

Ida pulled the book back. "I'm not sure, but this book is different than the others. The entries are by multiple people, not just one scribe. If I'm guessing right, I think this may be a journal written by past Seers."

Jacques' face brightened. "That's fantastic. There must be something in there."

Ida nodded in agreement, her pulse quickening at the excitement. "I should rest before class tomorrow, but I can't. I need to know what the Seers of old deemed important enough to record."

"Agreed," Jacques said. "I'll stay with you until you're finished."

Ida bit her lip, her heart warming at his never-ending kindness. "You don't have to. You must be tired from all that jousting earlier."

Jacques snorted. "I'll have you know Captain Blake made me stay up for almost three days straight to see how long I could last. And I almost made it too." He winked at her. "I'm not going anywhere. Let me know what you find out."

Ida smiled, her wall of self-doubt lowering as she crisscrossed her legs in her chair and laid the text in her lap. It was nice to not feel so alone.

From the corner of her eye, she watched Jacques stretch his long legs out before he settled into his chair. In a matter of moments, he was fast asleep. Ida chuckled to herself, hoping that he felt just as at ease around her as she did around him.

After saying another prayer of thanks to Tunri, Ida dove back into the words of the Seers. Her mind exploded with all the history and information she learned. Where the Seers originated, how they were the ones who founded Tenton and the four regions. Ida was baffled to learn Seers were actually the leaders of Tenton and delegated different jobs and positions of leadership to others with gifts as well.

Translators and Tinkers were just some of the gifts granted to Tentonians by Tunri. There were other gifts too, such as Marksmen and Shifters.

Ida couldn't drink in all the knowledge fast enough, trying to memorize it all in hopes of sharing it with Devora one day. Ida knew that feeling alone in their gifts was one thing her and Devora shared.

Then, a passage caught Ida's eye.

I am the one who brought the foretold prophecy. The prophecy that would spiral Tenton into war and disaster. It is with a heavy heart I bring this prophecy to the current king and queen of Tenton.

Ida gasped. Was this it? Was this the prophecy Jacques was talking about? The one Warden Hazor and Captain Blake wanted?

I have transcribed the prophecy in the Book of Ages. One day, a new Seer will read it and decipher its meaning to bring restoration to this broken land.

Ida blinked at the page, her eyes burning with having used her gift so much in one sitting. The entry she just read was the final entry in the book.

The morning sun peeked its head over the horizon, lighting the library in a yellow hue. Ida squinted at the light, feeling the lack of sleep. Now that the excitement of deciphering the text was over, exhaustion hit her like a boulder.

Closing the text, Ida rubbed her eyes and ran her fingers through her tight curls. Her mind ran over the last paragraph of the final entry again and again. The Book of Ages. Where was it?

As she tried to riddle out where a Seer's book of prophecies would be, a cacophony of voices gathered outside the library doors and Jacques woke up with a start.

He winced as he rubbed his neck. "What did I miss?"

"Three days without sleep, huh?" Ida commented with a tired smile.

Jacques gave her a sheepish grin before he saw the open book still on her lap. "What did you find out?"

"I know where the prophecy is—" was all Ida managed to say before a group of people burst into the library.

Ida slammed the book shut and hid it beneath her chair as the large group spilled toward their table.

Jacques shot up, his military persona taking over. Marching over to the nearest student, he asked, "What's going on?"

The young girl with straight red hair slicked into a bun, probably a First Year, looked up at him. "Haven't you heard? Hestia Sandje has been chosen for Assembly. Duke Sandje is here, at Vlacklear. He's demanding to see his daughters."

Fear struck Ida's core as she remembered Sergio's threat. Reese's and Hestia's father knew they were here. And it was all Ida's fault.

Chapter Sixteen

"Excuse me, please let me through!" Ida cried, pushing her way through the crowd in front of Reese's and Hestia's room.

In her state of panic, Ida fled the library without even telling Jacques about the Book of Ages.

It was her fault Duke Sandje knew his daughters were at Vlacklear. If she hadn't stood up to Sergio, they would still be here in secret.

Growing frustrated, Ida elbowed her way through the crowd toward the girl's dormitories.

"Hestia!" Ida pounded on the door. "Reese! It's Ida!"

The door opened a crack and an arm snaked out and grabbed Ida's wrist. Before Ida could react, she was yanked into Reese's and Hestia's room. The door shut before the clamoring crowd could get in.

Taking a breath, Ida faced her friends. Their room was far more lavish than Ida's at the end of the hall. Thick, velvet curtains draped from the windows, hitting the floor on either side. Intricately carved headboards stood behind each of their beds. Shining wooden desks sat between the beds, each with a plush velvet chair to sit upon. But all the luxury in the world couldn't stop the sadness and fear covering her friends' faces.

Hestia curled into a ball on her bed, her face staring into nothing. Her long shining hair sprawled out around her like a fan. Reese lowered herself in the fine chair, her back as rigid as steel as she flicked her abacus back and forth. Her hair was swept into the high, tight bun. And though her face was an impassive mask, Ida knew Reese was upset, as well.

Ida waited for one of them to speak. But the minutes ticked by, and no one said a word, allowing the clacking of the metal abacus beads to fill the silence. Biting her lip, Ida fiddled with her sleeve.

When she couldn't take the tension anymore, Ida confessed, "It's my fault your father knows you're here. Sergio threatened he'd reveal your location if I didn't help him with his Linguistics work. I didn't want either of you to be forced into marriage, so I agreed. But after I refused his offer yesterday..." Ida trailed off and burst into sobs before she could continue.

Covering her hands with her face, Ida couldn't face her friends. All she had to do was keep quiet and do what Sergio said. And she couldn't even do that.

Someone like you, Josef's mother's voice and look of disgust resurfaced in her memories.

Someone like you, the headmistress' arrogant glare came next.

Someone like me, her own voice said. *Has put her friends in harm's way.*

"Oh Ida," Hestia said, slowly sitting up from her bed. "We knew what Sergio was doing."

Ida's tears stopped. "What?"

Reese shook her head. "Sergio is the biggest gossip in Tenton. There was a ninety-five point nine percent chance he was going to blab about us being here. Plus, Father probably would've found out eventually anyway. Noble children are all gossips and will use anything to squash another noble. We thought you would come and talk to us about it."

Ida sniffed. "I-I didn't think I should. You guys were—are—so popular now. I didn't think you'd want to help someone—" she stopped before she added, "like me."

Reese tsked, crossing her arms over her chest. "You've got to stop degrading yourself, Ida. What's wrong with someone like you?"

Ida chewed her bottom lip. "I don't know."

Hestia stood and placed her hands on Ida's shoulders. "There is nothing wrong with someone like you, Ida. This place would be a lot better if there were more people like you in it."

Ida was at a loss for words. How could Hestia and Reese, two beautiful, wealthy women, care for her so much? Her, a poor girl from Lower Grenly who wasn't even Tentonian?

Tears pooled in Ida's eyes again and before she knew it, she was crying. Hestia wrapped her in a tight warm hug.

"We meant it when we said we're in this together," Hestia said. "All of us are still lieutenants in His Majesty's Army, remember?"

Ida nodded, remembering her true purpose here and how she needed to decipher the prophecy. But first she needed to find the Book of Ages.

Hestia released Ida from the hug and she decided it was time to be truthful. Maybe the twins could help her find the book. "Warden Hazor sent me here for a specific reason." Taking a breath, she continued, "Like Devora and Nadia, I have a gift too. I can translate any language, written or spoken."

Hestia gasped and smiled wide as Reese's face lit with surprise.

"Though I'm not being hunted like Devora, anyone with a gift is looked down upon, so I try to keep it quiet."

Hestia clapped her hands. "This is so exciting!" Her features then shifted, and a pout formed on her lips. "How come we're the only ones without a gift?"

Reese shook her head. "We do have a gift, Hestia. It's called knowing rich people because of Father's supposed wealth." She then turned to Ida. "What do you need to translate? I'm assuming it's something valuable or Warden Hazor wouldn't have sent us all here undercover."

Ida dove into the explanation Jacques gave her about the Seer's prophecy and the king and queen. She told them about the book Jacques had gotten from Captain Blake and how *he* had retrieved it from the Restricted Section.

"Ida," Hestia said with a mischievous grin. "Sneaking around the library with Sir Jacques."

Heat flared in Ida's cheeks. "It was nothing like that." But the intimate moment they shared in the greenhouse burned into her mind. Shaking her head, Ida proceeded to explain about the Book of Ages.

"The Book of Ages," Reese mused standing from her chair. She paced around the room, tapping her abacus on her thigh as she murmured to herself.

But before Reese could continue, a loud knock pounded on the door.

Hestia's face turned whiter than the snowflakes starting to fall outside. "The Assembly. It's time."

Reese strode over to her sister and squeezed her in a tight hug. "I'll think of something."

Hestia swallowed and nodded. "You always do."

Ida watched the twins with surprise and sympathy. Never had she seen Reese show an ounce of affection for her sister. But Ida always hoped that the twins were closer than they made it seem with all their squabbling. Ida was thankful she was right.

But as two knights from the Fortress burst into Hestia's and Reese's room, a new level of fear consumed Ida's heart. Without emotion or fanfare, one knight locked a pair of manacles around Hestia's wrists while the other grabbed her arm and escorted her toward the door.

"Wait," Ida whispered as she recognized the two knights. They helped train the other soldiers in the Theater of the Fortress.

Though Ida didn't know their names, she remembered their faces. "Wait, where are you taking her?"

The knights barely glanced at Ida as they yanked Hestia.

"Hestia!" Ida said, reaching forward.

"I'll be okay, Ida," Hestia said, her same smile plastered on her face, but her eyes shone with fear.

Before Ida could say another word, the knights pulled Hestia into the sea of gawking students until she was gone.

Ida's heart thumped in her chest as she pinned her gaze on Reese who stood there and did nothing. "What's happening? Why aren't you doing anything?"

Reese's lower lip trembled before she lowered her head, not daring to look at Ida's gaze. "Because I can't," she said, barely above a whisper. "I have no power to do anything for Hestia. It's too late."

Ida hurried to Reese and took her hands. "Why is it too late? What's happened, Reese?"

"She's being taken to stand trial at Assembly," a masculine voice said from the doorway.

Ida's stomach flip-flopped as she spun around to find Jacques leaning against the doorway, a solemn look on his face.

Ida's lips parted, but nothing came out.

Jacques straightened his stance. "I got worried when you fled the library, so I followed you. Naturally, I found out the rest." He motioned to the now-thinning crowd of students.

"Why is Hestia being chained like a prisoner to go to Assembly? What has she done?" Ida asked, fury rising in her chest as tears stung her eyes. Nothing made sense.

"The headmistress is not the proverbial woman she claims to be," Jacques started. "At random times, she takes the students who have the lowest ranks in their classes and puts them on trial. The students' families are brought in as well to witness the disgrace their children have placed upon their family."

"Jacques!" Ida cried, unable to believe he'd say anything so cruel about Hestia. "Hestia is not a disgrace."

Jacques shook his head and Ida noticed he hadn't stepped a toe into Reese's and Hestia's room. "The rules are different here, Ida. Especially for those of noble birth. All we can do for Hestia now is pray the headmistress will make a kind ruling."

Ida's throat tightened as she sat between Jacques and Victoria at the track where the jousting tournament had occurred. The stands were packed with students and Ida felt sick remembering the Regulus Protecti tournament. She'd prayed to Tunri endlessly that Devora would make it through each round. The same queasy feeling came over her now as she took in the black throne-like chair seated on a platform in the middle of the sandy floor below.

Ida placed one hand on her stomach, doing her best to not get sick.

Tunri, I don't know what's happening, but keep Hestia safe.

On either side of the black throne sat a booth where people of all different skin tones sat.

"Those are the families of the accused," Jacques whispered in her ear.

Ida wished she wasn't about to throw up, then she could enjoy their closeness more.

"Are you okay, Ida?" Victoria asked, her eyes laced with concern. "I was an absolute wreck the first time Patrick was put on trial during Assembly."

Ida turned toward Victoria, remembering what she said before. "How bad was Patrick's punishment?"

Victoria blew out a breath and drummed her fingers on her knee. "Even though Patrick's grades were horrendous, he luckily comes from a long line of nobility, so that helped him out in the end. He only got locked in the Tower for three days."

"What?" Ida gasped, her mind still comprehending the words Victoria said so nonchalantly. Students were given better treatment because of their social status? "What do you mean 'locked in the Tower?'"

Victoria slid her eyes over Ida's head to Jacques who was speaking to the student beside him. She then ducked her head and lowered her voice.

"The headmistress doesn't want anyone to know what happens there except the prefects." Her eyes darted toward Jacques again. "They try to scare students by threatening them with being expelled, but Patrick could care less about that, so he told me everything." Tears crested Victoria's eyes as she took Ida's hand. "Oh Ida, it's so awful. They chained him to a wall, and he wasn't allowed to eat or see the sunshine for those three days."

Ida placed her hand over her mouth. She really was going to be sick. How long had this been happening at Vlacklear? How could the headmistress allow this? How could King Atol and Queen Leza allow this?

"Ida." Jacques' warm hand lay gently on her shoulder. "Are you okay?"

But before Ida could answer, a large gavel pounded on the arm of the black throne.

Ida willed her stomach to calm, but still felt nauseous. She grabbed Jacques' and Victoria's hands and held them close. Fear consumed every fiber of her being, and she needed Jacques and Victoria to keep her grounded.

Forcing herself to look up, Ida's eyes locked on to the headmistress. Gone was the forced smile she pasted on her face every time Ida saw her. Instead, her lips curved in disgust and Ida found the look a lot more fitting for the woman.

"Bring in the accused," the headmistress boomed.

The room fell silent as a line of students shuffled onto the sandy track. Ida recognized a few faces from her classes, but most were students she didn't know. But then she saw a tall lanky boy with brown curly hair. When Patrick noticed Ida, he waved.

"Patrick?" Ida squeaked.

Victoria sighed and patted Ida's hand. "Yes. Even though Patrick is from a noble family, he hates the favoritism and special treatment the kingdom gives them over the lay people of Tenton. He makes sure to do badly enough that he is chosen for Assembly whenever it occurs. His parents stopped coming after the first trial. It's his personal way of fighting the system."

Ida couldn't help but notice a proud undertone in Victoria's words. "But you said what they did to him in the Tower was horrible," Ida said.

Victoria nodded. "It was. But now that he plans to do this, he somehow prepares beforehand."

"What?" Ida asked, when Jacques squeezed her hand. She hated that her stomach twisted in delight, especially during such a horrible event.

"There she is," he said, nodding at the line of students.

Ida held her breath as she took in the face at the very end of the long line. There with her head held high, like Ida had seen so many times at the Fortress, was Hestia.

Hope blossomed in Ida's chest. Though Hestia always joked and loved to flirt, her inner strength was just as strong and fierce as Devora's. Ida envied them and prayed she could be just as strong one day.

The headmistress assigned punishments swiftly as she worked down the long line of students. Some did poorly on only a few assignments, so they were sentenced to no dinner for a week. Others made low marks on larger assignments and had breakfast and dinner taken away for various days.

Ida felt her stomach churn again. Living in Lower Grenly made her sensitive to others who didn't have enough to eat. Just like First Lady Medee, Ama had always done her best to share what little they had with those who had even less.

To hear the headmistress so easily take away these students' meals ignited something within Ida that she didn't realize was there.

Ida watched with fury as the parents of each of the students readily agreed with the punishments. Some even asked for the headmistress to punish them more, so that they would learn from their mistakes and make higher marks.

Disgust wasn't a strong enough word for what Ida felt for this cesspool named Vlacklear Academy.

There were only four students left, two of whom were Patrick and Hestia. The headmistress dealt with the two other students swiftly, giving them both two days in the Tower without food or drink.

Ida was flabbergasted at how readily the students took their punishment and went on their way like they were going to a picnic. This was never how things were handled at the Fortress. Everyone there fought and clawed and beat each other up until a fair settlement was found. Here, everyone submitted and obeyed without question.

An uneasiness filled Ida's stomach as a dark feeling fell over her. Now that she thought about it, there was something odd about the way students readily agreed to everything at Vlacklear.

The only student she really knew that made trouble was Sergio. Everyone else complied with the rules.

"Why don't they do anything?" Ida whispered to Jacques.

The knight leaned closer, giving Ida a whiff of his alluring scent of honey. "Who?"

"The students. They just accept the punishment. At the Fortress, no one accepted anything without a fight."

A smile ticked at the corner of Jacques' lips. "The Fortress' regulations may seem twisted at times, but it's rather black and white compared to this place. As for accepting the punishment—" The knight paused, a crease forming between his brows. "I can't say I can blame them. Many students here are meant to carry on their families' names. It puts a lot of pressure on them to always succeed. The headmistress knows this and purposefully shames them, knowing they won't be at the bottom of their class again."

"That's why she dislikes Patrick so much," Victoria piped in.

Ida's gaze turned back to Patrick and Hestia, who both stood tall and strong, defiantly staring back at the headmistress.

"Mister Worthington, here you are again," the headmistress said, tapping her gavel on the arm of her black throne.

"Here I am again," Patrick repeated with a grin.

"I feel I've been too soft on you." An evil grin came to the headmistress' face and Ida squeezed Jacques' hand. "Instead of your usual three days in the Tower. We're going to make it five."

Victoria gasped, "No!"

"I'll take any punishment," Patrick said loudly, facing the crowd. "This is wrong, and you all know it. Don't succumb to the pressure of your titles. Use them for good!"

Patrick started to say more but was hurriedly dragged off by more knights from the Fortress.

It was then Ida realized that Warden Hazor must know what's happening in Vlacklear to have allowed his knights here. But why didn't he do anything about this?

Warden Hazor did allow your friend to almost be killed in a tournament to the death, Ida reminded herself.

Shaking her head, Ida felt Victoria's grip tighten around her own.

"We'll figure something out," Ida whispered. "We'll help him. Somehow."

Victoria nodded, but Ida knew her friend was about to shatter into a million pieces.

"Miss Sandje, one of the eastern region's famed twins. " The headmistress sighed in disappointment and Ida couldn't help but notice the small flinch in Hestia's posture.

"Who is here to claim Miss Sandje?"

Reese immediately stood. Next to her sat a man with midnight black hair pulled back in a low ponytail. A dark blue tunic and pants covered his tall, slim frame. He, too, rose, but a lot more slowly than Reese.

"Ah, Miss Sandje and the acclaimed Duke Sandje of Sandje Textiles." The headmistress grinned again. "How kind of you to bless us with your presence."

Duke Sandje gave a stiff nod but let no emotion pass on his face.

"Do you have a preferred punishment for your child who sullied your prosperous family name?"

Ida jerked back at the comment. There was something about the headmistress' statement that made Ida think of Sergio. It was then Ida realized she hadn't seen Sergio since the jousting tournament.

"Punish my child as you see fit," Duke Sandje said calmly before sitting back down.

Ida prayed for Reese to say something. To do *something*. But Hestia's twin only cast a worried look at her sister and sat back down.

Hestia gave her sister a nod in understanding then faced the headmistress once more.

"As the students and staff of Vlacklear Academy as my witness, I sentence Hestia Sandje for seven days in the Tower without food or drink."

Chapter Seventeen

Ida's breath left her lungs as she heard Hestia's punishment, unable to believe it to be true. Before she could stop herself, she leaned forward and tried to throw up. Nothing came from her stomach, but she dry heaved all the same.

Tears burned her eyes as her stomach twisted and lurched, not releasing anything to dull her pain. A soft hand laid on her back, rubbing soothing circles.

Seven days without food or water? Hestia would die.

No.

Ida took deep breaths until her stomach settled down.

No, Hestia was not going to die. Ida didn't care that she was poor or Kadeshian. She was going to save her friend.

Lifting her head, Ida saw that the track had cleared out save for her and a few other students.

"They took Hestia to the Tower," Jacques said softly, still rubbing her back. "We'll think of something. We're not going to let them keep her in there for that long. I promise you, Ida."

Ida nodded. She would personally break Hestia out of the Tower if she had to.

"Where's Victoria?" she asked, realizing the space beside her was empty.

"Probably trying to do the same thing as us: think of a way to lessen the punishment for a friend."

"They're more than friends, they just won't admit it," Ida sighed, closing her eyes.

"How do you know?" Jacques asked.

"The small looks they give each other when they think the other isn't watching. The way they make time to be near each other, even if it's inconvenient."

Ida opened her eyes and shook her head. "I wish they would see what was right in front of them."

She turned to find Jacques studying her with a look she'd never seen before.

"Maybe they just need a little more time to figure everything out," he replied quietly.

Ida bit her lip, remembering the moment they shared in the greenhouse. Jacques' eyes toward her lips. He, too, seemed to remember how they were interrupted before.

He moved toward her. "Ida, I—," he started before the sound of rushed steps came from behind.

Ida groaned inwardly, but Jacques made a point to let out his own frustration.

"Oh good!" Reese cried, coming up to them. "You're both still here. Follow me."

Before Ida or Jacques could respond, Reese raced back up the steps and out of the track.

With a sigh, Jacques stood and offered Ida his hand. "Shall we?"

Ida took his hand, loving the callouses on his creamy skin. They hurried up the steps to where Reese stood waiting for them. Her fingers madly slung her abacus beads back and forth as she whispered different probabilities under her breath.

"Reese, are you okay? We need to help Hestia," Ida said, wrapping her friend in a hug.

Reese typically didn't like hugs, but Ida didn't care anymore. To her surprise, Reese hugged her back tightly.

"Yes, I'm okay and I have a plan that will help us get Hestia out and help you get the Book of Ages."

"The Book of Ages?" Jacques asked. "What's that?"

Ida blinked. With everything that had just happened, she'd completely forgotten about the prophecy and the Book of Ages. And how she hadn't told Jacques about it before she fled the library.

"It's a book that apparently holds all the prophecies past Seers have had, including the one we're looking for."

Jacques' eyes grew wide as Ida turned to Reese. "How can we save Hestia and find the book?"

Straightening her shoulders, Reese said, "I'm sixty-eight point one percent sure it'll work and that's good enough for me." She spun around and headed down the hall.

Ida glanced at Jacques who shrugged before they both hurried after her.

"Where are you going?" Ida asked once they caught up to Reese's quick strides.

"I've been such a fool," Reese muttered, shaking her head. "Warden Hazor sent us here to distract everyone from you, but I can do so much more. I felt more useful when I was cleaning the Theater than I have here." Reese glanced over at Ida with a soft smile. "If Hestia needs to be saved and you need to find the Book of Ages, I'm going to do it."

Ida's heart swelled at the new fire in Reese's eyes. She'd grown so much from the rude girl Ida first met in the Fortress.

"So, where are we going to accomplish all this?" Jacques asked.

Reese lifted her chin. "To see Father."

Ida and Jacques walked quietly but quickly behind Reese as she charged ahead. Students passed by them occasionally, their gazes landing on Reese but looking away. Ida couldn't believe what Jacques had said was true. While a few days ago, people were worshipping the ground Hestia and Reese walked on, now that Hestia had been tried at Assembly, Reese had become a pariah.

As if reading her thoughts, Jacques leaned over and said, "Sometimes it's better not to be seen."

It was then Ida realized that her fingers were laced in his. Ida couldn't recall when this had happened, but she was so glad for it.

Reese sped through the school like there was a fire and Ida did her best to keep up the pace without breaking into a full-out sprint. Thankfully, there were no more students clogging the hallways. As Ida took in the thick-framed portraits on the wall, she realized this was an area of Vlacklear she hadn't been to before.

"Where is your father?" she asked Reese.

"The headmistress' office," Reese said over her shoulder. "I know Father won't leave until I come to see him. After the trial, he tried to barge into the girl's dormitories, but the headmistress stopped him before he could."

Ida's brows lifted as she studied Reese's tall, strong gait. If she'd acted like this at the Fortress, Captain Blake would've been ecstatic.

Yet, while Ida admired Reese's determination, she was worried about what they were getting into. From what Ida knew, Reese and Hestia did not have a positive relationship with their father. Ida didn't want Reese to do something that would ultimately harm her, even if it helped Hestia and resulted in finding the Book of Ages.

They continued past more portraits of aged men and women until they came to a set of double oak doors at the end of the hall. Shining gold handles gleamed back at them, waiting to be opened.

"Should we knock—" Jacques started before Reese ripped open the door. The knight shrugged. "Okay, then."

Ida couldn't believe the Reese before her was the same cool, calculating Reese she'd met and befriended at the Fortress. It was like she was an entirely new person.

With head held high, and abacus in hand, Reese stared down the man sitting behind the headmistress' desk.

Ida glanced around the office, taking in its minimalist decorations. The only picture on the wall was a large map of Tenton and Kadesh. A solitary window allowed the light to shine upon the thick, dark rug covering the floor. As Ida studied the room further, she realized the headmistress was nowhere to be found.

Strange. Why wouldn't the headmistress be in her office while we're here?

"I knew you would see things my way, Sachiko," the man with midnight-black hair said, breaking Ida's focus from her thoughts.

He didn't even bother to stand. Instead, he took another sip of his tea. If arrogance was a scent, Ida would be able to smell it oozing from this man.

This man is Hestia and Reese's father?

"Don't call me that name. I am not your good luck charm any longer," Reese snarled.

"It is such a lovely name," the man replied smoothly. "One your mother picked for you, Sachiko."

Reese's fingers tightened around the abacus, but she kept her composure. "I will here and henceforth be called Reese."

At that comment, the man's cool demeanor finally broke. Jolting up from his chair, he slammed his cup of tea down and growled. "I will not call my daughter by any other name than the one I chose for her."

"I thought you said mother named me," Reese countered, leveling her gaze at her father.

Closing his eyes, Duke Sandje pinched the bridge of his nose. "You've been hanging out with Michiko too long. What a waste she's turned out to be."

"She is not Michiko," Reese declared. "She is Hestia, and I am Reese. Those are the names *we* chose for ourselves when *you* sold us to be soldiers for the king's army."

Ida suddenly felt like she was eavesdropping on a very personal family conversation and should leave. She glanced at Jacques who had the same unease on his face as well. But as she started to signal to him that they should leave, the conversation continued, and Ida was curious.

"If you had married who I chose, I wouldn't have had to sell you to the army," Duke Sandje rebutted. "All the other noble daughters just do as they're told by the betrothal laws of Tenton. They don't fiddle with silly toys and numbers"—he gestured to Reese's firm grip on her abacus— "Or have their head so high in the clouds that they have no idea what's really going on."

Ida stifled her gasp at the cruelty of Hestia's and Reese's father. Though Ida's parents had adopted her knowing she was born in the enemy nation, they'd never spoken so harshly to her. Ida backed up into Jacques, fearful for Reese and her fate.

Jacques' hands held her shoulders, comforting her spiraling thoughts.

But as Ida took in Reese's stoic face, her heart broke. Reese was unfazed by Duke Sandje's insults because she'd heard them so many times. Ida wondered if Hestia would be numb to them, as well.

The memories of the cruel words said to her still pained her heart. But was it better to feel nothing at all? That couldn't be right either.

"Of course, Father," Reese said with a layer of condescension. "And since the only reason you have come to find us at Vlacklear is to gain something from your pitiful daughters, let's strike a deal."

Duke Sandje instantly righted himself. He smoothed back a few strands of dark hair that had fallen across his forehead in his aggravated state.

"You were always the smarter one," he said, and Ida saw her friend wince. "What is it you desire?"

"Name your terms first," she commanded, keeping her gaze firm upon her father.

"Ah, very good," the duke cooed, a wicked smile stretching over thin lips. "I've taught you well." He placed his hands palm up before him. "I only seek to see at least one of my daughters married by the betrothal laws of Tenton to a family of noble status within the next year."

"I want that in writing," Reese said before he could continue. She gestured to the wax and candle on the headmistress' desk. "With your signature and seal."

Duke Sandje clenched his jaw but kept an easy smile. "Of course, daughter. Now what is it you desire?"

"Now," Reese said, tapping on the desk. A confused look twisted her father's features. "I want it in writing, now."

"The Fortress has changed you, *Reese*," the duke replied mockingly as he grabbed a piece of parchment and quill and wrote his terms in quick hard strokes. "If you had always been like this, I would've taken you more as a business partner than collateral. That's what Cusha Medee did with his daughter."

For the first time since they entered the office, Ida saw Reese's strength waver at the mention of Devora. It suddenly dawned on Ida why Reese initially hated Devora when they met at the Fortress. How many times had Duke Sandje shoved it in Reese's face that Devora was a better, smarter daughter? Reese had decided to loathe Devora before she even knew her.

"Yes," the duke continued, not noticing Reese's reaction. Or he did notice and wanted to jab the barb in further. "Cusha was wise. His daughter was the entire package: smart, beautiful, and knew she was meant to rule over others." Grabbing a stick of red wax, Duke Sandje placed it over a flickering candle, allowing the wax to drip on the bottom of the parchment. "But *was* Cusha wise? His daughter is now a traitor to the kingdom. Mine are not." The duke shrugged before stamping his signet ring on the page. He waited a moment then handed it to Reese. "Done. Your terms."

Reese snatched the parchment from his hands and read it over. Once finished, she glanced up and said, "Since you want to see your daughters married, that won't happen if one of them dies in the Tower from lack of nourishment. I need access to the Tower."

Duke Sandje blanched for a moment, then regained himself. "Is this only to free Michiko?"

Ida held her breath, feeling Jacques' fingers squeeze her shoulders. Did the duke know something about the Book of Ages? Why else would he ask a question like that? Or were there other hidden things in the Tower that only high nobility knew about?

"Explanation is not part of the terms," Reese replied swiftly. "One of us marries within the year, you give me what I want, which is to go to the headmistress and say you've changed your mind and want Hestia to have another chance. She will agree and you will say you've already had your people set her free." The duke nodded steadily to the terms until Reese added. "And I want that—" she pointed to the ring on his finger.

Duke Sandje twisted the signet ring, showing uncertainty, but after a few moments, he slipped it off and placed it in Reese's palm. Before Reese could pull away, the duke gripped her wrist.

"Be careful of what you're getting into, Sachiko. Grown men often do not return from the Tower unscathed."

Reese wrenched her wrist out of his hands. "And you sent your daughter there without batting an eye. You should be ashamed of yourself. Do not act as if you care for my fate." Lifting her chin, she turned. "Sir Jacques, Ida, come on."

"The Amatas are still interested in your hand," he called behind her, but Reese kept walking. "And I've just received word that Duke Delequa's middle son is finally ready to marry. I'm meeting Lord Delequa soon to discuss the matter." The Duke smirked at Ida and Jacques, sending chills down Ida's spine.

Jacques gripped Ida's hand harshly as he tugged her toward the door, and she winced. He seemed to be just as unnerved by Duke Sandje as she was.

"Remember how I spoke of betrothing Hestia to the heir of Delequa when you were children?" Duke Sandje continued, focusing back on Reese. "Now's the time. You can be freed from your betrothal to Sergio Amata. Just have your sister agree to marry the young Delequa heir, and I will leave you alone. Forever."

Reese's steps faltered a moment, but she kept her head high and her mouth closed. She merely waved the parchment with the duke's signature and seal on it and fled.

Once they left the headmistress' office, Reese let out a huge sigh of relief, her shoulders relaxing. She turned to Ida and Jacques with a grin. "That man infuriates me, but I'm glad I picked up on some of Hestia's acting skills when she made me help her rehearse in grade school."

Ida stopped in the middle of the hall, utterly baffled, and confused. Everything in there was just an act? But the emotions felt so real, so raw.

"So that was all a lie?" Ida managed to get out. "You don't really mean those things you said about your father?"

Reese stopped and spun around. "No, it was all the truth. However, Father always wants to believe that he's getting the better end of the bargain. By acting arrogant and pompous like him, he believes I *want* his praise." Reese sighed. "I told you; we know what these people are like. It's all smiles and compliments until you turn your back and they're the first ones to strike you with a knife."

"Unfortunately, that's true," Jacques commented.

"The Fortress was refreshing," Reese continued, hurrying down the hall once again. "The inmates who hated you told you to your face and that was that. No backhanded compliments, no one starting rumors behind your back, just black and white." She sighed again, then plucked out the ring. "However, we got what we needed."

"So how does your father's ring help us save Hestia?" Ida asked, stepping alongside Reese. Jacques had taken to walking behind them, and Ida was starting to wonder if he was feeling all right. "And what does this all have to do with the Book of Ages?"

"The ring will help us get into the Tower without having to wait for the headmistress." Reese replied as she took a right at the next hall. "I don't know much about her, but I don't want anyone else casting suspicion on us."

Ida remembered what Duke Sandje said. *Grown men often do not come out of the Tower unscathed.* She shuddered, thinking of Victoria's words too.

"And you think the Book of Ages is there?" Jacques asked from behind. Ida glanced at him, noticing he seemed paler than earlier. Maybe the encounter with Duke Sandje rattled him as well.

"Are you okay, Jacques?" Ida asked, she placed a hand on his forearm.

He hesitantly placed his hand over hers then shook his head. "I think I need to lie down. Probably too many cinnamon rolls." He gave Ida a wink, but she knew there was something else beneath his smile that bothered him.

Reese nodded. "Meet us back here tomorrow night after dinner. I hate for Hestia to stay in the Tower at least one day, but we have to make it believable that Father needed to mull over his decision to give her another chance. When there's only one guard, we'll go in and free Hestia. My father should be good on his word to talk to the headmistress, especially since I have this—" she held up the parchment. "However, I don't trust him completely, so we need to work quickly. Once we're in the Tower, you two can go and search for the Book of Ages. I'm only fifty-four point four percent sure that it's there, but where else would you put a book you don't want to be found?"

Jacques nodded mechanically and was gone before Ida could even blink.

Sighing, Ida turned back to Reese. "I'm not sure about this," she said suddenly feeling wary about this entire thing.

Ida's head spun from lack of sleep and all the emotional events she witnessed today. Maybe she just needed to lie down. She then remembered the promise Reese made to her father and that the Amata family, Sergio's family, still wanted Sergio to marry Reese. But Reese promised only one of them had to get married. So which twin would it be? There was another family Duke Sandje had mentioned, but Ida didn't recognize the name.

"What about Sergio?" Ida asked, unfortunately unable to forget the playboy who blabbed about Hestia's and Reese's whereabouts. "What are you going to do about that?"

"I thought about that." Reese stopped suddenly. Her eyes darted in the direction Jacques had left before she focused on Ida. "That's why I had my father write his declaration down. He said only one of us had to get married and 'by the betrothal laws of Tenton.' I'm sure I can find a loophole in there somewhere."

"You mean you don't already have one?" Ida shrieked, placing her hands on her cheeks. How could she have allowed Reese to risk so much?

"I told you I was only sixty-seven point eight percent sure," Reese confessed with a shrug.

Ida rubbed her temples, trying to keep up with the conversation. The name of the other family Duke Sandje mentioned suddenly returned to her thoughts. "I know Amata is Sergio, but who is Delequa?"

Reese stiffened, twisting her father's signet ring in her fingers before she glanced in the direction Jacques had gone again. "You don't know?"

"I don't know what?" Ida asked. Her eyes felt so heavy. All she wanted to do was sleep.

Reese took a breath. "The Delequa Family is the second richest family in the eastern region," Reese explained, slowly, as if waiting—wanting—someone to stop her. "The oldest male of the Delequa house deserted His Majesty's Army and fled to Kadesh, leaving the second oldest, the middle son, heir to the entire Delequa fortune."

"Okay," Ida drawled out, closing her eyes. "And who is that?"

"Ida," Reese said quietly. "The heir to the Delequa fortune is Sir Jacques."

Chapter Eighteen

The ride from Totem back to the Fortress felt longer than it really was. As Matthias led his horse through the city of Juro, various scents constantly reminded him of Devora. A waft of chocolate resurrected memories of shared cocoa cake in the training room. The scent of sand and leather reminded him of the training uniform he gave Devora and how great she looked in it. And then the roses. Every time Matthias smelled a rose, he thought his heart would burst from agony.

Another week and a half passed and still there was no scent or sign of Devora. The wolf inside Matthias clawed with impatience, wanting to burst forth again. Without the imperial opal ring subduing the curse, the beast was getting more difficult to control. Matthias didn't know how or why, but somehow, his curse was getting stronger.

Gazing upon the familiar squared stones of the Fortress, Matthias dismounted Ater, his midnight-colored steed. He enjoyed returning to his duties here. At least it would distract his mind from Devora. Hopefully.

Guiding his horse to its stable on the east side of the Fortress, Matthias was surprised to see Warden Hazor waiting there for him.

"How long was it this time?" he gruffed, crossing his thick arms over his chest.

Matthias released a sigh. He was planning on sneaking back into the Fortress before the warden could find him. Warden Hazor, Jacques, and now One Shot were the only ones who knew of his curse. While Warden Hazor allowed Matthias to spend his time as a wolf with his hunting wolves, the warden still kept Matthias accountable for his wolfish actions.

"Three weeks," he replied, keeping his focus on unsaddling Ater. "Give or take a day or two." He waited for the harsh reprimand. Even if Matthias hadn't gutted any innocents, Warden Hazor still chastised him for his lack of control over the wolf.

Instead, Warden Hazor took a heavy breath. "Did you find her?"

Matthias shifted his gaze to the warden, detecting an unusual amount of concern in the harsh man's voice. "Not yet."

"You had better find her soon, Blake," he huffed. Unfolding his arms, he added, "When you're finished here, come to my office. Things are unraveling quicker than we anticipated."

"How could this have happened?" Matthias exclaimed, crumpling the coded message in his hand. "And right under our noses too."

Warden Hazor leaned back in his wooden chair and stroked his white mustache. "I can only think whoever did this knew the reclaiming of Yekel would be a big enough distraction that no one would notice the king's murder."

"But shouldn't people know by now?" Matthias questioned. His mind spun like a whirlwind. "Wouldn't his personal guard or the queen report this? We shouldn't have had to find out King Atol was murdered from one of our spies in the palace."

"I agree with you, Blake," Warden Hazor commented, tenting his fingers over his lips. He paused for a moment then continued, "I have several plans in motion and am just waiting to see which one comes to fruition."

"You mean like sending Nadia to Yekel?"

The warden nodded.

"Who else do you have working undercover?" Matthias asked, suddenly curious about how deep into espionage the warden had gone.

Warden Hazor only smiled slyly. "All will be known in due time, Blake."

Matthias took a deep breath, trying to control his frustration. It wasn't really directed at Warden Hazor. It was mostly at everything else. This corrupt kingdom, Devora's disappearance, his curse. All of it aggravated him. But nothing set him off more than what was said next.

"The queen has requested your presence." Warden Hazor kept his gaze void of emotion as he stood from his desk.

Matthias scrubbed his face with his hand, his composure unraveling quickly. He didn't want to play assassin for the monarchy any longer. Hadn't he paid his dues? When would he finally be free from this burden?

Matthias suddenly felt a strong hand grip his shoulder. Surprised, he glanced over to find Warden Hazor standing beside him.

"Just a little longer, Blake." The warden gave him a hardy thump on the back. "You're strong and have already saved countless lives with that strength. The end is nigh, I can feel it."

"Yes, sir," Matthias replied, baffled at the warden's encouragement.

As if suddenly realizing his out of character compliment, Warden Hazor returned to his stern persona once more.

"Don't keep the queen waiting, Blake. And make sure you report back to me whatever happens. Understood?"

"Understood, sir."

While the trip from Ballear seemed to take forever, it felt like Matthias was waiting at the entrance of Maldove Palace in mere minutes. Though the palace was a short ride from the Fortress, it wasn't *that* short.

A stoic palace guard stood at the entrance. There were usually two, but sometimes, when things were peaceful, the palace only stationed one outside the gates. And the palace was probably trying to keep the death of the king under wraps.

As he strode up the palace steps, Matthias resisted the urge to reprimand the guard about his sloppy posture. But when he stepped closer, he almost tripped over his own feet.

"Conan?" he questioned in disbelief.

"Quiet, Blake!" Sir Conan scolded. "Or do you want the whole palace to know who I am?"

Blake lowered his voice. "What are you doing here?"

Warden Hazor said he had multiple plans in play. This must be one of them.

"What does it look like I'm doing?" Sir Conan sneered under his breath. "I'm guarding the entrance of the palace."

Matthias ground his teeth, trying not to slug Conan in the jaw like he had the last time he was disrespectful. "Why are you not at the Fortress?"

"You're not the only one who does things of importance for the warden, Blake." Sir Conan sniffed and puffed out his chest.

"You mean, this is your punishment for weaseling out of the Battle of Edo?" Matthias goaded, unable to help himself.

He expected Sir Conan to snarl back, but instead the knight's face fell. "I was a coward. But the warden has given me an opportunity to redeem myself."

Matthias studied the knight, careful not to let his surprise show. "Very good, Conan. Is there anything I should know before I meet with the queen?"

Sir Conan adjusted the mech on his belt. "You know about what happened?"

Assuming Sir Conan meant the death of the king, Matthias nodded.

"Well," the knight's dark eyes darted around before he continued. "I've seen plenty of ladies in my time who have lost their lovers and they're always bawling their eyes out for weeks."

Matthias tempered his patience, hoping this anecdote was going somewhere useful.

"But the queen hasn't looked one bit upset. She's not even in mourning." Sir Conan shook his head. "Either she didn't love him, or she knows something."

"Or both," Matthias replied. "Thank you, Conan. That was actually helpful."

"I'm not a total dunce, Blake," the knight rebutted.

Matthias found himself smirking. "I suppose not. Maybe just half of one."

Sir Conan cursed at Matthias before opening the entrance to the palace.

"Watch yourself, Blake. Strange things are happening here."

Matthias gave a nod of appreciation and stalked inside.

A grand room made of shining marble laid before him. Tall columns lined the perimeter of the space while glittering golden sconces hung on the walls. The palace was eerily quiet, save for Matthias' boots clacking quietly across the slick marbled floor. Gold chandeliers with shimmering crystals swung above him and he half expected one to come crashing down upon his head.

When he'd been summoned by King Atol before, servants and councilmen usually buzzed about, completing their daily tasks, or waiting for an audience with the king. But the king was gone. Did the palace staff know about the king's demise? Did the King's Council know?

Matthias kept his eyes and ears open, temporarily tapping into his wolf's power to see and hear beyond his human capabilities.

As he turned the corner and passed by one of the washrooms, a scullery maid cursed about the king's filthy stockings to another maid who laughed.

So, they don't know he's dead.

Matthias focused on another part of the palace while he continued toward Queen Leza's meeting chambers.

The kitchen staff busied themselves, preparing for an upcoming event. Matthias took a few strides toward the commotion, wondering what event could have all the cooks in such a hurry. He knew he'd been gone for longer than usual, but even when he was traveling, word of palace events spread through Tenton like wildfire.

"Captain Blake," an elegant female voice called out to him, and Matthias snapped to attention.

Queen Leza stood a few paces before him, draped in a rich scarlet gown that plunged too low. Matthias hated how she wore the same color as Devora had the night of the ball when he betrayed her. He would never forget the pain in her beautiful violet eyes at his lies.

"My queen," Matthias replied, bowing low.

He knew the formalities expected of him. And he would be a good soldier until he got what he wanted: to find his mother and Devora, safe and alive.

"You flatter me, Blake," Queen Leza said with a flirtatious smile.

Her silver crown twinkled as she held out her hand for Matthias to kiss. The crown was different than the one she wore at the ball honoring Devora. That one had an imperial opal on it. Many nobles flaunted the gem to show their wealth, for it was extremely rare. But when Matthias had seen the queen's crown at the ball, a dark aura pulled from it. He was convinced the only reason he could even feel the aura was because of his curse.

Matthias glanced at the queen's outstretched hand, despising aristocratic etiquette. He didn't want his lips anywhere but on Devora's mouth. But, like all his other desires, he pushed them away and gave the queen's gloved hand a quick peck.

The queen's smile grew in triumph as she retracted her petite fingers and held them in front of her.

"Come with me, Captain, we have much to discuss."

Like the dog he was, Matthias complied without question, hating that this was his part to play in finding his loved ones. And though he obeyed, he still loathed every moment of it.

Queen Leza led Matthias to her meeting chambers. That she met with him alone always made him uneasy. Whenever he met with King Atol, there were always guards or servants or someone around. But never with the queen. It was almost as if she were afraid someone would overhear what she had to say. That, or she *wanted* him alone. Matthias didn't even allow his mind to continue that thought.

"Please sit," the queen gestured to a plump green velvet chair lined with gold tassels.

Before the emerald chair sat an ornate gold table set with afternoon tea for two. Matthias held his breath, unnerved by the intimacy of the meeting. He wanted to refuse but knew it would make matters worse.

"Thank you, my queen," he replied. He first pulled the queen's chair out, knowing this was more ridiculous etiquette required when in the presence of royalty. Thank goodness he had spent *some* time at Vlacklear or his cover with the king and queen would've been blown long ago.

"Always such a gentleman," the queen cooed. "Is that why you have so many young ladies after you?"

Matthias thought she batted her lashes at him, but he decided not to entertain the thought. His mind then focused on the question. A definite trap. Queen Leza knew of Matthias' affection for Devora and wanted to know if he was still in contact with her.

Even if he knew where Devora was, Matthias would never rat her out to the queen. Never again would he be the one to bring such pain to the woman he loved.

"Between working for the warden and Your Majesties, I hardly have time for female companionship, my queen," he replied carefully.

Queen Leza's eyes gleamed with something Matthias couldn't decipher, but he hoped she picked up on his plural use of majesty; thus, including King Atol. It was better if she thought he was ignorant on the matter of the king's death.

"We do keep you busy," she giggled.

Matthias gave a curt nod. He would rather slay a thousand giants than be stuck having tea with the queen. Anxiety itched at him from every nerve. He needed to get back to his office and try to figure out what happened to his mother and to Devora. Devora must have seen a vision about his mother to leave Yekel on her own. But what was it? And why didn't she tell him—or anyone—more about it?

"Is there something you require of me, my queen?" Matthias asked, politely inferring for her to hurry up.

"Always straight to the point," Queen Leza mused. She ran her fingers through her silky black hair.

When Matthias was unfazed by the gesture, the queen pouted.

"Very well," she sighed. "Congratulations, Captain. You're being promoted."

Matthias blinked, taken aback. "What?"

"His Majesty and I were so impressed by your reclamation of Yekel, we thought this was the best honor we could bestow upon you. In two weeks, there will be a promotion ceremony in your honor with a celebration ball to suit."

Matthias sat completely baffled. This was not what he was expecting. Usually, the king would send him on an errand to dispose of more citizens accused of treason. But a promotion? Matthias couldn't remember the last time he'd heard of anyone being promoted. The war had stagnated many customs that came with being in His Majesty's Army, promotions being one of them.

"I can see you're surprised and I'm glad," Queen Leza grinned before taking a sip of tea. "Please be sure to invite all your friends and family. I'm sure they won't want to miss it."

Chapter Nineteen

Rae couldn't believe how similar Ben and his father looked. Other than the foot of height Ben had on Byron, the men were basically twins.

Though Rae was pleased with Ben's family's reaction to him returning, she still felt unease clouding the air. She noticed Mara giving her glances out of the corner of her eye and Byron continuously wiping sweat from his brow.

Was their warm welcome just a façade?

Though Rae was used to not trusting others, Mara and Byron seemed completely genuine in their love for Ben.

While she studied the humble home, Rae took a sip of hot tea from the clay mug Mara had given her.

As the backroom of a bakery, it was more spacious than Rae would've expected. A glowing hearth sat cozily against the far wall where an oval table stood before it. To the right was the back door Rae and Ben had entered. The wall around the door was bare save for a few cross-stitched pictures. To the left was the entrance to the kitchen and storefront of the bakery.

"Would you like another scone?" Mara asked, placing the half-finished plate of scones before Rae.

Rae had to admit she was shocked to find Ben's little sister not so little. Though she knew Mara's incident with the men in the village was years ago, she never expected to see a fully grown woman ready to have a child. A fully grown woman who was younger than Rae, already healed and moving on with her life while she was still waking up with nightmares from her time at the Temple.

Pushing the thoughts from her mind, Rae offered Mara a kind smile. She knew she shouldn't take advantage of Mara's hospitality, but the scones were a delectable treat, so she helped herself to another.

"Thank you," Rae said, biting into the flaky yet smooth crust of the scone. The pastry melted in her mouth and Rae resisted the urge to eat it all in two bites.

"So," Mara said, easing herself into a chair next to Rae. She shifted her glance to Ben, as if making sure he was occupied first before speaking.

Rae followed her gaze to find Byron telling Ben an elaborate story about a runaway cow a few weeks ago. Ben chuckled along, fully engaged in the anecdote. Rae's heart warmed at the sight.

"Yes?" Rae asked, bringing her eyes back to Mara as she took another bite of her scone.

Mara hesitated, looking nervous, then blurted, "Are you Ben's wife?"

Rae choked on the piece of scone she'd eaten. By the time she finished coughing and caught her breath, the room had gone silent. Mara sheepishly handed her a cup filled with water.

Rae took a long gulp of water, not knowing how to respond.

A wife? Me? Could I actually be someone's wife?

Placing the cup down, she glanced at Mara. Her rosy cheeks and simple dress were beautiful on her. And her swollen belly completed the perfect image of the ideal wife. That's not how Rae looked.

Scars covered Rae's arms and legs from her fights in the Dark Market. Her hair wasn't even at her chin, not long and fashionable the way most women wore it these days. Rae stared at her purple dyed fingers. Balling her hands into fists, she hid them beneath the table in her lap. She wasn't most women, but Ben still cared for her anyway. Rae couldn't understand it. But she tried not to place her insecurities about herself on him.

"I apologize," Mara said quietly, looking down at her own hands.

Rae then noticed the rough patches and burn scars covering Mara's hands. Probably from baking for so long. Rae, too, had several scars from touching a pastry or bread pan fresh out of the kiln too early. Her heart softened.

"It's all right, I just wasn't expecting it." Rae smiled then added. "Ben and I haven't known each other very long, so I was surprised at the thought."

"I see," Mara said, relieved at Rae's response. She cast a glance toward Ben who was watching Rae closely.

Rae turned her eyes toward him, interested in the question lurking behind the curious gaze.

Before either of them could say anything, a loud pounding came from the back door, almost shattering the thin wood.

"Byron! It's me, Eustace. Some folks have got some questions for ya."

Byron wiped the sweat from his brow again, his hands shaking. "I knew he would be coming. Mara, quick, hide them where we store the butter."

Mara jumped up and nodded quickly. "This way, hurry."

Anxiety lodged itself in Rae's throat and she was back in her home in Yekel where General Yada and his men barged in, trying to find Devora—the Seer—and Ben. If it hadn't been for Master Monham's help, Rae wouldn't have been able to get Ben and Devora to safety.

Rae tried to move to follow Mara, but she stayed plastered in her seat, afraid. Fear like a knife drove itself into her back, paralyzing her. She felt herself crawling within, shutting the world out until a soft hand laid on her shoulder.

"Rae?" Ben said gently. "Are you okay?"

Like a flame banishing the night, Ben's voice warded away the bad memories of General Yada. Shaking her head, Rae stood and grabbed Ben's hand.

"Yes." She turned to Mara. "Please lead the way."

Mara took another curious glance between them before hurrying toward a door in the back wall.

"Mara, is that Eustace Stibbs?" Ben asked.

Mara nodded her head as she opened the door. Inside lay sacks upon sacks of flour, salt, and other baking necessities. "He usually doesn't give us trouble, but since the captain came by recently, too, well," —she sighed— "You know how people are here."

"Unfortunately," Ben grumbled before he stalked forward and moved three bags of flour to reveal a door in the floor. He turned to Rae.

Rae, momentarily distracted by the ease with which Ben moved such heavy sacks of flour, eventually realized the plan. Stepping forward, she peered into the small space.

"We usually keep our extra butter down there, but we haven't gotten our order yet so you will have a little more room," Mara said with a small smile.

"I'll go somewhere else," Ben said. "My legs are too long. I'll take up all the space."

Just as he started to leave, Byron's voice welcoming Eustace into the backroom of the bakery traveled against the walls.

"There's no time," Rae said grabbing his hand. "Just go in first."

"Where will you go?" he immediately replied.

Rae sucked in a breath. "I'll fit, just hurry."

With a sigh, Ben crawled down into the dark hole.

Rae yanked the bags of flour as close as she could to the open door before she said, "As soon as I get down, close the door, and slide these back on top as best as you can. But don't hurt yourself. You shouldn't be lifting anything."

Shock covered Mara's face before she nodded hesitantly. "I wish I could do more."

"Be just as hospitable as you were to me and you'll be fine," Rae replied with a quick smile. "Oh, and please don't forget about us."

"I could never," Mara replied, shaking her head.

Taking a breath, Rae eased herself into the small space.

Mara's face was the last thing they saw before the door closed and darkness enveloped them.

Every single one of Rae's nerves set on fire as she realized she was sitting directly on Ben's lap. It didn't matter which way she moved; he was always there.

"I'm sorry," Ben whispered, and she could hear the embarrassment in his voice.

"Why are you sorry?"

"I'm so big, there's no space for you."

Rae frowned at him, even though she knew he couldn't see it. "Maybe I'm too small."

His hair brushed against her cheek as he shook his head. "No, you're perfect."

Rae couldn't help but bark out a laugh then covered her mouth with her hands. She waited a moment and when the voices continued, she relaxed.

Lowering her voice, she whispered, "You and I both know I'm hardly perfect."

Rae finally decided to sit with her back against Ben's chest and her legs crisscrossed in front. It was the most comfortable for both of them.

"Is this okay?"

"Mm-hmm," Ben strained.

"Are you okay?" she asked, suddenly concerned. "Am I too heavy?"

"Yes," he said quickly. "I mean, no! I-I've just never been this close to...well..."

Heat ignited Rae's nerves again as she realized the intimacy of their position. "Oh, right. I can sit a different way."

"No," he said and suddenly two long arms wrapped around her. "I want—" he stopped, and she felt his Adam's apple bob against the back of her head. "I want to be close to you," he confessed quietly.

"Oh," was all Rae was able to manage.

Her heart felt like it was beating faster than a hummingbird's wings. Every nerve on her skin knew exactly where Ben was and how it was affecting her. *What is this feeling?* Even with all the street fights she'd won, she'd never experienced something quite as exhilarating before. *Is this love?*

Rae pushed the thought from her mind. They had just met a few weeks ago. How could this be love? But everything in her heart—in her soul—was telling her it was.

Taking a breath, Rae decided to change the subject. "Who's Eustace Stibbs?"

Ben gave a frustrated grunt, his breath tickling Rae's neck. Tiny bumps rose across her skin, but she tried to ignore them.

"He's the brother of one of the men who violated Mara. Unfortunately, he's the sheriff. He dared to testify and say Mara lied about the whole thing to get attention. I almost killed him too. Pa knew he'd be sniffing around here. If Eustace knew I was out of the Fortress, he'd do whatever it took to send me back."

Rae found herself placing her arms over Ben's and pulling them tighter around her. Ben's arms went rigid, but he allowed her to move them until he hugged her close.

"I'm glad you didn't kill him," she whispered. "One more burden on your soul."

Ben's rigid position relaxed, and he placed his chin on her shoulder. "Thank you."

"For what?"

"For caring about my soul," he whispered, sending pleasant shivers down her spine.

"Thank you," she breathed.

"For what?"

"For caring about mine," she responded, turning her face toward his.

Ben's breathing became husky. "Rae."

"Yes?"

"I know I said I'd wait until you're ready, and I will. But I really *really* would like to kiss you. Right now."

Rae couldn't help but smirk at the honesty. Her heart felt as if it would burst out of her chest and for the first time, she *wanted* to kiss a man, this man. This amazingly kind and gentle man who would listen if she said no. But she didn't want to say no.

"I think I would like to try," she admitted softly.

Ben's arms tightened around her. And, even in the pitch black of the small cellar, his lips found hers.

The kiss was soft yet passionate all at the same time, exactly how Ben was. And Rae knew that if she wasn't falling in love with the gentle giant before, she definitely was now.

Ben pulled back too quickly for Rae's liking, but she accepted the action. Her lips tingled from the kiss, and she wondered—hoped—she'd get to experience it again soon.

"I'm glad my first kiss was with you," Ben said, and the happy bubble Rae placed around herself popped.

She didn't want to remember her first kiss. It was a forced and ugly thing. She suddenly felt tears in her eyes, emotions building up inside of her. She tried to contain them, but they seeped out too fast.

"What's the matter?" Ben asked against her ear, still trying to be quiet, but his voice was filled with concern all the same. "I didn't think I did that awful."

Rae laughed through her tears. "You were perfect and wonderful. You've always been that way. Even when you fought against me in the Dark Market, you were kind." Rae wiped her tears on her sleeve. "Ben, I'm not perfect. I'm not a dainty little wife who has rosy cheeks. I'm scarred and broken. And I'm trying to heal. I'm trying to learn who Tunri is and His goodness, but I'm still so hurt. I can't be the woman you deserve to have."

As Rae tried to quiet her tears, she thought Ben would release her, agree with her. But he held her closer.

With a sigh, Ben explained, "Ever since we were kids, Mara would always blurt whatever was on her mind. But I never said I was ready for a wife, much less one with rosy cheeks." He pressed his warm cheek against Rae's, and she giggled. "We both have a lot to learn about ourselves, Tunri, and each other. And though I've been using every ounce of self-control to not kiss you, I *want* to take the time to get to know who you are, Rae Salvar, scars, and all."

"I don't even know who I am," Rae whispered.

Ben pressed his lips against her cheek and held her close. "We'll find that out together."

Chapter Twenty

Jacques scooped up the stack of restricted texts Ida had left as she rushed out of the library. At least he had another excuse to see her again. Warden Hazor placed him in the ideal position of being a prefect as well as a tutor to excuse why he was spending so much time with Ida. Not that Ida needed the extra help. She was amazingly quick and efficient with her work. He always knew there was something fascinating happening behind those beautiful big eyes of hers.

Sighing, Jacques sauntered down the hallway, now cleared of the commotion of students. He overheard something about the Assembly, but, since he was still trying to fully wake up, the details were foggy.

Whistling as he strode along the barren hall, Jacques remembered when he'd first seen Ida after her Categorization Call. She looked at him as if Jacques himself had killed her most beloved pet. And Jacques was heartbroken to watch the beautiful girl from Lower Grenly cry. Before Ida's Call, he'd witness countless others be overjoyed at the color patterns they categorized or violent at their results. Most of the violent ones were those being forced to enlist in the military instead of attending Vlacklear.

Ida was the only one who cried and cried but still accepted her fate without a fuss. Jacques couldn't believe the strength it took for someone so small to be so brave. And then she and Lady

Devora were attacked by that giant and still Ida stood strong. He expected that behavior from Lady Devora, but after he'd seen Ida a mess of tears only a day before, Jacques was shocked to find Ida well after the attack.

Jacques rounded the next corner and ended up in one of the larger rooms meant for studying. Structured with peaked arches, the room was spacious so students could spread out among the wide wooden tables and plush chairs. Though it wasn't as silent as the library, the study hall was almost empty of students. Jacques was thankful classes weren't in session today, and he could have a break from being a Vlacklear prefect.

As he strode across the thick scarlet carpet, Jacques wondered when he should try to seek Ida out again. It was by chance he ran into her at the joust the other day. He hadn't even planned to be there, much less defeat Sergio in a match. Jacques grinned as he remembered the shocked look on the usually cocky Third Year's face. He was thankful father had made him, Raphael, and Charles, all attend Tinwa's annual joust and even practice against one another when they were younger.

Jacques thought back to Sergio's desire to dine with Ida alone. He didn't know why Sergio was so fascinated with Ida, but he didn't like it.

After he was halfway through the study hall, Jacques decided to take a seat by the window. It was almost time for lunch. He would seek Ida out then and maybe they could continue to decipher the texts. Ida was just about to tell Jacques what the book said earlier before she ran off.

As Jacques eased into the soft, crimson-colored chair, he placed the restricted texts in his lap. Matthias had checked them out a while ago, trying to decipher what they meant. Once he had gone to reclaim Yekel, Warden Hazor told Jacques of his new assignment and sent him on his way to Vlacklear. Though Jacques sometimes got lost in the details of the warden's plan, he did his best to obey.

As Jacques thumbed through the thick pages of parchment—not understanding a word—he recalled how Ida defended Warden Hazor. Almost as if she knew him personally. It was odd and Jacques wanted to know more.

Crossing one leg over the other, Jacques continued to turn pages when a solitary set of footsteps approached him from behind. His first instinct was to jump up, draw his mech, and threaten whoever came near. Instead, Jacques willed himself to stay seated. It was probably only another student passing by. This wasn't the Fortress or the battlefield. No one here would harm him. At least, they hadn't so far. And he obviously didn't have his mech anyway.

But when the footsteps came closer and started to slow down, Jacques grew more anxious.

"After all this time and you still slouch in your chair," a familiar voice from the past commented. "I would have thought the military taught you better than that."

Jacques sprang out of the chair and spun around.

A middle-aged man with slicked back sandy-blond hair and hard blue eyes stood before Jacques. A light green tunic and brown pants covered his slender form. His father was thinner than Jacques remembered.

It seemed like yesterday Jacques told his father he was leaving home and would never return. But it wasn't yesterday, it'd been four years and Jacques had stayed true to his promise.

"What are you doing here, Father?" Jacques demanded.

He allowed his posture to relax but was ready to flee if he needed to. The gossips at Vlacklear Academy were almost as bad as the King's Council. Jacques knew it would only be a matter of time before Father discovered he was here.

There was only one reason why Lord Emanuel Delequa was here, and it was to marry his second son off to the highest bidder.

"I won't bore you with details," Emanuel stated plainly. He strode forward until he was about a foot from Jacques.

Though Jacques was a few inches taller than his father, he felt his inner child cowering at the man's presence.

"Duke Sandje has requested to continue with the betrothal between you and one of his daughters, as discussed when you were children."

Jacques paled. "Duke Sandje? Of Sandje Textiles?"

When Reese and Hestia entered the Fortress as lieutenants, Jacques was shocked. Even with the change in the category colors, he couldn't understand why Duke Sandje would allow his only daughters to be sentenced to the Fortress. Especially when the duke could easily convince the king otherwise. Jacques had seen it done before—many times—when he was learning about his father's business as a child. Wealth always paved a way out.

"The very one," Emanuel replied with a nod. "I have agreed to this match. It will be beneficial to both of our families. You and his daughter—whichever one you marry—can leave this Fortress nonsense behind and you can reclaim your place as head of the Delequa *and* Sandje fortunes." A greedy grin spread across Emanuel's thin face. "Think of the power and influence you'll have over Tenton."

"I refuse," Jacques replied without allowing his father to continue.

Crouching down, he grabbed the restricted texts and strode away from his father. Maybe Jacques would seek out Ida earlier than he expected. After this news, he needed to see her, to be reminded that there were still pure, genuine people in the world.

"Don't walk away from me, Jacques," Emanuel commanded, but Jacques kept walking.

After four years, his father hadn't changed. He was still utterly obsessed with money and would do anything to get it. After the sickness took Mother—and Helene—Father got worse.

As Jacques got older, he realized why Raphael, Jacques' older brother, defected from the military and ran to Kadesh. Everything—his children, the people of Tenton—were second to Emanuel Delequa's greed. Jacques knew Emanuel sold iron to Kadesh, and he loathed his father even more for aiding the enemy.

"Jacques, please," his father said once more and the hint of desperation in his voice made Jacques pause.

But he wasn't ready for the final blow Father had planned. "I'm dying."

A sudden burst of anger and fury exploded in Jacques' chest. He spun around. "Don't. Don't try to play me to get your way. It's bad enough you never cared when Mother died. You didn't even mourn when Helene, the bride *I* chose, passed. But lying about your health?" Jacques scoffed. "That's a new low. Even for you."

Emanuel's shoulders sagged as he reached up and pulled the blond wig from his head. Jacques took a step back as deep, scarlet spots covered his father's head where his hair used to be. Flashbacks to Mother gaining the spots and then losing her hair entered Jacques' mind. He shook his head, unable to believe it.

At first, the physician thought it could be contagious and that Raphael, Jacques, and their cousin, Charles, would get it too. That's when they were sent away to the eastern countryside, away from their home in the city of Tinwa. Not one of them was able to say goodbye to Jacques' mother before she passed.

"No," Jacques said. "The physician said—"

"They were wrong, Jacques," Emanual said, defeated. "It wasn't long after this that your mother passed. I have, maybe a few weeks, possibly a month or two. Thankfully, the disease isn't contagious, like we thought." A weak smile came to Emanual's lips. "I'm just another lucky one, I guess."

The air grew thick around Jacques, his whole world crashing down upon him. With Raphael gone and Charles still too young, Jacques was the only one left to control Delequa Iron.

"Why didn't you find me sooner?" Jacques breathed; thankful he was still standing on his two feet.

He wished Matthias were here. Matthias was always quick with his answers and responses. Jacques always fumbled when trying to make the right choice, never knowing if he really made the correct decision.

"You told me not to," Emanual replied, simply.

Jacques resisted the urge to roll his eyes at his father's pettiness. "What about Charles?"

Charles, Jacques' and Raphael's younger cousin, came to live with them when Jacques' aunt and uncle passed. Though Charles wasn't Jacques' real brother, Jacques always thought of him as such. It pained him to leave Charles behind when he left home. He wished he had a plan to somehow take Charles with him. But being four years younger, Charles was still young and Jacques knew he'd be better off in the Delequa mansion rather than following Jacques to the Fortress after Jacques categorized to work in His Majesty's Army.

"Charles categorized for the Fortress a few months back," Emanuel replied, replacing his wig. "I thought he would've sought you out."

The room spun and Jacques found the nearest seat to plunk down in. He placed his head in his hands, trying to force himself to breathe. *Charles was at the Fortress? Why hadn't I seen him? Why hadn't Charles sought me out?*

Jacques ran a hand through his hair and breathed deeply. He'd heard Lady Devora speaking about Tunri, a God who listened to prayers. Though Jacques never refuted the existence of a god, he never embraced it either.

But with his world crashing down upon him, now seemed like a good time to reach out.

Tunri, I know I'm not the best with prayers, but I don't know what to do.

"Even if Raphael were still here," Emanuel continued, taking a step toward Jacques. "You were always the best one to take over the iron ore business."

Jacques glared up at his father. Emanual knew very well that Jacques wanted nothing to do with the family business. It was all about cheating and taking advantage of people. Two things Jacques hated most.

"People have always loved you, wherever you go," Emanuel continued with a soft smile. "I can see Delequa Iron growing exponentially under your guidance. You've always had a charming personality, just like your mother."

Just then, something inside Jacques clicked. He didn't want to marry Hestia or Reese, but if *he* were in control of Delequa Iron, he would have pounds of iron ore at his disposal. That alone could be what ended the war with Kadesh. Once and for all.

Trust.

It wasn't a voice that spoke to him, but more of a feeling tugging at his soul that everything would be okay.

Running his hand through his hair again, Jacques took a deep breath and stood. He straightened his tunic and stared at his father. In his surprise, Jacques hadn't noticed the deep bags under Emanuel's eyes and how gaunt his face looked. His clothes bagged around his thin frame, almost swallowing the lord up.

The little sympathy and love he still held for his father struck Jacques' heart and he made his decision.

Unable to believe the words coming out of his mouth, Jacques said, "I will renounce my knighthood and return to Delequa Manor. I will become the head of Delequa Iron and—" he hesitated, Ida's kind eyes and gentle smile flashing in his mind.

Trust.

Jacques continued, barely above a whisper, "I will marry a Sandje sister and unite our families as one, for the good of Tenton."

Emanual strode forward and wrapped his arms around Jacques. Jacques stood stiff, not knowing how to react to the first hug he'd ever received from his father.

"I'm proud of you, my boy. I'll draw up the paperwork and have it sent to Duke Sandje immediately. As soon as it's signed, you can leave all this behind."

As soon as Emanuel left, Jacques flopped back into the chair. Placing his head in his hands, he wondered how he could ever face Ida again.

Chapter Twenty-One

After talking with Reese last night after the Assembly, Ida ran to her room and cried herself to sleep, hoping what she'd learned was all a bad dream. Was Jacques really the heir to Delequa Iron? Did that mean Jacques would marry Hestia? But why hadn't he said anything to her about it?

She then remembered how he practically dragged her out of the headmistress' office once Duke Sandje spoke of the arranged marriage between the Delequa and Sandje families. Had Jacques known beforehand about the agreement?

Unfortunately, when Ida awoke the next morning—or early afternoon—and headed to the dining hall for lunch, the gossip proved even worse. She almost ran the other way when she heard.

"Did you hear?" a tall, thick girl with dark brown hair asked.

The shorter, slim girl to her right flicked her bangs out of her eyes. "No, what?"

"One of the Sandje twins is getting married!" The tall girl could barely contain her excitement. "I believe it's Hestia!"

Her friend gasped. "Who is she marrying?"

Leaning in, the tall girl—who was pretending to whisper but really almost yelled the information, knowing all ears were listening in— "The new heir of Delequa Iron."

Ida and a boy with frizzy blond hair a few feet ahead of her both froze. There was something about the boy that was familiar, but Ida was too shocked at the news of Jacques' upcoming nuptials to register his face. She hadn't realized the arranged marriage had been finalized so quickly.

Ida's thoughts were a whirlwind as she backed out of the dining hall and ran down the hallway. Students chittered with one another, not sparing a second glance at the crying girl sprinting through the academy.

Ida had tried to be strong. She tried not to develop feelings for Jacques, knowing he would be taken away from her, and she fell for him anyway. And, just like Josef, Jacques had been taken from her too.

Finally, she arrived back at her room, thankful to be alone and sob her heart out.

Locking the door behind her, Ida jumped on her bed, buried her face in her pillow and cried. Thankfully, classes were done for the day. After Sergio's betrayal, she crumpled the work she had done for him and threw it out the window. He could be locked in the Tower for all eternity for all she cared. But Ida knew that wasn't true, and she would still try to save Sergio if the Tower were his fate.

Glancing at her textbooks, Ida couldn't imagine focusing on aristocratic etiquette or linguistics at a time like this. After the horrors of Assembly, Duke Sandje, and Sir Jacques' lineage, Ida just wanted to crawl into a hole and never come out.

Tears flowed freely down her face as she tried to erase the few but cherished memories she shared with Jacques. How kind he was when she'd been sent to the Fortress. How he always sent her a special smile in the dismal prison. And the wire bracelet Nadia made. Ida couldn't contain her smile when his fingers brushed against her arm as he wrapped it around her wrist when they were back in the Fortress.

Butterflies soared in her stomach at the memory, and Ida hated how she still wanted only him.

And then their almost kiss. *If Jacques knew he would be taking over Delequa Iron and marrying Hestia, why did he try to kiss me?*

Knowing what she did now, Ida wished she could go back to that time at the greenhouse where she didn't know anything about Jacques' upbringing, and they could just be knight and soldier once again.

Sighing, Ida sat up and wiped her face with her palms. A pounding throb vibrated against her skull. She always hated the aftereffects of crying. But after many years of hardships and tears, Ida had grown used to the sensation.

Ida thought of her small lily doing its best to thrive in the harsh northern environment. She and the flower really were one and the same.

A seed must be broken to create a beautiful flower. Professor Mal's words entered Ida's thoughts and she frowned. Right now, she'd rather be a weed that could grow anywhere than a finnicky desert lily.

Slowly rising from her bed, Ida reached for a cold cup of tea on her desk. She didn't know how long it had been there, but some liquid was better than nothing at all. Gulping down the lavender chamomile blend, Ida strode to her frost-covered window. Just before the horizon sat the Fortress, it's dark, looming architecture a stark contrast to the fresh layer of snow.

Though adjusting to the Fortress was difficult at first, Ida had grown used to it. In fact, she enjoyed the regimented schedules of training and eating times. She didn't mind her job cleaning out the cells—although some were a lot worse than others. And she absolutely loved the friends she made there. She considered Devora, Nadia, Hestia, and Reese more like family, like sisters, than just friends. Maybe that's why the news of hearing Hestia's betrothal to Jacques hurt so much.

Ida took the last sip of tea. Reese had just made the agreement with her father that she or Hestia would marry within the year by the betrothal laws of Tenton. Once she thought about it, Ida remembered how Reese hesitated for a moment when Duke Sandje brought up the heir of Delequa Iron. And when they left the headmistress' office, Ida asked who the heir was and Reese glanced in the direction Jacques had gone, as if willing him to return and tell Ida the news himself.

Brushing her wild curls back from her head, Ida strode away from the window. Maybe she was just slow, but nothing made sense anymore. She thought she was following Tunri's direction, but maybe she had gotten it wrong somewhere along the way.

A soft but quick knock sounded at her door.

Hope sparked Ida's chest that it was Jacques coming to explain everything, but as she opened the door and Reese rushed in, Ida's hope was squashed.

"Before you say anything," Reese said as Ida closed the door. "I found out when you did in the headmistress' office yesterday."

Ida slowly faced Reese, unsure of how to react to the statement when she gazed upon her friend's face. Bloodshot eyes and puffy cheeks replaced Reese's usual stern face. Streaks of tears ran down her cheeks as the tall, slim girl threw her abacus on the bed, burying her face in her hands and crying.

Any anger Ida held toward her friend vanished as she strode forward and wrapped Reese in a hug.

"It's okay, Reese. I believe you."

"I told you not to cry at the joust and here I am, a blubbering mess," Reese said between sniffs. "I'm so sorry, Ida. I've been trying to change, to view the world differently than how I was raised. You must understand, we were taught to look down upon anyone who was a lesser class than us."

Ida led Reese to sit on the bed then gave her friend a spare handkerchief. Reese wiped her tears before blowing her nose.

The trumpet sound caused Ida to giggle, breaking the sullen atmosphere in the room.

Reese gave a small smile before it fell. "I was eighty-eight percent sure Father was going to bring up marriage again, especially to Sergio, so I was prepared. But when he mentioned Sir Jacques' family, I completely froze. I should've thought of a different plan and probability that didn't include marriage. Now I've made a horrible mess."

More tears fled down Reese's face and Ida took one of her hands. "I think you're being unfair to yourself. It's not like you knew Jacques' family was ready to marry him off."

Reese paused and considered the statement. "There were talks when we were children, but nothing concrete. But I still could've done something else than promise Father marriage. I hope that my probabilities of finding a loophole in the marriage law will increase."

Ida bit her lip, not wanting to ask what the probability was. Her own heart was breaking inside, but focusing on Reese was far easier than confronting her own pain. "Please let me know if I can help in anyway."

Reese stared at Ida, then shook her head. "You're too good for this world, Ida. We all know you and Sir Jacques are together. This is a horrible circumstance and you're still being kind."

Ida bit her trembling lip and turned away, hoping to squelch the coming tears. "Unfortunately, Jacques and I are not together. We never were." She fumbled with the hems of her sleeves. "And I'm not from a noble lineage so thinking we ever could be was just a silly dream anyway."

Reese spun toward Ida. "If Hestia were here, she would say, 'Wanting true love is *not* a silly dream.' And I agree with her. We all noticed Sir Jacques ogling you since we arrived at the Fortress. It was so obvious."

"What?" Ida asked, shocked by the statement.

Reese tapped her fingers on her thigh. "While I'll admit he's attractive, I definitely do not want to marry him or Sergio for that matter. And though Hestia is a flirt, her heart has been set on someone else for some time."

The declarations made Ida feel better, but it didn't change the facts. Even if the marriage between Jacques and Hestia didn't happen, Ida wasn't a noble and Jacques was. This wasn't a fairytale where her prince would leave all his riches behind and live in poverty with her. Plus, she wouldn't want that for Jacques anyway.

"I wish he would've told you," Reese said suddenly. When Ida glanced over at her, Reese explained, "We knew each other growing up but tried to avoid each other at the Fortress. It was like reopening a wound none of us wanted to endure again." Reese then furrowed her brow as she grabbed her abacus and swatted a few beads to the right. "Given how affectionately he looks at you, I'm seventy-nine point four percent sure he would've told you if he had foreknowledge of the marriage agreement."

Ida nodded but still wondered if Jacques would explain every-thing himself. But then she remembered he didn't have to ex-plain himself to her. They were from two different worlds, two different countries. Because if being poor wasn't enough, Ida was Kadeshian. Jacques would certainly run from her if he found out the truth.

"Thank you, Reese," Ida said. "I hope you're right." She reached out and squeezed the girl's hand. "You're a good friend and I wish you so much happiness." Ida couldn't stop her tears as she said the final statement.

This time Reese wrapped her long arms around Ida and held her close. "Ida, I know Hestia will refuse to marry Sir Jacques. Even if it wasn't obvious he is hopelessly in love with you, she still wouldn't. She has other plans for her future. And I have other plans for mine."

"Really?" Ida asked, her throat scratchy.

Reese nodded as she pulled away. "I don't know how it will all come to pass, but there's one thing I do know." Reese stood, wiping the tears from her eyes, and transforming into the noble daughter she was born and bred to be. "Devora is the only person who has defied my probabilities but other than that, I have always been spot on. My plan may not be one hundred percent foolproof, but it's enough of a chance that I'm willing to risk it and find happiness for all of us. You, me, Sir Jacques, and Hestia."

Ida noticed the certainty in Reese's dark eyes. Though the twins seemed to bicker more than get along, Ida realized that they were still sisters and would support and protect each other to the end. And, somehow, Ida had been invited into that relationship.

Ida reached out and hugged Reese again, thanking Tunri for providing her friends after being alone for so long.

"Enough of all this," Reese said as she playfully pushed Ida away. "It's almost time. If we are to save Hestia from the Tower and allow you to search for the Book of Ages, we need to go soon. Are you ready to speak to Sir Jacques?"

Ida bit her lip, not knowing what she could say. How could someone like her question Jacques? A noble, the next *Lord* of Delequa Iron? While Ida was just Ida. A poor Kadeshian who—for some reason—Tunri decided was worthy of a second chance at life.

"I'm not sure if that's a good idea," Ida said quietly. "He doesn't owe me an explanation."

"Ida, I don't know why Sir Jacques accepted a marriage proposal into my family. But I know enough about this noble world to realize this deal probably has a lot more to it than we think."

Ida swallowed and nodded, knowing Reese was right but still terrified of seeing Jacques.

"We better get going," Reese said, standing. "Are you ready?"

Ida swallowed all her fear and pain, hoping—praying—that everything she thought was true was really false.

Holding her head high, Ida nodded and followed Reese out the door.

Chapter Twenty-Two

Devora, Somewhere in Tenton

There was one thing Devora hated worse than not being able to bathe. It was not being able to bathe while being stuck in a dark, dirty tunnel. She cringed when she thought about the layers of dirt caked beneath her fingernails.

Devora lost track of how long she'd been underground when she followed the tunnel from beneath the Temple of Pahga to a dead end. She had searched relentlessly, not understanding how Kanna and her captor could have vanished from the tunnel. But try as she might, Devora didn't see the streak of purple light leading her to Kanna anywhere.

Devora frowned at the dank dirt and stone walls around her. She hated diverting from her original plan, but it had to be done. The trail was cold, so it was useless for her to stay underground if Kanna wasn't down here anymore.

Placing the lightweight pickaxe Nadia made over her shoulder, Devora backtracked a few feet. She wasn't an expert at tunnel building, but she noticed what looked like the start of another tunnel a little way back. With Nadia's pickaxe, she could dig through a bit more and see where she came out on the other side.

The small light of the lantern swung from her fingertips as she walked. She had just enough fuel for a little longer. Devora couldn't believe it had lasted this long and would have to give her compliments to Nadia once they were reunited again.

During her time underground, Devora found a lot of time to think about everything. With no one to talk to and nothing really to see, she focused her energy on planning what she would do once she found Kanna, how she would find Princess Haden after that, and what she was going to say to Matthias. She winced at the last thought.

Devora turned into the half-dug tunnel. It was almost as if someone wanted to go this way and stopped. Unease crawled up her spine. She prayed there weren't any creatures lurking in these underground tunnels, ready to eat her.

Shaking the thought from her head, Devora lifted the pick-axe and struck the rock. Just like all the other rocks she chiseled at before, the stone fell away with ease. But though the pickaxe did cut stone like butter, there was still a lot of it.

Preparing herself for the long task ahead, Devora struck the rock repeatedly. Her thoughts soon slipped back to Matthias. She knew he would come to Yekel to find her. Devora was surprised he hadn't found her yet. When that man set his mind to something, he didn't give up until he reached his goal.

She found herself smiling at the thought. She couldn't wait to see him again; she only prayed it would be under joyous circumstances. And, though she had several plans for when she found Kanna and Princess Haden, her mind always went blank when it came to Matthias.

Taking a quick break, Devora wiped the sweat from her brow. Of course, she had explored several scenarios and practiced what she would say to him, but nothing seemed quite right.

There was the betrayal scenario. As soon as she saw him, she could slap him across the face and demand an apology for his actions.

Devora picked up the axe and continued tunneling her way out. It had been some time since Matthias betrayed her and he'd already apologized, so that pitch didn't sit right with her.

Then there was the romantic scenario. As soon as Devora saw Matthias again, she would wrap her arms around him and kiss him until he couldn't breathe.

That scenario always flip-flopped her insides. *Could I ever do something so bold?* She wouldn't know if she didn't try. Her stomach flopped again, and Devora decided to focus on digging rather than on passionately kissing the captain.

Then there was the third scenario, and this was the one that scared her the most. That she would find Matthias again and he would no longer care for her. That everything really was a ruse. That he *was* using her to better his position and as soon as he saw her, he would arrest her like he had before.

Devora hated the thought, but she couldn't shake it from her mind. Matthias betrayed her once. What would stop him from doing it again?

Doubt nagged in her soul for weeks now, and it was draining. But until she knew without a doubt what Matthias was thinking, she couldn't get rid of the feeling.

With her biceps begging for another break, Devora placed the pickaxe on the ground and sat next to it. Rummaging through her pack, she picked out the last few rations Master Monham had supplied. She had been careful in only eating what was necessary. Thankfully, Kanna's captors also needed food and water and left barrels throughout the tunnels filled with different provisions. Though they were almost empty, the water and scraps of food were enough to keep Devora going. It was good she was trying to get out of here. Who knew how much longer she would've lasted if Kanna's escape tunnel kept going?

As she nibbled on a piece of dried beef, Devora wondered about the sudden disappearance of Matthias' mother from the tunnel. It was almost as if Kanna and her captor somehow transported elsewhere. Devora pursed her lips. It was a mystery she had yet to solve, but she was anxious for the answer. Every day she didn't find Kanna was another day King Atol and Queen Leza ruled Tenton without restraint.

With that thought, Devora packed away the last of the rations and stood up once more. She needed to get to Kanna and find out the prophecy she delivered to the king and queen all those years ago. Hopefully, the prophecy would explain why the kingdom ordered all the Seers to be slaughtered.

Rearing back the pickaxe, Devora struck the wall again before a stream of water spurted back in her face. Realization hit her like a boulder as more water sprung from the rock. This was the reason why the tunnel hadn't been completed.

Scooping up the lantern and pickaxe, her mind raced for a solution. She could run back the way she came and hope to outpace the water. But judging by the inch already surrounding her boots, it would catch up to her long before she could find her way back to Yekel.

The water was now at her ankles and Devora's panic intensified. She could try to tunnel out a different way. But, once again, she knew there wasn't enough time.

A small tug pulled at her heart, and Devora immediately shook her head in embarrassment.

"Forgive me, Tunri," she said as the water came to her calves. "I should've asked for Your direction first."

Closing her eyes, Devora prayed for guidance. Sometimes Tunri answered immediately. Sometimes He took His time. As the water quickly approached her knees, Devora prayed Tunri would give her direction as quickly as possible.

An idea then popped into her thoughts. It was so insane, Devora knew it had to be from Tunri.

"I hope you know this is extreme faith," she said aloud.

Praying she'd deciphered Tunri's promptings correctly, Devora swung the pickaxe straight at the crack spurting water. A massive piece of stone splashed into the liquid below, dousing the rest of Devora. Though she was just wishing for a bath, this was not what she had envisioned.

But the prompting came again, and Devora struck the stone a second time. More water drained into the tunnel at rapid speed. It would probably take one more blow before the water filled the tunnel entirely.

Protect me, Devora prayed before taking a breath and swinging her axe for a final time.

The water burst through the stone in a fury, completely overwhelming Devora. Then, almost as if supernatural, the water drained out of the tunnel, whisking Devora away with it.

Though she was thankful she'd taken a large final breath, with her body being tossed to and fro, Devora wasn't sure how much longer she'd last.

Yet, just as her lungs were going to shrivel from the lack of oxygen, a beam of light streamed through the dark, murky water. With newfound hope, Devora kicked and swam as best as she could toward it, praying she would break the surface soon. After five more kicks, she burst through the rippling waves, gasping for air.

"Thank you," she gasped to Tunri as she drifted along the now steady river.

Devora learned that Tunri's plans were usually the opposite of hers and rarely made sense. But she'd also learned that Tunri's plans were never wrong; she just needed to have faith and trust.

Now that Devora was finally out of the dark tunnel, she took in her surroundings, trying to gauge where the water had taken her. One glance around and she realized she was neither in the southern region nor the northern region. There wasn't an overabundance of lush trees with stifling humid heat. And there wasn't an under abundance of trees with a frigid chill.

Paddling with the current, Devora tried to ease her way toward the shore. She was either in the western region or the eastern region.

From her geography lessons, she didn't remember learning about such a large river in the western region, so she was going to assume she was in the east.

Grasping on to a nearby branch, Devora took a few moments to rest before using all the strength she had left to haul herself up on the riverbank. Panting, she lay in the green grass for what seemed like ages, thankful to be alive.

Suddenly, cautious footsteps approached, and it was then Devora realized her violet eyes were fully exposed. Closing them quickly, she rummaged through her pack, trying to find anything to cover her face with. Though soaked through, she still had the extra scarves One Shot bought her at the market in Yekel from Rae.

Sopping wet, just like the rest of her, Devora slapped the scarf over her head. It was difficult to see through, but she could just make out two pairs of small boots. Judging by their size, a pair of children had found her.

Devora breathed a sigh of relief. "Hello," she started before they screamed and ran in the other direction.

"River monster!" one yelled as the other one continued to scream uncontrollably.

Devora lifted the dripping wet scarf from her face, just then noticing the mud and muck covering her from head to toe. No wonder the children ran off screaming. She shook her head as she tried to clean off the mud on her boots in the grass. She would have to think of another way to hide her eyes.

Once she'd fully cleaned herself of all the mud, the twilight light of dusk set upon the river. Sighing, Devora grabbed her pack and scarf and followed the river's edge. It was bound to lead somewhere. And the scarf was now dry enough that if someone approached her, she could cover her eyes. She had yet to come up with an excuse as to why she was hiding her face though. In Yekel, most women wore scarves around or on their heads, so Devora's disguise there was easy. But she was unsure of the customs regarding headwear in the east.

Just as she was around the river bend, a village greeted her vision. Relief filled her wet and weary soul as she trudged toward it. It was bad enough she had to sleep on the hard tunnel floor for the past few weeks. But sleeping outside in a foreign place? Devora probably would've stayed awake until sunrise before she allowed that.

As she quickened her steps, Devora's stomach let out a loud growl. She placed her hand on it. She was more famished than she realized. Glancing at the small buildings ahead, Devora found the will to carry on. Where there were villages, there were places to eat and rest. She knew Nadia had packed several trinkets in her pack. Hopefully, she could use one of them to barter for a hot meal and a warm bed.

Finally close to the village, Devora placed the black scarf on her head just before she approached the first shop.

If anyone asks, I'll say I'm from Yekel, she decided, knowing she could easily explain away the scarf by claiming the Yekelian customs as her own.

But as the village people swept the front of their shops and made their final sales for the day, no one approached Devora at all. She also noticed there were a few others who wore scarves around their heads.

Curious, she thought. Though she was thankful, she was a bit unnerved by the flippant attitudes of the people walking by her.

After passing another store, a hand carved sign caught Devora's attention. *Beatris' Bed and Breakfast* was a humble establishment with its seemingly well-built, yet simple wooden structure, but it looked like Maldove Palace to Devora.

Sending up a quick prayer for guidance to Tunri, she entered the building. With a few men playing cards in one corner, two women chatting near the fireplace, and a couple giggling in the opposite corner, the bed and breakfast wasn't nearly as busy as Devora expected.

She sat down at the nearest table and started searching through her bag for something to barter for a hot meal and room. As she moved aside a set of metal tongs, Devora's fingers grazed a thick leather pouch. Curious, she pulled it out and opened the pleats to find it busting with golden coins. She audibly gasped, causing the women in the corner to eye her suspiciously.

Devora took a few coins out and hid the rest within the sack. *How had Nadia gotten so much coin?*

Before she could dwell on the thought, a plump woman with kind eyes approached her table. She reminded Devora of the Kadeshian woman in Yekel who explained to Devora about the goddess, Pahga. Devora's heart ached, knowing that even though the woman worshipped a god who required human soul sacrifices, she was still kind to a complete stranger.

"Hello there, dearie," the woman said with a smile. If Devora's covered face bothered her, the woman didn't react otherwise. "What can I get ya?"

"Just a hot meal, please, and a room for the night," Devora replied.

She slid three gold coins toward the woman, hoping it would be enough to cover everything.

"I'll only need one of those, dearie," the woman said quietly. "Best to keep the others out of sight."

Devora heeded the warning and swiftly scooped the other gold coins up.

The woman gave her a nod of approval. "I'll be back with your food in a mo'."

Devora wasn't quite sure what the term meant but when the woman was back in less than a few minutes, she was delighted. Steaming chicken smothered in a white cream sauce made Devora's mouth water. Bright orange carrots sat on the side with a plump golden biscuit.

"Thank you," she breathed to the woman and Tunri at the same time.

Living off of only dried meat and fruit for the past few weeks had taken a toll on her stomach and now Devora was ready to make up for lost time. She plowed right into the meal, bringing her fork beneath her scarf to her mouth.

"So," the woman said with a satisfied smile. "Are you traveling for the captain's promotion?"

Devora's thoughts froze, the glorious food turning bitter in her mouth. Forgetting all decorum and etiquette she asked, "Whose promotion?"

With a chuckle, the woman replied. "Why Captain Blake's, the hero of Tenton! He reclaimed Yekel and united Tenton once again! The king and queen are honoring him by promoting him to colonel! He'll be second to General Teague in leading Tenton's troops against Kadesh." The women took a breath, then continued, "The kingdom announced there would be a ceremony in just a week's time. And a magnificent masquerade ball, as well! Who knows, maybe the new colonel will find a special lady there."

The woman fanned herself from all the excitement while Devora sat awestruck. Matthias was being promoted to colonel? Had he given up on finding her already? Was he really looking to find someone special at a ball?

At Devora's silence, the woman added, "I just assumed you were traveling from Yekel." She kindly motioned to Devora's headscarf.

"Oh yes," Devora said quickly. "Yes, I'm most excited for the ceremony."

"Well, I don't want to take up anymore of your time, dearie," the woman said, her cheeks flushed. "Leave your plate when you're done. Your room is ready for you: number five." She gave

Devora a wink and headed off to serve the couple in the corner another round of drinks.

A different feeling, one Devora had never felt before, spread over her heart. It wasn't anger or fury, but it was slippery and if she didn't control it, she knew it would consume her. As she finished her plate and headed to her room, Devora realized, for the first time in her life, she was jealous and would be attending Matthias' promotion and masquerade ball no matter what.

Chapter Twenty-Three

If Ben had to stay cramped in the tiny cellar with Rae forever, he wouldn't mind. His body was on fire as she snuggled against him. It took all his strength to not wrap his arm around her and hold her close. He'd wanted to for ages. So, when Rae finally placed his arms around her herself, Ben didn't argue in the slightest.

He knew he was being bold when asking to kiss her again. But the moment seemed right. Ben was still shocked when Rae agreed and once again, he didn't argue.

But, as the door to the small cellar lifted open, beaming in a bright ray of light, Ben knew all good things, especially for him, always came to an end.

"Well, slap me with feathers and call me a chicken, Mara wasn't lying," Ben's old comrade, Jonathon, laughed as he crouched over the cellar.

Ben squinted up at him, waiting for his eyes to adjust to the light. Jonathon had changed in the few years Ben was at the Fortress. Not only had he lost all his baby fat, but now Jonathon also had a thick brown beard. Ben grinned, remembering how jealous his friend would get when Ben could grow a full beard in a week, while Jonathon barely sprouted a few hairs.

"I see you've finally grown a beard," Ben replied with a grin.

Jonathon laughed, proudly stroking the fine hair on his chin. "I think it's what finally won Mara over."

"I wish he'd shave it off," Mara called from the other room.

Jonathon laughed again. "Well, the coast is clear. I wasn't sure what was going on when I walked in and saw Eustace Stibbs, but Byron and Mara did a great job getting him off your trail. I almost didn't believe it when Mara said you'd come home." His eyes shifted to Rae, still seated on Ben's lap. "And with a friend, no less."

"This is Rae," Ben said as Rae quickly jumped out of Ben's arms. He already missed the feeling of her against him.

"Hi," Rae said with a small smile, her cheeks far pinker than they usually were. "This was the only place we could hide on such short notice."

Jonathon nodded, but something devious twinkled in his eyes. "Nice to meet you, Rae. How about we get you out of there? I know Ben doesn't need my help getting out."

Rae grabbed Jonathon's offered hand and climbed out of the hole. Ben easily hoisted himself up and out of the cellar right after her.

"Have you grown?" Jonathon asked, peering up at Ben. "I could've sworn I was at least to your shoulder."

Ben laughed. He hadn't realized how much he missed his best friend. "No, you've always been short."

Jonathon playfully punched Ben in the shoulder before walking back toward the dining and living area. Ben turned to find Rae and caught her watching him closely.

"What?" he asked, suddenly self-conscious of his actions in the cellar. Was she upset he kissed her?

But Rae smiled softly and grabbed his hand. "I like seeing you happy."

Ben squeezed her hand, knowing she was the core reason he felt so happy lately. He knew he was falling for Rae hard and fast. When they spent time together, the minutes went by too quickly. When they weren't together, he only thought of the next time he'd see her.

Ben knew he should slow down and guard himself. Rae wasn't ready to jump into something serious so fast. But it was too late. His heart committed to this love. Thankfully, he hadn't said anything. And he was glad he hadn't. After Rae's reaction to Mara's wife comment, Ben confessing his love to Rae would scare her away.

"You make me happy," was all he could muster before they joined the others in the living area.

Jonathon sat next to Mara at the table, their fingers intertwined. Ben thought it would be strange to see his best friend with his little sister. But surprisingly, he was okay with it.

"Now, son," Byron said, closing and locking the back door. "Care to tell us what you and your lady friend are doing here?"

Ben rubbed the back of his neck. "It's a long story."

"I made apple muffins earlier today," Mara said, prancing up. "And I'll put on some tea."

"If we stay here much longer, I'm going to gain some serious weight because of your sister's baking," Rae whispered to Ben.

Ben smirked before leading Rae to the table. They sat down just as Mara came out with a tray of muffins and five clay mugs.

Jonathon swiped a muffin off the tray. "Since she found out about the baby, Mara has been testing out new recipes. And I have been fully supporting her."

Mara playfully nudged Jonathon in the shoulder before she set the tea kettle on the woodfire stove in the corner.

Ben watched them closely. It was like night and day. When he'd been arrested, Mara was a shell of a woman. She wouldn't talk, she wouldn't eat. Seeing her so lively—laughing and smiling—brought joy to Ben's heart. He'd only wished he'd been around to help her through the hard times.

"Why don't you start from the beginning," Byron said, before taking a bite of his muffin.

Ben hesitated, then felt Rae squeeze his hand, giving him the confidence he needed. He had been alone for so long; he was glad he wasn't alone any longer.

"I was almost halfway through my sentence at the Fortress when I met a Seer," Ben started.

"What?" Jonathon, Mara, and Byron all exclaimed.

Rae nodded. "It's true, I've met her as well."

"Were you at the Fortress, too?" Mara blurted.

"Mara!" Jonathon exclaimed.

"It's an honest question, Jon!"

Rae laughed and Ben was thankful she handled difficult situations with such ease. "No, I come later in Ben's story."

Mara grinned. "I can't wait."

Heat crept up Ben's neck as he tried to figure out how he could speak about meeting Rae without divulging his heart. Thankfully, Pa cleared his throat, motioning for Ben to continue.

"Yes, Devora," Ben continued and hurried into his explanation about her Seeing power, and the Regulus Protecti tournament. How Devora was victorious but used her win to pardon him. The Battle of Edo came next and then Matthias' betrayal of Devora *and* Ben. How Warden Hazor charged Devora with finding Kanna Blake, the Seer who delivered a life-threatening prophecy to the king and queen. Then he described how they were on the run when they made it to Grenly, how Matthias left a note leading them to Yekel where they met Tristan and entered the Dark Market to find more information about Kanna.

Ben hesitated, knowing the next part of the journey was when he met Rae as the Crimson Cord. Not only did he not want Rae to relive her time as the Crimson Cord, but he also didn't think she'd want three strangers to know about her time in the Temple of Pahga.

Mara, Jonathon, and Byron were on the edge of their seats. No one had touched the muffins, too engrossed in the story to eat anything.

"Then what happened, Ben?" Mara asked, clutching on to Jonathon's arm. "You can't just stop there!"

Rae gave Ben a questioning look then said, "Then Ben met me in the market. I sold different fabrics and scarves. He saved me from a very unfortunate incident. We became good friends after that."

Ben breathed a sigh of relief, thankful for Rae's quick thinking.

Mara gave Ben a suspicious look, knowing there was more to the story, but she let it go.

"Rae hid me and Devora when the Kadeshian troops came looking for us," Ben added on. "When Tenton reclaimed Yekel, Captain Blake gave her and many others the option to start a new future elsewhere."

"We just met him," Mara said cheerfully as she stood to grab the screaming teapot. Carefully, she poured the steaming water into the clay cups. "Not too long ago."

"Yes." Rae nodded. "He's actually why we're here."

Ben scratched his neck, wondering how to explain Lucas', Rae's father, invention. "Matt—er—Captain Blake has a...friend...who made a...device...that can nullify the effects of imperial opal," he awkwardly murmured.

Mara and Byron looked confused, but Jonathon realized why they were actually in Snoken right away.

"I was wondering why he took such an interest in this," Jonathon said as he unhooked the knife from his belt.

Ben stared at the shining blade handle in awe. A metallic sheen glistened over the smooth surface. Other than Matthias' ring and the giant statue of the Goddess Pahga, Ben had never seen the stone close up. There was something mesmerizing about it.

"Have you always had that?"

Jonathon shook his head. "A year after you left, I stumbled on a small cave a few miles east while hunting. Never been there before, and it would be almost impossible to find if I haven't found it by accident, but it was filled with the stuff." Sliding the knife toward Ben, he added, "I didn't realize what it was until the captain told me."

Reaching out, Ben took hold of the knife. A heavy weight suddenly fell on his shoulders, almost as if a sack of flour had been dropped on them. The longer he held on to the knife, the heavier the weight got. His eyelids drooped. Why was he getting so sleepy?

Suddenly, the knife was ripped out of his hand and thrown against the wall.

The weight immediately lifted from Ben's shoulders as he regained his energy.

"What was that?" Rae asked, her eyes wide with fear.

Ben placed his hand on his head. "I-I don't know. I just suddenly felt so tired."

Rae pursed her lips but said nothing. Ben wanted to say more, but by her rigid posture and hard features, he decided to stay quiet.

"I can take you there," Jonathon said, prying his knife from the wall. "If that's what you want."

Ben shifted his gaze to Rae, who wouldn't look at him. What had he done wrong?

"Yes," he said. "We just need enough to test the device and see if it actually works."

Jonathon nodded. "I've heard great stories about Captain Blake. He's done a lot of good for Tenton, so if this is my small way of helping, I'd be happy to."

Mara joined Jonathon as he headed back to their house to gather a few things for the journey while Byron tended to customers at the front of the shop. Ben and Rae were left alone at the table.

Rae still wouldn't look at Ben, which hurt and frustrated him all at the same time. After a few more moments of silence, Ben finally said, "I'm sorry." He wasn't sure what he was sorry for, but he thought it was a good way to start.

Rae folded her arms over her chest. "Why didn't you tell me?"

It was then Ben noticed a trickle of tears rolling down her cheek. Now he was more confused than ever. He always tried to be honest, and it usually helped him, so he would try again. "Tell you what?"

Rae turned her tear-filled eyes on him. "You've been blessed by Tunri! After everything we've been through, I thought you would tell me something as important as that."

Ben's mind went from confusion to completely blank. "I'm what?"

Rae growled at him, and, for a moment, Ben was taken aback. But he then shook his head and replied, "How can someone like me be blessed? I'm not special. I don't have a gift."

"Imperial opal drains the power out of the gifted," Rae explained. "When I touch it without having taken *menta* first, it doesn't affect me at all because I don't have a gift. Though, when under the influence of *menta*, I can feel its drain." She glared straight at Ben. "So, unless you've been taking menta, which I highly doubt, you have a gift."

Ben blinked, trying to keep up. "I really didn't know, Rae. Honest."

The fire in Rae's eyes settled at his honesty. "You really didn't know?" He shook his head and Rae sighed. She ran her hands over her hair and closed her eyes. "I'm sorry for overreacting."

Ben reached out and grabbed her hand. "I would never keep something so important from you, Rae. I would never keep anything from you."

"I know," she whispered, glancing over at him. "I was just hurt, thinking you'd lied to me."

Ben stroked the top of her hand with his thumb. "I wouldn't lie to you. But I would like it if you didn't growl at me again."

Rae wiped the tears off her face and laughed. "Deal."

A gust of wind burst through the back door as Jonathon threw it open with Mara right behind.

Ben and Rae whipped their heads around, seeing the panic written all over Jonathon's face.

"Eustace didn't buy the act. Fortress knights are on their way here. We need to go now."

Chapter Twenty-Four

Ida did her best to keep up with Reese as the pair hurriedly walked down the hall. On their way to the Tower she had stopped by Victoria's room before leaving the girls' dormitories. After Patrick had been taken to the Tower with Hestia, Victoria was a wreck. Ida wanted to make sure her new friend was okay. But much to Ida's surprise, she found out that Victoria had left Vlacklear Academy. Victoria's roommate told Ida after Patrick was sent to the Tower again, his parents decided to pull him out of Vlacklear and do his lessons at home. Victoria apparently decided to do the same. A brief smile descended over Ida's lips as she thought about Victoria and Patrick. Though she hadn't known them long, she prayed Tunri would guide their paths and, hopefully, guide them together.

Reese and Ida whipped around another corner so fast, Ida thought she would lose her footing. After all the tears she and Reese had shed, it was well past dinner. Thankfully, Ida and Reese were able to scrounge up some food before it was all gone. The rest of the students had already poured out of the dining hall and were in their rooms or the library studying. All students except one.

As if knowing they were heading toward the Tower, Sergio leaned against the far wall of the hall. Reese blew past him, not giving the playboy a second glance. But Ida's steps faltered and that was enough for Sergio to approach her. A new fury overtook Ida. It was Sergio's fault all of this happened. If he would've just left Ida alone, she wouldn't have gotten wrapped up in this entire mess. No one would've found out where Hestia and Reese were, and Jacques wouldn't be betrothed to one of her best friends.

"How could you?" Ida asked before he had even said a word, fuming. "You broke our agreement. How could you squeal about Hestia's and Reese's location?"

Instead of being angered, Sergio grinned. "My my, Ida, I didn't know you had a temper. I have to say I like it. Maybe I should anger you more."

He took a step closer, and Ida took a step back, ready to use the wire weapon around her wrist. After the day she'd endured, she wasn't in the mood for Sergio's games.

"Our agreement is void. You broke your word. Leave me alone."

Lifting her chin, Ida marched past him. Reese had already rounded the next corner and Ida wished she would've continued with her friend.

"Ida, wait," Sergio called and grabbed her wrist.

She tried to wrench it away, but he tightened his grasp.

"Let me go." Ida struggled, ready to do anything within her power to subdue him.

"Wait, please," Sergio said gently.

At the change in his tone, Ida stopped squirming. Something different, something soft, gleamed in Sergio's eyes.

Sighing, he bowed his head, his dark hair falling into his eyes. "I just wanted to spend time with you. I didn't know how else to do it."

"So, you blackmailed me with my friends' secret?" Ida questioned in disbelief. She shook her head. "That's not a good enough reason. Unhand me now."

"It's the truth, Ida," Sergio cried, pulling her closer. "The moment I set eyes on you, I couldn't breathe."

Unease danced over Ida's skin, noticing how Sergio still hadn't unhanded her. She needed to think of a way to get out of here and fast. There was something warning her that this interaction could turn bad very soon.

"While I'm flattered," Ida started, trying a kinder approach. "There is somewhere I must be."

Sergio's genteel expression changed from lovesick to fury. "Are you still pining over that Fourth Year prefect? He won't have you, Ida. Everyone knows he's the heir to Delequa Iron. He's not going to want some poor First Year on a scholarship."

Though Ida knew Sergio's words were true, they stung all the same. But it was enough encouragement for her to rip her wrist out of Sergio's grasp and shove him away.

"You're an awful liar," she barked at him, thankful she was too mad to cry. "All that talk that you wanted to be near me was just pretty lies. Leave me alone."

Without looking back, Ida stormed away. When Sergio didn't follow, she breathed a sigh of relief. Her hands were still shaking from the confrontation, but she had successfully stood up for herself without crying. Adrenaline pumped through her veins. The feeling was exhilarating. *Is this how Devora and the others felt all the time?* No wonder Devora could take on giants and Captain Blake.

But as Ida rounded the next corner, all her excitement drained, for standing there waiting for her with Reese was Jacques.

Upon noticing her, the knight quickly straightened from his slouched position against the wall. Though his academy tunic was finely pressed, his hair was a mess and his shoulders drooped like they was carrying a weight larger than they could bear.

Reese awkwardly slid to the other side of the hall and fiddled with her abacus as they stared at one another for a moment, neither knowing what to say until Jacques cleared his throat.

"I wasn't sure you'd come; I was getting worried."

Ida gave a side eye to Reese, who seemed to be too busy studying her father's signet ring to notice. "I was highly encouraged to come."

Jacques gave a quick smile before it fell. "I would like to explain—"

"Should we head to the Tower first?" Ida asked, quickly walking past him. Though she had agreed to see him, her heart was already aching at the sight of him. "I don't want Hestia locked up any longer than she needs to be."

Ida clasped her hands in front of herself as Reese understood and led the way toward the Tower.

Ida's heart cracked as she realized she would never be able to wrap her arms around Jacques. Or fix his messy hair. Or kiss his lovely lips. Those luxuries were all going to go to Hestia, and Ida couldn't bear the thought of it.

Jacques didn't argue with her as she and Reese strode quickly down the back hall toward the doorway leading to the Tower. Just as Reese said earlier, a solitary guard stood outside it.

Ida remembered Victoria's terrible stories on what happened to students in the Tower. She was thankful she'd scored high enough on assignments so that she wouldn't be sent there. Until now.

A shiver ran over Ida's skin, and she did her best to be brave. She didn't want to admit it, but she was thankful she didn't have to venture into the Tower alone.

"Unless you've been sent here by the headmistress, go back to your dormitories," the guard said without sparing them a glance.

A bored look crossed over his face as he reached up and scratched his thick black mustache.

Reese casually placed the signet ring in her hand behind her back, where Jacques easily picked it up.

"Good evening, sir," Jacques said with an easy smile. "I am Prefect Jacques and a Fourth Year here at the academy. We were sent by one of the headmistress' friends, Duke Sandje of Sandje Textiles."

Jacques nudged Ida, who stood like a statue staring at the guard, trying to think of something to say. Instead, she nodded in agreement, while Reese stood regal and reposed.

"To convince you of our friendship with the duke, he has given me his ring," Jacques continued without pause. He held Duke Sandje's ring out on his palm for the guard to assess.

Ida stood awestruck at how easily Jacques could speak to anyone. He was formal yet kind. Convincing but not overpowering.

The guard took the ring in his hand and studied it. With a shrug, he gave it back to Jacques. "I don't know what the duke would want in here, but it's not my job to ask questions." He stepped aside and opened the door.

The eerie creak of the rusted hinges sent Ida's nerves on edge, but she resisted the urge to grasp on to Jacques' arm.

"Thank you, sir," Jacques said with a salute. "We appreciate your work here." "Nobody else does," the guard muttered under his breath as Jacques nodded at Ida and Reese before the trio headed toward the staircase.

With a small smile at the guard, Ida hurried behind Jacques and in front of Reese. A spiral of stone steps twirled upwards, farther than Ida could see. *Is there only one room in the Tower? Or are there many?*

"Great job, Sir Jacques," Reese whispered. She held out her hand and Jacques placed the ring in her palm.

"Hestia will be up the stairs," Jacques said. He rifled through his pocket then pulled out an iron key. "I was able to procure this as well. The duke's ring could only get us *in* but not *out.*"

Ida looked at the key, wondering where Jacques had retrieved it.

"Excellent thinking, Sir Jacques." Reese took the key and headed up the stairs.

Ida started to follow when Jacques grabbed her hand.

"Not that way," he whispered, gently pulling her back toward him. "Come on."

Confused, Ida allowed Jacques to lead her in the other direction of the Tower. Apparently, there were not only stairs spiraling up, but rotating down, as well.

"I didn't think there was a lower level to the Tower," Ida said as Jacques grabbed a lantern from the wall and started to descend the steps. Ida noticed that he hadn't let go of her hand. And since she couldn't find the strength to release her own hand from his, she didn't bring it up.

"It's not one many know about, but I remember Matthias talking about it one time."

"Who's Matthias?"

Jacques paused, embarrassment flushing his cheeks. "Guess I can't back out now. I promised no secrets." He smiled at her then explained, "Matthias is Captain Blake's first name. He was a student at Vlacklear before he gave up his position to help his younger brother."

Ida blinked in surprise. "Captain Blake attended Vlacklear? But he's so scary and angry. Perfect for the military."

Jacques chuckled. "It's amazing how many times I've heard that. But yes, it's true."

"So, he was sent to the Tower while he was here?"

Jacques shrugged his shoulders. "That, I'm not quite sure about, but when he was searching for his mother, he stumbled upon an old map of Vlacklear Academy. It sketched out the top room of the Tower, where misbehaving or low-scoring students are now sent. But it also had a sketch of the lower part of the Tower."

Ida kept her eyes on Jacques as he walked and explained the story, intrigued about the knight's and the captain's friendship.

"So," Jacques continued. "If I were a secret book that no one wanted to find, I would hide in a place that hardly anyone knew about, right?" He glanced back at Ida and gave her a wink, sending her insides twisting in knots. "At least, that's the conclusion I believe Reese came to as well."

At the mention of Reese, the thick tension from before returned, and Ida was suddenly very aware of Jacques' warm, strong hand holding hers. Delicately, she released her hand from his grasp. She shouldn't be holding the hand of a man betrothed to another.

But once she released his hand, Jacques stopped. Due to him being a few steps below her, his face was right in line with hers when he spun around. A turmoil of emotions swirled in his eyes until finally he blurted, "I don't love Hestia *or* Reese for that matter."

Ida's brows rose and she blinked at the comment, unsure of how to respond.

Jacques shook his head. "No, that didn't come out right."

"So, you do love one of them?" Ida asked.

"No, absolutely not," Jacques replied making a face. Ida couldn't help but laugh. "They are wonderful women and good friends, but that's it," he added.

Ida decided if she was going to be bold, it was now or never. "Why are you marrying Hestia then?"

"I don't want to, Ida," he said quietly. "I have to."

"I see," Ida replied, keeping her tears at bay.

She knew she wasn't of noble birth and didn't understand all it encompassed. She just wished Jacques would be honest and tell her the real reason for the marriage instead of dancing around it: someone like her wasn't good enough for someone like him.

Giving him a nod, Ida tried to walk past him so she could get to the lower part of the Tower without him, when Jacques raced ahead of her, blocking her path.

"Please let me pass," she said quietly, not able to look into his eyes. She knew if she saw his kind hazel eyes pleading with her to understand, she would. And she would never forgive herself.

"Ida, please," Jacques pleaded, desperation in his voice.

It was odd that Ida had just heard the same phrase from Sergio a few moments earlier. When had she gained suitors begging her to understand? Why couldn't everyone be truthful? Why couldn't they just tell her to her face what they really thought of her instead of hoping she'd understand?

Furrowing her brows, Ida lifted her chin. "No."

Jacques quirked a brow. "No, what?"

Folding her arms over her chest, Ida replied, "No, I don't want to understand. I don't want to sit by and say nothing. I don't want to be 'quiet and cooperative Ida who never makes a fuss.' I've done that my entire life."

She wanted to stop the words coming out of her mouth. She was baring too much of her heart, too much of her soul, to Jacques. If she didn't stop now, it would be too late.

But she didn't stop.

With tears freely flowing down her cheeks, Ida continued, "I finally found someone I love spending time with and want nothing more than to spend *more* time together. But just like last time, he's been taken away. Why can't *I* be the winner for once? Why can't *I* have my heart's desire? Is it because I'm poor? Is it because I'm quiet? I don't understand why things never work out for me. Every time I get something good in my life, it's taken away and I'm tired of it."

Her cries turned to sobs, and she buried her face in her hands. She never thought she would declare her feelings for Jacques, much less in a dark gloomy secret stairwell of Vlacklear Academy.

But it was out there and there was nothing she could do about it now.

Yet when she felt Jacques' arms come around her, her sobs quieted down. In that moment, she didn't care if he was betrothed to someone he didn't love. She just wanted to stay there, together, for as long as they could.

He didn't answer any of her questions and Ida wasn't sure if she wanted him to. After a moment, Jacques pulled away enough to cradle Ida's head in his hands.

His beautiful hazel eyes searched hers. "How can a collection of scattered moments feel like an eternity?" Reaching down he brushed his lips against her cheek.

Ida's eyes fluttered closed at the gentle kiss wanting—hoping—for more.

Jacques continued; his voice low. "It must be that time ceases when I'm with you. I never want our moments to end."

Before Ida could register the words, Jacques' lips were on hers. She melted into the kiss like wax to a flame. Wrapping her arms around his neck, she brought him closer, wanting to savor the kiss.

Jacques pulled her closer still, his arms around her waist, holding her tightly. He kissed her again and again and Ida didn't want it to end. They stood in each other's embrace for what seemed like mere moments until Ida remembered why they were there.

Regretfully, she pulled away from Jacques, knowing that was their first and last kiss. She should feel ashamed for kissing a man promised to another. But she didn't. Somewhere in her heart, she knew kissing Jacques was the right thing to do and she would lock the cherished memory away forever.

"Ida," Jacques whispered, placing his forehead against hers. "I'm so sorry."

She didn't want him to continue, but she had to ask, "Why?"

Jacques swallowed. "My father is dying. This is his last wish."

And suddenly Ida understood Jacques' turmoil. She wanted to fight against his decision, to stomp her foot like a child and say it wasn't fair. Because it wasn't. But that was never her way. And as she held the man she loved for the first and last time, she knew she couldn't stop fate.

Reaching up, she ran her fingers through Jacques sandy-blond waves. Just once, she wanted to feel them before she forced herself to stay away from him and accept his choice. Jacques leaned into her hand as she gently caressed his cheek. Ida pulled her hand back, knowing she had to stop, or her heart would break even further.

"We should continue with our mission," she whispered before striding past him.

This time, Jacques let her go.

The stairwell fell silent save for their boots shuffling along the stone steps. Ida stifled the rest of her tears, knowing she would cry herself to sleep again that night.

Finally, the stairwell opened into a small space. Ida was surprised to find it fairly tidy for a hidden room at the base of the tower. On one side of the room stood a few filled sacks and a stool.

Maybe this used to be a storage area of some kind, Ida thought.

But as she turned to the other side of the room, she saw stacks of wooden boxes heaped upon one another. Some were broken in half, others had a few slats missing, but all contained bundles of parchments.

Excitement invigorated Ida's depressed spirit as she rushed to the boxes. Inside lay a plethora of scrolls and manuscripts, all in different languages. Anticipation consumed her thoughts with the new information pouring in from parchments. As she dug through the pile, her fingers grazed upon a stack of papers bound together.

Hesitantly, she pulled it out. Her eyes grew wide as she prayed to Tunri and the text translated into the same script as the restricted texts. Excitement pumped through her veins, assuming she'd found the Book of Ages. But as she made it to the last page, she read a note in different, elegant handwriting. It wasn't in a foreign tongue, but Tentonian.

To whoever is reading this page, the Book of Ages is gone, and you will never find it.

Chapter Twenty-Five

It was extremely difficult to wake up for class the next day. Not only had Ida stayed up too late *not* finding the Book of Ages, but she also kept replaying Jacques' kiss in her mind until she was a puddle of tears.

On her way to breakfast, Ida stopped by Reese's and Hestia's room to make sure Hestia was okay. Poor Hestia was exhausted from the Assembly and her night in the Tower and was fast asleep. Reese quietly closed the door to her room as she stepped out into the barren hall.

"So did you find it?" she asked in a hushed tone.

Ida shook her head. Another disappointment to add to her many disappointments.

Reese frowned and tapped her fingers. "I'll keep thinking, Ida." She reached out and squeezed Ida's hand.

Ida was thankful for the small comfort. After Jacques' betrothal and not finding the Book of Ages, Ida was glad at least her friends were safe.

As Ida floated through the hall, she tried to focus on something other than Jacques but couldn't. Though they shared their desires in private, public knowledge was all that mattered. And news of Jacques' betrothal to Hestia was everywhere. The gossip vines claimed the betrothal would be officially announced at Captain Blake's promotion celebration ball at the end of the week.

The students buzzed with the news of a masquerade ball hosted by Queen Leza at Maldove Palace. Ida overheard the chatter in the breakfast line before she'd seen the notice posted on Vlacklear's main board for schoolwide announcements. Ida thought it was quite generous of the queen to invite the entire school but did think it was odd that the invitation was signed by Queen Leza alone. Though Ida hadn't been raised in aristocratic society, she would've thought King Atol would be the one to share the news about Captain Blake. But as Ida strode through the halls, eavesdropping on others, no one else seemed to notice or care that the invitation was only from the queen.

Ida missed Victoria and Patrick as she sat alone in the dining hall. When she finished the last of her breakfast, Ida sent a prayer of safety for them to Tunri then headed to her first class. Hestia and Reese decided to stay in their rooms and complete their assignments there until the betrothal news died down.

As she clutched her books to her chest, Ida readied herself to see Jacques. She didn't know how he'd react to her after what happened between them in the Tower, and she also didn't trust herself to react indifferently.

Please help me, Ida prayed to Tunri.

But as she entered the classroom, she was surprised to find Jacques wasn't there. As a Fourth Year and recent aide to Professor Trudoe, Jacques was usually the first one in the room, ready to take attendance or writing that week's quiz questions on the board.

But Prefect Eric had returned, and Jacques was nowhere to be found.

Unfortunately, Sergio was in class and as soon as Ida sat down, he sidled next to her.

What does this man not understand about no? Ida thought, annoyance creeping from her thoughts onto her face.

"I think we started off on the wrong foot," Sergio started, leaning his temple on his palm.

He gave Ida a dashing smile that she had to admit was hand-some. But the fact that Sergio never listened to her made him the most undesirable man in the world.

"Are you talking about how you blackmailed my friends or about all the other times you've bothered me?" She smiled sweetly back at him. After everything that happened in the past few days, she was in no mood to deal with Sergio.

But once again, her salty words had the opposite effect on him, and he scooted closer.

"My prosperous Ida, you never cease to amaze me. Here I thought you would be in tears over the betrothal of that prefect to one of your dear friends. But you're just as strong as ever."

The statement took Ida by surprise. No one had ever equated her to being strong. She was always kind and quiet Ida. Ida hated to admit it, but she enjoyed the compliment, even if it was from Sergio.

"Listen," Sergio continued, lowering his voice as more stu-dents filed in. "I just wanted to apologize for the idiot I've been, and I'd like to make it up to you. No strings attached."

Ida gave him a skeptical glare to which he lifted his hands innocently in response.

"Cross my heart," Sergio said with another winning smile as he traced an X over his chest.

Ida closed her eyes and sighed. Maybe, if she just appeased him one more time, he would leave her be. Hopefully, she would be able to read over the restricted texts soon and get another lead on where the Book of Ages could be. Then she could get away from Vlacklear for good. No more terrors of the Tower, no more Sergio, and no more Jacques.

Opening her eyes, she found Sergio studying her face. It was the first time she hadn't seen him trying to look mischievous and, for once, she thought he was handsome.

"Okay," she replied, earning that devilish grin of his again. "I'm listening."

Reaching out, he grabbed her hand. Ida immediately wanted to pull it away, remembering his actions in the hallway a few days ago. But Sergio's grip wasn't firm and commanding. It was soft and gentle. Ida wasn't sure why—maybe it was all the heartbreak she suffered lately—but she enjoyed the delicate touch.

"Ida," Sergio whispered, leaning in so only she could hear. "Will you do me the honor of attending the masquerade ball with me?"

Ida's eyes widened in surprise, and she jerked back. "What?"

Sergio tilted his head to the side. "You heard me."

Ida studied him. There had to be a catch. She knew Sergio flirted with her only to torment her. He knew she hated his attention and that's why he did it more. But this time he actually seemed genuine.

Ida wished she had the confidence to accept his invitation, but instead she asked, "But why me? What about Reese? Shouldn't you go with your bethrothed?"

Something flickered in Sergio's green eyes. Was it sympathy? Or pity? Ida couldn't tell. But he simply replied, "It is you I wish to go with." He paused before adding, "Your friend has called off our betrothal and I am at a loss of what to do now."

Ida felt her cheeks grow warm at his boldness then felt a zing of shame. Were her feelings for Jacques so fickle that she could be easily swayed by a few flattering words?

Then again, Jacques was marrying someone else and apparently, Sergio was not. Couldn't she try to have some fun and find happiness too? Plus, she had always wanted to go to a ball. Even if she didn't care for Sergio, it would be fun to attend the masquerade.

All her emotions were a swirling storm in her chest, waiting to burst forth. But finally, she made a decision.

"I have nothing to wear," she admitted, and Sergio's grin grew wide.

Ida wasn't sure why he was so genuinely happy to go with her. She'd wanted to go to the masquerade but wasn't sure if she would be able to keep it together when Jacques' and Hestia's engagement was announced. But maybe with someone as handsome as Sergio on her arm, the pain would hurt a little less.

Sergio gently lifted her hand and kissed the top. "Not to worry, my dear. I will take care of everything."

Shocked, Ida didn't lower her hand until Professor Trudoe came into the room, and Sergio returned to his seat.

The lecture flew by, and Ida couldn't remember a word of it. Her thoughts were completely consumed with Sergio's sudden change of character and if it were really all a ruse. But still, the small seed of hope that maybe everything would turn out in the end started to bloom in her heart. This wasn't what she'd pictured when she came to Vlacklear Academy. But her life had never turned out the way she thought.

The rest of her classes spun by just as fast as the first and Ida found herself in her final class of the day, Horticulture.

"The end of the term is right around the corner," Professor Mal explained. "I know you all have been working hard on your final projects, but now is when you really need to focus and make your plants shine."

Ida smiled at Professor Mal's confidence in them. She seemed like the only professor who cared about her students. Professor Trudoe of FLAB came to class late, taught his lesson, and left as soon as it was over. It was much the same with Ida's other professors.

Are the professors punished if one of their students is sent to the Tower?

Ida had never thought about that. Maybe that's why the professors tried to keep their distance from the students. Either way, Ida was thankful for Professor Mal's kindness.

Ida sprinkled additional fertilizer on her lily, which, to her excitement had miraculously grown and was almost blooming. Tunri Himself had to have grown the flower, for the last time Ida saw it the desert lily was only a sprout. As Ida smiled at the bright white petals beginning to open, Professor Mal's shuffled footsteps approached.

"I never thought I'd see the day where a desert lily bloomed in the northern region," the elderly woman said with a laugh. "But you've surprised me Ida and I'm glad for it."

Ida smiled at the beautiful white lily just opening its petals. It would hopefully be fully bloomed by the end of the term, after the masquerade ball.

"Thank you, professor," Ida replied. "But it was really under your tutelage that I was able to learn how to care for such a delicate flower." *And with Tunri's hand*, she wanted to add.

Professor Mal stepped up and examined the lily. "Though a lily is beautiful, it is not delicate. You've taught me that. It's strong and able to withstand even the harshest of winters but still stay just as beautiful, inside and out."

Ida couldn't help thinking that Professor Mal was speaking of something more. The professor had caught her and Jacques in here before. There was no doubt in Ida's mind that she had also heard the news of his betrothal to Hestia.

"Professor, what if a lily doesn't want to withstand the winter. What if it doesn't want to stand tall and just wants to wilt?"

Ida couldn't bear the thought of watching Jacques marry one of her best friends. All she wanted to do was find the Book of Ages and return to the Fortress. After she completed her five years in His Majesty's Army, she would return to Lower Grenly and live a happy and simple life with Ama and Jil.

"A flower cannot determine where its seed lands," the professor replied. "It must learn to bloom where it's planted."

Professor Mal gave Ida an encouraging smile before she continued to the next student.

Snipping a few dying leaves off her lily, Ida sighed, knowing she would have to endure the gossiping halls of Vlacklear for just a bit longer.

The next few days soared by as the students in the academy prepared for the masquerade ball. Ida had yet to see Jacques since their parting in the Tower. She'd dreamt of their kiss every night since.

Even though she was attending the masquerade ball with Sergio, her heart still loved and wanted Jacques. Ida ran her hand along her slicked back bun and adjusted her uniform in the mirror. But maybe spending time with someone else would help her not think about Jacques so much.

Gathering her books, Ida left her room and headed toward Hestia's and Reese's room in the middle of the hall. It had also been almost a week since she'd seen them as well. Ida knew she should've spoken to them before today—the day before the ball—but she couldn't bring herself to face Hestia again. Guilt wrought Ida's chest. After Hestia had been put on trial and taken to the Tower, Ida should have pushed past her selfish feelings and cared for her friend.

But Reese had sought Ida out and told her they wanted Ida to see their dresses for the masquerade ball, so Ida obliged.

When she arrived at their room, Ida took a breath, said a prayer for strength, and knocked on the door.

Ida didn't know what to expect when the door opened, but being pulled inside by a swath of fabric was not it.

The rich emerald green wrapped beautifully around Hestia's slender form, hugging her in all the right ways. Ida always thought the twins were beautiful, but Hestia was breathtaking,

Jacques would love her in this, Ida thought before she could stop herself.

Jealousy and pain stabbed her heart, but Ida pushed it away with a smile. Jacques was not hers to own.

"You look amazing," Ida said with a smile. And she meant it.

"Ida!" Hestia cried, stumbling down from the pedestal she was on.

"There are pins, Lady Sandje!" the seamstress squealed through the multiple pins held by her teeth.

But Hestia didn't care. She waddled over to Ida and squeezed her in a tight hug.

"Ouch!" Hestia cried, pulling away and examining the inside of her arm.

"She told you there were pins," Reese snorted from the corner.

Hestia stuck out her tongue and Reese laughed.

"We're so glad you're here," Hestia said with a big smile. It then turned into a frown. "And you've got some explaining to do. What's this that you're going to the masquerade with Sergio Amata?"

If Hestia could've shouted any louder, Ida's eardrums would've ruptured.

"Hestia, please," Reese said. "I'm sure Ida has her reasons."

"Are you going with anyone?" Ida asked Reese, hoping to stave off Hestia's probing a little longer.

Reese shook her head, flicking a single abacus bead to the left. "No, I'm not going at all. I have other plans."

Ida furrowed her brow, about to ask more when Hestia grabbed Ida's shoulders. "Sergio is a playboy. Why are you going with him? You should be going with Jacques."

"Hestia," Ida said, feeling tears in her eyes. "You know I can't go with Jacques. He's betrothed to you. He explained everything to me, and I understand his reasoning." Ida needed to change the subject, or she would fall apart right now. "How are you doing since the Assembly and the Tower?"

"Ida," Hestia said, ignoring Ida's question. "Not everything is set in stone. There's still time."

Ida shook her head as she backed away toward the door. "I wish you both so much happiness. I must go."

And before either of the twins could stop her, Ida raced out of the room. Fresh tears rolled down her cheeks. Some lily she was. She couldn't survive this harsh winter Tunri had sent her. All she wanted was to wilt away from everything. To hide in the background like she always had.

Ida needed to get away. Just for a moment. The academy, classes, the Book of Ages, Jacques, Sergio, the masquerade, it was all too much. If Ida didn't compose herself now, she was going to break down.

Turning around the next corner, Ida hurried toward the greenhouse knowing it was the one place she could find solace. But as she wiped the tears from her eyes, not focusing on where she was going, she bumped right into someone.

"Oh, I'm sorry," she managed to say before she looked up into the concerned gaze of Sergio.

Chapter Twenty-Six

Jacques stayed away from people as best as he could. But still, every time he turned a corner or fled to an obscure place, someone was there, asking questions about his betrothal to Hestia.

He finally had enough and barked at a poor Second Year. Jacques ran his hands over his face as he slumped in a chair at the back of the library. He wasn't usually prone to anger so quickly. Matthias flew off the handle quicker than he did, so Jacques had grown accustomed to being the "calm, cool, and collected" one of the pair.

But after his past resurfaced, Jacques felt like his life was spiraling out of control.

When Warden Hazor first assigned him to attend Vlacklear Academy, Jacques was confused. The warden had previously given him time off from the Fortress to attend classes and be a real student and blend in. It wasn't until Warden Hazor approached him about keeping an eye on Ida that Jacques was ecstatic. He'd wanted to learn more about the beautiful girl with sorrow tinging her eyes. This was the chance he was waiting for. And everything was going well too. He was able to get to know her better under the guise of tutoring. He so looked forward to their evenings together. And then that worm, Sergio, let everything go to ruins. Jacques didn't know how the annoying

Third Year had gotten word to Duke Sandje about his daughters' whereabouts so quickly, but he had. And as soon as Duke Sandje knew where the twins were, he found out Jacques was here too; thus, notifying Jacques' father, Lord Delequa.

Jacques ran a hand through his hair, wondering how everything had unraveled so quickly. Once mother and Helene died and Raphael deserted, Emanuel Delequa paid no mind to his second son. Fortunately, Charles did come to stay at Delequa manor after Uncle Francois and Aunt Clair passed. But Charles was three summers younger than Jacques so finding a companion in him was difficult at times. Though Jacques still tried to befriend the young boy just the same.

Jacques couldn't understand how Charles had come to the Fortress without him knowing. Jacques was even in charge of the new recruits. He rubbed his eyes, frustrated. Unless Charles didn't want to be found. The Fortress was huge. A soldier could very easily stay hidden in plain sight if they didn't want to be seen or heard.

Sighing, Jacques slumped back in the chair and closed his eyes. So, he had failed as a son to his father, failed as an older cousin to Charles, and he had failed as a friend to Ida.

Jacques found himself frowning at the last thought. They weren't friends any longer. Not after that incredible kiss in the Tower. But, because of this ridiculous betrothal, he was stuck as only being Ida's friend. How could he bear not being able to hold or kiss her again?

Grunting, Jacques stood and stared out the frosty window. Maybe coming to the library to try to think through everything wasn't the best decision. Instead of clarity, he was just getting more and more angry.

"This is a fine mess you've made," Warden Hazor's stern voice said.

Jacques almost jumped out the window in fright but was proud he managed to keep his face calm as he faced the warden.

"Apologies, sir," Jacques replied, thankful he had chosen to be in the back of the library where no one else was. "Permission to speak, sir."

Warden Hazor strode next to Jacques and peered out the frosty glass. "Granted."

"What are you doing here, sir? Everyone knows who you are. Our mission will be compromised."

Warden Hazor stroked his white mustache. "And you think your engagement hasn't found us out already?"

Blood drained from Jacques' face, suddenly realizing his stupidity at goading Sergio and how the consequences had not just affected him but Ida and the twins as well.

"I apologize, sir," Jacques replied, molding back into the perfect soldier he always was. "I wasn't thinking."

"No, Jacques," the warden replied. "You weren't. Your mission was to assist Ida in finding the prophecy. Have you found it?"

Jacques refrained from lashing out at the warden, trying to find the calm he always had at the Fortress. "One of the books Captain Blake had speaks of the prophecy. It's said to be in a book called the Book of Ages."

The warden's eyes lit with interest. "And?"

Jacques prepared himself for punishment. "We have yet to locate the Book of Ages, sir."

Warden Hazor clasped his hands behind his back and faced the window once again. "So, while you're off getting betrothed to one of the Sandje twins, Ida has been trying to find the book on her own? Why did I send you here then?"

"The betrothal was something I didn't foresee, sir," Jacques tried to explain, doing his best to keep his temper in check. "I thought when I left home, my father would nullify it. The agreement was only discussed between mine and the twins' family when we were children, but nothing was ever solidified."

But Warden Hazor didn't seem to be listening.

"You are one of my most trusted soldiers, Jacques. That's why I sent you here, especially to protect Ida. I'm disappointed."

His words were a dagger in Jacques' gut. Though Warden Hazor was hardly kind, he had always rewarded obedient behavior, something at which Jacques excelled. But what snagged Jacques' thoughts was the warden's concern for Ida. He had paid the girl no mind when she was at the Fortress. But as soon as Lady Devora and Matthias were sent to battle, it was like a new person took over the warden's body.

Jacques then remembered Ida's defense of the warden and before he could stop himself, he asked, "Sir, did you know Ida before she came to the Fortress?"

Warden Hazor's gaze cut to Jacques. Jacques wasn't sure what he thought was going to happen, but the warden revealing the truth was not it.

"I was part of the battalion that invaded Renta, the capital of Kadesh, years ago. It was also where Ida grew up. Many fled when they saw us coming, but after the destruction, she was the only survivor."

Jacques' lips parted in shock. "Ida is Kadeshian?" As if Jacques life wasn't already complicated enough.

Warden Hazor looked at Jacques like he was a fool. "Of course she's Kadeshian. I saved her against my commander's wishes and brought her to Tenton. I knew there was something special about her. On our journey back from Kadesh, I found her sifting through pieces of parchments I collected from various cities and villages, all different dialects. She was able to read them all without hesitation." The warden sighed. "I knew if her gift and her heritage were discovered, she would be killed, and I couldn't allow that to happen."

Jacques blinked, trying to control the thoughts swirling through his head. "But you wanted to kill Lady Devora."

Warden Hazor frowned at Jacques. "If I wanted Devora Medee dead, she'd be dead."

Jacques shivered at the comment before he asked, "So, you sent Ida to live in Lower Grenly. But why didn't you take notice of her when she came to the Fortress?"

"I knew life in Lower Grenly was hard, but the couple she stayed with were kind. I also learned of her adopted father's death and that life had gotten harder. I didn't want to add anything else to her already difficult life."

"She remembers," Jacques said plainly, finding himself angered for Ida. "And she defended you. You need to speak with her."

"You don't give orders, soldier," Warden Hazor growled back. "Even before this conversation, I'd already decided: you're off this mission. You're to report back to the Fortress tomorrow evening to get your affairs—or betrothal—in order." The warden turned and started walking away.

Jacques' jaw went slack. "What?" He ran to catch up. "You can't take me off the mission. What about Ida?"

If Jacques left now, how would he see her again? She had to know how he felt. He had to find a way to convince Warden Hazor to give him more time to find the Book of Ages, more time to try to break his betrothal and more time to spend with Ida.

"Ida has obviously done fine without you since no one has found out she's a Translator or a Kadeshian whereas all your secrets are out in the open," the warden snapped back.

Jacques knew he shouldn't press the warden further. He'd witness soldiers being flogged for saying less than he already had. But he wouldn't leave Ida.

"Give me until after Captain Blake's promotion. Please, sir." Jacques bowed his head, praying for the warden to grant his request.

Silence weighed like an anchor between them until Warden Hazor replied, "You have until after the masquerade. I need you at Blake's promotion the next day. Something's not right about it."

Joy radiated throughout Jacques' body. Crossing his fist over his chest, he bowed. "Thank you, sir. I won't disappoint you again."

"You better not, Jacques. Or it will be your head. We can't afford another mishap." Before retreating from the library, the warden sent a glare at Jacques that could scare even the bravest of men.

But Jacques took the glare with ease, overjoyed to see Ida and to have another chance to find the book—and a way to stop his marriage to Hestia—before tomorrow night.

Forgetting everything else, Jacques ran out of the library to find Ida. He raced down the halls, ignoring the confused stares thrown his way. As he searched for Ida in her usual places, he realized the fact that she was Kadeshian didn't even bother him. Yes, he was initially shocked, but to him, she was still Ida. His wonderful, beautiful, kind Ida. He didn't care where she came from, only that she would wait for him until he could be with her.

After he searched the greenhouse and another study area without finding Ida, Jacques slowed his quick pace. Vlacklear was big but not as big as the Fortress. He should've found her by now. But as he turned the next corner, he heard a familiar voice.

"What can I do to help, my dear?" Sergio asked softly, and Jacques found himself rolling his eyes.

The Third Year was probably trying to seduce another girl with flattery until they bent to his will. Then he disposed of them. Jacques had heard all about it in the male dormitories and didn't wish to hear anymore.

"It's nothing, I'm fine," Ida replied, and Jacques did everything in his power to run to her aid as fast as possible.

Sergio always liked to force females to rely on him and create a false sense of security, but Jacques wouldn't allow it to happen to Ida.

But before he could utter a word, his feet stopped cold. Ida wasn't pulling away from Sergio. In fact, it was the opposite. She was embracing him.

"It seems we have an audience, my dear," Sergio whispered loudly against Ida's soft skin.

Skin that Jacques had kissed and caressed not a week ago. Jacques' blood boiled beneath his own skin as he watched Sergio wipe a tear from Ida's face as she pulled away. The Third Year was goading Jacques, and it was working.

"Jacques," Ida said with surprise. "What are you doing here?"

She took a step away from Sergio and it made Jacques insanely glad. "I was actually looking for you, Ida. There was something I needed to discuss with you about your tutoring sessions."

Jacques knew Ida would understand his code and hoped she would get rid of Sergio before Jacques threw him out the window.

"Ida, do you really still need his help? I can't imagine someone as smart as you to need so much assistance."

Jacques watched Ida smile at the compliment and forced every muscle in his body not to punch Sergio square in the jaw. Pretty words covered a multitude of lies. Of course, Ida was smart, but Jacques knew Sergio didn't want Jacques and Ida spending any more time together.

"Sergio is right, Jacques," Ida said quietly to Jacques' disbelief. "Plus, you'll be busy with your wedding plans. I'm sure I can figure my studies out on my own from now on."

Jacques couldn't believe what he'd heard. First, Warden Hazor, now Ida? He'd been nothing but a loyal soldier to one and loyal friend to the other and after one mishap he's cast aside.

"You also have me if you need assistance," Sergio said, tapping Ida on the nose.

Jacques gritted his teeth. If he didn't get Ida alone soon, he was going to lose everything he worked for by murdering Sergio right then and there.

"Ida," Jacques said through clenched teeth. "Please allow me to discuss one final thing with you."

Ida eyed Jacques suspiciously then nodded. "Okay." She turned to Sergio. "I'll see you tomorrow."

Sergio grabbed Ida's hand and lifted it to his lips. Jacques knew the Third Year gained great pleasure in angering him.

"I'll see you then, my prosperous Ida."

As Sergio passed Jacques, he gave him a wink and continued.

Once Sergio was out of earshot, Jacques couldn't contain himself any longer.

"Out of everyone you could've chosen, you chose him?"

Hurt flashed across Ida's face before it morphed into an emotion Jacques had never seen Ida wear. "What did you need to discuss?" Her voice was cold and hollow.

Jacques ran his hands through his hair. "Warden Hazor is taking me off the mission because of the betrothal. I have until tomorrow night. Please, Ida. I don't want to leave. If we can find the book together, I can stay here. With you." He reached out to her, but she evaded his grasp.

"Maybe Warden Hazor is right," she said softly, averting her gaze. "Maybe it's better if I continue the mission alone. I'm sorry, Jacques." Ida gave him one last look before walking away.

Jacques found his world crumbling around him. The future he'd once dreamed of was slipping from his grasp and there was nothing he could do about it.

Chapter Twenty-Seven

Rae, Snoken, Ballear

Rae pushed her legs to try to keep up with Ben's long steps. Outrunning soldiers was something she'd done before but never across such distances. Jonathon gave Ben directions and a quick sketch of where he found the cave with imperial opal. He would go the opposite way to try to steer the soldiers in the wrong direction. Jonathon also suggested Ben and Rae go on foot rather than horseback, that way they could hide among the scattered trees. But as Rae's lungs squeezed, she wished she would've had a horse just to keep up with Ben.

"Rae, come on," Ben said over his shoulder. "We're almost there."

"I'm trying," she huffed. "If you haven't noticed, my legs are significantly shorter than yours."

And I haven't been training like I usually did as the Crimson Cord.

Ben stopped short and spun around. Before Rae could react, he took three steps forward, scooped her over his shoulder and ran.

Rae bounced up and down on Ben's shoulder, trying not to hit his crossbow attached to his back. She wasn't sure she liked being slung over his back like a sack of potatoes. But they were moving a lot quicker than before.

Shouting echoed in the distance and Ben picked up more speed than Rae ever thought possible for a mortal man. Keeping her head down, she squeezed her eyes shut and wrapped her arms as best as she could around Ben's waist as he zigzagged over the rolling hills and through the trees.

The voices died down and soon Ben slowed when they entered a thick patch of tall oaks. Shoulders heaving, Ben gently grabbed Rae's waist and lowered her to the ground. He then laid in the grass and cast an arm over his eyes. Sweat poured down his face as he tried to regulate his breathing.

Rae sat down beside him and offered him her waterskin. "I don't think I've ever seen anyone run that fast before."

Ben peeked at her from under his arm with a smile. Slowly sitting up, he took the waterskin and downed a hefty gulp. After wiping his mouth with the back of his hand, he replied, "Me either. But I couldn't risk us getting caught. I don't think I've ever ran that fast before."

"And with an additional person weighing you down," Rae added.

"I didn't mind that," Ben replied with a smirk.

Rae felt herself blush as she took a drink of water. The silence stretched between them, and Rae wasn't sure how to break it. Their kiss in the cellar was the best kiss she'd ever experienced. Though she wanted to kiss Ben again, her fear kept her from doing so. The ever-present thought that he would leave her behind played continuously in her mind. And though Ben had never left her since they were reunited in Totem, Rae was still unsure. However, when she glanced up at him, she found him watching her carefully. As if he, too, thought that *she* would leave *him* behind.

Rae chuckled and shook her head. They were both a mess, but a beautiful mess that she loved being a part of.

Placing the cap back on her waterskin, Rae stood and brushed off her pants before offering Ben a hand. "Come on, we need to find the cave and get some imperial opal for Papi to test his machine."

Relief covered Ben's face as he took her hand and stood. They walked through the trees for about an hour until the soft dirt turned into hard stone. Rae followed the ground until her eyes landed on a cave.

"That has to be it," she said, squirming with excitement. She couldn't believe they'd finally found the cave. As she darted forward, she felt Ben's hand reach out and grab hers.

"Just a minute," he said quietly. "Jon said he was hunting around here. I don't know what kind of animal he was hunting this far away from home, but let me take a look around before you go in."

Rae frowned. "You know I can take care of myself."

"I know," Ben replied simply. "But I like taking care of you. Please let me."

Rae's heart melted at the honest and genuine comment. All she could do was nod and watch as Ben unlatched his crossbow from his back. He crept forward slowly, his feet not making a sound. It always impressed Rae how quiet he was for such a tall man.

Ben glanced around again then darted into the cave. Rae held her breath, not liking being the one waiting on the other side of the unknown. And she was surprised at how much relief she felt when Ben's dark hair exited the cave as he waved her inside.

Darkness bled around Rae as she entered the cave. Anxiety shot through every one of her nerves when she tried to find Ben. But thankfully, he found her.

As soon as she was at his side, he grabbed her hand. "I need to show you this. It's incredible."

Comforted by his presence, Rae breathed a sigh of relief and followed him through the darkness. In a matter of moments, they came upon a large opening.

Rae gasped as she gazed upon an entire cavern glittering and sparkling with imperial opal.

"It's beautiful," she said, reaching her hand out to the stone.

Part of her wanted to feel its effects, to know that she too had been blessed with a gift by Tunri. But as her fingers grazed over the metallic sheen of the stone, nothing happened. Just as she knew it would.

Sighing, Rae retracted her hand. "So, how are we going to get a piece out?"

They were in such a hurry to flee the soldiers, neither of them had brought any sort of tool to chisel out the stone.

Leveling his crossbow at a section near the ground, Ben shot a multitude of arrows before Rae could blink. When Ben stopped shooting, the arrows formed a perfect circle in the stone.

"That should be enough for your Pa's machine," he said, lowering his crossbow.

Rae shook her head, amazed. Of course, Ben was gifted by Tunri. No ordinary man could shoot so accurately every time. Striding forward, Rae yanked each arrow out one by one. When the final arrow was out, a smooth cylinder of imperial opal fell into her hands. A sensation of something—power? desire? —flowed into Rae's thoughts, but she pushed it aside before she could dwell on it. She knew this stone did nothing but evil and wouldn't be swayed by its promptings.

Opening her pack, she pulled out an extra scarf and wrapped the stone up before placing it back in her bag. She picked up all of Ben's arrows then faced him.

"I didn't want to almost pass out again," he said, motioning to the stone. "Or I would've gotten it. Thank you."

Rae shrugged. "You did most of the work anyway. I don't mind."

"Rae, I'm sorry if the kiss was too much and that I have a gift. I know how you feel about both things," Ben rattled off before Rae could take another step.

Rae glanced up at him to see the same worried expression he always wore after he made a confession. It was adorable and Rae had grown fond of it.

Reaching up, she laid her hand on his cheek. "I enjoyed the kiss and am pleased you have a gift. You don't need to apologize for either thing."

It was time she started not only fully trusting Ben with her heart but trusting herself with his. If they were going to overcome the terrors of their pasts, they were going to have to do it together.

Ben leaned into her hand and smiled, and Rae felt as if they had solidified another stone in the foundation of their relationship. Hopefully, they would be able to layer many more stones upon it.

The journey back to Totem seemed longer because it was. Ben held extra caution due to the number of soldiers now scouring the hills of Ballear. Thankfully, both Rae and Ben were good at hiding and moving quickly in short periods of time.

Eventually, they made it back to Totem. Rae never felt so thankful to see the familiar tents covering the vineyard. But when Liam found them in a rush, her fear from her days at the Temple resurfaced.

"Thank Tunri you're back," he said, his eyes swimming with worry. "Ben, a messenger from Matthias is here for you. Something has happened but he won't tell me what."

Ben's face turned to stone, and he nodded. "Where is he?"

"At the main house."

Ben gave Rae's hand a squeeze. "I'll find you as soon as I'm done."

Rae nodded, her apprehension rising as Liam waited for Ben to leave before he continued. "Rae, it's your mother. She's become terribly ill since you left. Nothing we've done has helped. Your father fears the worse."

Fear like a knife split Rae's heart in two as she raced past Liam and headed toward her parents' tent. All the while the cackle of her fear echoed between her ears.

You thought you could leave the Temple unscathed? Did you forget how you got into the Temple in the first place?

Rae gasped as she remembered the skeleton key she received from the old hag. It was General Yada's key he used to keep all the women confined to the Temple and their rooms. Rae never questioned the hag on how she procured it.

Rae ran with everything she had, hating how foolish she was. Devora had said there was something off about the key. The Seer even warned Rae to be careful. But Rae had been too distracted by the happiness in her new life, she forgot about the mistakes of her old one.

Panting, Rae flew through the flaps of her parents' tent. Mami lay on her cot on the far side, a pile of thick blankets layered over her shivering form. Papi sat next to her, holding a bowl of broth.

"You need to eat, my love. Just a little bite."

A round of phlegmy coughs escaped Mami's lips in response. She jerked up, trying to dispel whatever was in her lungs, but nothing came out. Dark purple circles lined Mami's eyes. She tried to open her swollen lids but failed. Exhausted from her coughing fit, she lay back down on the cot and fell asleep.

Rae rushed to Papi's side. "Papi, what happened?"

Placing the bowl of broth on a small table, Papi rubbed his tired eyes.

"I'm not sure. As soon as you left, the cough she's had for a few weeks grew worse. It was as if your presence kept her well." Papi sighed. "I'm not sure what to do. A few of the others are healers and have tried everything they can think of, but nothing has helped."

"I'm so sorry for leaving," Rae whispered, grabbing Papi's hand. "I won't leave again. Not until Mami is well."

Papi squeezed her hand back. "As much as I would love for all of us to be together forever, I would be a selfish father to allow such things. Especially when you have a bright future ahead of you."

"But—"

"Speaking of futures," Papi interrupted. "Where's Ben? I thought you two went to Snoken together."

Standing, Papi strode toward the table near the entrance of the tent where a steaming kettle sat. He plucked a few dried herbs from the drying rack above and placed them in two clay cups.

Rae watched as he poured the steaming water over the herbs and left them to steep. "Liam said a message had come for him from Captain Blake. He said he would find me after."

Papi nodded as he swirled the herbs in the cups. "He's a good man. Ben, I mean. Captain Blake is too."

"How do you know the captain, Papi?"

Papi carefully placed the cups on a tray and brought it over to Rae. "When King Atol ordered the best Tinkers in Yekel to be taken to the capital, Captain Blake was one of the soldiers ordered to round us up." Papi handed her one of the cups. "We made it all the way back to the capital. I was there for only a small amount of time when he approached me with a crazy plan."

Rae took the hot cup in her hands, casting a worried glance at Mami's sleeping form before asking, "What was it?"

Papi motioned around him "This. A place where those who had been unfairly tried or taken against their will could seek refuge and use their gifts and talents without consequence. I don't know how he did it, but he managed to save a handful of Tinkers that day. We were some of the first to come to Totem."

Rae blew on the steaming cup, realizing she had misjudged the captain. All she had known when she first saw him was that he had taken Papi away. She'd never forgotten his cold gray eyes. But appearances didn't make a man. And ultimately, Rae was thankful that Papi had been safe all this time.

Mami spun into a fit of coughing again, causing Papi to rush to her aid. He was able to get her to drink a few sips of tea but nothing more.

Rae remembered the key from the hag and the thought that entered her mind when she first heard Mami was sick. *Could the hag somehow have poisoned Mami? Cursed her?*

Blowing on the tea again, Rae took a sip. But what Papi said also struck her thoughts. Could it be that *she* was the one who cursed Mami instead? Rae was the one who took the key from the hag. Maybe her actions had caused Mami to fall ill.

Closing her eyes, Rae tried to find any solution to helping Mami heal but came up short. The only thing that made sense to her was to destroy the key from the hag. When Ben returned, she would talk to him and see if there was some way to grind the key into dust.

As if hearing her thoughts, the tall man strode through the tent flaps. His skin shone whiter than it usually did, his eyes filled with worry and sorrow.

"I heard about Sara," he said softly. Kneeling, he sat next to Rae. "I'm so sorry this happened while we were away. I shouldn't have had you come with me."

A flame of irritation spiraled in Rae's stomach. "I came because I wanted to. I didn't want you to face your past alone. I know what that's like. Mami falling ill is not your fault, Ben." Rae stared at her cup of tea.

I think it's mine, she wanted to add but kept the thought to herself.

Papi came over and clapped Ben on the shoulder. "I pray your mission was successful?"

"Oh!" Rae said fumbling through her bag. She'd forgotten about the imperial opal from the cave.

Carefully, she lifted the wrapped stone out of her bag and handed it to Papi.

His exhausted eyes lit with excitement. "Smart to wrap it up, *mija*. A piece of imperial opal this large would definitely take a toll on me."

Rae remembered the effect of Jonathon's imperial opal knife on Ben. "Papi, I think Ben has been gifted by Tunri." Rae turned to Ben, who gave her a shrug. "When he held imperial opal in Snoken, he almost passed out."

Papi carefully rewrapped the chunk of imperial opal and placed it on the table by the entrance before striding up to Ben. Even while Ben was sitting, his head almost reached Papi's shoulders.

Papi scrutinized Ben carefully. "Your hands, please, Ben."

Ben obediently lifted his palms to Papi. Papi turned Ben's hands over a few times. "I was wondering when I first heard of your abilities. Have you ever missed a shot?"

Ben shook his head. "Not that I can remember."

"And I thought they had all died out," Papi muttered to himself.

"What is it?" Rae asked, anticipation bubbling in her chest.

"As you know, there are several gifts Tunri can bestow upon His followers," Papi began. He eased himself back into the chair beside Mami and took her hand. "The ability to create, which is the Tinkering gift, and the ability of foresight, which is the Seeing gift, are just two of the many gifts that Tentonians used to have." Stroking Mami's hand, he continued, "The ability to decipher and read any language is the Translator gift. But I haven't heard of anyone having that gift in ages."

"But I can't do any of those things," Ben replied, his brows furrowed in confusion. "Why am I still affected by imperial opal?"

"Because you have a different gift, Ben. One that King Atol already thought he'd destroyed."

Papi took a long sip of tea, leaving Rae bursting with questions.

Finally, he said, "When I was younger, the king originally required male citizens to serve for two years' time in the military. If we did our time, and survived, we would be free to live our lives how we pleased afterward. And while I was a scrag, there were several officers who had the ability to shoot several men down with only one arrow."

Rae glanced at Ben, her eyes wide. But Ben stayed focused on Papi.

"I don't know what their official title was, but we called them the Marksmen." Papi grinned, recollecting his days of youth. "They were amazing and all of us scrags wished we could be like them but knew we could never practice enough to be so talented. They had to be blessed by Tunri."

Papi's face turned somber. "But then, after one battle, they all were killed. I remember being shocked. How could a Marksman be killed when they could never miss?" He shook his head. "I was too young to realize the corruption of our kingdom because not long after the Marksmen were gone, King Atol declared his 'observation of Seers' next."

"And the Tinkers were after that," Rae added, the memory of Yekel burning forever branded in her mind. Papi nodded and took another sip of tea.

"But how can I have a gift if all the Marksmen were killed before I was born? No one in my family has a gift. Isn't that how they're passed down?" Ben asked.

"Tunri blesses who He chooses, Ben. Our lineage does not always grant our gift." Papi gave Rae a knowing look. Rae focused on the empty cup in her hands. Papi knew how badly Rae wanted to be a Tinker as a child. How badly she wanted *any* gift from Tunri. But, since she met Ben, she realized that maybe all gifts weren't something so tangible. Maybe just caring for another person could be a gift.

"Though, I am pleased to know that there are still Marksmen among us," Papi added, giving Ben a smile.

"It's gotten me into a lot of trouble," Ben replied, rubbing the back of his neck. "But it's also helped me a lot too."

"I'm sure it will help you with whatever Captain Blake needs too, yes?" Papi asked.

Ben's face sagged again, and he nodded before turning to Rae. "Matthias needs me at the capital. Something suspicious is going on, but he can't say what." Ben hesitated before adding, "I'm leaving at first light."

Chapter Twenty-Eight

Devora kept the sack of gold coins tied inside her tunic, just to be safe. Though the small village she happened upon seemed safe enough, she didn't want to test out what the waitress from the bed and breakfast said. Placing the dark veil over her head, Devora hoped everyone would assume she was from Yekel and traveling for Matthias' promotion ceremony.

Today Devora had two goals: find out more about Matthias' promotion and find a way into the ball.

She almost laughed at the thought. Not long ago was she attending a ball in her own honor. Now she was trying to sneak into one without being arrested. Again.

Shaking her head, Devora kept to the sides of the main street, doing her best not to garner any attention. She engaged her soulsight to see most of the men and women in the village were hopeful and happy with their lives. Devora was thankful; she had already seen too many sorrow-filled souls.

As she continued down the street, a shop filled with exquisite gowns and fabrics caught her eye. She knew she shouldn't confine herself in such a small space, but if there was one thing Devora learned growing up as a noble, it was that the best gossips always loved fine dresses. Convinced, she made her way to the shop and entered. Thankfully, there was a gaggle of women already inside, making it easier for her to slip in unnoticed.

Another thing Devora knew about gossips were their keen eyes and lack of tact. She always admired how Mama was able to divert assuming questions and backhanded compliments with kindness and grace; two things Devora was still learning.

Maneuvering around a mannequin swathed in gorgeous white and black silk, Devora sent a prayer to Tunri for her parents. When she had last seen them in Grenly, they were still under house arrest even though King Atol promised they would be freed. Devora didn't like it, but she was thankful they were alive, even if they were prisoners inside their own home.

The sparkles on the black and white fabric distracted Devora from her thoughts. She'd not seen a gown so beautifully made in months. As she admired the material further, a trio of women skittered to the back of the already long line in the shop.

"Isn't it odd that the *queen* approved of the masquerade ball instead of the king?" a thin woman with high cheekbones and stringy cornsilk hair asked. A bundle of shimmering blue fabric plumed in her grasp.

"I did think it was strange to see her seal alone at the bottom of the announcement," the second woman admitted.

She was a bit shorter than the first, and rounder. But there was a kindness in her brown eyes and plump cheeks. Devora glanced at the woman's soul to find it was mostly yellow and hopeful, but a small swirl of blue tinged the edges. The woman wrestled with her own bolt of sparkling green fabric as it spilled out of her arms.

A tiny speck of a woman bent down and helped the second woman with the green fabric. "Maybe the king's illness is worse than we thought," the third woman commented. She pursed her small lips as she studied the smooth yellow fabric in her hands.

Illness? Devora thought. She'd certainly missed a lot while underground. Pretending like she was checking the price of the black and white fabric, Devora scooted a bit closer to the women to eavesdrop.

"If the king can't even put his seal on the bottom of a piece of parchment, he may be almost to the grave!" the thin woman exclaimed.

"Shh!" the second chided, glancing around the shop. She lowered her voice. "Don't say such things. We wouldn't want anyone to think we *want* anything to happen to the king."

"But we do," the third piped in. "Everyone does. The king has brought Tenton to ruins. Does anyone even know why the war with Kadesh started in the first place?"

The plump woman's eyes grew wide with fright, and she clamped her hand around the third one's small mouth. Another woman further down the line glanced back at them, and the trio just smiled and waved back.

Devora's mind whirred with the new information.

What happened to King Atol? He didn't seem sickly when he sent Devora to her death on the battlefield or condemned her to prison in Level Five of the Fortress. *Did the same thing happen to Princess Haden and that's why no one has seen her?*

"The queen has been gracious to invite us to the masquerade ball," the plump woman said with a sigh. "Let's enjoy her benevolence until it runs out."

Devora's brows rose as she watched the women continue down the line and order three dresses from the bolts of fabric. An idea then pulled at her thoughts. It wasn't the most honorable plan, but she needed to get to that ball, especially now that she knew something strange was happening with the king. Each woman was handed a white card with their name and dress order on it. When they headed toward the exit of the shop, more women tried to enter as the door opened and Devora took her chance.

Ripping the tag off the black and white gown, Devora headed toward the trio of women. As a new wave of chittering females tried to enter the shop, Devora "accidentally" bumped into the plump woman. She'd already seemed so frazzled, Devora figured she'd be the most distracted and wouldn't notice when her dress order card was swapped with a price tag.

"Apologies," Devora said, trying to mask her voice as she made the slip.

The plump woman was taken aback by Devora's veiled appearance, she didn't even notice the different paper being placed in her shaking fingers. Before the woman could react, Devora joined the crowd floating further into the shop. The trio of women were soon swept out of the dress shop, the plump woman none the wiser.

Devora waited in the shop until the crowd died down. The masquerade must be soon for so many women to be placing orders. When there were only a few women left scouring the shelves of brooches and gloves, Devora stepped up to the counter.

"How can I help you, miss?" the kind seamster said. A long measuring tape slung over his thin shoulders, dangling as he removed his glasses to wipe his tired eyes.

Devora wasn't sure if he could see well through his thick oval glasses, or her veil just wasn't as obvious as she thought it was since he didn't react to her oddly.

"I would like to make an alteration to the dress order I requested earlier." She placed the plump woman's card on the counter, praying the seamster had seen so many women that day, he wouldn't remember the plump one.

"Ah, I'm glad you came before I started on the order," he said, squinting at the card. "Miss Agatha?"

"Yes," Devora nodded. "I had a change of heart about the fabric."

The seamster nodded as he gave her back the card. "Happens all the time. May I ask you a question before I submit your order?"

Panic clawed up Devora's throat. This was it. He was going to ask her to remove the veil and she would be killed for her

Seeing gift, for capturing the princess—which wasn't true—and escaping prison—which was true.

But she remembered the lessons Papa taught her on diplomacy: "Do not assume you know what the other person is going to say. Stay calm and confident," he told her not too long ago.

Taking a breath, Devora took a chance. "Of course."

The seamster gave her a kind smile. "Are you from Yekel? I heard Captain Blake recently reclaimed the city and some of its citizens would be finding new homes throughout Tenton until the city was restored."

Devora stared in disbelief at the man. No wonder no one batted an eye at her disguise. If they didn't think she was traveling for the ceremony, they would have thought she was a refugee from Yekel. Devora would take the backstory and run with it.

"Yes," she replied, relaxing. "We are so grateful for everything Captain Blake has done for Yekel. He truly is a great man."

Devora blushed at the statement, knowing she'd thought this for longer than anyone else attending the masquerade ball in Matthias' honor. She didn't want to think about all the frilly females flocking around him, vying for his attention.

"That he is, miss," the seamster said with a nod. "And I'm grateful his ball has mustered up so much service for me. It's been quite dry here for some time if you know what I mean."

Devora nodded, remembering the waitress' warning to Devora to hide her coin from view.

"Now, which fabric would you like? It would be an honor to create something in Yekelian fashion."

Devora didn't know a thing about Yekelian fashion other than headscarves, but she didn't want to push her luck, so she pointed to the shining black and white fabric in the corner.

"An excellent choice, miss. I will start working on it right away. Please come back the day of the ball and it will be ready for you."

"Thank you," Devora said, still unable to believe her luck. "Please forgive my frazzled brain, but what is the date of the ball?"

The seamster chuckled. "Why in two days' time, miss."

Devora thanked the seamster again and left the shop feeling accomplished. She hadn't been arrested and she had secured a dress for the ball. The only question now was: how was she going to get there?

Chapter Twenty-Nine

Ida hurried down the long corridor, clasping the note from Sergio in her hand. Though she agreed to meet with the suave Third Year, she couldn't push her meeting with Jacques yesterday from her mind. Ida was proud of herself for not bursting into tears as soon as the knight reached toward her. In fact, she was shocked she had the self-restraint to not rush into his arms.

But Sergio was right. Jacques needed to fulfill the commitment he made to Hestia. Ida wouldn't be the one to mess up his perfect future.

Swallowing, Ida did her best not to think of Jacques' pain-filled hazel eyes as he pleaded with her to continue with their mission to find the Book of Ages together.

She shook her head. Warden Hazor said Jacques was off the mission. That meant it was up to Ida, and Ida alone, to find the book. Thankfully, she had been able to translate more of the restricted text last night when she couldn't sleep. The text was fascinating. It described life in Tenton before King Atol, *before* the war with Kadesh. From what Ida understood, the two countries used to be at peace. But still, the restricted text didn't say anything about how the war started.

As Ida rounded a corner, she came upon the back hallway of the lower level of Vlacklear. A few students tittered about, but the hall was mostly bare.

Frowning, Ida read the note Sergio pinned to her doorway earlier that morning.

Meet me in the lower hall at two o'clock.
S.A.

It concerned her that it was the day of Captain Blake's masquerade ball, yet she still didn't have a dress to wear. Ida glanced down at her standard black academy dress. She still hated how tight and scratchy the uniform was. It was almost as if the designer *wanted* her to feel uncomfortable every time she wore it.

Starting down the now vacant hall, Ida tried to stay positive. Regardless of what happened, she would get to attend the masquerade. Ida had never been to a ball, and after hearing all the fairytales Ama told her as a child, Ida had always wanted to be a princess.

She sighed at the thought, knowing she would never be a princess. An image of Jacques' kind grin and gentle eyes swam through her mind before she could stop it, and Ida's heart fell to her feet. Why couldn't he have just been a regular guy like the one Hestia liked at the Fortress? Ida couldn't remember the frizzy blond boy's name, but knew Hestia was heartbroken at not being able to see him since she came to Vlacklear.

As Ida's black boots clicked softly against the stone floor, an eeriness crept over her skin. When had the hall gotten so quiet? Was she just imagining things, or did it seem colder than before? And where was Sergio?

Ida checked the note again and knew she'd gotten the time right. It made sense that he wanted to meet earlier to prepare for the ball, but Ida still was unsure about the whole endeavor entirely.

Trying to find her confidence, Ida trekked on, looking this way and that until a figure exited a door at the end of the hallway. Relief relaxed Ida's tense muscles as she recognized Sergio's broad shoulders and sturdy frame. But what made her stop her gait was the next figure who exited from the doorway.

"Headmistress?" Ida asked, confusion rattling her thoughts. *Why is the headmistress with Sergio? Alone?*

Ida glanced past the two toward the door behind them. Dread coiled its way around her. Behind Sergio and the headmistress was the door to the Tower.

"Right on time," Sergio said with a predatory smile.

Unease rippled across Ida's skin. Every lesson she'd learned at the Fortress told her to run, but her feet stayed planted to the floor.

"Hello, Ida," the headmistress said, a new coolness overtaking her usual pleasant demeanor.

"What are you doing here?" Ida asked, forgetting to add honorifics. Ida wasn't sure it was possible, but the headmistress' gaze grew colder.

"I know why you're really here, Ida Shabawn."

Fear like ice froze Ida's core. *Has the headmistress found out I'm a spy? What's going to happen to me? What about the others?* Ida thought of Jacques and vowed to never rat him or Hestia and Reese out, no matter what.

Ida thought she would immediately cower and lower her gaze, just like she always did. But a comforting presence wrapped around her heart.

You are enough. You are not alone.

Raising her chin, Ida looked the woman square in the eye. "And why is that?"

The headmistress sneered. "The Book of Ages has been lost since the beginning of the war. You'll never find it *or* the prophecy. I don't know who sent you, but I will find out. I know you were snooping in the Tower when the Sandje brat was released."

The venom in her voice surprised Ida. Though she was always suspicious of the headmistress, the middle-aged woman usually went out of her way to appear kind to Ida. Was this why? Was she trying to gain more information?

Pinching her lips shut, Ida would never tell what the restricted text revealed to her in the late hours of the night: *The Book will reveal itself to one who is worthy. Though it may be hidden, the key lies within the crown.* The Book of Ages wasn't lost. It was waiting.

"And then what?" Ida found herself saying, surprised at her own confidence. "If Tunri wants the book and the prophecy to be found, it will be. There's nothing you can do to stop it."

The headmistress cackled, taking on a completely different persona than the one Ida had grown used to while at Vlacklear Academy.

"Oh, how foolish youth are." She snapped her slender fingers. A coil of black smoke wrapped around her wrist until a thick skeleton key lay in her palm. "Tunri doesn't reign in Tenton any longer. This land is all for the Goddess Pahga."

Ida gasped. She'd read several archaic texts about Pahga and her cultish religion. While some of her followers weren't as devoted, the most loyal would do anything—sacrifices of souls, sacrifices of their own lives—to please the goddess.

Fear got the better of her and Ida took a step back only to find Sergio there. Like the headmistress, Sergio's playful demeanor had changed. Cruelty and malice lingered in his usually impish eyes.

Before Ida could react, Sergio grabbed her wrist. "Who else is working with you?"

Ida winced as the wire bracelet Nadia made dug into her skin. "No one. I was sent alone."

Sergio growled and pulled her forward, his aquiline nose inches from her own. "I know you're lying. And when I found out who it is, I will make them pay."

"Sergio, lock her in the Tower until after the ball. We'll get our answers then," the headmistress said, handing Sergio the key that had appeared out of nowhere.

Ida could've sworn she saw the headmistress' eyes flash violet before she spun around, leaving the two of them alone.

Sergio tugged Ida down the hall toward the doorway. The stories Victoria told of the Tower filed through her mind, escalating her fear.

Ida yanked against Sergio's grasp. "Stop, let me go!"

But Sergio didn't reply. The next thing Ida knew, a piece of cloth was forced over her mouth and within a few breaths, everything went dark.

Ida groggily tried to open her eyes, as her head spun. She shut her lids again, her head hanging like a pendulum between her shoulders. What happened?

The clinking of chains echoed around her, and Ida forced herself to lift her heavy head. Shining manacles clung to her ankles. She tried to move her legs, but felt so tired and drained. As she lifted her hand to her forehead, Ida realized her wrists were chained in the same type of manacles.

"If you would've fallen for me like you were supposed to, none of this would've happened, Ida," Sergio commented from the darkness.

Ida squinted into the void, trying to find where he was. But with nothing but black surrounding her and her head feeling like a boulder, she gave up.

"Why are you working with the headmistress?" she asked, her voice barely above a whisper. "Why are you doing this? I thought we were beginning to become friends."

Ida closed her eyes, trying to preserve as much strength as she could. She had to think of a way out of here. But with her wrists and ankles bound in the shining metal, she wasn't sure what she could do.

"We were friends," Sergio answered softly. "But we can't be friends any longer." It was as if Sergio's inner light was able to break through for just a moment. But just as quickly, a coldness overtook him again.

Ida felt the cuff on her ankle clench a hair too tight and she whimpered.

"My aunt, or the headmistress as you know her, would never allow me to fraternize with someone like you."

The three words shattered what hope Ida had accumulated in her heart that she could survive this. Of course, this was a fitting end for someone like her. The tears Ida had been trying so hard to hold back finally broke through. Like gushing waterfalls, tears rolled down her cheeks.

"The imperial opal should work fast," Sergio said, his voice void of emotion. "Your end will be fairly painless."

His footsteps faded away from her.

"Wait, Sergio!" she cried, trying to pull against the restraints. "Don't leave me here! Don't leave me alone!"

As Sergio pulled open the door, Ida caught a glimpse of his face from the light outside. A flash of regret whipped across his features. But just as fast as it came, it disappeared.

"Goodbye, Ida."

A strip of light drew over Ida's face and as Sergio closed the door, it grew thinner and thinner until it was gone entirely.

All at once Ida was back at the orphanage on the day Josef left. The day she'd lost her only friend. She'd already lost her parents—or they didn't want her, she didn't know—but to lose Josef had shattered her world.

Ida curled in on herself, snuffing out any joy or hope or light she'd gained since Josef left. Everyone left her eventually: Josef, Apa—her adoptive father—and even Jacques.

The manacles' draining force increased and Ida felt her strength wane further. *What did Sergio say? Imperial opal? What is it and why is it affecting me so much?*

Ida wasn't sure how much time passed. Had it been hours? Days? Or only a few minutes of agony?

Either way, her hope was gone. With her limbs being bound, and her energy depleted, she couldn't move. Whatever the imperial opal was doing to her was working because she could hardly think at all—much less figure out an escape plan.

Devora escaped from the Fortress. She always had a plan and knew what to do. Now more than ever did Ida wish she was someone else, someone stronger.

"Why have you allowed all this to happen, Tunri?" Ida sobbed. "I've never questioned Your ways. I follow the rituals for my gift. Is it because I got distracted by Jacques?"

She paused; her pain too harsh to utter another word. She cried and cried and cried. It was as if the Tower wasn't big enough to cage the grief in her heart.

Ida regretted how she treated Jacques yesterday. If she'd known she would die today, she would've told him she loved him.

Ida's tears eventually slowed as she gathered her breath. Her headache grew even worse as tiny stars danced in the corners of her vision. Her toes and fingers started to numb. Is this what it was like to die? Why had Tunri sent her here for her to die in the Tower of Vlacklear Academy? Was she really that useless to Him as well?

But, as always, Ida bowed her head and accepted her fate. What was the use of trying to fight when she'd already lost?

"Forgive me if I've done something wrong," she breathed to Tunri.

A cold tingle crawled up her ankles, but Ida felt peace. Tunri had guided all her steps to this point. If He wanted her to escape, then He would provide a miracle for that to happen. And if not, well, Ida didn't want to dwell on that thought.

As the numbness worked its way up her limbs, encroaching on her heart, Ida unleashed all the memories she tried to suppress. Ama, trying to figure out what to do with Ida's hair when she was a child was the first that came to her mind. Ida remembered the fit of giggles she fell into when the hairstyle Ama tried made Ida look fuzzier than a lion.

A small smirk cracked across Ida's lips as she remembered Jil's first steps and all the times they played together.

When Apa passed but Ama still held their little family together with evening fairytale stories while they preserved fruits and vegetables.

Ida's memories shifted from her childhood to her time at the Fortress. How she watched in awe as Devora stood up to the giant and Captain Blake. How vivacious Hestia was in such a dark situation. How much she admired Reese's quick mind with numbers and wished she could be as smart. And how much she loved watching Nadia tinker and create amazing gadgets out of nothing. Nadia was always so generous in giving them away too. And of course, there was Jacques. His kindness even before he knew her, his playful demeanor, how he always looked out for her even when she didn't notice.

Ida found herself crying again. Tunri had blessed her so. Of course, there had been bad times, many many bad times. But there had also been so many good times. And throughout them all, Tunri was there, weaving her path. Just like the seedling of her desert lily fought its way through the soil to the fresh air and sun, Ida would continue to fight too.

"I don't know how, Tunri," she prayed. "But please free me from these bonds. Help me find the Book of Ages and finish what Warden Hazor sent me here to do."

Only a sliver of her strength returned, but it was enough for Ida to think clearly and remember the wire bracelet Jacques wrapped around her wrist weeks ago. Slowly, she twisted her wrist and was able to release one of the pins from the wire. Elation excited her tired nerves as she fumbled to stick the pin in the lock securing the manacles. What Ida hoped would be trivial turned out to be more difficult due to her numb fingers. But eventually, the pin found its home and Ida was able to pry her hand out of the manacle.

A wave of energy rushed into her spirit and Ida hurriedly worked on her other wrist. In a few moments, it was free as well.

Yet as she unlocked her left ankle and started working on her right, hurried footsteps rushed outside the locked door. Her joy deflated, churning into fear.

Is Sergio returning to check on me? Is it the headmistress, ready to kill me off once and for all?

Ida quickly finished unlocking her right foot and slipped against the far wall. She'd seen Nadia use the weapon before and Ida wouldn't hesitate to practice on whoever came through that door.

Yet as the door crept open, a tall thin figure with shining black hair stepped inside.

Ida's mouth opened in surprise as she gazed at Reese.

"Expecting someone else?" Reese questioned with a quirked brow, but a small smile cracked her lips.

Before Ida could think to speak, she rushed forward and barreled into Reese with a hug, her eyes brimming with tears. "Thank you."

"I'm not sure why you're thanking me, seeing as you rescued yourself." Reese patted Ida on the head then pulled away. "No time for tears, Ida. There's a ball you must attend."

Chapter Thirty

Ida and Reese raced down the quiet halls of the academy. Just a few weeks ago, Ida was lost and confused on how to navigate through the large building. Now she seemed to know Vlacklear Academy like the back of her hand.

Reese paused before they turned a corner. The tall girl searched around before signaling to Ida. "This way."

"Where are we going?" Ida asked, rubbing her wrists. Though she'd broken free of the imperial opal irons, her skin was still raw.

Reese didn't reply. She bolted down the hall toward the girls' dormitories. Ida followed quickly, noticing the corridor was too quiet.

Is the ball already over? Did I miss it? Though she was excited for the masquerade, Ida needed to get into the castle and search for the Book of Ages.

Reese suddenly reached out and yanked Ida into an adjacent doorway.

With a squeak, Ida was pulled into Reese's and Hestia's room. She braced herself to face Hestia, wrapped in her elegant gown, ready to take Jacques' hand in marriage. But instead of seeing Hestia, Ida only saw Hestia's gorgeous gown still hanging on a mannequin.

Confused, Ida glanced out the window. The sun was just setting. She knew the ball would begin at dusk. But dusk was here, and Hestia was not. Only her dress.

"Reese, where's Hestia?" Ida asked, cautiously. "Is she already with Jacques?"

Shaking her head, Reese carefully, yet hurriedly, pulled the gown off the mannequin. "She's gone."

Ida's lips parted in shock. "She's gone? Where did she go?"

Reese sighed as she undid the trail of buttons cascading down the dress's low back. "I have a seventy-three point eight percent chance of knowing where. But, for this probability, I need to be one hundred percent sure before I tell you." Reese held the opened dress out to Ida. "Here."

Ida stared at the dress with a blank look.

Reese huffed. "Ida, get in the dress. We both know you need to go to the ball and sweep Jacques off his feet. In."

Ida blinked. Maybe Hestia had started to rub off on Reese because they were starting to sound the same.

"Reese, Sergio and the headmistress locked me in the Tower," Ida said. Chills ran down her arms at the drain of energy she felt from the shining irons. "They don't want me to find the Book of Ages. I know it's somewhere in the palace, but I don't know what they'll do if they see me at the ball."

Reese pinched the bridge of her nose and closed her eyes as if Ida were annoying her. "It's a masquerade, Ida. Everyone will be wearing a mask. They won't know it's you."

Shaking her head, Reese laid the gown on the bed and stomped to Hestia's desk. Throwing open the top drawer, Reese pulled out the most beautiful mask Ida had ever seen. Intricate swirls of gold covered the white mask, twirling and swirling this way and that. It was simple yet elegant. But what Ida loved the most was the white lily pinned to the side of the mask. Three delicate white feathers fanned from the blooming flower, completing its glamourous look.

"Hestia picked this?" Ida gasped, reaching out to the mask. "But why?"

The lily looked almost identical to the desert lily she grew in Horticulture. Only Hestia would know that.

"Hestia may seem like she only cares for flirting and fun, but she's extremely clever." Reese held out the mask, which Ida took immediately. "I'm eighty-one percent sure she'd been planning this for some time."

Ida delicately ran her fingers over the soft feathers. She'd never seen anything so beautiful. Could someone like her really wear this? Did she deserve to wear this?

"We've wasted enough time," Reese said. She shoved the opened dress at Ida again. "In. Now!"

A tear trickled down Ida's cheek as the mask glittered up at her. It was as if Tunri was saying, "Go."

And Ida didn't need to hear Him twice.

"Okay," she said as she grabbed the dress from Reese.

Taking the gown behind the dressing wall, Ida stripped off her soiled academy dress and slipped on the ballgown. The green silk was so fine and smooth against Ida's skin as it wrapped around her small form. The only problem was it was too long.

Ida couldn't help but laugh as silk rushed at least a foot past her toes. It was then she noticed its dark green color faded into a sparkling white. While Ida was admiring the shimmering dress, a soft knock rapped on the door.

Ida went rigid. *Is it Sergio? Did he find out I escaped?* Staying hidden behind the dressing wall, Ida listened as Reese slowly opened the door.

A female voice spoke in a language Ida hadn't heard before. Reese promptly replied, and the door shut.

Ida waited a moment until she peered around the dressing wall to find a petite woman, shorter than her—if that was possible—standing with a basket full of thread and a hand full of sewing pins.

"I deduced we would have this problem, so I called Mei to help. She's the finest seamstress in the eastern region and practically raised Hestia and I when our mother died." Reese placed her hand on the woman's hunched shoulder. "She's efficient and will have that hemmed before the ball even begins."

Before Ida could react, the small woman hurried toward her.

"No move," she instructed, pointing a crooked finger at Ida.

And, like the good soldier she was, Ida obeyed.

Time flew as Mei measured, pinned, and finally hemmed Hestia's gown to fit Ida. As soon as she clipped the final thread, Reese slapped the mask in Ida's hand and pulled her out the door, kissing Mei on the cheek as they left.

"Time is not on our side tonight, Ida," Reese explained as she ran down the hall.

Ida did her best to keep up with Reese's long steps, but it proved difficult, especially in the form-fitting dress.

"The ball has already begun, but there is still time for you to find Sir Jacques and the Book. From what you explained earlier, it's somewhere in the palace."

Ida nodded then asked, "But why can't I just search for the Book?" After how she treated Jacques yesterday, she didn't want to have to face him again.

They rounded a corner and fled down too many stairs before Reese answered.

"The only way my plan will work is if you find Sir Jacques *and* the Book *tonight*."

"What plan?" Ida questioned, growing weary of not understanding what was happening around her.

Shoulders heaving, Reese finally stopped when they reached the exit of Vlacklear Academy.

Ida did her best to catch her breath, as well. She hoped she hadn't torn any of Mei's fine work while Reese yanked her through Vlacklear like a cat after a ball of string.

"Warden Hazor charged Hestia and I to support you in your mission. We didn't know what it was, but when you told us about the Book of Ages, we knew we had to do everything within our power to help you get it. This" —Reese motioned to the dress—"was the plan with the highest probability." And for the first time, Reese gave Ida a genuine smile.

Reaching out, Reese hugged Ida tightly. Ida was so shocked at the gesture; she didn't know what to say.

Clearing her throat, Reese stepped back and opened the door to reveal a fine carriage waiting among the freshly fallen snow.

Ida gaped in amazement. What other glorious surprises would be waiting for her tonight?

"I may not have prophetic visions or have the ability to translate languages," Reese chuckled, noting Ida's surprise. "But I do know numbers and—thanks to my terrible yet somewhat still rich father—a lot of people."

With a nudge, Reese pushed Ida toward the carriage. "Go, you don't have much time."

Unable to feel the snow around her slippers because of her excitement, Ida rushed down the steps.

It wasn't until she was in the carriage and waving to Reese did she wonder: why didn't she have much time?

Ida couldn't stop her jaw from dropping as the carriage pulled in front of Maldove Palace. Shining marbled columns gleamed against the bright moonlight. Droves of people dressed in fine fabrics and silks hurried up the steps. It seemed most of Tenton had been invited to the ball, which was perfect for Ida to blend in.

Carefully, Ida placed the mask on her face before the driver helped her out of the carriage. Once she thanked him, she headed toward the palace but stopped. This fairytale all seemed too good to be true. Could everything really work out so well?

Ida felt the same cool presence in her heart as she had in the Tower. Tunri wanted her to trust Him. Trust His guidance and His plan.

With her newfound confidence in Tunri, Ida melded into the crowd. There were so many people entering the palace, the Herald at the front had given up on announcing every single one. Ida was thankful to see all the people of Tenton represented, so her darker skin wouldn't be such a contrast to the paler citizens of Juro.

Keeping to the middle of the crowd, Ida entered the palace with hardly any issue. And though she was still anxious at everything working out *too* well, she enjoyed watching all the beautiful finery and people laughing and dancing around her.

Yet, although she was wearing a mask, Ida was concerned about being recognized, so she stayed to the edges of the grandiose ballroom. She smiled as couples paired off and danced in what seemed to be beautifully choreographed routines. Her imagination took hold for a moment as she pictured herself with them, twirling the night away with her handsome prince charming.

But she'd been here for a little while now and there was no sign of Jacques. Ida's hope dwindled. It was difficult to find anyone in a crowd so large, but she would've thought, if this was indeed Tunri's plan, *somehow*, He would guide them to one another.

Ida shook her head at the silly thought. She should focus on finding the Book of Ages. *That* was her real purpose here. Not to spend the night swooning over Jacques.

Running her gloved hand over her head, Ida realized she had never changed her hair from the tight, confining bun forced upon her by the headmistress' rules. In an act of defiance, Ida ripped the pins from her hair, setting her wild ebony ringlets free.

Shaking her head, Ida massaged her scalp. Though her hair follicles were sore from being tortured into a cinnamon roll shape, she was thankful they were loose again.

Even though it was a small rebellion, Ida's confidence bloomed within her as she set off to search for the Book of Ages.

As she hurried around the edge of the ballroom, Ida made sure to stop occasionally, and pretend she was part of a group's conversation. She didn't know who would be watching, but after discovering how Sergio and the headmistress knew her mission, Ida didn't want to risk anyone else finding out.

After her third stop, Ida had almost reached the doors leading out of the ballroom. Her nerves flitted with excitement as she remembered the passage she just translated last night.

The Book will reveal itself to one who is worthy. Though it may be hidden, the key lies within the crown.

Ida wasn't a huge fan of the cryptic message, but she was pretty sure that meant the Book of Ages was in the palace. And the crown could only mean it was somewhere in the throne room.

As Ida swiveled around a man who had one too many glasses of wine, a woman with a dress the color of peacock feathers grabbed Ida's hand and thrust her into a circulating line of dancers.

Panicked, Ida didn't know what else to do besides follow along. She didn't know much about ballroom dancing, but the lessons she'd learned in class at Vlacklear were enough for her to pass through the dance unscathed.

As Ida spun and twirled around, her arms linking with different partners each time, she found herself enjoying the dance. And though she previously decided to leave the dance when she was spun toward the exit again, Ida changed her plans and danced and laughed a little while longer.

The conductor of the orchestra indicated that this would be the last round of the jig before he played a soothing tune. More people joined the rambunctious circle. Ida was twirled and hooked and twisted so many times, she could hardly register the faces of the masks dancing around her.

But then, her gloved hand slipped into the crook of a familiar arm. One that had been offered to her many times before. Her fingers recognized the tone of the bicep and the exact angle of the elbow.

The music began to slow, transitioning into a steady waltz. Ida's heart jumped to her throat. Jacques didn't hesitate at all as he spun her around until she faced him. Ida's eyes widened as she admired his white and gold mask covering the top half of his face. His sandy blond hair was slicked back, allowing Ida to study the beautiful swirling designs of the mask. A pristine white tunic with a light green sash covered his toned chest, indicating his position of nobility.

Ida tried to speak, to say something, but she couldn't find the words. What could she say? She'd practically told him to leave her alone and here she was, melting in his arms.

Jacques' hazel eyes searched hers behind his mask as he pulled her closer, moving them to the slow, steady beat.

"I don't know how you got here, but I'm so glad you did," he breathed in her ear.

His warm breath sent pleasant chills down her neck.

They stayed silent for a bit longer until Ida worked up the courage to say, "I'm sorry. About yesterday."

Jacques' hand tightened around her waist. "No, you had every right to say what you did. I've been a fool. It wasn't right of me to ask you to wait for me. Especially if you want to be with Sergio."

Ida wasn't sure whether now was the right time to tell Jacques about the headmistress and Sergio or not, but she did enjoy how his words became tight at the mention of the Third Year.

"I don't want to be with Sergio," Ida whispered.

Jacques swallowed. "I don't want to marry Hestia."

"Then don't," Ida said. For once, she wasn't surprised at her forwardness. Finally, she decided to be bold, to say what her heart had been screaming since she found out about the betrothal.

"Don't marry Hestia," she repeated, pulling away from Jacques enough that he could see her. Her eyes searched his before she added. "Marry me instead."

Chapter Thirty-One

Rae, Totem, Ballear—Two days before the Masquerade

Mami hadn't gotten better since Rae returned from Snoken with Ben. In fact, she was worse. Instead of just chills and coughs every now and then, Mami's limbs constantly shivered. Her once bronzed skin was almost as pale as the clouds. Thick drops of sweat pooled from her forehead.

Rae wrung out the damp cloth from Mami's forehead, replacing it with a clean dry one. Although Mami claimed she was cold, her fever was too high for Rae's liking. Several healers who'd found refuge in Totem tried everything from tinctures and salves to saunas and inhaling smoked tea leaves. Nothing helped Mami.

But what worried Rae even more was that the key from the old hag in the Dark Market had disappeared. Rae ripped the tent apart trying to find it, but it was gone. Panicked, she searched everywhere she'd been in the last week before she left for Snoken, but it was nowhere to be found.

Mami is dying because of me. Rae held her head in her hands. She knew there were going to be consequences after taking the key from the hag. Devora even warned her about the evil aura surrounding the skeleton key, but Rae had no other options to free the women who were enslaved in the Temple of Pahga.

Mami erupted into a coughing fit that lasted longer than the last, and this time little droplets of blood spotted the handkerchief Rae lifted to Mami's mouth.

Fear plunged into Rae's heart like a knife, shaking the hope she'd fought so hard to find.

This can't be happening. Tunri, please, show me what to do. How do I save Mami?

A rustle sounded behind her. Rae hadn't quite rid herself of her reflexes from her fights in the Dark Market. But when she whipped her arm around to stop whoever had entered their tent unannounced, Ben's hand was there, waiting for the blow.

Rae thankfully was able to stop it this time. There were many times in the not-too-distant past when Ben took the blow at full force.

If Rae's heart wasn't already burdened, the sight of him wearing his cloak and crossbow strapped to his back further worried her.

She tried to muster up a smile. "Leaving so soon?"

Ben didn't release her arm. Instead, he dragged his fingers from her forearm to her palm, entangling their fingers together.

"She's not any better?" he asked, his voice low.

Rae bit her lip to prevent it from trembling. She shook her head then looked away.

Ben's other hand gently laid against Rae's cheek and pulled her face toward him.

"We'll figure this out, okay? Tunri didn't have us both survive through our lives for everything to crumble now."

Those few words were enough to break Rae's barriers and she ran to Ben and cried in his chest. His long arms wrapped around her shuddering shoulders as she sobbed.

"It's all my fault, Ben, I'm the one who made Mami sick."

"What do you mean?"

Rae then explained to him about the old hag and the key, how Devora warned her, and Rae ignored it. She then told him about the voice she'd heard that sounded just like the hag's voice, blaming Rae for killing her own mother with her selfishness.

"Are you sure you heard the voice?" Ben asked after Rae had finished.

Wiping the tears from her eyes, she nodded her head.

Ben frowned. "What if I told you I heard something too?"

"What?"

Ben rubbed the back of his neck. "Something is happening at the palace, but Matthias can't say what. He just said he needed someone there he could fully trust." He paused and checked Rae's reaction. When she didn't respond, he continued, "And I would like someone to come with me that I trust completely too." He sighed. "I didn't really hear any voice, but I have this feeling that you need to come with me." Ben shook his head. "I don't think I'm making any sense."

Rae glanced back at Mami, her heart tearing in two different directions. The moment Ben told her Captain Blake summoned him to Maldove Palace, she immediately felt it was her responsibility to go with him. But knowing Mami was getting worse, Rae wasn't sure what to do.

"I want to..." she started then trailed off.

Ben's dark eyes softened. "I understand your decision either way."

"Well, I don't," Papi's voice came from the tent flaps.

Unashamed of eavesdropping on his daughter's conversation, Papi strode into the tent with a tray of broth and tea. Placing it down, he faced his daughter.

"Rae Salvar, you spent too many years sacrificing your own life for others. If you feel led to go with Ben, go."

"But—" Rae started but Papi held up his hand.

"No, Rae," he interrupted. "For too long I wasn't there to help guide you. But I am now." Papi reached behind a chair and pulled out Rae's Crimson Cord uniform.

Rae gasped. "Where did you find that?"

Rae had hidden the uniform when she arrived in Totem, not wanting to resurrect that part of her life again.

"I may have told your Pa about our fight in the Dark Market," Ben replied sheepishly.

Rae shot him a glare before focusing back on Papi. "I vowed not to be the Crimson Cord again. Because of me, an innocent man died."

Rae would never forget when she heard the news about the death of the Wizard Wankle. All because General Yada wanted to punish her for hiding Devora and Ben from him.

"But," Ben said, coming next to her. "Maybe we still need the Crimson Cord."

His fingers skimmed hers and Rae felt her heart race. Would it be okay for her to leave Mami *again*? She'd already left her in the Temple when she'd escaped. But Rae also hadn't known Mami was in there.

"Rae," Papi said, pulling Rae from her spiraling thoughts of guilt. "Your mami would want you to go. Imagine what she'll say when she heals and discovers you didn't go save our country. Again!"

Papi laughed and Rae couldn't help but smile. Although, she did notice a subtle sadness in his usually bright eyes. He had faith that Mami would be healed, but a speck of doubt still lingered.

Papi extended his hand, handing the Crimson Cord disguise to Rae.

Rae stared at the black fabric. *Can I really use my fighting skills to help Tenton?*

"How long is this going to take?" a voice whispered a bit too loudly outside the tent.

A sound like a hand clapping over a mouth followed. "Shush!"

Rae's brows rose and she stalked to the tent flaps. Yanking the fabric open, she caught Nadia and Tristan crouching outside the tent, listening in on their conversation.

Rae crossed her arms over her chest. "What are you two doing here?"

Tristan raised his hands in innocence then pointed to Nadia.

Nadia rolled her eyes and stood. "Ben told us about the Cap's orders and we're coming too."

"Ben also said that if you didn't agree to come, we needed to help convince you," Tristan added with a grin as he stood.

Ben rubbed his eyes with his fingers and groaned.

"Ignore him," Nadia said, shoving Tristan away. "Rae, admit it. You miss fighting."

Rae pursed her lips, not wanting to give into Nadia's claim. Although it was true. Rae loved her fights in the Dark Market. Not just the coin, but the thrill of beating an opponent. But that was before she'd found Tunri. Could she still follow Tunri *and* fight?

"You're not answering, so I'm right," Nadia continued as she strode into the tent. Nodding to Papi, Nadia took the Crimson Cord uniform in her hand. "If you were looking for a sign, this is it. The Cap, Devora, and so many others need us."

Rae lifted her chin, remembering the easygoing little girl she grew up with. Now Nadia had blossomed into a fearsome and lovely woman.

The two friends eyed each other until Rae snatched the uniform back out of Nadia's hands. Nadia grinned in triumph before she strode over and embraced Rae in a hug.

"Tunri will save Mami, Rae. I know it."

As Rae packed the rest of her things and joined the others, she prayed Nadia's statement would prove true.

Chapter Thirty-Two

Devora, Eastern Region—The Day of the Masquerade

Devora slipped in and out of the seamster's early the day of the masquerade, thankful the streets were quiet. Most people had already traveled to the capital in preparation for the masquerade ball honoring Matthias.

Thick paper wrapped the shimmering black and white gown, protecting it from any mud or wrinkles that may occur on the journey to Juro. After she'd ordered the gown earlier in the week, Devora went straight to the village stables, praying there would be at least one carriage available to get her to Maldove Palace in time.

And luckily, there was.

Folding the gown over her arm, Devora paid the young driver and stepped into the carriage. It wasn't the most luxurious carriage she had ever ridden in, but anything was better than trying to walk to Juro. How she missed Vinn! She had tried calling out to the elk-like creature in her mind, but, so far, he hadn't responded. Devora prayed he was safe and that they would be reunited again soon.

The carriage rolled out of the stable, the sun barely kissing the horizon on a new day. By that evening, Devora would be at Maldove Palace.

As the carriage bounced steadily along the road, Devora relaxed and took the headscarf off her face. Though the scarf had saved her life, she was tired of suffocating in the fabric.

Taking a deep breath, Devora was thankful to not have her air filtered by the scarf. She wondered how Rae was able to fight as the Crimson Cord with the red mesh covering her entire face.

Placing the headscarf in her pack, Devora rummaged around until she saw the bag of coin. It was strange how the dark leather sack appeared in her pack. She hadn't remembered it before and knew Nadia hadn't given her all the extra money. So where had it come from?

Devora held the sack in her palm. Bringing it up to her eyes, she examined it and found nothing out of the ordinary. Not satisfied, she opened it and examined the inside. She'd been so exhausted and rushed the past few days, she hadn't had a moment to really do anything besides lay low.

Yet as Devora searched through the pouch, her fingers ran over two small c's branded into the leather. Smiling, Devora closed the leather sack and tucked it away in her pack, thankful Rae, the Crimson Cord, had helped her in her time of need.

Dusk approached and the pointed spires of Maldove Palace's towers were just within Devora's line of sight. The trip from the eastern region to Juro had lacked giants and anything out of the ordinary, and for that, Devora was grateful.

Knowing she was less than an hour from the palace, Devora started to unwrap her dress. The black and white fabric was stunning. The seamster had done an excellent job at arranging the contrasting light and dark pieces. The top was entirely black, twinkling like the night sky before it faded into a beautiful white, shimmering like stars.

A simple black lace mask was tied to the fabric of the dress. Pinned to the back of the mask was a small piece of parchment. Plucking it off, Devora read.

May Tunri guide your path, young Seer.

Devora's brows lifted in surprise. She had wondered why the seamster had taken her request so easily. Still, she was thankful there were some people who did not want to hunt her down and arrest her for her gift.

Thanking Tunri for his guidance, Devora lifted the mask to her eyes and was instantly greeted by a vision.

Devora strode into the ballroom. Hordes of people filled every crevice. Though the ball in her honor after the Battle of Edo had been crowded, it wasn't as packed as the masquerade ball.

Devora shuffled through the crowd until the vision started moving people around her. Faces blurred and she couldn't make out if it was the crowd or herself moving.

The vision stopped momentarily on a woman swathed in a beautiful jade dress with a lily mask. She was dancing closely with a blond man dressed in white.

"Ida?" Devora gasped at the transformation of her friend.

What is she doing here? And with Sir Jacques of all people? Have I been so blind as to not have seen the connection between them?

The vision didn't give her time to dwell on the thought before it whisked her out of the ballroom and outside the castle. Devora didn't feel the chill but was amazed to see a flurry of snowflakes spiraling from the sky. She'd wanted to see snow when she came to the north, but the Fortress hardly allowed her time to frolic in the snowflakes.

But the vision didn't care for Devora's love of snow. It pulled her toward the outside of the castle where four hooded figures were grouped. Fear lodged itself in her throat as she recognized her friends all too well.

An eerie feeling crept across Devora's skin. Ida and Sir Jacques, One Shot and Rae, Nadia and Tristan. What were they all doing here?

Devora's thoughts shot back to her time at the Fortress when her suppressed Seeing abilities were revealed, and she feared her power would harm her friends as well.

But, as far as everyone knew, she was still missing. So, they all had to be here for Matthias. But why?

Why are One Shot and Rae dressed in their fighting leathers? Why does Nadia have more weapons than Devora had ever seen? Why was Tristan even there?

Devora shook Tristan's confusing presence from her mind. Something was up and she had to figure out what.

As if she'd prompted it, the vision flung her back into the castle. But instead of the ballroom, Devora landed in the throne room. A group of guards scuffled with a couple, but Devora flew by too fast to know what had happened.

Up into the palace the vision took her until she entered a large, elegant room. Velvet drapes lined the high arched windows. Gilded frames of past kings and queens lined the walls. A roaring fire blazed between two plush chairs. And seated within them were Queen Leza and Matthias. Queen Leza sat poised and calm, but ready to pounce like a tiger. Matthias, ever the soldier, mirrored an iron rod, firm and rigid even while seated.

Devora's heart leapt at the sight of him. How she wished she could rush to him and explain her actions in Yekel. But the vision kept her planted in her spot.

Queen Leza said something with a coy smile and Matthias didn't respond, although Devora noticed the tightening of his fist on his knee.

What are they saying? And where is King Atol? He was usually with the queen.

Confused, Devora urged the vision to get her closer, but it refused. Instead, it pulled her further away, just as Queen Leza stood and tightened something around Matthias' neck.

Dropping the lace mask, Devora gasped as she emerged from the vision, wiping the cold sweat from her forehead.

What was Queen Leza trying to do to Matthias? Was she trying to kill him?

Rage, dark and swirling, rumbled in Devora's soul. *Have I been a fool this whole time?*

Her mind filtered over the events of everything that happened at the Fortress: Regulus Protecti, being sent to battle, the queen offering her handmaidens, the ball in Devora's honor, and being framed for Princess Haden's disappearance. Could it really have been the *queen* orchestrating everything all along?

All this time Devora thought King Atol had been the one who hated her and wanted her dead. But the vision clearly showed Queen Leza threatening Matthias. And based on what the women at the seamster's shop said, there were already rumors that something had happened to the king.

Could Queen Leza have harmed King Atol as well?

Devora pressed her palms against her temples. But what did it all mean? Was this why Tunri was guiding her back to the palace? Was the queen involved with Kanna *and* the disappearance of Princess Haden?

Closing her eyes, Devora took a deep breath. There were too many questions and not enough answers. Either way, she needed to get to the masquerade and find Matthias before it was too late.

Chapter Thirty-Three

Matthias, Maldove Palace, Juro

Matthias hated social events. And worse than most social events, a masquerade ball. He glared at the plain white mask on his desk. The queen herself had highly encouraged—threatened him, as it were—to wear it.

He always dressed in black. It was his comfort, his security. The black of night hid secrets and lies. White was light, exposing everything in the darkness. Matthias had too many secrets in the dark and didn't want any of them exposed. Especially since his allies would be at the ball.

He was thankful Warden Hazor was able to contact Jacques. Matthias knew his friend had keen eyes and would be able to scour the ballroom for anything amiss.

Matthias was also grateful Tocha, his right-hand man at the Battle of Edo, retrieved One Shot. Eyes in the ballroom were important, but those hidden in the castle were even more deadly.

Placing the white tunic over his black slacks, Matthias grunted at the outfit. He hated bowing to the queen's every whim, like he was her personal pet. But he knew she was up to something and until he could figure out what, he had to stay close to her and keep her happy.

The echo of chattering nobles vibrated throughout the castle walls. The masquerade began well over an hour ago, and

Matthias knew he had to make an appearance soon. It was, after all, in his honor.

Combing his hair back, Matthias grabbed the white mask and placed it on his face. The sooner he went downstairs, the sooner he would get this over with.

A flurry of council members in sparkling coats surrounded Matthias the moment he stepped into the ballroom. He had specifically tried to enter without being noticed but wearing black and white in a sea of colors did nothing but make him stand out.

"Captain, captain!" A short man with slick black hair and a vibrant blue coat grabbed Matthias' arm. A mask resembling a jester was secured to his face.

Matthias thought this was an accurate mask for the man.

A cascade of azure glitter floated onto Matthias' white sleeve. He frowned at it. He hated glitter almost as much as he hated social events.

"Captain," the man said again with a wide smile. "You've finally arrived! The queen has been looking all over for you." The man whipped a hand fan out and waved it in front of his glistening face.

Matthias quirked a brow at the gesture before pulling his arm out of the man's grasp. "Why does the queen wish to see me?"

He kept his voice steady, but inside, his heart was pounding. He'd already endured the queen's company far more in the last week than he liked. The woman never had an interest in him before. He usually did business with King Atol. But now that the king was dead, it seemed Queen Leza had become far too comfortable with taking over the throne.

The short man laughed, waving his fan at Matthias. Matthias dodged the rain of glitter that came with the gesture.

"Why to announce you, of course! This is a ball in *your* honor."

Matthias sucked in a breath, knowing he wouldn't be able to leave the masquerade unnoticed. Sighing, he replied, "You may tell the queen I have arrived."

"Of course, sir," the man said with a bow and bounced off into the twirling couples on the dance floor.

Matthias observed from the far corner of the ballroom. The back corner was always the most powerful position in any room. He could see and hear everything going on around him.

Yet, as he watched noblemen and women drink far too much wine and dance horribly with one another, nothing seemed out of the ordinary.

His wolf's hearing picked up on a gait he recognized, and Matthias' tense demeanor relaxed slightly.

"Still hiding in the shadows?" Jacques asked with a grin, handing Matthias a glass of wine.

He took it but didn't drink. Though tempted to drown his worries and heartache, he needed to be sharp.

"The shadows conceal everything that doesn't wish to be seen," Matthias replied, taking a quick glance at Jacques before keeping his eyes on the crowd.

"Ah, and the star of tonight wouldn't want anyone to know he's actually present?" Jacques replied, taking a sip of wine.

"Unfortunately, they already do," Matthias answered as he caught sight of the queen at the far end of the ballroom.

She strode down the stairs in an elegant silver gown. A long trail of sparkling fabric flowed from her shoulders, meeting the long train of the starry gown.

The crowd oo'd and ah'd at the sight, but Matthias hardened his gaze.

"I heard you were getting married," he said to Jacques, trying to keep his mind off the queen for as long as possible. He didn't like the woman being in his thoughts more than necessary. "Congratulations."

Jacques rubbed the back of his neck before chugging down the last of the wine. "I'm hoping not to marry. Not yet."

Matthias glanced over at Jacques again. It seemed as if his longtime friend was searching for something—or someone—in the crowd.

"Are you now? I thought you met the love of your life at Vlacklear." Matthias laid the sarcasm on thick, knowing very well how Jacques thought of his family and arranged marriages.

Jacques sent Matthias a deadly glare that had him chuckling. Not many people could get under Jacques' skin and Matthias was pleased he was one of the few that could bring another emotion out of the man besides positivity.

"The betrothal agreement is idiotic, but I don't know what to do about it," Jacques replied. He stared into his empty wine glass, as if hoping it would magically refill. "With my father dying, I'm stuck."

Matthias reached out and clapped Jacques on the shoulder. "You won't find any answers at the bottom of that glass, my friend. Trust me on that."

Jacques frowned but lowered the glass with a sigh.

The queen was halfway across the ballroom and Matthias didn't want her to know anything about Jacques being here. Or One Shot, for that matter, so now was the time to meet her head on.

"Regardless, I'm thankful you're here," Matthias continued. "If there's anything I can do to help you with your predicament, say the word."

"Thank you, sir," Jacques replied.

Defeat wasn't a good look for Jacques and Matthias hoped something could be done about his situation soon.

"Blend in as much as you can. We'll meet at midnight on the terrace."

"Yes sir," Jacques replied and the two strode in opposite directions.

Matthias was glad he departed from Jacques when he did because in no more than ten steps he was face to face with the queen.

"Captain, you're late," Queen Leza said, donning her feline smile.

Matthias refused to let his true fear show and was suddenly thankful for the mask covering the top half of his face. "Apologies, Your Majesty. I wanted to make sure my attire was appropriate for tonight's event."

The queen extended her hand to Matthias. "All is forgiven."

Reluctantly, Matthias took her hand and kissed the top of it, wishing to be anywhere but here.

But he had to be obedient. He knew he was close to finding Devora *and* his mother. Something in his soul kept encouraging him, he was almost there. If he played his cards right, they would all be reunited soon.

Clearing his throat, Matthias offered his hand to Queen Leza. "May I escort you to your throne, Your Majesty?"

Queen Leza nodded, the large imperial opal in her crown taunting Matthias. She slid her thin fingers into the crook of his arm before they strode across the floor.

The crowd parted like water as they came near. Matthias hated their looks of approval and gossiping lips. He knew how it looked, and it was nothing but a lie. A façade.

Thankfully, the queen's throne was closer than Matthias thought. After he guided her there, he quickly broke all contact with the woman and stood as far away as possible. Queen Leza chuckled and sat on her gilded throne.

There were usually two thrones, one for the king and one for the queen. But since the announcement of King Atol's "illness," it was as if the palace had forgotten him entirely. Matthias noticed most of the servants didn't even speak of the king anymore, as if their memories had been erased.

Unease raked over Matthias' gut, but there wasn't enough evidence to prove what his heart was telling him to be true. There actually wasn't any evidence at all and he couldn't figure out why.

Queen Leza stood, and the orchestra quieted down. All eyes turned to her, wide with genuine awe and admiration.

Matthias' frown deepened. Something felt strange about the reaction. He'd seen people fawn over royalty before, but this was different.

"Welcome, honored guests, to the masquerade ball honoring Captain Matthias Blake," Queen Leza announced as she gestured to Matthias at the far end of the platform.

The crowd applauded wildly and focused their attention on him. Matthias did his best to block out all the curious and judgmental stares, but even for someone like him, it was hard not to buckle under the large crowd's scrutiny.

"As you all know, Captain Blake played a pivotal part in reclaiming the citadel of Yekel and uniting Tenton once again."

The crowd roared in applause again and Matthias hated the sound. These people didn't care about what happened to the Yekelians or any other region outside of the palace. They didn't care that it was the king who left Yekel to its doom after he ordered it to be burned to the ground, making them vulnerable to Kadesh's siege.

But, just like they seem to have forgotten King Atol, the crowd also appeared to be unaware of these facts.

Matthias kept his face stoic as the crowd continued its applause. He thought of all the people he had saved and hidden in Totem. He was grateful the numbers were so large. But the thought just behind that one was of how many lives he hadn't saved. How many people he'd ruthlessly killed in his cursed form. Each death was a wound on his heart and soul that would never heal.

Once the crowd died down, Queen Leza continued, "As you all know, our own General Teague was killed recently by the savage Kadeshians."

The crowd gasped and even Matthias was taken aback. He had received no report of General Teague's death. And, as far as he knew, there were no attacks by the Kadeshians. In fact, Kadesh had been laying low since the recapture of Yekel.

"He was a brave general who won many battles for Tenton. My heart is grieved at his passing, but his position will be empty no more, for tomorrow, you will have a new general!"

The queen lifted her hands and dread constricted Matthias' throat.

Please, no, he sent a desperate thought to Tunri, hoping the God that he often ignored would hear him.

But just like when he begged to find his mother and Devora, the answer was silence.

"Tenton, meet your new general who will bring us victory and claim Kadesh as ours, General Matthias Blake!"

The crowd roared with approval and Matthias almost fainted from shock. In addition to the fact that he was too inexperienced to become a general, it didn't make sense. His mind whirled at high speed as foolish nobles in sparkling frocks congratulated him.

Unless that was the point. He *was* inexperienced and the queen knew that. He remembered General Teague and King Atol having several arguments on which places were the best to attack Kadesh. Maybe, like King Atol's "illness," General's Teague's death was planned.

Matthias' mind latched onto the thought, rooting it within him. When he first became a knight at the Fortress, he never thought he would become a puppet and pet to the queen. Maybe he wasn't the only one being controlled by the monarchy.

The glittering nobles continued to pat Matthias on his shoulders and back. Annoyance rattled over him, and he shoved them away, not caring if he offended anyone. He needed to get out of here.

Queen Leza spoke again, but Matthias blocked the sound from his ears. The wolf riled inside of him as his mind focused on one thing: escape.

But as he looked around, people stuffed every inch of the ballroom. It was suffocating and if Matthias didn't leave soon, he would transform and kill every person in sight.

Shoving more sparkling people out of the way, Matthias finally found the exit to the balcony.

It wasn't a full escape, but it would do until he could get the wolf under control.

Bursting through the tall, arched doors, Matthias made sure to close them behind him. As soon as they shut, the cold silence of night overwhelmed his senses. Stalking to the edge of the balcony, he placed his hands on the railing. He ripped the stupid white mask off his face and launched it into the night sky. Growling, he shut his eyes. The wolf was there, gnawing at his soul, begging to be unleashed. Matthias wanted to let it out. He wanted to terrorize the palace and make the fools inside wake up and see the web of lies being spun before them.

But he couldn't.

The queen had his mother somewhere and for all he knew, she'd captured Devora as well. In order to keep the women he loved safe, he had to keep playing this awful game, no matter how battered and bruised his soul became.

Matthias took in a chilling breath, enjoying how the piercing air froze the fury inside of him and quieted the raging wolf.

After a few more breaths, Matthias was ready to return to the masquerade, but he didn't. The coolness of night brought peace to his weary soul, and he didn't want to forget the feeling just yet.

Peering up into the sky, a slow trickle of snowflakes spiraled down from the clouds. Matthias always loved the snow, especially when he first came to the capital. Snow was pure, blanketing all the muck and mess in an iridescent shine. When it snowed, the darkness of the land showed no more.

Closing his eyes, Matthias allowed the flurries to kiss his cheeks. Just a few more minutes and then he'd go back to playing his part.

The doors behind him cracked open and Matthias' wolf instincts shot awake. He barely controlled himself from whipping around and grabbing whoever dared to interrupt his peaceful solitude. But thankfully, his only reaction was a rigid stance.

The footsteps were soft and steady. Whoever approached him wasn't trying to hide, but they weren't trying to attack him either.

They stopped about three feet away from him and Matthias wasn't sure whether he should face them or not until they spoke.

"I hear congratulations are in order, General."

The confident tone of Devora's voice sent all of Matthias' decorum out the window. For a moment, he thought he was hallucinating. He had many times in the past months—thinking she was there when she wasn't.

But as he spun around and laid his eyes on the beautiful woman wrapped in sparkling black and white fabric, he realized she was, in fact, there. And glitter never looked more appealing.

Chapter Thirty-Four

Jacques stared at Ida in pure shock. "What?"

Ida swallowed. "Marry me instead. I know I'm not rich or as beautiful as Hestia, but I—" She took a breath. It was now or never. She had set herself up and wasn't going to back down now. "I love you. I have for a while."

Ida didn't think Jacques could look any more shocked after her proposal, but her confession widened his eyes so much, she thought they would pop out of his head.

As the couples continuously twirled around them and each passing moment ticked by without an answer, the sting of rejection bit into Ida's heart hard.

Mustering a smile, she held her tears back. "It was a silly thought. I need to go."

Jacques finally snapped out of his daze as Ida pulled away from him. "No, Ida, wait."

But it was too late.

Ida pulled free of Jacques' arms and rushed through the crowd. The corset cinching her waist suddenly felt like a tourniquet, cutting off her air supply. Ida forewent pleasantries and nudged and bumped the excited crowd out of the way. Thankfully, Queen Leza was about to make an announcement so all eyes would be in the opposite direction Ida went.

She thought she heard Jacques say her name again as she reached the exit, but she didn't look back.

Silly, stupid girl, she thought to herself. How could someone like her think of proposing to Jacques? She couldn't even imagine what Ama would say. That was if Ida ever got to tell her.

Only a few tears rolled down Ida's cheeks as she burst through the doors and out of the ballroom.

She had been so infatuated with Jacques that she hadn't noticed the humid, suffocating atmosphere of the masquerade. The cool air of the hallway adjacent to the ballroom calmed Ida's frantic pulse.

The double oak doors leading into the ballroom slowly closed behind her, silencing an eruption of applause. Something exciting must have happened, but Ida didn't care. She took a chance and had made herself a fool. The last thing she wanted to do was celebrate.

Removing the beautiful lily mask from her face, Ida wiped the few tears that had fallen from her eyes. Hestia and Reese worked so hard to get her here, she wouldn't waste her time dwelling on Jacques' rejection. There would be many days in the future she could cry about it, but tonight, she wasn't a heartbroken girl, she was a soldier.

Replacing her mask, Ida quietly hurried down the dark hall. Grand portraits of Tenton's line of royalty hung on her left, highlighted by the light of the moon streaming through the grandiose windows on the right. Ida glanced at them every now and again, but kept her mind focused on what the restricted text said about the Book of Ages.

The Book will reveal itself to one who is worthy. Though it may be hidden, the key lies within the crown.

She surmised the crown meant the king and queen and the throne room. But beyond that, the text gave no other clues. Ida searched endlessly trying to find any other information about where to look for the Book of Ages, but there was nothing.

But now that she was in Maldove Palace, walking the halls of the kings and queens of Tenton, she felt Tunri guiding her steps.

Ida had never been to the palace before. Why would a poor Kadeshian girl want to visit the home of the king who'd killed so many of her people? And, more realistically, *how* would a poor Kadeshian girl make it to a place as grand as Maldove palace?

And yet, here she was.

Life—or Tunri, rather—had an interesting way of forging one's path.

Ida succumbed to Tunri's promptings and continued down the hall. A few giggles came from a dark corner she passed, but Ida didn't have any desire to know what was happening there.

Blushing, she quickened her steps until she came to an intersection of three halls.

Closing her eyes, Ida focused her thoughts, hoping Tunri would continue to show her the way.

It was a small, quiet prompting, and Ida needed to concentrate to be sure, but the hall to the right was the correct path.

Breathing a word of thanks, she hurried down the hall. More paintings covered these walls, this time portraits.

Ida stopped at the one of Princess Haden, wondering what had happened to her. It was said Devora captured the princess for ransom. But the ransom timeline came and went, and the princess never returned. Ida thought the kingdom would be in uproar about the disappearance of their beloved princess. But there had been no word about the princess' whereabouts in weeks.

Ida studied the light-skinned girl with bright emerald eyes and striking white-blonde hair. She looked nothing like her parents. Although Ida looked nothing like hers either, but she was adopted.

Saving those thoughts for another day, Ida continued down the hall until she came to two forest green doors. The painted wood reached from floor to ceiling, branded with the symbol of

Tenton—a crown with two antlers protruding from it with five colored interlocking circles between the antlers.

Ida stared at the doors, knowing the throne room was just beyond her reach. She started to reach for the golden handle when she stopped.

Wasn't it a bit odd that she'd gotten this far without being caught? In fact, she hadn't seen a single guard since she left the ballroom. The instincts she'd honed at the Fortress were buzzing that something was awry, but Ida still felt Tunri's push to continue.

Keeping her faith, Ida grabbed the cold handle and opened the door. The throne room was larger than she imagined. Like the first hallway she entered, large, peaked windows stood tall behind the marbled platform holding two golden thrones. Deep green flags, shimmering with Tenton's seal, hung from the windows. A set of candelabras stood on either side of the platform, casting a haunting glow over the room.

Ida wished to experience the throne room during the day. She was sure it would be stunning and not as frightening. Swallowing her nerves, Ida plunged on. Her silk slippers glided quietly along the thick, velvet carpet, the same shade of forest green as everything else in the room. Everything was so fine and lavish in the castle, even the mice probably lived like kings.

Ida chuckled at the silly thought.

She searched around the high columns standing like soldiers on the sides of the room. Running her fingers along the walls, Ida checked for trap doors or hidden spaces where something of significance could hide. Ida looked as high and low as she could in every area of the dimly lit room but found nothing.

Frowning, she placed her hands on her hips. She still felt this was where Tunri was leading her. And the throne room made sense with what the restricted text had said. Ida turned, her eyes scanning every area of the room until her gaze landed on the one place she hadn't checked: the king's and queen's thrones.

Suddenly a bout of fear clouded Ida's thought. *What if someone comes in? What will happen to me? Will I be sent to the Fortress as a prisoner?*

Biting her lip, Ida realized that if she continued to argue with herself, she wouldn't complete her mission from Warden Hazor. And if she could save Devora and the others by finding the Book of Ages, she would.

Gathering her courage, Ida pulled up the hem of her dress and started toward the thrones. After only a few steps, she was there. Just like almost everything else in the room, the velvet lining on the throne was a dark forest green, making the dust upon it look like a layer of snow atop a forest of evergreens.

Ida thought it odd that the chair King Atol was meant to sit in on a regular basis would have a layer of dust. Wouldn't the servants have cleaned it regularly? However, when she turned to the throne on the right, Queen Leza's throne, the seat was perfectly plumped and free from any dust. The gilded armrests shone, as did the backrest of the throne. Though the throne was exquisite and lovely, nothing seemed out of the ordinary.

But Ida still felt she was missing something.

Ida scanned the throne again, searching for something—anything—that would show her where the Book of Ages could be hidden.

She was about to give up when she noticed the cushion of Queen Leza's chair wasn't as perfectly aligned as King Atol's.

Ida's pulse increased, adrenaline flooding her veins as she placed her hands on the askew seat and pried it up. The cushion lifted with little effort, cluing Ida in that this had been done many times before.

Licking her lips, Ida crouched on her knees and peered inside the throne. Her heart almost exploded with joy. There, seated beneath the throne, sat a thick leather-bound book. But there was something odd. Surrounding the book, as if chaining it down, were thick strings of black smoke. An eerie aura pulsed from the smoke and Ida was reminded of the headmistress' hidden power.

Trust.

Holding her breath, Ida stared at the bound book, praying the smoke wouldn't fly out and strangle her. As she reached into the seat of the throne, the smoke hissed, and Ida stopped. Once she found her hand still intact, she reached in again. This time, the smoke hissed then disappeared. Ida's pulse raced. Remembering to breathe, Ida reached in and grabbed the Book of Ages. It was heavier than she thought, and she quickly heaved the book onto her lap as she sat with her back against the throne.

The tome was beautiful, looking as if it had just been bound. On the front cover, a delicate image of an elk was carved into the leather. Ida ran her fingers along the image, remembering what the book Jacques had given to her said about the white elk she'd seen in the Fortress.

The white elk, the soul of Tenton. *Is that why the elk looked so ragged in the Fortress? Is Tenton, as a nation, dying?*

Ida shifted her gaze to the thick strap of leather holding the book shut. Pulling the book closer, Ida examined the lock. It didn't look particularly difficult to open, yet it seemed to be undisturbed.

The phrase from the restricted text rang in Ida's mind again. *The Book will reveal itself to one who is worthy. Though it may be hidden, the key lies within the crown.*

"If I am worthy," she prayed aloud to Tunri. "Please reveal the prophecy to me."

Holding her breath, Ida pinched the leather next to the lock between her fingers and pulled. The lock binding the book easily opened and Ida almost squealed with delight.

She was worthy. Someone like her was worthy to open the Book of Ages.

She knew she should probably leave the throne room before opening the book, but excitement flooded her veins. Forgetting where she was, Ida said a prayer and carefully peeled open the front cover. As she flipped through the sacred pages, a plethora of sentences and languages flooded Ida's mind. The words of so many Seers, so many leaders, from Tenton's past flowed into her like a steady stream, filling her mind with the wisdom of voices past.

Until suddenly, the words stopped, ending with the prophecy that endangered the entire line of Seers for years to come.

Ida's eyes widened in surprise and fear at what she read until a voice interrupted her thoughts.

"Ida?"

Shrieking, Ida slammed the book shut and closed her eyes. So many words still floated in her mind, but she couldn't forget the prophecy. There had to be more to it. It couldn't end in such a horrible way.

Ida rubbed her eyes, shaking her head.

"Ida, what is it?" Jacques' steps came over in a hurry.

Ida then remembered her proposal to Jacques and really wished he hadn't followed her. She didn't know what to say to him after he so blatantly rejected her heart and confession of love.

"You found it," he whispered, crouching down before her.

Ida watched Jacques as he gazed at the book. He'd removed his gilded mask, looking like the same kind man she admired in Lower Grenly.

"Did you open it? What did it say?"

Ida parted her lips to answer when the throne room doors barged open.

"There they are! Guards! I told you there was a spy in the castle and there she is!"

Ida barely had time to push the book into Jacques' hands before Sergio ordered the knights to clap her in irons.

Chapter Thirty-Five

Matthias could hardly believe his eyes. He'd never witnessed a more beautiful sight than Devora standing before him. Her dress shimmered like the stars in the night sky then faded into snow white. The exact opposite of him.

How fitting the gown was, for together, they were complete. And that's exactly what Devora was to him: his other half. She was his light in the darkness, the goodness that kept the shadows away. And he wanted nothing more than to tell her.

Devora started to speak again, but he rushed forward and pressed his lips against hers. All his thoughts, all his apologies, nothing would emit his love and desire for her more than his kiss did. Her words silenced immediately as she reciprocated the kiss.

Matthias deduced gratefully that she'd forgiven him for his horrible betrayal as he ran his fingers through her long hair. He'd never seen it loose and free, and he loved it. Threading the thick strands between his fingers, he cupped her neck and deepened the kiss, not wanting this moment to end. Because as soon as it did, he would have to face reality again.

But the moment had to end, and Matthias regretfully pulled away. "I'm sorry," he breathed against her cheek. The black lace of her mask rubbed against his skin.

"That was a wonderful way to apologize," Devora replied, and Matthias smiled for the first time in weeks.

But he soon snapped back into his usual demeanor and asked, "What are you doing here? You're still wanted for treason."

Devora's eyes searched his own. Their violet shade striking against the black lace mask. Matthias hadn't realized how much he missed those eyes.

"I had a vision from Tunri prompting me to come here. And I wanted to see you," she added with a small smile.

Matthias' heart skipped a beat, but a frown marred his lips. "You went out on your own in Yekel. We were supposed to meet there."

Devora snorted. "First, your Counter Code never said that. Second, if I were still there, you would have never reclaimed Yekel and reunited Tenton."

"Exactly!" Matthias said throwing his arms in the air, frustration lacing his tone. He didn't want this moment to be ruined by his words, but they wouldn't stop. "I'd probably be a lot happier too. I wouldn't be here, stuck in this position."

Devora lifted her chin in the defiant way she always did when she was about to reprimand him. "I thought you wanted to lead Tenton's armies."

Matthias stalked toward her, and he loved the way she never cowered from him. He loved her strength, determination, and stubbornness. Gently, he cupped her face in his hands.

"I would rather spend my life with you, the woman I love and so dearly miss, than lead any soldiers ever again."

He leaned in and kissed her again, wanting to make up for all the ones they missed.

"You're going to have to stop doing that if you want to hear what I have to say," Devora said with a sly grin on her face.

"So far, your visions have not brought me any good, so I would rather keep kissing you than learn of my inevitable doom," he said jokingly, but when he peered down into her worried eyes, he stepped back. "I see."

"No," Devora cried, latching on to his arm. "No, you don't. Tunri's visions only tell me part of the story. I believe He was telling me to come here to warn you. To save you."

Tears rimmed her beautiful bright eyes, and it was too painful for Matthias to bear.

He carefully removed the lace mask from her face and wiped the two tears that had fallen.

"Devora," he sighed, drinking in her face. "I don't know if I'm worth saving. If Tunri has told you my fate, maybe it's best to let it be."

That same fire Devora always held exploded in her eyes as she narrowed her gaze. "Everyone is worth saving, especially you. No one's past is too shadowed for Tunri's healing."

Matthias started to speak when Devora sprang on her tiptoes and kissed him. Surprise whisked his words away.

"See? That's what it's like," she said with a coy smile. "Now, listen. I don't have much time."

Matthias didn't have a chance to utter another word before Devora dove into her vision about the ball, Ida and Jacques, and him and Queen Leza. Matthias felt the queen's grip on his life tighten as Devora told him about Queen Leza putting something around his neck, as if to hang him. It terrified Matthias to no end.

The queen already held him on a tight leash, evoking his powers to transform into a wolf whenever she pleased. But with his new promotion to general, Matthias felt as if his freedom was disappearing even further.

"You need to be careful, Matthias," Devora pleaded as she gripped his hands. "I don't know what's going on with the queen or what happened with King Atol, but this is not good."

Matthias studied Devora, wondering how a woman as bright and wonderful as her could care for the life of someone as cold as him. And she didn't even know about his curse.

Matthias thought about telling her through the Counter Code, but what use would it be? Would Tunri reveal to Devora how to break Matthias' curse? Matthias didn't even know how to break the curse. As far as he knew, so long as the queen lived, he would be forced to transform into a wolf and kill whomever she deemed necessary.

"I know," he said softly.

He was never able to be vulnerable to anyone besides Jacques. Even with One Shot he stayed guarded. But with Devora, he wanted to pour out his entire soul. He wanted to laugh with her, he wanted to cry with her, he wanted to experience life with her. And now, he didn't know if he would be able to do any of that.

"Devora," he said, deciding he would rather her know everything about him than keep lying to her. After he betrayed her, Matthias vowed he would never lie to her again, and he was a man of his word. "You need to know that I've been cursed."

Devora blinked at him, confused.

Matthias took her gloved hands in his. "When I won one of Warden Hazor's tournaments, I was able to become a knight of the Fortress instead of a prisoner. For some reason, the king and queen took an interest in me and wanted to personally congratulate me and perform the knighting ceremony. But before my ceremony, something happened to me." Matthias shook his head, the details of that day still fuzzy.

Then it dawned on him.

The nobles in the crowd forgetting King Atol, his own memories wiped before he was cursed to turn into a wolf. The connection between them was the queen. But he already knew that. The real question was how? How was the queen wiping people's memories and why?

"What do you mean 'something happened to you'?" Devora asked, squeezing his hands.

"The queen cursed me to shift into a wolf," he said bluntly.

He waited for her to laugh at him or call her crazy. But just like their time in the Fortress, Devora surprised him.

"A gray wolf?" she asked quietly.

Matthias' brows rose. "Yes."

"Like Warden Hazor's hunting wolves."

He nodded.

She paused for a moment, and he could see her mind working. "You were there. When I fed the wolves."

Matthias smirked. "I had to make sure you were doing your job correctly."

Devora pursed her lips. "I always wondered why you were so fast and strong."

With his pride hurt, Matthias explained, "I have *always* been fast and strong, even before I was cursed. Why are you taking this so well?"

Devora shrugged and ticked off her fingers one by one. "One of my best friends can make weapons out of anything she lays her hands on, another one can shoot an arrow hundreds of feet without missing, I can see visions of the future, and now the man I love can shift into a wolf." She held up her hands. "I don't know what else could really surprise me at this point."

Matthias tilted his head back and laughed, enjoying the warm sensation of joy rumbling through his soul. He glanced back at Devora, his mind replaying her words: *the man I love.*

"Do you really love me?" he asked, his voice serious.

"I don't lie or cheat," she said with a smile, referencing their game of Kings that seemed like years ago.

He cupped her face again. "How? Why?"

"Does there need to be a reason?" she asked, gazing up at him. "I have them, of course, but you just need to know that I do. Would I risk coming here if I didn't?"

Matthias didn't need any more explanation as he bent down and kissed her again, savoring the taste of her lips on his own.

"Sir!" a voice cried.

The doors to the balcony swung open and Matthias flung Devora behind him so fast, he feared she would fly off the balcony. But when he glanced over his shoulder, she was still there, keeping her eyes hidden from view.

"What is it?" Matthias growled, allowing the wolf's anger to overtake his own.

"Apologies, sir," an extremely uncomfortable and embarrassed knight said as he bowed deeply. "There has been a spy caught in the throne room. You're needed immediately to make judgment."

Matthias controlled his features, but irritation radiated through him. He couldn't ignore a spy in the palace. He hated to leave Devora, but they both knew their time would end eventually.

"Very well," he said regretfully. "I'll be there shortly."

The knight bowed again, making sure not to glance at the flowing skirt hidden behind Matthias' frame.

Once the knight departed, Matthias turned around to find Devora's lips on his once more. She wrapped her arms around his neck and held him tight. Matthias returned the embrace before it ended all too soon.

"Make that one last," she whispered, placing a hand on his cheek. "Remember what I said. I know we'll meet again."

"I love you," was all he could manage to say, his heart breaking as she released him from her grasp.

"And I, you," Devora replied before placing her mask back on her face and fading back into the glittering crowd of the ballroom.

Chapter Thirty-Six

Jacques, Maldove Palace, Juro

"Unhand her immediately," Jacques roared, ready to skewer Sergio like a fish.

When would this annoyance of a man leave him and Ida be? Jacques had already messed up by agreeing to an engagement with Hestia, then even *more* when he failed to respond to Ida's proposal.

Jacques still couldn't believe that beautiful, kind, caring Ida would admit to loving him after everything he'd put her through. He was frustrated and irritated at himself for his actions, how could she not be?

She had misinterpreted his silence as rejection, which was the opposite of what Jacques felt. And now that he'd finally found her, Sergio barged in—*again*—and had the audacity to have Ida arrested.

"Stand aside, prefect." Sergio puffed out his chest as the palace knights placed shining manacles on Ida's wrists.

Jacques recognized the imperial opal stone of the manacles from when Babshee was brought to the Fortress. It had taken him and the other Fortress knights ages to chain the giant down.

Jacques remembered how Babshee fought tooth and nail against the imperial opal, knowing what it would do to his powers. At the time, Jacques didn't care what the giant thought, he only wanted to be done with the job. Obey orders, that's what he was good at.

But now that he saw the same stone locked around Ida's thin wrists, Jacques' heart twisted. To the untrained eye, one wouldn't notice the drain the stone had on Ida because of her Translator gift. But Jacques knew her. And he also knew the effects of the stone if worn too long.

A tornado of fury erupted from deep inside Jacques and for once, he didn't want to obey anyone's orders but his own.

Rearing back, he balled his fingers and barreled his fist into Sergio's jaw. Sergio flew across the floor, landing on his backside before the two thrones.

"Jacques, no," Ida cried, though it was a weak plea.

Jacques knew he should stop, but Sergio had been an annoyance since day one. Even the long patience of a man like Jacques came to an end eventually.

Sergio scurried away from Jacques, like the coward he really was.

"Stand up," Jacques commanded. "I want a fair fight."

Sergio grinned that coy smile that Jacques had come to despise. "I don't want a fight at all. I just want that filth arrested." Sergio pointed at Ida, and Jacques had enough.

Grabbing Sergio by his tunic, Jacques lifted him off the ground then plowed another fist into his chin. Sergio fell back again, and the coy smile knocked from his face.

"You want to fight? For her?" Sergio flung his arm toward Ida, who was now chained between two guards.

Jacques was surprised the guards weren't assisting Sergio. Maybe they thought him just as annoying as Jacques did.

"I would fight for her any day," Jacques growled.

Sergio laughed. "Oh, Jacques, you have no idea who she really is. What she's really done."

Jacques needed to stop this fool from talking or he would kill him outright. He was on the brink of losing control. The only other time he had lost control of his anger this much was when Helene died. Jacques didn't want to fall back into that darkness again.

But one more punch wouldn't hurt.

Swinging his fist, Jacques waited for it to crack against Sergio's nose when a hand came out and absorbed the blow.

Jacques paled as he looked into Matthias' eyes, not wanting to think about his friend and superior officer seeing him in such an unraveled state.

"I think your point has been made," Matthias said coolly, releasing Jacques' fist.

Jacques returned his hand to his side, shame filling his heart. Every time he tried to make something better, it got worse and worse. He should've just kept his head down, completed Warden Hazor's assignment of watching out for Ida, then returned to the Fortress. He never thought his feelings would tangle up everything so horribly.

Matthias raked his gaze over Sergio's form, unimpressed. "Who would care to tell me why three guests of the masquerade are in the throne room?"

Sergio scrambled up like the weasel he was, sidling up to Matthias. "That woman is a threat to Tenton, general. She is not only a spy, but a Kadeshian, as well!"

Matthias analyzed Sergio with the same cold stare he gave all the soldiers at the Fortress until Sergio squirmed.

Jacques smirked, but it fell once Matthias turned to him. "A Kadeshian spy?"

Hopefully, Warden Hazor had clued Matthias in on the mission he placed the twins, Ida, and himself on at Vlacklear. But Matthias' stoic face was so unreadable, Jacques wasn't sure.

"I know nothing of this, general," Jacques replied, the new title for Matthias feeling odd. "As far as I know, Miss Shabawn has been attending Vlacklear with myself and Mister Amata. He can attest that she has done nothing out of the ordinary."

"She's a spy! I know she is! I have proof!" Sergio wailed like a cat.

Matthias spun around to him. "Show me."

Sergio's face paled whiter than the snow falling outside. "I—I don't have it with me."

Matthias sighed, pinching the bridge of his nose. "I was interrupted for this," he muttered under his breath.

"Take this young woman out of those irons," Matthias started to say.

Relief flooded Jacques' veins until Matthias continued.

"Give her regular irons and place her in the upper cells until we can figure out what's going on."

"What?" Jacques claimed as the guards switched Ida's bonds to regular metal manacles. "But sir—"

Matthias sent Jacques a cold glare, shutting Jacques' lips immediately.

Sergio smiled smugly at Jacques. "Thank you, general. I believe you will have a long and prosperous career."

"Guards, get this idiot out of my sight," Matthias flicked his wrist at Sergio.

"Hey, wait, but I—" Sergio started as the three guards surrounded him. They latched onto his arms and yanked him through the throne doors, kicking and screaming.

Once Sergio was disposed of, the guards began to lead Ida away when Jacques stepped to Matthias' side.

"Wait, let me talk to her. Please, sir."

An understanding crossed over Matthias' usually cold gaze as he nodded at the guards to wait.

Swallowing, Jacques stood before Ida.

She turned her beautiful doe eyes on him, and it pained his heart to see the hurt swimming inside them.

"I'll get you out of there. We'll figure this out. Yes?" He tried to smile, but it wouldn't come.

But what was worse was Ida's lack of response. She only nodded and let the guards take her away.

Once they'd exited the throne room, Jacques faced Matthias with fury.

"Why are you imprisoning her? She hasn't done anything wrong."

Matthias dropped his hard exterior, his shoulders slumping as he strode to the platform the thrones rested on and sat down. He rubbed his eyes.

"What did you expect me to do with so many witnesses, Jacques? She was clearly trespassing in the king's and queen's throne room. The only reason you're not in chains right now is because you're a knight of the Fortress."

"Then arrest me," Jacques practically screamed, his anger hot. "I would rather be in the dungeon with her than here with you."

Matthias glared up at him. "My previous company was far superior to you as well. Now settle down before we both do something we regret."

Jacques took a breath and stalked away, his anger dulling to a simmer.

"What was she looking for?" Matthias inquired.

"The Book of Ages," Jacques responded, swatting his hand in the air. "Apparently, it's the book that holds all the prophecies from Tenton's past Seers."

Matthias' whole form went rigid, and he stood. "Did she find it? Was it here?"

"Yes."

"Where is it now?"

Jacques shrugged. "I don't know. She was just about to tell me something when that idiot came in."

Matthias' eyes narrowed. "Is she really Kadeshian?"

Jacques nodded. "The warden confirmed it."

"Not a spy?"

"As far as I know, she's spying for Warden Hazor alone."

"Aren't we all?" Matthias grumbled under his breath. "I knew of her gift, so I removed the imperial opal chains. But the fact that she had them on in the first place meant that man knew of her gift as well. Be careful, Jacques. I don't know what he wants, but he doesn't seem likely to give up easily."

Jacques ran his fingers through his hair. "He's been a thorn in my side since I was put on this mission. He constantly flirts with Ida. It's maddening."

Standing, Matthias straightened his tunic. "I can give you until tomorrow to prove Ida's innocence." His face softened as he placed a hand on Jacques' shoulder. "Be smart, my friend. I don't know who the enemy is here, but they may all be allied against us."

Jacques nodded, knowing he should salute, but didn't have the strength. Matthias took in a breath then exited the throne room, leaving Jacques alone with his tormented soul.

How could he prove Ida's innocence? She was Kadeshian *and* she was a spy. She just wasn't a Kadeshian spy.

Jacques could reveal that Ida was really a spy for the Fortress, but that would open a whole different box of troubles. And he really didn't want to get on Warden Hazor's bad side more than he already was.

Jacques scrubbed his face with his hands, trying to force a solution to come to his thoughts, but all he could think of was Ida proposing to him.

He'd never heard of a woman proposing to a man before, but he had to say he felt extremely flattered by it.

If only Ida was his betrothed instead of Hestia. Then, by Tenton law, Ida would be a true citizen of Tenton and none of Sergio's threats would hold any weight.

Jacques' head shot up, excitement pumping through his veins. Could he really get out of the betrothal *and* save Ida? He had to try.

With a new determination in his heart, Jacques raced out of the throne room.

Chapter Thirty-Seven

For all the strange twists her life had taken, Ida never expected to be imprisoned twice in one day. Though she did suppose it was well after midnight now. But even being imprisoned twice in two days was too many times for her.

She stared down at the simple black pants and white tunic she was given to change into. At least Hestia's beautiful gown wouldn't get soiled.

Ida thought she would cry after being placed in the cell, but surprisingly, she felt more comfortable in the cell than she had at Vlacklear.

Settling on the cot, Ida realized Captain Blake had placed her in a nicer cell than most. In the Fortress she had been tasked with sanitation, meaning she had to clean out the inmates' cells. Which wasn't the most pleasant job, but Ida was a hard worker and most of the inmates were more courteous than she first realized.

But the inmates in Level Five didn't receive as nice cells as the prisoners on Level Three. Of course, the soldiers were housed on Level Two, so Ida assumed they were the nicest cells out of them all.

As Ida studied the palace cell again, she realized this cell was just as nice as the one she called home in the Fortress. She was thankful for Captain Blake's kindness, especially that he changed her chains. She hated the heavy drain the imperial opal manacles had on her. It must have something to do with her Translator powers, apparently something Captain Blake also knew.

Ida shook her head. How many people had Warden Hazor told? For a man who seemed so secretive, he sure did tell a lot of people *her* secrets.

Ida sighed, wondering what had happened to the Book of Ages. Just when she pushed it into Jacques' hands, it disappeared. As if it knew Sergio was coming and the wrong hands would seize it. But if it could appear and reappear, why hadn't it just appeared to her when she discovered the restricted book's clue?

Ida remembered the smoke chains binding the book inside the base of the throne. Maybe the Book had tried to come to her but couldn't.

Closing her eyes, Ida sighed. Too many intense things had happened in such a short amount of time. She wished she could go back to Lower Grenly. Back with Ama and Jil. Back to a simpler life when no one knew who she was, and she could be plain, quiet Ida.

"I don't think it would be wise of me to break out another one of my soldiers," a gruff voice called from outside of the cell, giving Ida a fright.

She squealed and scurried to the back edge of her cot, her heart pounding against her rib cage. After she took a breath to settle her pulse, she recognized the broad form of Warden Hazor.

"Sir?" Ida asked, confusion flooding her thoughts. "What are you doing at the palace?"

Warden Hazor held up the iron plated mask in his hands. "Did you think I wouldn't celebrate the promotion of my right-hand officer?"

Ida hummed, unconvinced. "I've noticed you always seem to have alternative plans."

Warden Hazor shook his head with a smirk. "Figured me out already?"

"Why else would you save a Kadeshian girl with no future or purpose?"

Warden Hazor blinked at her frankness. But Ida was tired. She'd been imprisoned by Sergio, saved by Reese, tailored by Mei, rejected by Jacques, and arrested by Captain—General—Blake. She had no more energy for manners and games.

The warden regained his composure as he stroked his mustache. "I could say it was out of duty and honor. Doing the right thing. But the reasons were purely selfish."

Ida scooted to the end of the cot where she was only a foot away from the warden on the other side of the cell bars. Ama had told her a captain brought Ida to her and Apa, but nothing more. The only reason Ida knew it was Warden Hazor who saved her that day was because of her own memories.

She'd often wondered why the captain with the thick mustache wanted to save an orphan from the enemy.

"A few weeks before my company was sent to Renta, a group of rogue Kadeshians attacked a small border city outside of Shaldo. They set fires to the buildings and slaughtered anyone who was unlucky enough to be there."

Warden Hazor paused, and Ida watched as the iron-strong warden she'd come to know in the Fortress began to weep.

"My wife and young daughter were killed in that attack. I'd just been sent on patrol. I would have returned in two days. But it didn't matter. They were gone and there was nothing I could do about it."

Ida's heart shattered at the horrible injustice that happened to Warden Hazor. She now understood why he had become a hardened man. How could he not have?

"When I was assigned to attack your home nation, I was ready." A fire lit in the warden's piercing eyes as he continued, "I wanted to make Kadesh pay for what it did to my family."

Ida shuddered, remembering the destruction of her home citadel. The awful screams, the smoke. She still remembered everything even though it had been so many years ago.

"But when we took the city, the hollowness inside didn't waver. It only grew." The warden sighed. "When my soldiers found you in that destroyed building, still alive after two days, I felt it was my duty to save you. Though no one saved my daughter, I could not condemn someone else's to that same cruel fate."

A lump lodged in Ida's throat at the warden's raw words. Even though she had no family, even though she was no one special, the warden still chose to save her.

"Why did you stay away? Why weren't you a part of my life?" Ida asked. "Don't you think I wanted to know the man who saved my life?"

A pained look crossed the warden's face and he turned away. "Again, pure selfishness. I was glad I found you a good home, but every time I saw you, I could only think of Hanna. And when Cyrus wrote me and said your Translator gift had grown, I couldn't bear to come anymore." Warden Hazor turned away from Ida, to hide the continuous stream of tears rolling down his cheeks.

With her heart shattered, Ida stood and strode toward the cell bars. Cautiously, she reached out and held the warden's hand. She was surprised when he didn't shove her off or push her away. Ama taught her long ago that sometimes, a comforting hand was all a person needed to know they weren't alone.

"Hanna had just started translating the month before she was killed. When I saw you reading the parchments in my pack on our way back to Tenton, I knew I was right to save you. But I couldn't bear to see you, to be a part of your life, and try to replace my own daughter with you."

Ida wasn't sure how to respond to the comment, but she often wasn't sure how to respond to many things. It was one of the reasons she didn't speak much. She'd discovered long ago that most people just needed a listening ear instead of a jabbering mouth.

So that's what Ida did. And she was thankful for that decision because, especially in moments like these, she'd learned so much by listening to someone, rather than trying to talk over them.

Ida patted Warden Hazor's callused hand and waited until he dried his tears and regained his hard exterior once more.

His piercing eyes analyzed her, and Ida only smiled. She wasn't angry or upset with the warden. In fact, she felt the opposite. She could finally confirm her thoughts that Warden Hazor was the one who saved her. Maybe he saved her for selfish reasons, but Ida didn't care about the reason. She was just grateful.

"If something horrible doesn't happen to me in the next few hours," Ida started, releasing his hand. "I would like to begin a friendship, if that's all right with you." She held her hands in front of her.

"Do you think something horrible is going to happen to you?"

Ida paused and thought about the question. She really didn't feel fearful or frightened about her future. Though she was locked in a cell, she'd been in a cell before and Tunri sent someone to release her from prison, both in the Fortress and the Tower.

With a smile, Ida shook her head. "No, I don't think so."

The warden smirked. "Faithful to the end."

"Tunri hasn't failed me yet, warden. And He won't fail you."

Warden Hazor gave a curt nod. "We'll see." He extended his arm through the bars. "I accept your offer of friendship."

Giddiness sputtered in Ida's heart as she placed her small dark hand in the warden's large pale one. She thought his grip would crush her fingers together when instead he was gentle as they shook on their agreement.

"Blake will make his judgment on you after he is officially promoted," the warden said, releasing Ida's hand. "The queen, I believe, is using this trial to test him out. I suggest you start praying to your God for a miracle."

Ida's back felt like an iron rod when she awoke the next morning. The cot in the palace cell was not nearly as comfortable as hers in the Fortress. Twisting back and forth, she worked out the kinks, causing the chains still secured around her wrists to clink around. Thankfully, a small meal of a hunk of bread, some dried meat, and water was placed in her cell. She devoured it without a second thought.

Ida wasn't sure what time it was or how long she'd slept. Warden Hazor said Captain—General—Blake would make his judgment on her arrest after he was promoted. But when would that be?

Ida shuddered at the memory of Sergio shouting she was a Kadeshian spy. Would the newly promoted general be merciful to her because she was his soldier? Or would he be ruthless because she was his enemy?

Either way, she knew Tunri would guide her path. If today was her last, she was thankful she'd found the Book of Ages and told Jacques she loved him.

Her heart sagged at the thought, remembering his words to her before she was taken to her cell.

We'll figure it out, you and me.

You and me. Ida sighed. If only it could have been. But Jacques was still betrothed to Hestia and Ida was locked away in the dungeon.

A few moments later, a knight came to escort her from her cell. Ida held her head high. She wasn't ashamed to be Kadeshian and she wasn't ashamed to be a Translator. If the discovery of one of those things got her killed, she would accept it. But she still prayed to Tunri for deliverance, just for good measure.

The knight led Ida down the dimly lit corridor of the dungeon then up a set of spiraled stone steps. A bright stream of light blinded Ida as she shuffled into the lower level of the palace. Raising her hands, she rubbed her eyes, waiting for them to adjust.

Once they did, Ida lowered her arms and gasped. She found herself in a large room, almost as large as the Theater in the Fortress. Rows upon rows of people sat all around. Some were on a balcony circling the room, but most were seated in chairs on the floor. It reminded her of the indoor track in Vlacklear Academy, where the headmistress conducted her trials during the Assembly.

Fear crept over Ida as she saw Captain Blake standing on a platform before the crowd, Queen Leza eerily close to his left side. Was he General Blake yet?

"A Kadeshian spy was caught in my throne room last night during the masquerade," the queen announced to the crowd.

The crowd gasped in shock and Ida winced. For all her training at the Fortress, she'd done a horrible job at being stealthy.

"I call up our witness to the event to provide the details of what happened and allow our new general to make his judgment on the case."

Ida scowled as Sergio strutted to the platform, enjoying the attention the crowd gave him. She wished now more than ever that she'd been a better soldier, and that General Blake liked her. While she never failed at any of his tasks, she certainly wasn't one of the best soldiers in the group. And now her life was in her former commander's hands once again.

Sergio recounted the scenario of last night, adding several embellishments and lies. Apparently, Ida had a band of spies with her that were planning on sabotaging the general's promotion ceremony and to kidnap the queen. But Sergio—alone—defeated them and held them off until the guards came. That's why he wore so many bruises on his face.

Ida snorted at the tall tale and the guard beside her smirked. It was then Ida recognized Sir Conan. It was too dark in the dungeon before and he had his faceplate on, but now that she was in the light, and his faceplate was up, she recognized him. She wondered if he had been there last night and had seen what really happened: Sergio getting the tar knocked out of him by Jacques. Ida wished she hadn't been so dazed by the imperial opal irons so she could've enjoyed the fight more.

As Sergio added several more embellishments to his account, Ida searched around the room, looking for Jacques' sandy blond hair. But after several scans, he was nowhere to be found.

Her shoulders drooped. Why would she expect him to be there? He wasn't bound to her in any way. He said they would figure it out, but that could've just been more pretty words.

Another person suspiciously absent was the headmistress. After the woman ordered Ida to be locked in the Tower, she would've thought the headmistress would be front and center at the trial. But the woman was nowhere to be found.

"Bring out the accused," General Blake's voice boomed through the room.

Ida held her breath. *Help me be strong, Tunri.*

"Good luck," Sir Conan whispered as he led her down a set of stairs into the open forum.

The crowd sent nasty glares at Ida, hurling uncouth insults at her as if she were the one who'd ravaged Tenton's lands and killed its people. What they didn't realize was that Ida had suffered losses on both sides. She had lost Josef and Apa. One Kadeshian and one Tentonian. Both lost lives broke her heart. The pain didn't differ based on their nation.

Ida held her chin high, doing her best to be the strong woman she hoped she could someday become.

Sir Conan stopped them before the platform. General Blake peered down at her with a look of sympathy, one Ida had never seen while under his command at the Fortress. Queen Leza's face held great apathy, as if she would rather be anywhere but here. But Sergio's look was the one that riled her the most. Smug arrogance marred his handsome face, and Ida wanted nothing more than to smack it off.

General Blake waited a moment too long, and the crowd started to stir. Ida studied the man. He had always been punctual when leading their exercises. Was there a reason he hesitated this time?

Ida prayed the miracle she so desperately needed would come soon.

But another moment passed by, and Ida knew the trial would continue.

"Ida Shabawn," General Blake started, taking a quick look around before gluing his eyes on her. "Are you Kadeshian?"

"Of course, she's Kadeshian," Sergio interrupted.

Ida glanced down at her dark skin. Though the people in Grenly had darker skin, Ida was always the darkest. But that never made her feel ashamed about it.

"Mister Amata, I suggest you hold your tongue before I have you arrested, as well," General Blake said coolly.

Sergio promptly shut his lips and Ida was grateful General Blake wasn't a fool.

He then focused back on her. "Well?"

Ida swallowed. "I am Kadeshian."

Sergio's face lit with triumph as the crowd tittered with murmurs.

Ida did her best not to hear the slanderous verbiage of the audience.

General Blake didn't silence the crowd but waited for them to die down on their own. Ida still felt the nudge that he was waiting for something. Or—hopefully—someone.

The general waited a moment longer and Ida watched his resolve drop. He'd given all the time he could for whoever he was expecting. Ida's fate would be sealed in the next few moments.

"Do you plead innocent or guilty to the accusations of being a spy for Kadesh?" The general gave Ida a slight tilt of the head.

She caught the gesture and his specific question. She *was* Kadeshian and she *was* a spy. But she wasn't a Kadeshian spy.

A bloom of hope blossomed in her soul once more.

"I plead innocent. I am not a spy for Kadesh."

Quick relief cast over the general's face, knowing she'd understood his olive branch to her.

"This is preposterous!" Sergio cried, stomping down the steps.

Before anyone could react, he grabbed Ida by the arm and shook her. "This woman is a spy. Sent here to destroy us all! You're all fools!"

Ida felt herself yanked back and forth before the doors at the back of the room slammed open.

As she was being whipped back and forth, Ida's eyes landed on Jacques sprinting toward her.

Rearing his fist back, Jacques plowed it into Sergio's cheek, sending him crashing into the nearest row of nobles.

Panting, Jacques glared down at Sergio. "Don't ever touch my wife again."

Chapter Thirty-Eight

Ida blinked at Jacques, unable to think about anything other than the question: *Wife?*

The crowd stared at Jacques in horror at his declaration, but he ignored them all and strode up to Ida.

Taking her hands in his, he looked her in the eye. "No more lies, remember? I love you and I have for a while." He smiled, repeating the words she'd told him the night before. "It just took me a little longer to say it."

Tears gathered in Ida's eyes, and she couldn't help but smile. "But we're not married. What about your betrothal?"

"You're not married *yet*," a voice said from behind.

Ida spun around to find Reese holding a stack of parchment and wearing a determined look. Behind her stood Hestia and the frizzy blond-haired boy who always followed her around while they were at the Fortress. Ida's brows rose at their interlocked fingers.

"Charles?" Jacques gaped, staring at the frizzy blond. "What are you doing here?"

Charles tilted his head to the side with a grin. "I could ask you the same thing, cousin."

"Cousin?" Ida asked, feeling extremely confused as to what was happening.

"General Blake," Reese announced, marching passed Ida and Jacques. "I have come to declare the innocence of Ida Shabawn and annul the betrothal of Jacques Delequa to Michiko Sandje."

"What?" a new voice popped up from the crowd.

Ida whipped around to find Duke Sandje storming from his seat heading straight toward Reese.

"You ungrateful child! I will deal with you properly later," he cried as he reached for Reese, but General Blake stood.

"Duke Sandje, I advise you not to lay a hand on any member presenting a case to me. If you do not return to your seat, I will send you to the dungeons."

Duke Sandje retracted his hand but cast a scathing glare at Reese.

Ida breathed a sigh of relief, remembering witnessing the duke's wrath before. But she still prayed her friend knew what she was doing.

"Thank you, General," Reese said, paying her father no mind. Hurrying up to Ida, she lowered her voice and said, "I didn't stand up for Hestia during the Assembly and I've regretted it every day. I *will* stand up for you and I *will* win this case." Reese squeezed Ida's hands as she continued toward the platform holding the general and the queen.

Ida sent a prayer for Reese and admired her friend's fierceness and grace as she began her argument.

"Miss Shabawn has been accused of espionage and this claim is completely false. I would like to call Professor Mal, the Linguistics and Horticulture professor from Vlacklear Academy, as a witness."

Murmurs dispersed through the crowd as Professor Mal was led into the grand hall by another knight.

The professor gave Ida a wink as she passed before shuffling up to the platform. She bowed to the queen.

"Proceed," General Blake said, looking extremely interested in the events happening around him.

"Thank you, General," Reese said, handing her stack of papers to Hestia who reluctantly released Charles' hand. However, the boy was still only a hair away from her.

Ida couldn't believe her friends had rushed to her aid. She was so overwhelmed with emotions; she didn't know what to think. Ida always thought she was alone, and no one cared for her. But Tunri had proved her wrong again. Jacques loved her! Reese and Hestia came to defend her. Even General Blake tried to help her out.

Tears brimmed Ida's eyes, but she held them back. She trusted Jacques, Reese, and Hestia with her life. There was nothing to cry about. Not anymore.

"Professor Mal," Reese began, facing the professor. "Is it true that Miss Shabawn attended every one of your classes?"

The professor nodded. "Yes, Ida is one of the few students I have that has perfect attendance. She never missed a day."

"And is it true that you are considered one of the most difficult professors when it comes to assignments?" Reese added on. "I've calculated that more than sixty-eight percent of students fail out of at least one of the classes you teach."

Professor Mal snickered. "Yes, that is true, as well. My assignments take up most of my students' time."

A few murmurs rose from the crowd, but one glare from General Blake had them silenced immediately.

Reese held up the piece of parchment in her hand. "This is Miss Shabawn's class schedule. Along with Linguistics and Horticulture, she also had several other classes. Professor, how are Ida's class marks?"

"She never was sent to the Tower, if that's what you mean," the professor replied frankly.

General Blake interjected. "Explain what the Tower is."

"The Tower is where students who make poor marks on their assignments are sent for punishment," Reese explained.

General Blake's eyes narrowed. "I see. Please continue."

Reese nodded then turned to Professor Mal once more. "Is there any way a student of high standing with a schedule like this could find time to 'spy' on the king and queen?"

"I would think not," Professor Mal replied without hesitation. "And if you ask me, if anyone's a spy, it's that Amata boy. He's always goofing off, never getting his assignments done, yet he was never sent to the Tower once."

Sergio made a face from his place between the guards but didn't refute the comment.

Ida felt a surge of confidence flow through her and the need to speak up on her tongue.

"Reese," she whispered. "Can I say something?"

"If it's not detrimental to my case, then sure," Reese replied as she took the papers from Hestia's hands, filing through them.

Ida nodded, knowing the words she spoke were not from her, but Tunri. "General, I need to correct one thing my defendant said. I have been sent to the Tower."

The crowd gasped. Some nodded like they knew it all along. Jacques gave Ida a confused look, but she continued.

"You were sent to the Tower although your marks were satisfactory?" General Blake asked.

Ida nodded. "Sent is a kinder word than what actually happened. Sergio and the headmistress of Vlacklear Academy, who is his aunt, lured me to the Tower, drugged me, then locked me in there."

"What?" Jacques cried; outrage written all over his face. He sent a murderous glare to Sergio before taking Ida's still chained hands. "Why didn't you tell me?"

"You can't prove anything," Sergio sneered.

"Thank you, Ida," Reese nodded with approval as she stepped forward once more. "That leads me to my next point, General. I found Ida bound in the Tower, alone, the day of the masquerade ball. I hadn't seen her for a few hours and knew she had gone to meet Mister Amata earlier." Reese rifled through the parchments and held up the note that Sergio left on Ida's door.

"Here is a note signed by Mister Amata himself asking Ida to meet him in the back hall of Vlacklear, exactly where the entrance to the Tower is." Reese handed the parchment to a knight, who handed it to General Blake.

The general scrutinized the note before asking, "How do we know this is his handwriting?"

Reese grinned and handed the knight another parchment. "Here is a copy of Mister Amata's notes from Linguistics. The manuscript matches perfectly."

General Blake scanned both documents then nodded.

"Oh, and just for good measure, Sergio was blackmailing Ida to do his assignments for him," Hestia piped in from the side.

Sergio's face paled as the crowd whispered to one another. Ida didn't hear any slanderous words cast toward her, but toward Sergio.

"That was only because Aunt Beta told me too!" Sergio whined and the crowd's whispers increased.

"Silence," General Blake boomed before speaking to Reese. "You've made a strong argument toward Miss Shabawn's innocence toward espionage but she's still a Kadeshian illegally in Tenton."

"That's right!" Sergio cried.

A vein ticked in General Blake's neck. "Gag him."

"What?" Sergio squeaked before the knights flanking his sides filled his mouth with cloth then tied a piece over his lips and around the back of his head.

Muffled cries came from Sergio's mouth but thankfully, no more words came out. With the headmistress nowhere to be found, Sergio was on his own.

"That's where we come in," Hestia said, holding up Charles' hand with a wide grin. "We're married!"

Reese ran her hand down her face as confusion passed around the room.

"Married?" Jacques questioned with a quirked brow. He stalked up to Hestia and Charles. "What about the betrothal law?"

Reese flipped through more of her papers until she found an unrolled scroll. "The betrothal law states that a member of each of the willing families must be united by their twentieth birthdays. Neither Charles nor Hestia are past twenty yet and they represent the Delequa and Sandje families, as the original contract agreed upon."

Ida's eyes went wide, as she grasped what Reese was saying. They didn't have to break the contract because the contract had been fulfilled. And Jacques wasn't bound to marry Hestia any longer.

"Hestia," Ida said, reaching out to her friend. "Is this what you truly want? I don't want you to marry someone else so I can be happy."

Hestia laughed and squeezed Ida's hand. "I would be lying if I said I'd done this all for you, Ida. When I met Charles at the Fortress, we immediately recognized each other from childhood." Hestia shrugged, "This was a great way for all of us to have our cake and eat it too."

"Miss Sandje and Mister Delequa being married does not help Miss Shabawn's case in residing illegally in Kadesh," General Blake announced. "Unless she proves citizenship by documentation or marriage, I will have to continue with the charges."

Before Ida could comprehend General Blake's words, she was spun around. Jacques placed his hands on her shoulders, then slid them down her arms and held her hands. His hazel eyes burned with anticipation and worry.

"I know I didn't answer you right away yesterday, but my answer is yes. I will marry you." His shaky hands pulled a gold band with a shining diamond on it from his pocket. "But will you marry me?"

Ida swallowed at the knot in her throat, unable to find her words as she gawked at the ring. She had never seen a diamond so huge. She had never seen a diamond *at all.* Ida didn't need time to think as she nodded her head violently and Jacques smiled.

"General, I would like to ask for a formal recognition of the engagement of Lord Jacques Delequa to Miss Ida Shabawn," Reese said, grinning widely.

General Blake did his best to keep his face stern as he replied, "Granted. Release Miss Shabawn from her chains. You have one month to sanctify this marriage before the Court of Tenton's recognition expires."

The crowd erupted into applause, loving the drama of the trial.

As the audience cheered and clapped around them, Ida's breath left her lungs. *A month? Would she really marry Jacques in a month?*

Once the guards unlocked her manacles, Ida turned to Jacques, wondering if he was just as overwhelmed as she felt. But his gaze held nothing but happiness.

As soon as Ida's chains were gone, Jacques scooped her up in his arms and kissed her. Ida melted into the kiss, wrapping her arms around his neck, pulling him as close as she could.

Some of the crowd aw'd but Ida couldn't care less what anyone thought anymore. Someone like her would be marrying the man of her dreams.

"General, if I may add an additional request," Reese said, glancing up from her stack of papers.

General Blake took a breath. "Proceed."

Ida watched Reese and this time when she spoke to the general, she seemed nervous. "I wish to file charges against Duke Gou Sandje of Sandje Textiles for tax evasion."

Ida gasped. Duke Sandje erupted from the crowd again, sputtering all sorts of threats at Reese for being a disgrace to the Sandje name, at Hestia for being a loose woman, and a whole plethora of cruel comments Ida couldn't believe left the mouth of a man of his position.

Jacques' hands tightened around Ida's waist as the duke came near them, but he paid them no mind.

"Guards, restrain Duke Sandje while I hear what Miss Sandje has to say," General Blake said calmly.

Sir Conan and the other knight who had previously guarded Ida grabbed Duke Sandje before he could slap Reese across the face.

"Not a word or you'll be escorted to the dungeons," General Blake threatened. "Continue, Miss Sandje."

With shaking hands, Reese gave another parchment to the general. "Here are the last three seasons of financial reports for Sandje Textiles. As you can see by the places marked, there has been an increase in profit that is the exact amount due to the kingdom for taxes." Reese held up another huge stack of papers. "I researched the rest of the accounts and discovered Duke Sandje has been evading taxes for the past ten years."

Cries of outrage rumbled through the grand hall as the duke squirmed in the guards' hands.

General Blake assessed the parchments. "How do you plead to this accusation, Duke Sandje?"

"If my worthless daughters had only married rich, I wouldn't have to evade taxes. They've only ever brought grief to my life."

Ida's heart broke for Reese and Hestia at their father's cruel words. Though she never knew her own father, her adoptive father had been nothing but kind to her.

Nodding, General Blake stood. "Duke Sandje is found guilty of tax evasion and will be sentenced to time in the Fortress. From this day forth, Sandje Textiles will be withdrawn from his holding and given to his only living heirs, Michiko and Sachiko Sandje."

Reese breathed a sigh of relief as Hestia jumped up and down, hugging her sister. Duke Sandje stared in disbelief at his loss but was escorted from the grand hall without a fuss.

Ida couldn't believe the miraculous turn of events. Just a day ago she had been arrested and wasn't sure if she would make it to see another day. Now she was engaged to a Lord and her best friends were Duchesses. Tunri certainly knew how to keep her on her toes.

"This session is officially dismissed," General Blake declared and the crowd watching applauded at the exciting and dramatic events of the proceedings.

Although Ida was overjoyed with the way things had transpired, an uneasy feeling tugged at her soul. There was something that still wasn't right.

Ida spun toward where Sergio was being held to find him gone.

"Ida, what is it?" Jacques asked, taking her arm.

"Sergio is gone," Ida said, searching around the room. Where could he have gone?

Ida turned toward the platform where General Blake was readying to leave. She watched as the queen—who had been disturbingly quiet throughout the whole proceedings—stood behind him and whispered something in his ear that made the general's entire stance lock up.

And before Ida could figure out what was said, an arrow crashed through the high peaked window, striking General Blake.

Chapter Thirty-Nine

Ben, Maldove Palace, Juro—Before the attack on Maldove Palace

Ben, Rae, Nadia, and Tristan arrived at Maldove Palace the night before Matthias' promotion. The sun had yet to rise, but Ben was on full alert. The group scouted around the castle, searching for anything suspicious. But when they concluded that all was clear, they each found places to keep a lookout while the ceremony commenced.

Ben knew Matthias needed his sharp gaze to warn him of anything awry during the ceremony. But so far, the ceremony had continued and nothing out of the ordinary had happened. Ben overheard that a legal case was to be brought before Matthias after the ceremony, so Ben and the others would have to guard in the shadows just a bit longer.

Standing in the castle keep, Ben knew Rae and Nadia had an eye on things below. Relaxing his crossbow on the edge of the window, Ben sighed. He wouldn't mind guarding the castle if he wasn't stuck with Tristan.

While Ben desired blissful silence, Tristan kept yammering the whole morning about nonsense. Ben didn't care to hear how Tristan could've been a great soldier if he'd been allowed into the military and an explanation of how he left Vlacklear Academy without anyone noticing.

While Tristan discussed his heartbreak over Devora's rejection of his proposal, Ben's mind flowed back to Rae and their discussion about marriage. Though he wasn't ready for marriage now, he would be lying if he said he hadn't thought about it more recently than before. But he knew not to rush things and he didn't want to. He wanted to take his time and learn who Rae was outside of all the madness of Yekel.

Ignoring Tristan's new babbling about the latest gossip, Ben peered down the window. Rae and Nadia stood poised and alert, but he could tell they were chatting with one another by the way their hands flew back and forth. They were both so expressive. Something he wished he was better at.

He was doing better, now that Rae was in his life, but he still had a long way to go.

As Tristan dove into yet another topic Ben didn't care to listen to, he ran his fingers through his hair, wondering when he could take a break. He'd been up all night, scouring the towers of the castle for potential threats while Rae checked the lower levels. Nadia had been stuck with Tristan last night. Now Ben understood why she demanded he go with someone else while they guarded the castle today.

Rubbing his eyes, Ben internalized his groan. Would the man ever stop talking?

But Tristan paid no mind to Ben's obvious annoyance and continued chatting like Ben wasn't even there.

Grunting, Ben stalked back to the window to pick up his crossbow when he saw something in the distance. All his senses went on alert as he peered closer.

"Quiet," Ben said to Tristan.

But Tristan continued.

Growling, Ben roared, "Shut your mouth!"

Eyes wide, Tristan finally closed his mouth. Ben hurriedly turned to the window. Orange flags with the seal of two interlocking circles and a sparrow in between marched on the horizon. The Kadeshian army.

Fear and panic jittered through Ben's body as he whistled down to Rae and Nadia. They both immediately looked up at him.

"Find the king's guards," he yelled. "We're going to need reinforcements."

Nadia took off toward the inner wall of the castle, leaving Rae alone at the bottom. Ben didn't need to think twice before he ran down the stairs to join her.

"What are you doing?" she said, stretching her arms. "You get a better vantage point from higher up."

"I won't leave you alone down here."

Rae swatted her hand at him. "I'll be fine."

"No, Rae," Ben said, cupping her face in his hands. "I've fought Kadeshian soldiers before. They're ruthless. I would never forgive myself if something happened to you."

Rae placed her hand over his. "*I've* fought Kadeshian soldiers too, Ben. I know exactly what they're like. But if you're asking me to have come all this way to just hide in the tower and watch you fight, the answer is no."

Ben smiled and nodded.

"Go," Rae said nudging him back toward the tower. "Be my eyes above."

Bending down, he kissed the top of her head. "Be my strength below."

Rae glanced up at him, grabbed his face, and pressed her lips against his. Ben was so shocked, he stood paralyzed until she released him.

"Now, go, I'll need you to take out as many as you can before reinforcements arrive."

Ben stared at Rae in amazement, wondering how he could've won the heart of such an amazing woman.

Almost as soon as Ben returned to the tower, the Kadeshian arrows rained upon the palace. Ben cursed under his breath, knowing he, alone, couldn't stop the hundreds of archers coming against him.

He let loose a string of arrows. But killing six archers was a drop in the bucket to the thousands of soldiers marching over the hill. A whimper came from the corner of the room where Tristan huddled, his face pale.

Ben was thankful Nadia had made him a vast number of arrows before they departed from Totem. Reloading his crossbow, he unleashed another round. Still, more and more Kadeshian arrows came.

Reaching into the sack, Ben pulled out an extra crossbow.

"Just in case," Nadia had said with a wink.

Ben always wondered if Nadia knew more than she let on.

Ben held the crossbow out to Tristan. "Make yourself useful."

Tristan stared at the crossbow like it was a disease. "I'm not a soldier."

Ben took a step forward and shoved it in Tristan's hands. "You are now. Point and shoot. If you hit Rae, I will kill you without a second thought."

With trembling hands, Tristan took the crossbow. He fumbled as he loaded the arrows, but eventually shot a single arrow out the window.

It wasn't a horrible shot, but Ben needed more help than just that. The soldiers were closing in, and Nadia hadn't returned.

Cursing again, Ben double loaded his crossbow, hoping his plan would worked. Praying to Tunri to guide his arrows, he launched twelve arrows into the oncoming line of soldiers, taking out the middle column of soldiers.

"Thank you," he breathed.

He'd given Rae just enough time to react before a Kadeshian soldier attacked her.

Ben did his best to keep his eyes on the soldiers and on Rae, but his attention was split. He couldn't do both.

"Go," Tristan said, loading his crossbow. "Help her. I'll be okay."

Ben raised his brows, impressed with how quickly Tristan managed to learn how to load and launch the bow.

Ben nodded in thanks, grabbed half the arrows, and raced down the stairs, skipping three at a time. For once, he was thankful for his long legs.

He barely made it to the bottom when a Kadeshian soldier raised his sword against Rae. Ben shot his arrow straight into the heart of the soldier.

Rae whipped around, a fire in her eyes. "I had it handled."

"I know," Ben replied but continued to shoot the soldiers around her.

"Who's defending the tower?" Rae asked, kicking another soldier in the gut. He flopped forward before she kicked him in the head.

"Tristan," Ben replied, shooting four more arrows.

"What?"

"He's all we've got," Ben grunted, smashing his crossbow against another soldier's head. "He's not a bad shot actually."

Rae snorted at the comment before she took on another soldier.

But although the three of them fought their hardest, three people couldn't take on an entire army.

"We can't last much longer," Rae grunted. "We have to retreat."

"We have to find Matthias." Ben prayed that was where Nadia had gone first. Yet she still hadn't returned.

Rae nodded. "Now?"

"Now." Ben grabbed Rae's hand and ran through the lower level of the castle. "Tristan!" he yelled. "Retreat!"

Tristan sprinted down the tower faster than Ben had ever seen him move and joined them. They ran hard and fast and were able to get to the inner wall before the soldiers did.

But as they caught their breath, the line of Kadeshian arrows were just behind and the soldiers were ready to breach Maldove Palace.

Chapter Forty

Matthias, Maldove Palace, Juro

"You were always loyal to the king," Queen Leza whispered in Matthias' ear after Ida's trial commenced. "And that's the problem, sweet little captain."

Standing, she ran her pointed fingernail across his neck and Matthias immediately went rigid. Something cold and sticky pierced his skin, breaking the flesh enough to inject a cool liquid into his skin. Matthias' limbs numbed as he felt a chilled metal chain slide around his neck.

"You are now loyal to only me," Queen Leza claimed, and the chain tightened around his neck.

He didn't have to see the chain to know it was made of imperial opal. The metal bit and stung his skin, antagonizing the wolf inside of him. Matthias wanted to claw the chain off and throw it as far away as possible, but he couldn't move. Even his lips were numb from whatever the queen had injected into him. Why had she waited until the trial was finished to kill him? Why not finish him off before?

Matthias' eyes darted around the grand hall. No one was paying any attention to him and the queen. They were all too busy chatting or congratulating the happy couples. While Matthias was glad things were working out for Jacques, he wished his friend would care to glance back just for a moment.

But Jacques didn't turn around, and Matthias stayed paralyzed, knowing that at any moment, the wolf would become angry enough to burst out.

It seemed time had slowed around him, and he was the only one who could see what was really happening. Not one occupant of the grand hall looked his way, as if he had been blocked—erased—from their view.

"You may have dismissed the Translator who found the Book of Ages," the queen continued, stepping to Matthias' side. She ran another nail down his cheek, drawing blood. "But I have who your heart so deeply desires. You won't be able to save either of them now."

Matthias' heart cried out. The queen already had his mother, how had she found Devora?

His mind spun, remembering his encounter with Devora. Unless Devora knew the queen would capture her. And she came anyway. To warn him.

Matthias wanted to scream, but he only sat there, unable to do anything as his soul shattered inside of him. He didn't know what the queen wanted with his mother or Devora, but the fact that she had two Seers in her grasp was not a coincidence.

Queen Leza smiled down at Matthias. "Such a pity too. You look so much like your mother. She would've been so glad to see you again." She sighed then glanced up at the row of windows lining the top of the grand hall. "Ah, it's time for me to go." Bending over, she kissed Matthias' cheek and whispered in his ear, "Long live the queen."

As soon as Matthias blinked, the queen was gone.

He'd always wondered if Queen Leza dabbled in some sort of sorcery, and with her sudden exit his suspicions were confirmed.

Though the queen was gone, Matthias still sat paralyzed in his chair, but time had raced back to its normal speed. And then, finally, he saw Ida studying him with a concerned face. She knew something was wrong. He wasn't sure how, but just her taking notice broke whatever the queen had done to him.

His fingers grabbed at the chain around his neck when a sharp pain jabbed into his left bicep. Matthias jerked back from the blow of the arrow protruding from his arm. Where had it come from? Had someone in the crowd shot him?

But as more arrows shattered the grand hall's windows, glass raining on the people below, Matthias' worst fears came true.

Kadesh had breached Maldove Palace.

All other thoughts flew out the window as Matthias' mind focused only on strategy and saving as many people as possible.

Blood oozed down his arm, the pain stinging, but bearable. In moments like these, he was thankful the wolf lent him its strength.

Clutching his left bicep, Matthias barked, "Jacques, Ida, get as many citizens out of here as possible. Get them to the lower wings then out through the servants' quarters. If you can, get them to the Fortress."

The couple saluted then ran to corral the frantic people.

"Reese, search the upper balcony and evacuate everyone there. Lead them to the east wing, away from the attack then circle back toward the Fortress as well."

"Yes, sir," Reese cried and sprinted toward the stairwell.

"Charles, go to the training center and tell every knight you can find to suit up and defend their kingdom. Go now!" Matthias screamed as more arrows crashed through the windows, these tipped with roaring flames.

Charles saluted and sprinted away.

"Hestia, put out those fires as best as you can, with anything you can find. Cloth, water, go!"

Hestia snapped to attention and ran off as well.

Matthias' gaze darted around the chaos. The seats were on fire, the people were screaming, and the love of his life had once again slipped from his grasp. He had to find her, he had to save her. But how?

Matthias stumbled down the platform and raced out of the hall. The ground rumbled beneath him, shaking the foundation of the castle. As he exited the grand hall, a fury of panicked people raced around outside. Matthias tried to give orders, but the frightened crowd ignored him.

"Matthias!" a familiar voice called.

Matthias whipped around to find One Shot, Rae, and Tristan.

"What happened? Why didn't you send a warning?" He strained through his teeth.

"There was no time, brother," Tristan said, panting. "They came so fast, we barely had enough time to make it here."

"Tristan's right," One Shot agreed. "We sent Nadia for reinforcements, but she never returned. I was hoping she'd found you."

Matthias shook his head, wincing at the arrow protruding from his arm. If he waited just a few more minutes, the wolf's quick healing would push the arrow out enough that Matthias could yank the weapon out. "She didn't reach me."

"What?" Rae shrieked; panic written all over her face. "What happened to her?"

"We'll find her," One Shot said, placing a hand on Rae's shoulder. He turned to Matthias. "What are you orders?"

Finally, Matthias felt the arrow push away from his muscle and toward the surface of his skin. Placing his tunic in his mouth, he waited only a moment more. Just as the two base prongs of the arrowhead broke through the surface of his skin, Matthias bit down on his tunic and yanked the arrow out.

He threw the arrow on the ground, flinching from the pain, but already feeling the wolf healing the wound. Sometimes being cursed on the battlefield wasn't half bad.

One Shot, Tristan, and Rae stared at Matthias in utter shock. He ignored their stares and readied to bark out a string of orders when his eye caught something in the distance. A familiar long black braid, struggling and fighting against the Kadeshian soldiers.

"Devora," he whispered, before he screamed, "Devora!"

He then saw Nadia's blonde head not far from Devora, kicking and punching whoever was in her sight. Next to her was Ida, twirling some sort of weapon, as well.

Matthias didn't have time to comprehend why Ida disobeyed his order before he started toward the trio. But Rae had already caught on to his line of sight and sprinted past him. He couldn't believe how fast she was and understood why she'd won so many fights in the Dark Market.

"She'll bring her back, Matthias," One Shot said confidently.

A new wave of Kadeshian soldiers flooded over One Shot, Tristan, and Matthias, elongating the distance between them and Devora even more. As reinforcements from the Fortress finally came, Matthias was whisked away to order another squadron of soldiers. The only thing he could do was pray that One Shot was right.

Chapter Forty-One

Ida intended to follow General Blake's orders as she always had. But when she and Jacques had begun escorting citizens and Ida caught sight of Devora, a new feeling came over her. Although Ida wasn't the best fighter or the best soldier, she knew she needed to help Devora.

"Jacques, I have to go," she called to him.

Jacques spun around and grabbed her arm. "Go where? I can't lose you. Not when I finally have you." Agony and fear swirled in his beautiful hazel eyes and Ida still couldn't believe those strong emotions were for her.

"I'll return," she assured, and she knew she would.

Although Jacques wasn't happy about it, he let her go. "You'd better. I can't plan a wedding in a month all by myself." He tried to smile.

Ida ran up to him and kissed him hard before sprinting away.

The wire bracelet on her wrist burned like fire as she got closer to where Devora was.

She knew Nadia had given it to her for a reason and now was the time. Unwrapping the wire from her wrist, Ida twirled it around her head and launched it into the nearest soldier. The pointed needle sliced through his armor like butter before Ida retracted it.

As Ida hurried toward Devora, she knew she should feel sympathy for battling the soldiers of her own country. But she didn't. Instead, she felt sympathy for every person—soldier, layman, and child—on both sides that were strung into this horrible war.

Twirling the wire again, Ida caught sight of Nadia, kicking and punching like it was any other training day in the Fortress. Ida's heart warmed at the sight, realizing it had been weeks—months—since she'd seen her dear friend.

"Ida!" Nadia said with a smile as she locked her arm around a Kadeshian's neck. Nadia jabbed her bladed hand into the soldier's neck before he went limp. "It's been too long, I've missed you!"

Nadia gave Ida a quick hug before spinning around and kicking a Kadeshian in the gut. Another soldier was ready to strike when Ida spun the wire and launched it around his leg. Ida yanked with all her might and the soldier fell on his backside.

Nadia laughed wildly. "I love when my inventions work." A mischievous gleam shined in her eyes as she looked at Ida. "Let's go get some more."

Ida grinned, unable to understand the excitement pumping through her veins as she fought alongside Nadia. Another woman, someone Nadia seemed to know, assisted them in defeating the final soldiers blocking them from Devora. The three of them were almost at Devora when the sight of the soldier before her Seer friend stopped Ida dead in her tracks.

Standing before Devora in shining bronze Kadeshian armor was the headmistress of Vlacklear Academy.

Chapter Forty-Two

Rae sprinted past the captain—or general now—before he could utter another order. She immediately recognized Nadia's striking blonde hair and ran as fast as her legs would take her.

On her way to find reinforcements, Nadia must have run into Devora and tried to help her escape.

Rae couldn't condemn Nadia for her actions when she would've done the same thing.

Pumping her legs, Rae jumped into the fight between Nadia, another girl she seemed to know, Devora, and a group of Kadeshian soldiers trying to overwhelm them.

Rae jabbed a soldier in his pressure points, causing his arms to go limp. She then kicked him in the chest, making him stumble into three more soldiers.

"Hey Rae," Nadia said, panting with a grin. "Welcome to the party."

"Thanks," Rae deadpanned, dodging a large knife coming toward her throat from a nearby soldier. She disarmed him and kicked him in the back. "Devora, what are you still doing here? You need to get out of here. Your captain is about to tear the castle down to find you."

Before Devora could respond, two soldiers flanked her sides and Rae watched in awe as Devora disposed of them with ease.

"I was about to say the same thing," Nadia yelled as she ducked under the blade of a screaming soldier. "Devora, you need to leave, now!"

"Please!" The other girl with amazing ebony curls added on to Nadia's cries.

"She isn't meant to leave," a cool voice announced.

Rae watched as Devora's body straightened, her chin lifted high. But the Seer didn't lower her blade. Rae turned toward the voice. A tall thin woman with pin straight hair and a beak-like nose grinned at them.

"Who's that?" Nadia asked, smacking another soldier in the face.

Devora breathed steadily, slowly lowering her sword.

"Headmistress?" The girl with curls questioned her eyes wide. "Your eyes they're—"

"Violet," Devora finished. "She's not the headmistress of Vlacklear Academy, Ida," Devora said, keeping her gaze glued on the woman. "She's General Beta, King Redore IV's most trusted general and Seer."

"What?" Rae, Ida, and Nadia asked at the same time.

"Exposing all my secrets?" General Beta asked with a conniving grin. "That won't do." The general pulled out a long sword. She jutted the tip toward Devora's heart. "I shall see you pierced through so you can speak your false prophecies no more."

The trio jumped forward.

"I'd like to see you try," Rae said, blocking Devora with her body.

Ida held a long wire with two spiked ends, she twirled one end, ready to strike. Rae instantly recognized the design as Nadia's and felt a surge of pride for her friend.

As Rae faced General Beta once again, her heart stopped. Hanging on the Kadeshian general's neck was General Yada's iron skeleton key.

"Ah, so you're the one Leza gave the key to in the Whispering Hall," General Beta chuckled, flicking the key around her neck. "I see you're still alive. That's impressive. Usually, my key takes something from its holder."

Fear wrapped around Rae's throat like a noose. "What do you mean?"

General Beta swatted the tip of her sword. "Nothing is free. You want power, you must pay for it."

Rae felt the blood from her face drain to her feet. Mami had become sick as soon as she and Rae were reunited. Had the key somehow taken Mami's health instead of Rae's? But why? How?

General Beta noticed Rae's surprise and used it to her advantage. Before Rae could react, the general stabbed her leg and kicked her out of the way.

Rae cried out and tried to gather her footing beneath her but stumbled onto her back. Nadia tried to intervene and met the same fate.

Ida raised her weapon, swinging it high above her head and letting it fly. It launched into the Kadeshian general's shoulder, but General Beta yanked it out, unphased.

"You can't defeat me, Ida. It doesn't matter that you're a Translator. It doesn't matter that you found the Book of Ages," General Beta sneered. "You're still poor and worthless, like you always have been."

"That's not true," Ida said, spinning her weapon again. "Someone like me will always have more heart and faith than someone like you."

She let the weapon fly, and Rae watched as it sunk into the general's chest. Rae expected General Beta to fall from the impact, but instead the woman cackled.

She wrenched the speared end out of her chest, blood dripping, and yanked on the wire, reeling Ida in like a fish.

General Beta grabbed Ida by the neck and held her up, so her feet dangled. "Heart? I don't have a heart. Not anymore."

Rae struggled to stand. She didn't know Ida well, but she'd heard enough stories about her to know she was a good woman and didn't deserve to die in the hands of a monster.

But as Rae tried to put weight on her bleeding leg, it buckled beneath her. The general cut her leg deep enough to inflict a serious injury. Rae watched helplessly as Ida struggled to breathe.

"That's enough, general," Devora said, her voice cool and commanding. "Let Ida go. You have no purpose for her."

General Beta squeezed Ida's neck once more, causing Ida to claw at the gloved hand before she threw her to the ground.

Rae dragged herself toward Ida, her leg screaming the entire way. She quickly checked for Ida's pulse and was relieved to find a faint but steady heartbeat.

"You're right, my Seeing sister." General Beta wiped her blade clean of Rae's blood with a handkerchief. "Come, the queen awaits."

Shock parted Rae's lips as Devora dropped her sword and strode forward.

"Devora!" she cried. "Don't!"

Devora turned her bright violet eyes on Rae. A small smile came to her lips. "It's okay, Rae. Tunri goes ahead, my job is to follow." Devora then rummaged in her pocket and pulled out Rae's leather sack.

Before Devora helped Rae and Ben free the enslaved women in the Temple of Pahga, Rae had a feeling she wouldn't be seeing Devora again for some time, especially after noticing Nadia making Devora so many different weapons and tools.

Rae felt Tunri urging her to give her bag of coin from her Dark Market winnings to Devora. She didn't know how the coin would help Devora, but she followed the prompting.

Devora bounced the sack in her hand then tossed it to Rae. "Thank you for your help, Rae. I wouldn't have gotten to see Matthias again without you. Tell him I'll see him when the sparrow flies."

Rae frowned at the message but nodded just the same.

With a pained smile, Devora faced General Beta and nodded. Rae's lips parted in shock as Devora took the general's hand and disappeared into a cloud of black smoke.

Chapter Forty-Three

Matthias sat with his head in his hands in the center of the Theater. All the citizens who had been evacuated from Maldove Palace had finally been sent back to their homes. After Rae, Ida, and Nadia fought alongside Devora, Matthias and a slew of other officers, led their companies against the endless waves of Kadeshian soldiers.

Matthias ran his hands through his hair. He wouldn't call it a victory, but they had pushed the Kadeshian troops out of Juro far enough that they retreated into the Edo desert. Though Matthias was thankful the battle was over, his soul felt more burdened than ever.

Devora was gone. His soul knew she was gone. He just didn't know the details yet.

The doors of the Theater cracked open. One Shot ducked his head before walking through the threshold. He then extended his hand to whoever was behind him. With a crutch under her arm and a bandage on her leg, Rae grabbed One Shot's hand and limped into the Theater. Nadia came in right after with a similar bandage but not as bad of a limp. Clutched in her hands were a piece of wood and a small pocketknife. Though her fingers were bandaged and bruised she continued whittling all the same.

Both women approached Matthias with tears in their eyes.

"I'm so sorry," Rae whispered, bowing her head.

"We tried to stop her, Cap," Nadia said, trying to hold her tears back. She wiped her eyes with the sleeve of her shirt before focusing on the piece of wood. "We tried."

Matthias turned his heavy, bloodshot eyes on them. "If Devora's mind was set on something, there was no changing it."

Nadia smirked slightly and nodded.

Rae nodded as well but looked forlorn anyway. One Shot guided Rae to one of the seats Matthias had dragged into the center of the Theater. Nadia sat beside her.

Matthias didn't know why he had called this meeting, or what they would accomplish, but something inside of him told him he needed it. He needed these people who were so ready to follow his orders. For once, he didn't have to stand and make decisions alone.

One Shot sat down between Rae and Matthias. Leaning his elbows on his knees, he said, "So, what now?"

Matthias rubbed his eyes. "That's what I'm trying to figure out as well."

The door to the Theater creaked open again and in walked Jacques, Ida, and the twins. Matthias was still impressed with their readiness and efficiency when Kadesh attempted to siege the castle. He would've never thought those fear-stricken girls who entered the Fortress would transform into some of his best soldiers.

"You look terrible," Jacques commented as he took the chair on Matthias' other side.

"Jacques," Ida scolded with a gasp. "The general has been through a lot. Be kind."

The corner of Matthias' lips ticked up. Even after everything crumbled to dust, Ida was still Ida.

"Thank you, Ida, but I have to say your soon-to-be husband is right. Although he looks far worse than me."

"It's true," One Shot commented with a nod and Jacques scoffed.

"Stunning case, by the way, Reese," Matthias commented, turning his gaze toward the weary-faced twins. "I was thoroughly impressed with your evidence and thought process."

"Thank you, sir," Reese said with a firm nod, sliding her abacus beads back and forth. "Ida deserved to be found innocent and, for the first time, I was one hundred percent sure I would be able to prove it."

Matthias nodded, amazed at the loyalty of the people around him. How each one of them was willing to give everything for the people they loved. Himself included.

The door creaked open a final time and Tristan swaggered in. All eyes watched him as he slumped into the last vacant chair. Dark bags ringed his eyes as he crossed his arms over his chest.

"What? Why is everyone staring at me? I was invited to the secret circle meeting too."

"Only because of nepotism," Nadia said, but she nudged Tristan playfully in the shoulder.

Matthias heard One Shot groan and couldn't help but chuckle under his breath.

The group silenced and turned to Matthias for direction. Matthias called them all here and he figured they expected him to have a plan. But, for once in his life, he didn't. He didn't know what to do, what the next step was, or where to go. Just like in his game of Kings with Devora, he was usually three steps ahead. But now he wasn't even close to being ahead. He felt so far behind.

These people had risked their lives not only following his orders, but for each other. He knew what One Shot, Devora, and Nadia had done for Rae in Yekel. He knew what Rae had sacrificed for the women in the Temple of Pahga. Warden Hazor had told him about Reese's and Hestia's insistence to help Ida in her mission. And Jacques. Jacques had given so much of his time helping Matthias when he transformed in and out of his cursed state.

Matthias reached up and tugged the chain around his throat. It no longer burned his skin like when Queen Leza first put there, but when he tried to take it off, it sent a pulse of pain through his body. There had to be a way to break the chain, but Matthias couldn't think about that now.

Dropping the chain, he cleared his throat.

"I don't have a plan for what to do next," Matthias said plainly. "Kadesh hasn't infiltrated Tentonian ranks in years. I can only assume the attack that just occurred was planned by the imposter headmistress of Vlacklear who we have confirmed as King Redore IV's head general, General Beta. She is also a Seer." Matthias glanced at Ida, Rae, and Nadia who all nodded in confirmation.

Leaning back in his chair, Matthias crossed his arms over his chest. "Based on what I've been told, Devora went willingly with the general upon threat to others. But we have no idea what a Kadeshian general would want with another Seer when she is a Seer herself." Matthias extended his hand. "Does anyone have any theories?"

They all looked at him blankly, as if too scared to respond.

Matthias hung his head. "No one will be punished for speaking their mind. This is an open forum."

"Devora said that she would see you again when the sparrow flies," Rae said quietly. "She wanted me to pass that on to you."

"A sparrow?" Jacques jumped in before Matthias could speak. "Like the one on the Kadeshian crest?"

"That would make sense," Reese added, flicking four abacus beads to the right. "There's an eighty-nine point four percent chance that Tunri granted Devora a vision about General Beta seeking her out."

"Good ole, Dev, keeping us in the dark again," Nadia chuckled as she sliced off another chunk of wood.

"Eighty-nine point four?" Tristan questioned with a quirked brow, staring at Reese. "What are you, a human abacus?"

Reese blinked at him. "Yes, of course."

Hestia snorted and burst into a fit of giggles, relaxing the tense state of the room.

"When we were helping Rae in the Temple of Pahga, I had a feeling Devora knew more than what she was telling us," One Shot added. "But Rae and I also knew Matthias was coming and we needed to free the enslaved women."

Rae nodded. "She made sure we didn't follow her to where I told her Kanna was kept."

"You knew our mother?" Tristan asked, disbelief lining his features.

"Yes," Rae nodded again, her face solemn. "She helped me during one of the darkest times of my life."

One Shot held Rae's hand in his own, squeezing it tightly.

"Our mother is also a Seer, for those who don't know," Matthias offered to the group. They might as well all be honest. "The king and queen have held her captive for longer than I can remember. I've made it my life's work to try to find her, but I never have."

Pained looks crossed over the circle of faces around him.

"Why are they holding her captive?" Hestia asked.

"She delivered the prophecy that would bring doom to the current monarchy," Matthias replied. "They didn't appreciate it. But I could never figure out why they didn't kill her outright like they did the other Seers."

Then Tristan asked a most profound question: "Does this Kadeshian General-Seer-woman have mother, too?"

Matthias blinked at his brother in astonishment. Out of all the thoughts and scenarios Matthias had thought of, their mother being in Kadesh was not one of them.

"I...don't know," Matthias admitted. "There were leads that she was in Yekel, which were confirmed by Rae, but after I arrived, the trail was cold."

"What if the king and queen were working with the general of Kadesh?" Tristan proposed. "I mean, doesn't it seem odd that as soon as they got Devora the soldiers suddenly backed off into the desert? What if, for whatever reason, they need Seers and that's why they kept mother alive."

The circle silenced as everyone processed Tristan's thoughts.

"That actually makes a lot of sense, Tris," Nadia admitted, giving him an impressed look.

Could he be right? Matthias thought. *Could something so far-fetched be the truth?*

"Sir," Ida spoke up. "Your brother is, unfortunately, correct."

And as Ida spoke the sentence, a shimmer of light appeared in her lap in the form of a book.

"Is that the book?" Hestia asked, her eyes wide. "You found it?"

Ida nodded and Hestia squealed with delight. "The Book of Ages reveals itself to one who is worthy and wishes to find it. Unfortunately, a spell had been cast over it, binding it to the queen's throne." She cast a look at Matthias. "That's why I was in there."

But Matthias didn't respond. His eyes stayed glued to the Book of Ages. He'd been searching for it for years. But, as Ida confirmed, he was never worthy enough to find it. Everything he needed to find his mother, and hopefully, Devora was in there.

"Please explain how Tristan is correct," Matthias asked, anticipation crawling through his veins.

Carefully, Ida opened the book. Her lips moved, as if saying a prayer before her eyes glowed gold and she read over the pages.

"The prophecy your mother gave to the king and queen is as follows: *The tyranny shall last for years, shedding more than blood and tears. But one day a Seer's heir will arise and bring the monarchy to its demise.*"

Ida's eyes faded back to their normal brown color. The circle stayed silent, no one knowing what to say.

Rae was the first to speak. "That's it? The king and queen killed Seers and imprisoned Tinkers and others with gifts for two lines?"

She snorted and muttered under her breath a few choice words about the monarchy.

Matthias agreed with her frustration. But it did make sense that the king and queen ordered all Seers to be killed. They didn't want any Seers to have children that would rise and end their reign.

"Captain—er—general," Ida said. "There's one more thing. I know why they need your mother and Devora."

Matthias scooted to the edge of his seat.

Jacques gave Ida an encouraging look before she took a breath and flipped a few pages of the book. Her eyes glowed gold again as she translated. "This is a diary entry from a past Seer. 'A Seer's gift is found within. Not the blood or the heart but etched on their very soul. If this power can be extracted, the Seer will die, and the power will deform into something evil. I know not of a way to do this, but I have heard rumors of the discovery of a stone that can suppress and extract any gift given by Tunri.'"

The chain around Matthias' neck burned as his mind connected the pieces. His pulse increased as his fear rose alongside it.

"I don't know why," Ida said, closing the book. "But I believe the Kadeshians and the queen are going to try to extract Devora's and your mother's powers to use for their own gain."

Matthias shot up and paced the room, not caring about the nervous glances his comrades were giving him. Though it sounded absurd, it made sense. The imperial opal ring Devora received, the imperial opal tincture, the manacles, maybe they were all a part of the plan to siphon Devora's power.

"In the Temple of Pahga, there was a giant imperial opal statue," Rae explained. She shifted uncomfortably in her seat. "I've seen it extract the souls of innocents. It's a terrible thing.

Though we destroyed—or rather, your catapults—destroyed it, I wouldn't be surprised if Kadesh had another one on their land."

Matthias absorbed the information, his previous blank mind already forming a plan. It was a crazy plan. It was an outrageous plan. But, by Tunri's grace, if He thought Matthias reliable enough to carry out this plan, it just might work. As he was about to reveal this plan, a voice from the stands in the Theater called out to him.

"So, General Blake. What are you going to do?"

They all glanced up to see Warden Hazor striding down the steps. His black tunic and slacks contrasted his stark white mustache and hair.

Matthias studied the warden. The man who'd guided his path—albeit a little forcefully and painfully at times—but guided him all the same. Matthias wondered if the warden really knew the outcome of all the events at play and was waiting for the rest of them to catch up.

"Sir," Matthias said, saluting the warden. "We're going to do what any good commander does when one of his soldiers is taken captive behind enemy lines."

The warden quirked a brow. "And that is?"

Matthias faced the circle around him. They were all so different from one another, but each of them was connected by a single person. And that person needed them now more than ever.

Turning back to the warden, Matthias yanked on the chain around his neck, hoping the queen could hear him loud and clear. "We're going to bring her home."

Chapter Forty-Four

Darkness dominated Devora's vision for longer than ever before. She didn't think she'd been drugged. She didn't feel drugged. Yet her sight was still black. She thought that maybe General Beta had blinded her. But she could still see faint lights occasionally, so that wasn't likely either.

When Tunri granted her the vision of Queen Leza killing Matthias, he'd also shown her about General Beta and why she was really a spy at Vlacklear Academy. It was to find Devora. When King Atol changed the color categories, it completely derailed General Beta's plans to capture Devora at Vlacklear Academy.

Devora was thankful she hadn't gone to Vlacklear but knew that this time her fate was inevitable. She had to go with the general. It was the only path leading her to Kanna and Princess Haden, who was still very much alive.

Devora felt herself rumble along before she was led forward. The familiar sound of iron cell bars closing echoed behind her.

Frowning, Devora reached for the sack that had to be covering her head and obstructing her vision, but she found nothing there.

A new panic set in as Devora realized she was actually blind.

"Don't worry," a calm voice said. "Your sight will come back momentarily."

Devora jerked away as a cool hand reached out to touch her.

"Who are you?" Devora demanded.

"A friend," the voice replied.

Having no other choice, Devora allowed the owner of the voice to place a cool hand over Devora's eyes. A chilled sensation poured over Devora's face before a pop sounded. Springing her lids open, Devora gasped as her vision returned.

She blinked and looked at her hands, making sure she wasn't dreaming.

"Thank you," she said, glancing up to the stranger. "How did you—"

But the question died on her lips, for the person seated in front of her was none other than Kanna Blake.

This is usually the time when I have finished a series. But, of course, I must challenge myself and write a tetralogy instead of a trilogy! I have loved writing this story so far and cannot wait to share the ending with you in the fourth and final book of The Legacy Chapters.

Sanctified is different from *Fortified* and *Justified* because it focuses less on action but more on the politics and secrets hidden in Tenton. I was worried it wouldn't be as exciting as books one and two, but I think you'll still enjoy all the twists and turns I've added. As always, I have many to thank who have supported me this far.

To David and my boys, I love you all! Thank you for being super impressed that Mommy writes books.

To my family, thank you for always encouraging me to follow my dreams.

To my college friends, thank you for your constant support!

To C.A.V.A., thank you for always being there to bounce ideas off of and being willing to read manuscripts before everyone else.

To April and Quill & Flame Publishing, thank you for taking on this beast of a story! I hope it has brought success to the company.

To my amazing readers, thank you to all of you, old and new! I have loved watching you all enjoy my stories from day one and I hope you continue to do so.

To God, my Creator, and Christ, my Savior, thank you for inspiring me to write stories that glorify You.